THE T

A Reagan Moon Novel

τ

By Mike Duran

THE THIRD GOLEM
A Reagan Moon Novel
© 2020 Mike Duran
Published by Blue Crescent Press
ISBN: 978-1-7351608-0-1 (paperback)
ISBN: 978-1-7351608-1-8 (ebook)

ACKNOWLEDGEMENTS

I'd like to thank Jill Domschot for her editorial work, Teddi Deppner for her story insights, the members of my writing group—Merrie Destefano, Paul Regnier, Rachel Marks, and Becky Miller—for their encouragement, prayers, and modeling of endurance, Kirk Dou-Ponce for his brilliant cover art, my wife and family for putting up with my eccentricities, and my readers. Thank you!

OTHER BOOKS BY MIKE DURAN

The Ghost Box: A Reagan Moon Novel (Book One)
Saint Death: A Reagan Moon Novel (Book Two)
Christian Horror: On the Compatibility of a Biblical Worldview and the Horror Genre
Wickers Bog: A Tale of Southern Gothic Horror
Requiem IV (novella)
Other Voices, Other Tombs (story included in anthology)
Winterland: A Dark Fairy Tale (novella)
Subterranea: Nine Tales of Dread and Wonder (anthology)
Disciplish: My Unconventional Pilgrimage through Faith, Art, and Evangelical Culture (memoir)
The Telling
The Resurrection

"I do not believe in a fate that falls on men however they act; but I do believe in a fate that falls on them unless they act."

—Chesterton

CHAPTER 1

Some people have tried to label me a hero. Thankfully, those who know me well make no such mistake. They see me as I truly am—a troubled soul with special gifts and a bad attitude hoping to make peace with my past, my future, and whatever joker has chosen me to be the Seventh Guardian of the Imperia.

Okay, so my attitude has actually improved a little since the Accident. Ellie would appreciate that. But making peace with all the weirdness in my life has been rather difficult. The most immediate reminder was my hanging on for dear life in the back of an urban assault vehicle as it raced to Chinatown to capture a humanoid creature of unknown origin.

Did I mention that my life has gotten really weird?

"One o'clock!" Mace barked from the driver's seat, pointing to a commotion ahead of us.

The storm gifts coursed through my body. I hadn't mastered these unusual powers yet and doubted I ever could. I only hoped I would not kill anyone. At least, not intentionally. The Tau scar throbbed beneath the Ndocron vest. I wiped sweat off my forehead and shook out my hands, attempting to work the chill of energy from them. Unbuckling myself, I leaned over and peered between the front seats of Mace's van.

At the intersection ahead, past Chinatown's famed archway, people were scattering. Groceries and handbags spiraled across the asphalt as pedestrians fled from an unspecified disturbance. Some stumbled, fell, and then leapt back to their feet, all the while looking frantically over their shoulders. Horns blared as cars braked to avoid the chaotic crowd. Mace zig-zagged his vehicle through traffic, swerved into the opposite lane, broke free from a cluster of cars, and sped toward the bustle.

"Sit back, Moon." Mace cast a stern glance over his shoulder. "And be ready to roll."

He could tell that I was edgier than usual. Not that this superhero gig should have been a cakewalk. Whereas most people instinctively flee from trouble, I was still getting used to running towards it. And despite a growing catalog of impromptu adventures, I remained on the front end of that curve.

I leaned back, trying to control my emotions.

Kanya turned and looked at me. "You okay?"

Even though my mind was racing, I gave her a thumbs up.

She sat shotgun. Her straight black hair was pulled back into a tight ponytail, accentuating those piercing hazel eyes. Turning back to the road, she removed one of the retractable polycarbonate pulse wands from the overhead rack and slipped it into her belt. It was her only weapon. Should she choose to unleash Cricket, her freakishly ornery alter ego, Kanya probably wouldn't need another weapon. Even though she appeared outwardly calm, my second sight told me the adrenaline was roiling inside her. Thankfully, I wasn't the only team member still human enough to feel fear.

Mace hit the brakes and laid on the horn. I slammed sideways and toppled from my seat. The van skidded into the intersection and came to a stop.

I scrambled onto my hands and knees, poked my head between the front seats again, and peered through the windshield. Through the tangle of cars and fleeing pedestrians, a glint of steel flashed in the summer sun, and with it came a whir of motion. A fleshy, shimmering creature bound into the crosswalk.

"What in the hell?" Mace kept his foot crunched on the brakes. He nudged the brim of his U.S. Army ballcap up and leaned over the steering wheel, peering at the thing before us.

A pale bald human head rose on a mechanized serpentine torso, swaying in the crosswalk.

We craned forward and tried to make sense of what we were seeing. The head swiveled from side to side, eyes wide in seeming panic. The spinal column was in the process of unspooling from the base of the cranium, expanding as it went, forming a python-like trunk. Moisture lubricated its metallic vertebrae. Small, almost microscopic gears and pistons etched the serpentine surface and glistened in the sunlight.

I gaped. "You have gotta be—"

"Don't move," Mace growled, his tanned, rock solid body poised. "That is our target."

"Ya think?"

The head swiveled upon this odd anatomy, looking to-and-fro with wide, pained eyes. Barbs like that of a small dragon appeared along the crest of the spine. Despite its steely trunk, the head appeared entirely humanoid. As its transformation ceased, the steel snake man slithered forward and stopped. Its head swayed, eye level with our windshield, as its gaze moved between me and the other passengers inside the van.

Kanya muttered something and recoiled back into her seat. Her flesh rippled, as though she was about to morph. However, she restrained herself. Mace retrieved another pulse wand from the floorboard without moving his gaze from the creature.

"It wants something," Kanya said, breathlessly. "Look. It's trying to say something."

She was right. The creature's mouth was moving, opening and closing in a voiceless appeal.

Until its gaze locked upon me.

Even in broad daylight, its pupils glowed with a luminous silver, almost metallic in appearance. Though no one else could see it, a bluish aura emanated from its cranium, suggesting that this was not a machine. At least, not entirely. The metallic skeletal serpent was partly biological.

But there was something else about it, something that left my mind reeling. Fiery spasms flared within the aura of its organic halo, indicating deep distress.

It was in agony. In torment.

You must understand something—in the invisible world, machines leave no imprint. Unlike humans, there is no emotional or spiritual penumbra cast by lifeless, soulless automatons. They are simply chunks of matter emitting electronic or audio signals. Yet this mechanized monstrosity appeared to have feelings! And whatever it was, I was dialed into its emotions.

A circle of spectators now stood aghast. Some

frantically snapped pictures of the robotic entity with their cell phones. Others just gaped. Mothers pulled their children to their sides, shielding them from the horrific sight. A voice from the crowd shouted *Terrorists!* causing some to dash for cover. In the distance, a drone soared over a pagoda and approached at high speed.

The creature looked up, and then turned and squared its body with our vehicle. A blazing pain gripped its eyes.

"What's it doing?" Kanya asked. "What does it want?"

Suddenly the heat, the crowd, and the nervous energy didn't matter. While I could not discern the exact nature of this entity, its intentions now seemed obvious.

"He wants us to kill him," I said matter-of-factly.

Kanya turned and stared at me.

"Say again?" Mace continued to stare forward.

"It wants to die," I said. "And he wants us to do it."

Now they were both staring at me.

"Klammer wants it alive," Kanya said, turning back. "That's what he said, right?"

"Affirmative." Mace jammed the vehicle into park. "We are *not* killing it. Not if we can help it."

He shifted the wand to his opposite hand and nudged the door open. "Moon, in that rack next to the door there is a DES rifle. Please, remove it. And be careful as you do." He motioned towards Kanya's door. "Kay, bring up the opposite side. Set your wand on medium charge."

Together, they slowly stepped down from the van.

Across from the bench seat was a bank of radio and video equipment, as well as an attached swivel stool. Mace had talked about using this vehicle during his cryptid hunts. The van was a sleek charcoal gray with aluminum roof rack and front bumper, grill protector, all-terrain tires, and tinted windows. Like its owner, this beast was jacked up on bravado and steroids. The only thing it was missing was a gun turret mounted on the rooftop. Although, knowing Mace, that was likely in the works. Near the back of the van, meshed gloves lay atop balled up nylon netting. Several mounted wall racks contained miscellaneous items including a modified football helmet, water-stained blueprints, and a clown mask. A trident was clamped to the interior ceiling and traced the length of the vehicle. Near the side door, three unusual-looking rifles stood strapped in place. Having sworn off guns and having no clue what a DES rifle looked like, I stared blankly. Finally, I shook my head, and returned my attention to the creature.

The crowd was now bustling, a dense mass of onlookers, pedestrians, bicyclists, and commuters encircled the van and the robotic serpent. Exhaust fumes filled the air. Horns honked. A street mime climbed atop a nearby statue of Bruce Lee and sat on its shoulders, filming the commotion with a cell phone.

Mace and Kanya crept toward the serpent from opposite sides, their wands extended. However, I was too enthralled to move.

"Moon!" Mace snarled, glancing back at the van. "The rifle. Now."

Apparently, the creature sensed that we had no intention of putting it out of its misery. A ripple passed through it and its entire torso began to reconfigure. Slight diaphanous tendrils bristled from the spinal column, forming a scaly sheath. The head swiveled from side to side, and then the mechanized serpentine creature whisked through the intersection like a massive cobra. The crowd erupted in shrieks and shouts, running in multiple directions again to make way for the monster.

Mace closed the telescoping rod and inserted it into his belt. Then he climbed back into the van and ripped his ball cap off, revealing his short-cropped bleached hair. He flung the hat onto the dashboard and cursed.

Kanya said, "I'll follow it on foot. Go!" She slammed the door shut and bolted toward the fleeing creature.

Mace put the vehicle in gear and laid on the horn. "Hang on, Moon!"

The vehicle jolted forward and I tumbled back, smacking my head on the swivel seat near the radio equipment. More horns and angry shouts erupted as Mace wove through the crowd and the congestion in pursuit of our prey. I climbed into the front seat, hung on, and watched the creature whip around cars, headed to the next intersection.

"What was that thing?" I said, checking the back of my scalp for blood.

"Some sort of biot. An older model. Black market commodity, most likely."

"Biot? I haven't—"

He jammed the brakes and I braced myself against the dashboard. Then the vehicle slowed to a crawl as the traffic bottle-necked.

Biot. It had been a while since I'd heard that term. Like most journalists, I'd been forced to do some investigation into the explosion of artificial intelligence and robotics technology. Along the way, I'd learned that biots were different from robots and cyborgs, which were inorganic in nature—machines, for the most part. On the other hand, biots were artificial or synthetic biological organisms comprised mostly of organic and lab-grown tissues. *Soft robots* they were sometimes called. This could explain why I had seen a life aura from the bizarre man-serpent.

"Moon! That thing is moving fast. I need you to stay focused or we're gonna lose it."

He was right. The traffic was crawling. Some people leaned out of their cars, craning to catch a glimpse of the cause of the commotion. Other anxious commuters honked at them to get moving. On the sidewalk across the street, screams sounded, and a briefcase sailed through the air.

"There!" I pointed.

Kanya hurdled an overturned trashcan in pursuit of the biot, which slid around the corner and headed in a northeasterly direction. She was some twenty feet behind and had to dodge pedestrians to keep up. At that pace, she would lose the creature.

"Hang on!" Mace spotted a narrow opening in traffic between a curb and a driveway and swerved into the opposite lane in an attempt to reach it. A horn bellowed beside us and a tour bus jolted to a stop just inches from my door. The driver slid her window open and shouted expletives. Mace lurched forward, attempting to reach the temporary traffic opening, but the van went over the curb and flattened several newspaper racks before resting in front of a storefront. The smell of roasted ducks and burning rubber met us.

"Let's go!" Mace turned the vehicle off, climbed into the back, and removed a rifle from the rack. Then he flung the side door open and leapt out, brandishing the weapon. However, with its thick square muzzle and transparent butt, the rifle looked more like a prop from a Battlestar Galactica set than a real weapon.

"Wait." I climbed down from the vehicle and scanned the area. "Here? You're bringing *that*?"

"Let's go, Moon!" He slung the rifle over his back and cut through traffic to reach Kanya.

I didn't need superpowers to know that this wasn't going to end well.

The store owner marched up and got in my grill. He shook his finger at me, chattering in an Asian dialect. I was pretty sure he was not explaining what today's specials were.

I bowed apologetically and backed into the street before turning and jetting after my friends.

Horns assaulted me as I wove through cars and pedestrians, apologizing as I went. I reached the corner and located Mace some thirty yards away. He was near an open-air produce market scanning the street. I caught up to him and stood panting.

"I lost 'em," he said.

People gawked at Mace and stumbled out of his way.

"You're going to use that here?" I objected again.

"It's on a shock setting. This won't kill it."

"Yeah, but I thought we were supposed to stay under the radar."

"I'm doing my best, Moon. Let's bag that thing

and get outta here."

Screaming sounded down the street and horns blared. Someone whistled loudly. Kanya stood halfway down the block, frantically motioning to us. I followed her gaze. About one hundred feet beyond her, a flock of pigeons burst into the air. The creature was whisking towards an alley near the end of the block. At this rate, we'd never catch it.

"It's getting away," Mace said. "Moon! Do something!"

I didn't need to ask what he meant.

"Here?" I said. "With all these people?"

"Yes, here. You have your vest on, right? Then do it."

He wanted me to jump. I stood staring at what was probably the length of a football field. I'd never jumped that far.

Some called it teleportation. I simply called it jumping. Because of the side effects, I avoided it as much as possible. With every jump, the Tau scar on my chest grew larger. Without my vest, the scar would eventually consume me. That was the reward I'd received for taking this job. Go figure. Spatial jumping seemed to exist at the top of my talent hierarchy; moving through space, both outer and inner. Rapha, second guardian of the Imperia and my default mentor, said that it was basically a self-generated tesseract; an ability to project an additional dimension for spatial transport. With a little practice, I'd developed the capacity to see or will into existence dimensional bridges from one spot to another. Rapha speculated that by learning to navigate a tesseract, someone could travel great distances in seconds. Orphana, our resident Loreist, told me of a boy who'd traveled the length of Hollywood Boulevard in a few steps. At the moment, I didn't need to go *that* far. But this would still be tricky.

"Moon! What are you waiting for? Do you see what is happening here?"

I was tiring of Mace's attitude. "Chill out. I'm thinking."

"We do not have time!"

"You want me to kill somebody?! Then gimme a second."

He huffed in frustration, looked back down the street, and prepared to continue his pursuit.

"What do I do when I catch it?" I asked.

"Don't let it go, that's what you do. Got it? Just wait for us to get there."

The Tau scar was already tingling. However, the thought of that human face and its odd synthetic frame made my stomach churn. It wanted to die. But why? What torment could a synthetic entity experience? And if I was able to intercept it, how would I restrain it without killing it? I didn't know the first thing about fighting a biot. However, I had the storm gifts.

Another whistle sounded and Kanya motioned for me to hurry it up.

"Okay." I exhaled deeply and glanced up to the sky. "Ellie? Are you watching?"

I would have to manage an arc, a flight that took me over the traffic. Now, if you thought I could explain the actual physics behind this action, you'd be wrong. Did my physical body reconstitute during this phenomenon, or did I just accelerate at light speed? Whatever the case, if I struck physical objects during my flight, they were sheared, melted, or nicely vaporized.

Maybe it was magic or some weird quantum instinct. I couldn't say. All I knew was that it was real and a rather normal part of my new alien way of life.

At the moment, several street lamps and telephone lines intersected my potential path. This would be tricky. If I flattened my approach, I had a clear window of perhaps twenty-by-twenty feet between cars, pedestrians, and high-power lines. I peered that way and the tesseract bent to my will, boring itself through space, shaping itself into the trajectory in my mind's eye. If all went well, and if the creature maintained his current pace and direction, I should land in front of it by some ten yards.

"Moon! C'mon!"

I nodded. Keeping my gaze fixed on my target spot, I willed myself there.

And let go.

That familiar rush of motion. My stomach dropped. I was struck with the sensation of being outside my body, in another field, unbound by time. No. It wasn't that I was actually outside of time, but in different proximity to it; time itself was, in this state, fluid and malleable. It was Einstein's theory of general relativity—the faster one travels, the more time slows down. Only in this case, I experienced the distinct possibility that time wasn't just slowing down but stopping. Freezing.

Perhaps time was even reversible.

"Hail to the Seventh Guardian!"

The voice was not unlike those I always encountered during my jumps. I had yet to learn where they came from. This one, however, sounded near. Within my very reach.

The tesseract whirled around me. Soft bursts of light and color swirled in the atmospheric canopy. Yet as my attention drew away from the fleeing biot and toward the source of this voice, my body grew dense, weighty. The roiling colors became a fantastical slow-motion tapestry. I turned my head. It was a struggle to do so, as if I was fighting against an invisible current. Once I managed to steady myself, I gasped.

A lanky brown-skinned man in a sequined vest stood there. *Inside the tesseract!* His chest was bare, his neckline braided with layers of jewelry and chokers draped with odd symbols. His hair was pulled tightly up into a ponytail that wafted in the kaleidoscopic tide.

"It's about time," he said, smiling at me. "We need to talk, Reagan."

That's when I noticed he was wearing a Tau.

CHAPTER 2

As I stared at the man, colors flared and folded in upon themselves, framing his silhouette in a liquid glow. I had never encountered such a phenomenon during jumps. Doctor Strange himself would have been impressed with the psychedelic lightshow going on around me.

I must admit, my first reaction was to worry this man was a genie or djinn. I had glimpsed them on occasion in the ether along with cytomorphs and other Invisibles, although I'd never interacted with one. In fact, I'd been warned about them. Djinn usually travelled alone. Though always colorfully dressed, their skin was ruddier than this man's, and their eyes were of volcanic fire. Rapha said they were often tricksters and that engaging them must be done with great caution. This man didn't look like a djinn. But further complicating matters was the Tau. Why was he wearing the same cross as the Imperia? Despite all these questions, my next thought caused panic to grip my mind, spiking energy through my body.

I had stopped mid-jump!

This had never happened before. I was parked mid-teleportation.

My heartbeat practically exploded in my chest. I

had to leave! Or keep going. Immediately! I had a mission to accomplish. My friends were out *there*, waiting for me.

I tore my gaze away from the man and fought to locate the end of the tesseract tunnel. But the weight of the moment bore down on me. Tentacles of cold blue electricity scorched the atmosphere around me. Good Lord! *If I didn't leave right now, I would become stuck in that state forever.* Terminally imprisoned in the Twilight Zone!

"Hey, hey! Reagan. It's all right. Calm down."

The man stepped forward with his hands extended. He didn't seem to fear the energy emanating from me. Or that we were frozen in space-time. I met his eyes.

"It's all right," he said. "You can do this."

I glanced back in the direction of my jump, then to him.

My body was tingling with energy. "D-do what, exactly?"

"Just slow down, man. Calm down. You can stay here as long as you want. Everything else will wait. Trust me."

I fought through the panic and peered into his eyes. Oddly, I sensed that I *could* trust him. Still, I stood panting, struggling to rein in the frenetic juice coursing through my body.

"That's why they call us Lopers," he said. "We have that in common. You and me. We're *interlopers*. We can jump. We can make a way, find the tunnels. The world is full of them! You'll get it before long. It takes practice. But you're doing good so far, brother."

Like the eye of a storm, his gaze seemed to center

me despite the turbulence all around. I yielded, making a conscious effort to dial down my energy.

"Good," he said. "Ease up. That's right."

He nodded, watching as the electrical tempest around me dissipated.

When he was satisfied that I had calmed, he continued. "I've been trying to get your attention for a while. See, there's something we need to talk about. Something way more important than all this. So, you have to listen closely. Okay?"

I nodded.

"It's the map," he said. "*The map*. That's what everyone's worried about. Felix spoke to you about it, right? Good. Well, that's what everyone's after."

I swallowed hard, trying to convince myself that I could remain in conversation with this person without compromising my jump. I glanced at the odd kaleidoscopic current encapsulating us.

"It's just a membrane," he said, motioning to the space around us and its meandering current of colors. "A membrane between Arcadium and Diades. The tesseract passes through this space. Like a tunnel... or a bridge. Something like that. The world is down there. Out there. But the tesseract is a separate structure. It crosses over... or maybe *through*. Things are different here—physics, time. It's an entirely different ballgame. We could stay here for days and the outside world will have barely moved."

I looked down the tunnel as it twined towards the biot fleeing on the streets of Chinatown. Was my destination miles away, or years away? Or maybe just a thought away? Though the light at the end of the tunnel remained distant, the image of the biot remained as I had last glimpsed it. Frozen. Unmoving. Paused in mid-jump.

Voices echoed somewhere, followed by a faint but audible, chorus of moans. But it wasn't coming from the street. He heard it too, because he furrowed his brow before returning his gaze to me.

The energy pulsating through me had subsided. Sensing that I could indeed stay here without compromising my mission, my mind and body calmed enough to ask him the obvious question: "Who are you?"

"I'm Ki."

"The Sixth Guardian?" I gaped.

He reached up and touched the Tau around his neck. "The *Wayward* Guardian. Isn't that what Felix likes to call me?"

I nodded dumbly, unsure what to say.

My mission and some of the prophecies allegedly spoken about me involved this man. I would return the Imperia to glory, lead us to destroy the Black Council. Felix Klammer, the reclusive billionaire who led our group, was convinced of that. However, this would involve reconciling Ki to the team. He had fractured the Imperia, abandoned them for reasons I'd not yet discovered. Some even said he was colluding with our enemies, the Summu Nura. Perhaps now that we were face to face, I would get some answers.

"Did you hear that?" Ki asked. "Those... voices?"

I nodded.

"Shh! Listen. There they are again."

This time, I felt a slight breeze. Cold. Rising from some unseen aperture. It brushed my skin and with it came the voices. Although, this time, the moans had turned to howls and shrieks, distant, but tortured. It sent gooseflesh rippling along my arms. What hellish dimension was this? And what guarantee was there that I wasn't dangerously close to being entombed in their torment? The breeze passed, and the cries grew silent.

After a somber moment, he said, "It's Diades— Earth's lower dimension. The outer rim, at least. It's a sort of limbo. An in-between place for those who've passed."

We listened, but the cries did not return.

"People end up there for all kinds of reasons," Ki said. "But the bottom line is, if you don't let go of your issues, if you don't get right with God, your soul descends to the Netherworld. The longer you stay there, the further you go into Diades. Become one with it. And the worse it gets. No one leaves the Netherworld. Ever. Hail is god there. And he makes sure that everybody stays. They live in a never-ending Veil of Tears. I can't imagine—" He caught his breath and his countenance darkened.

The moment quickly passed and, looking up at me, he smiled weakly. "You heard it, didn't you?"

I nodded again.

He paused and then said, sounding somewhat embarrassed, "Someone I love is down there."

I squinted. "In...?"

"The Netherworld? No. God, no. She hasn't gone that far. She's still in the outer rim, in limbo. Which means, there's still a chance."

I peered at him.

The crimson miasma swirled below me. I turned my gaze there, as if I might spot one of those lost souls pining for freedom. But the whirling kaleidoscopic fog was all I could see.

I had come to believe that hell was real. I mean, how could people like Hitler and Mao and Jerry Springer not go to hell? Of course, heaven was also for real! I'd seen it with my own two eyes. Matisse was there. And Ellie. And I'd do my damnedest to make sure I joined them.

"They think you possess the Fifth Essence," Ki said.

His words jolted me from my thoughts. "The *what*?"

"The Fifth Essence. They haven't told you? It's required to traverse all dimensions."

I gaped, and then caught myself. "Look, I'm not quite sure what that means. Or what it requires."

"Hm. Me either. Whatever it is, it's quite legendary. Some sort of universal element. An ability unknown to earth guardians. Been speculated about for centuries. Only a seventh guardian can possess the Fifth Essence. That's why the Seventh Guardian has always held a special place in their lore. But so far, none of them have delivered. So, the elders have kept waiting. And waiting. And then you show up... *with a Tau burned into your body.* If that isn't a sign, I don't know what is! See, the one who possesses the Fifth Essence can control the Crossroads of Time. And according to the prophecies, when the Seventh Guardian controls the Crossroads of Time, they pretty much control everything—past, future, every event and all potential outcomes. It's like godhood, or something."

"You sure you got the right guy?" I stared at him. "I mean, I'm just a reporter."

He ignored my objections, articulating his next words with precision. "The one who controls the Crossroads of Time can alter history, Reagan. Which means that they can even go back and save the lost."

A slight smile creased his lips.

I shook my head. "No. No way."

"She can be saved, man. And you can do it."

I peered at Ki. His sincerity was commendable. Yet I was unable to discern his motivations, much less the implications of his appeal. *The Crossroads of Time? Altering history?* It sounded like complete madness! But even more disturbing was the suggestion that I could descend into hell and rescue someone from their suffering. What made this thought so repulsive was not the possibility of plunging into the Netherworld, but of circumventing judgment. Only one person had the power to judge a soul's fate, and I was not that person. It didn't matter what kind of powers I'd been bestowed with. Playing God was not a power I wanted.

"The Imperia," I said. "Why did you leave them?"

"You're asking the right questions. Go on."

"That's it. That's what I'm asking. *Why did you bail on the other guardians?*"

"Well, first off, I didn't make a pact with Hail. So, let's stop that rumor right here, okay? And I didn't exactly leave. I mean, I'm around. Look, I'm right here! Besides, it's not like we made a blood oath. Remember when you first joined them? It wasn't exactly official, was it? You didn't sign a contract or something. And there was a lot of folks kinda nudging you along. Right? Rapha. Your Dad. Ellie."

I stiffened. "What do you know about them?"

"What do I—? Ha! Everything. I know everything

about them. I mean, we've been watching you."

"Who's *we*?"

"You gotta be—" He tipped his head back and laughed. Then Ki spread his arms wide. "Don't be so dense, Reagan. Everyone! Other lopers. Warpers. The elder ones. The Black Council."

"You mean, the Summu Nura?"

"The *Lightless Ones*. That's right. *Everyone*. You're on everyone's radar, Reagan. Ever since you took up the Tau and pledged to protect it. That got folks' attention. No one thought you'd do it. Sorry, but your reputation preceded you. You were always a bit of a slacker."

I cleared my throat. "Can't really deny that."

"Ah, but then—the transformation. That was a first—the Tau fused into a human body. Whew! It was a game changer. Maybe the prophecies were legit, they said. Maybe this would release the Fifth Essence. But it's the Black Council that has the most to lose. If you fulfill the prophecies, man, they're toast. They don't stand a chance. You'll knock them back into the Stone Ages."

"Is this for real?"

"They've got plans, Reagan. *Big* plans. They're trying to merge the worlds, break down the barriers between Arcadium and Diades. Set themselves up as Overlords. But you can stop them. You're about the only one who can! The Imperia—pfft!—we just put out fires. But with the map, you'd be invincible. And they know that. So, they've been waiting for you. Watching your moves. Recruiting. Plotting. Setting traps. If you only knew. You're a big deal, bro. *Huge*. That's why the map is so important."

Felix had spoken about the map, and about the Seventh Guardian possessing the Fifth Essence. But it had never registered in me. Honestly, it sounded like a pitch from some far-flung Hollywood script. Which is why I felt lost. This couldn't be real! If it was, this stuff was so far beyond my paygrade I'd need a brain transplant just to catch up.

Seeing my dismay, he said, "It's a lot to process. I know. Anyway, that's kinda how I felt when I first joined the team. I was a big deal. I had powers. I was a Nomlie. And I was caught up in this big cosmic drama, part of this rich history. Wow. It was the stuff of childhood dreams. *I could be an earth guardian!* So many had come before me, lost things, even died. And there were all these stories of courage and risk. You've heard 'em, right? Seven warriors endued with power from Heaven. Who wouldn't want to be part of that lineage? It was crazy."

He inhaled and exhaled deeply. "But then they started dropping like flies."

There was bitterness in his tone.

"One bit the dust, and they just recruited another. Removed their Tau, and found a replacement. That was it. Over and over again, for centuries. Literally. Sure, they had powers. And they were on the side of Good. But they were still very, very mortal. Don't get me wrong—I *wanted* to be a part of that. I wanted to represent and serve mankind. I wanted to be one of God's soldiers. I still do! But it was like... I dunno. It was like I was just a placeholder until the next guy, a stand-in. We were expendable. We all were."

Something had turned inside him, a hope deferred.

I caught myself scratching the Tau scar underneath my shirt.

"It's not winnable," he said flatly. "Not the way it's working now. Felix won't admit that, of course. Or Rapha. Mace probably would. But that good ol' boy enjoys the fight too much to quit. Either way, I got tired. We were all breaking down. You've seen it yourself! *You've felt it.* Every one of us—crippled, blind, infirm. It'd be funny if it wasn't so sad. But the bad guys just kept coming. More and more of 'em. With every victory came two new challenges—parasites, plagues, mad scientists. Whatever! One fire after another. Wave after wave. We couldn't keep up. I got tired. Really tired. And... I just had enough. There had to be another way, ya know?"

As much as Ki's words puzzled me, I sensed he spoke the truth. My body ached in confirmation. Yeah, he was spot-on with his appraisal of the Imperia and our mission. We were breaking down. Even though we were gifted, we were painfully mortal. It wasn't hard to see how someone could lose hope in our mission. Hell, I wasn't completely sold on it yet!

"But now we finally have our chance." He pointed at me and smiled. "With the map, we can change things. Turn the tide. We can finally get the upper hand. Reagan, you can save people. Lotsa people. You can avenge your father. And Ellie. We can stop the Summu Nura once and for all."

The confidence with which he spoke those words caught me by surprise. I needed to check myself. I was getting too caught up in his testimony. Yet it was hard to deny his contention—moving from one fire to the next would do little to turn the tide. Of course, the Imperia were supposed to battle evil. Typical superhero protocol. Yet we were spinning our wheels. Something more dramatic was definitely needed.

"The map," I said. "Refresh my memory."

"*Tabula Lumen*—the star chart. You've heard about it. Allegedly there's one for every human being, a chart of our destinies. Thing is, we aren't privy to our own futures, we're just destined to live them out. But the Stormsoul, the Twelfth-borne of Chaos, is different; he can control the map of his destiny."

I shook my head. *Stormsoul? Twelfth-borne of Chaos?* What the hell kind of sword and sorcery schtick was this?

"The Seventh Guardian!" he snapped. "Don't look so lost. That's who I'm taking about. He can stand at the Crossroads of Time. See? It's all falling into place. We're watching history unfold right before our eyes."

"That's... insane."

"Wild, isn't it?"

"So, you think I'm...?"

"It's not just me. It's Felix and the elders and the Black Council. It's anybody who matters!"

"Why is mine—my, um, map—floating around?"

"You'll have to take that up with Felix. The Great Archive is always guarded. Angels and seraphs— terrible things. You can't just waltz into the Archive. It holds all maps of every possible future. Well, some- how the Archive was breached and—*poof!*—the map got wings. From what I understand, Felix got care- less. Underestimated the Summu Nura. That happens when you're traipsing around in two different worlds. All I know is that it's changed hands. Lots of folks are interested in it. Lots of them have a stake. It's created quite a stir. The Black Council wants it. Lopers want it. Warpers and mages, too. Everybody wants the Seventh

Guardian's star chart. See, they think they can control you with it. Bribe you. Figure out what's going to happen. But as it stands, they can't do anything." He leaned closer and whispered, "*Because the map is mine.*"

His eyes sparkled.

"Wait," I said. "A map of my destiny?"

"That's right."

"*You* have a map of *my* destiny?"

"Yep. I have your star chart. Took a bit of wrangling to get it. But I'm convinced the deal will pay dividends. Amazing, isn't it?"

"So, with it, I can... what?"

"With it you can control the Crossroads of Time. Every possible future can be bent to your will."

"You're crazy."

"We can cripple the Summu Nura for good."

"Strike that—you're freakin' nuts."

"Just think of it. You can redirect the course of time—all events, tragedies, histories—tweaked to your choosing."

I shook my head. "I'm not listening."

"You *have* to listen!"

"Why me?"

"Don't question destiny, Reagan. Embrace it."

"That ain't destiny. It's freakin' madness!"

He shrugged. "It's definitely out there."

"And it sounds dangerous."

"Right?"

"What good does the map do you?"

His humor subsided, and his tone became serious. "It's a bargaining chip, that's all."

"So, *you're* trying to blackmail me?"

"That's too strong a word."

"What other word would you use?"

"Hm. Let's just say I'm trying to *persuade* you. Look, you've got choices ahead for you, Reagan. Big choices. I just want to encourage you to make the right ones. That's all."

"Like rescuing your...?"

"My sister." His features grew sullen. "Harleen."

"Why is she—?"

"She killed herself." He looked away. "She killed herself... and she shouldn't have."

With his words, the kaleidoscopic current shifted. The walls of the tesseract stirred, and gravity tugged at my body.

"That's not the only reason," he interjected, turning back to me. "But it's a big one."

I offered condolences, but he dismissed them.

"Before you get too excited about the prospects," Ki said, "there's a catch."

"Gee. What a shocker."

"There's someone else. He's a... wizard. A magician. Really, he's more than that. He's behind all this." He gestured to the end of the tesseract tunnel. "The biot. The murder. Man, he has some big plans. Anyway, we made a deal."

The tesseract whorled around me.

"Murder?" I wondered aloud.

"Afraid so."

"A... magician?" I said. "What the hell are you talking about? Like David Copperfield or something?"

"Dude."

"What kind of a deal?"

"One we had to make. Like I said—they're one step ahead of you, Reagan. The Summu Nura. They had the map. They've glimpsed the future. *Your* future. They know what lies ahead. And they always will. At least, until you get the map back. It's the only way."

I peered at him.

"Look, I can only hang on to it for so long," Ki said. "Everybody wants it. Lots of fighting. But if they get it again, game over. The Summu Nura will always be one step ahead of you. Like they are now." His body grew faint as if its molecular structure were reconfiguring.

"Wait!" I said. "Don't go. This is crazy! I can't—"

"You *can!* You can change things, man. For everybody. Reagan, with the map we can finally get ahead. With that power... you can save her. You can save whoever you want. Ellie. Matisse. You can restart the game. Reboot everything. Wouldn't that be cool? You can make good on all the promises. You can make us win again."

The image of Ellie, her body wafting in that cryo-tube, imprisoned by Soren Volden, hovered in my brain. Bring her back? Before the Accident? I swayed forward, stunned. Confused.

I watched Ki's body become little more than a spatial smudge. I opened my mouth to speak but the pull of the tesseract was too great. The tunnel's end yawned, an invitation to complete my jump. I could smell the street and hear the traffic again. Ki laughed as my mind returned to its previous trajectory.

Yet my thoughts reeled. The Fifth Essence? A star chart? The Crossroads of Time? Altering history?! What kind of lunatic funhouse was I living in?

As I snapped back into the jump, I heard him say, "I'll protect the map as long as possible. But there're no

guarantees. If you agree, let's hook up. The magician...
he'll be in touch. Trust me. He'll show you the way."

The atmosphere popped. No, it was more like a
mini-sonic boom. My mind caught up with my body
and I was back in real time. While I materialized where
I'd initially planned, I was unprepared for the gated
dumpster that I'd torn through. I stood wobbling between two halves of the sheared smoldering dumpster
in a shallow alley. The smell of spoiled food, wet cardboard, and hot metal formed a toxic combo.

As I recalibrated my senses, the biot swept
around the corner, stopped, and stood facing me.

CHAPTER 3

"**N**omlie!" someone shouted. "He's a Nomlie!"

I wasn't used to being called that. Perhaps it was time I got used to it.

Upon seeing my materialization, pedestrians scattered. Some peered at me from behind lampposts or parked cars while others stared, unsure whether to flee or get my autograph. The biotic serpent skidded to a stop and rose wobbling at the entrance to the alley. Sirens approached in the distance. However, it was the biot that captivated my attention.

We stood ten to twelve feet apart. My appearance had surprised it. I could see it more clearly now and make out previously unnoticed details. Its skin possessed a dull sheen and looked fleshy, but unnatural, like an aging celebrity who'd had one too many Botox injections. Slightly discolored circuitry-like panels framed the face. Our gazes met. Its watery eyes glistened, widening in both infantile recognition and wonder. Fear was clearly present in the creature. Despite its mechanized parts, this thing was not just a machine. It was human. Or part human. As close to a human as a synthetic life form could be. Where had it come from? And what was it fleeing? For, indeed, it was running from something.

My body was buzzing from the jump. My mind still spinning from the encounter with Ki, the Wayward Guardian.

I stepped between the remains of the smoldering dumpster, brushing debris off my clothing as I went. The stink of spoiled food turned my stomach. Everything was happening so fast. My encounter with Ki seemed dreamlike. A blur. An hallucination.

The magician... he'll show you the way.

A magician? And a map—Tabula Lumen. My own star chart. Good Lord, I had to be losing my marbles! The spatial jumps were playing tricks on my mind. Either way, what was unfolding was real enough.

The crowd watched, at the mouth of the alley, as I approached the biot. I instinctively began calculating how I could capture it. Odd calibrations skirted the periphery of my mind. If I could anticipate its next move, I could jump and block its path. However, jumping could land me in convo with Ki again, something I was not ready for. But unless I could summon the power to conjure a gravity bubble or Thor's Asgardian hammer, a physical confrontation with the biot was my only alternative.

A whirring sounded and the drone whipped around the building and hovered overhead, its eye focused squarely on us. *Great!* So much for staying under the radar. However, it did not appear to be a police unit. This one bore standard camo colorations, which left me wondering if it wasn't a civilian's or from an indie reportage outfit. Either way, Kanya and Mace should turn the corner any second. Which meant we'd likely be plastered all over someone's news feed or social media page.

I stared at the biot. "I-I'm not going to kill you."

It furrowed its brow. There was that infantile, innocent gaze again.

"I said, I'm not going to kill you."

The words didn't quell its apparent torment. It recoiled and slunk sideway towards the street, looking to flee.

"I know that's what you want," I said firmly, following it. "You want to die. You want to stop living. Why? Why!? Look, we can help you. You don't need to die."

Though it did not respond, I sensed it understood me. It continued slithering sideways, closer to the street, with its eyes fixed on me.

Now I could make out its machinery in detail. A nexus of micro circuitry and terminals encased along a glistening serrated spine. This looked less like an industrial bot or a military grade apparatus than a visitor from the future. And after my encounter with Ki, a futuristic transient seemed like a real possibility. Had I ripped open some bizarre portal during one of my previous jumps? Perhaps the tesseracts could tweak the fabric of time. Yet it was the appearance of the biot's skin and the uncanny likeness of the human head, not its inhumanness, which made the creature so disturbing.

Fearing that it would turn and bolt any second, I cautiously pursued, maintaining a seven to eight-foot distance between us. Close enough to engage if I needed to, but far enough away to give it space.

"We can help you," I said again, even though I was unsure *how* we could help. "You don't have to do this."

It opened and closed its mouth, trying to answer. *Wanting* to answer. Had I been a full empath, I might have doubled over in agony at the torment this thing seemed to be in. Thankfully, I was not an empath. Not fully. Which left me detached enough to continue to observe semi-objectively.

"What are you running from?" I said, closing the distance between us. "Why do you want to die? Talk, dammit!"

We had almost reached the street. Horns honked and bystanders clustered around the mouth of the alley watching us and snapping pictures. The drone hovered overhead.

Suddenly, the biot stopped. I did the same, now within a single stride of it. We stood staring at each other like alien species in a very close encounter.

Its mouth moved again, emitting throaty gurgling noises. Finally, it spoke.

"S-stop him." Its voice was airy and modulated abnormally between ranges. It swallowed, causing the neural strands along its throat and torso to quiver. "You m-must... s-stop him."

"Who? Who should we stop?"

"F-f-father. You must... s-s-stop... my father."

Father? This thing had a father? I prepared to query but Mace and Kanya bolted around the corner. The biot turned and darted into the street. Kanya stepped out of its way like a matador dodging a bull, as Mace lunged at the biot, apparently intenting to try to tackle it. At that moment, the biot sprang into the air as if it had launched from a trampoline. Clearing Mace by a good eight feet, the biot sailed over the first lane of traffic, unfurling in the sky like a metallic dragon, before landing in the center of the road. Horns and the screech of tires sounded as a delivery truck skidded to a stop, plowing into the biot as it did. A dull thud reverberated and the creature was slammed forward, striking another vehicle before collapsing into a moist heap. It lay unmoving.

I seethed with energy, too stunned to move. Mace, however, had already removed a folded canvas sack from his belt and rushed through traffic, motioning for us to join him. Pedestrians gasped and craned to see the grisly scene. As we reached Mace's side, the driver of the truck clambered out and stood gaping.

The biot remained motionless. A crevice sundered the brow and seeped fluorescent liquid. The spine was limp, and small metallic debris littered the area.

"I didn't even—" The driver's eyes widened. "What the hell is that?"

"Return to your vehicle, sir," Mace ordered, squatting down and snapping some surgical gloves on to recover the remains.

"Who are you guys?" the driver demanded. His attention went to the rifle strapped behind Mace. "Hey. That gun. What kinda gun is that?"

"Sir," Mace said firmly. "We'll take it from here. The authorities are on their way. Return to your vehicle."

"You're Nomlies, ain't ya? Those... those superpeople the news's always talkin' about."

Mace slipped the sack under the biot and, without touching it, scooped it up into the bag. He rose and faced the driver, dwarfing the man with his muscular frame. "Sir, I am *not* a Nomlie."

The sirens were almost upon us. Unless we wanted to be questioned by the cops, we had to get out of there.

"Hey!" the driver declared to the surrounding bystanders. "Hey, they're Nomlies. These three. Right here!"

"Let's go," Kanya said. "C'mon!"

She led the way and we followed, weaving our way through traffic and circling back to our vehicle. Any chance that our escapade would go unnoticed had been shot to hell. As I ran, Ki's words haunted me.

You can alter history, Reagan. You can change things.

Was that what this was all about—changing things? Is that why I'd been chosen? Is that why a religious icon had been fused into my sternum? So that I could alter history? How could that be possible?! In fact, how could *any* human be charged with such a weighty task? Then again, could I still be called a real human? I was a Nomlie. Something… different. Maybe I really *could* change things.

But perhaps the most immediate question was whether I should tell the others about my encounter with the Wayward Guardian.

By the time I got to his van, Mace had it off the sidewalk and idling at the curb. He motioned for me to hurry it up. The store owner stood at the passenger side, scolding Kanya. She was apologetic. I climbed in through the side door and Mace pulled into traffic.

"I hope you told him off," he said to Kanya.

"We were blocking his business," she replied. "Leave him alone." Then she frowned at a large grease smudge on the front of her pants. "Aw, man. I knew I shoulda changed before we left."

Mace shook his head and muttered to himself. He snatched his ballcap from the dashboard and put it on. Then he navigated our way back to the Asylum.

The Tau burned inside me. I lifted up my t-shirt enough to see the fiery scar fingering its way out from under the vest. Ghost flames of heat coiled from my solar plexus. I gingerly tapped my collarbone and the area surrounding the scar, wincing as I did so. Even with the Ndocron vest on, the scar had continued to expand. Over the last few months, the Tau scar had become an entity of its own, spreading its odd grey tentacles across my chest and pectoral muscles. The shape of the cross had become almost unrecognizable. I could feel it at night sometimes, like moths flitting about in my ribcage; on occasion it would make me sick to my stomach. The Ndocron vest seemed to slow its spread. Theoretically, if I didn't wear the vest, I would eventually be consumed by this phenomenon.

Kanya had turned around and was watching me. I let go of the shirt and slumped back into the seat, fighting a pang of despair.

"It looks bad," she said. "Worse than before. Does it hurt?"

"No. I enjoy scalding flesh."

She scowled. "You don't have to be mean."

"You're right. I'm sorry."

Kanya kept looking at me, her brow creased in suspicion. Did she know about my encounter with Ki? Could she sense that I was keeping something important to myself?

Before I could query her, she scrunched her nose. "Ew. Something stinks."

"It's me. I accidently landed in a dumpster."

"Ugh. That's gross."

By now, Chinatown was a frenzy of commotion. Emergency vehicles entered from opposite directions and the police chopper hovered overhead. A loudspeaker barked out some inaudible commands. Fortunately, we had missed the authorities. Just barely. However, this large show of force made me wonder if something much bigger than a fleeing biot was occurring in Chinatown.

Mace had tossed the canvas bag with the remains of the biot on the bench seat. I stared at it. Carefully taking one edge of the sack, I lifted it and peered inside. Amidst the serpentine bundles of moist fibroid detritus, I glimpsed the head, its lower jaw impacted, eyes rolled back to white, forehead cloven.

F-f-father. You must... s-s-stop... my father.

I let the sack close. What in the hell had Felix Klammer sent us to capture? And why? We would likely know soon enough.

The Asylum was located, inconspicuously, in the seat of L.A.'s warehouse district. Above ground, the area was little more than a urine-cured alley with loading docks and shuttered windows. Gangbangers swept through on occasion to smoke lerium, bust wine bottles, and spray-paint colorful monikers. Transients, on the other hand, typically stayed clear of the area. Probably because of its lack of proximity to food, water, and pedestrians with spare change. Adjoining the Asylum was a roll-up door. Years of graffiti layered its rust-laden surface. Mace pulled up in front of it, unlocked the door and hoisted it open.

Rapha's old Ford F215 was parked outside. He waited with Orphana, and they anxiously surrounded us when we stepped out. Rapha wrapped me in a bear-hug. He wore his familiar bandana around his head and smelled like smoke and solder. A welder by trade, the Second Guardian of the Imperia was gifted in Alchemy and could manipulate matter. But like all of us, his gifts came with a downside. Rapha stepped back, casting his broad gregarious smile.

"Brother Moon! You are well, yes?"

"I'm still in one piece, if that's what you mean."

"Excellent!" He clapped his hands together. "For now, we must begin another adventure."

"I think I've had my fill of adventures. Can I opt out?"

He squinted at me for a moment and then laughed. "I must not forget your propensity for sarcasm."

"It's one of my most reliable superpowers."

Rapha laughed again and slapped me on the back, sending me stumbling forward. He seemed to have gotten bigger since I'd last seen him. If that was humanly possible. Every time he exercised his powers, Rapha's physical being expanded. At the rate he was growing, I doubted he would be able to drive his truck much longer. Or walk through the average doorway without taking the frame with it. Becoming a literal giant was inevitable.

Orphana's limp was noticeably worse. She leaned against her cane, still dressed quite fashionably in Mod Squad 1970s garb—paisley bellbottoms and a wide white leather belt—and smiled broadly. The black woman was a Loreist and gifted in agglomeration. However, the ability to dissolve her body and reconstitute it in different forms had practically crippled her.

"Well, it's good to see all you fine folks," she said. "Seems like just yesterday that we were savin' the world from the angel of death."

"Time flies when you're kicking ass," Mace quipped.

"Indeed, it does." Orphana shook her head and chuckled. "Indeed, it does."

"The specimen?" Rapha queried us. "You don't have the specimen?"

"A live specimen? That's a negative." Mace reached into the van, retrieved the sack with the remains of the biot, and lifted it up. "Topped itself. Went straight to robot heaven. Jumped into the path of a moving vehicle. We'll need a sieve to find what we want." He shrugged.

"So, what do we *want*?" I wondered aloud.

Rapha glanced at me. "You're sure it was self-immolation?"

Mace responded, "Sure seemed like it. Besides, Moon said that's what it wanted—to be killed. Ain't that right, Moon?"

Before I could confirm, Rapha responded. "Strange. Very well. Come, friends, there is much to discuss."

Mace parked the van inside the garage, locking the roll-up door behind it. Together we descended into the Asylum. The doors opened and the overhead video cameras swiveled towards our location, running the facial recognition data on us. The Centaur Singularity blaster aimed down at us. With help from Quinn, Kanya had programmed it with enough safety features to circumvent false trigger events. While this would likely prevent another break-in, it also kept visitors on their toes. The threat of vaporization does wonders for one's attention. Tall aisles stretched in opposite directions, lit by overhead spotlights. Down these aisles thick pools of shadow were interrupted by glimpses of moldering statuary and magic weapons. Kanya led the way to the command center. At its entry, a large stone medusa head lay cloven in several parts. I stopped and stared.

"She looked in a mirror," Mace said as he passed.

I shrugged and then ducked under the camouflage netting and rosary beads, and joined the group inside.

Kanya approached a guttered steel table, moved a glass jar containing a large wet specimen, and pushed a stack of files aside, creating a spot for the remains. Mace emptied the contents of the sack out there. It flopped on the table into a mound of fibers, pistons, joints, and cartilage. The life I'd seen in its eyes was gone. The head lay limp, a bloodless split along the joint of the cranium revealing an interior mesh of some sort. A green oily liquid, much like radiator coolant, began pooling around the remains.

The five of us assembled around the table to have a closer look at this oddity. Kanya motioned for us to stand back, switched on a bright lamp, and began scanning the remains with a handheld bio-scan device.

She read from a data screen. "High levels of carbon, hydrogen, nitrogen. Basic components of the human body. The skin is some iteration of hydrogel—that touch-sensitive coating they use for robotic exoskeletons. Soft robotics. Radiation is non-existent. No outstanding toxins register. The frame appears to be a titanium compound." She adjusted the scanner and a thin orange light appeared, which she moved along the specimen. "I'm reading an inorganic energy source in the cerebral cortex. Most likely a data implant."

"A cyborg?" Mace asked. "Part human, part machine?"

"I'm not sure," she replied. "It's definitely part organic and synthetic material. But even the mechanized components appear to have organic analogs. As if the molecular structure was synthetically replicated."

Kanya set the scanner down and pulled up a swivel stool as the call box crackled. Quinn and Celeste were visible in the monitors. Apparently, whatever was going down was a big deal, for now the entire team, save Felix, had arrived. Mace buzzed the elevator and, in a few minutes, the two remaining earth guardians entered the command center.

Celeste made the rounds, her long auburn hair sweeping behind her. She hugged each of us as she went and spoke compliments and kind words. She exuded grace, and I always felt humbled in her presence. Indeed, as a Healer, Celeste's aura was warm and bright and when she embraced me, a shard of goodness always seemed to pierce the darkness of my soul. Quinn projected almost the opposite, a sort of cold omniscience. Like me, his cynicism was potentially toxic. Yet I'd discovered no reason to distrust him. As he shook my hand, I caught my reflection in his dark, oblong glasses. Just underneath them, small, uneven metal plates had been fused into his empty eye sockets. But he didn't need eyes to see anyway. He was gifted in Psionics, though I hadn't yet seen his powers on full display. As his grip lingered, I battened my mind against Quinn's intrusion. If I wasn't careful, he would read my thoughts and uncover my encounter with Ki. So I kept my brain shuttered. Beneath his Viking beard and thick, waxed mustache, Quinn smiled, likely amused by my resistance. He released his grip.

"Dude," he said, "you stink."

"Thanks."

He turned to the remains on the table.

"This better be good," Quinn said. "I was right in the middle of debugging a multi-platform first-person shooter game. And I'm up against a hard deadline." He approached the biot. "So, this is what all the commotion is about."

With his head tilted slightly, Quinn probed the being with his mind. He reached, touched its temple, and straightened. "A sentient model."

"You're sure of that?" Rapha asked, sounding somewhat surprised.

"It has latent memory imprints. Not strict data. It *knew*. It *experienced* things. It *felt*."

"Fascinating." Rapha returned his gaze to the biot.

"It's similar to those Terminator knock-offs we tangled with in Kashmir. Remember that? Colonel Razavi was tied in with that tech firm trying to protect the border with robotic arachnids. They'd been implanted with memories—human memories—for advanced battlefield instincts. It didn't turn out so well. 'Specially when they became self-aware. Yeah. This thing's way too advanced to be a simple grunt."

Rapha nodded. "That could explain why it would seek to kill itself, if it indeed did. Unless it was programmed to self-destruct, sentience would be the only other explanation. The average robot has no motivation to cease its own existence. But why?"

"The bigger issue is protocol." Mace repositioned the light and retrieved some surgical gloves. "Sentience has been outlawed."

"It is," Kanya said, as she also slipped on some surgical gloves. "But that hasn't stopped anyone. The black market for biots is bigger than ever. The government's too invested to wage an all-out war on the underground production of sentient models. They covet the technology too much. The first chance they get to develop a sentient line that won't suffer or turn on us, they're on it. Is that why Klammer wanted us to intercept this?" She glanced at Rapha.

"We would do well not to speculate, sister." Rapha scanned the group. "Our directives were to acquire a live specimen. That was the single transmission. Now we must gather as much information as possible and prepare ourselves for any new developments. Felix will undoubtedly deliver further orders."

"Dear Lord," Quinn folded his hands in mock prayer, "please, not a robot war."

Orphana plopped into a chair and released a heavy sigh. She laid her cane atop her lap. She was weary. I could see it in her eyes. Slight discolorations dappled her forearms, and I knew it to be the side-effects of her gifting. Her entire physical body was likely compromised due to the particle agglomeration. How in the world could she continue like this? At some point, Orphana would become a hindrance to the Imperia, rather than a help. A sickening sense of helplessness settled in my gut. How could we ever hope to complete our mission like this?

We're all breaking down, Ki had said. *Every one of us*

—crippled, blind, infirm. It'd be funny if it wasn't so sad.

Perhaps his defection had been legitimate. Maybe we *were* all just deceiving ourselves. If so, then a new course of action might indeed be in order.

Mace flipped his cap around, stepped to Kanya's side, and gripped the biot's head with both hands. Kanya traced the circuitry creases with her fingertips before slipping them in the fissure in the skull. She gently plied the fleshy exterior away from the head, revealing something like a fine mesh protecting the contents of the cranium.

"Whaddya know," Quinn exclaimed. "It's got a roll bar for a skull."

Retrieving some heavy pliers, she gripped the mesh, testing its strength. It didn't budge.

"Titanium?" Mace asked.

"Or some equivalent. Almost seems like... bone, rather than metal. Really strong bone. It might take some work to crack this nut." She tapped the mesh with her pliers.

"And its body." Mace pointed to the mound of limp fragments that comprised the serpentine torso. "Where was the neural casing?"

"Had to have been close by. The shelf-life of an unsheathed biot is limited. My guess is that it was removed from its torso a very short time before capture."

"So, its chassis was in the vicinity," Quinn conjectured.

Kanya set down the pliers and unraveled a length of the moist, jointed material. With her opposite hand, she swung a large magnification lamp over and switched on its light. Swiveling it toward the spine, she studied the material's contours. Finally, she turned the light off and leaned back.

"Someone's been busy. Wow. I've never seen anything like it. It's incredible."

Quinn nodded. "There aren't very many places something this state-of-the-art could come from. I mean, they ain't making these in Podunk. Celeste, does any of this ring a bell?"

Along with being a Healer, Celeste was an Archivist and had a photogenic memory. She was a virtual walking library. If she'd ever collected data about such advanced robotic operations, she was likely able to recall it.

"Hm." Celeste stepped closer, allowing her eyes to roam along the strange carcass. She bent over, eyeing the base of the skull, and straightened. "BioGen. I'm almost certain."

"The Rothbards," Quinn said with disdain. "It figures."

I peered at the biot. "BioGen has been out of commission for years. At least their sentient line. I did a piece on the old downtown factory four or five years ago. But there was nothing like this. Got a very limited tour of the facility. Basically, we toured the lobby. Saw a single assembly line, but only through a big window. I never managed to get an interview with Balfour Rothbard himself. Talked to a few of his inside team, but no pictures or video was allowed. You needed top secret clearance just to reach the front door. So that was a big deal. Back then, BioGen was the leading maker of factory bots, and the household prototypes. The operation was in its infancy, kept loosely under wraps. Shortly after that, they got shut down.

"Allegedly, Rothbard was developing a line of

sentient robots. Took over from his father, Hiram. But apparently, they were violating the Commission's AI protocol. They've been off the grid ever since. Rothbard started tinkering in other technologies, from what I understand. But the old BioGen complex is like a ghost town now."

I turned to Celeste. "You're suggesting that BioGen is still operational?"

She shrugged. "All I know is that this is identical to some of the models of theirs that I've seen. Early models. See this?" She bent down and pointed to the base of the skull. The skin had been sheared and pulled back, revealing the titanium. "If you look closely, there's some very fine rivets that form letters and trace back toward the spine. See?"

She pointed to fine, detailed imprints. Indeed, a sequence of Hebrew letters appeared there:

נִשְׁמַת חַיִּים

Celeste continued, "They spell out *nishmat chayyim*. It means *breath of life* or *spirit*."

"Wow," Quinn crossed his arms and smiled. "You're also a Hebrew linguist? I'm impressed."

"I just know a little." She brushed her hand dismissively at him.

"Breath of life," I said. "What does it mean?"

"I'm not sure," she said. "The Rothbards are Jewish, of course. It could be a direct reference to the Book of Genesis."

Orphana nodded. "God breathed into the First Man the breath of life. And Man became a living soul."

We remained silent for a long moment and let that sink in.

Finally, I said, "So you're saying that thing—" I

pointed at the biot "—is a living soul?"

Celeste shrugged. "I dunno. Apparently, they were getting close. Hiram started all the way back in the early 1970s with brain hacks—deleting bad memories, interfacing with other brains. By the end of the century his scientists were copying and uploading human consciousness into synthetic torsos. They called them *neural skins* which were, basically, just organic sacks that mechanized skeletons could climb into, house themselves in. The bodies were interchangeable. But entire stalks of brain and neural framework were developed that would be assimilated into these bioengineered bodies."

"The robot revolution." Quinn nodded. "I learned about it in grade school."

"The Rothbards weren't just players, though," I said. "They had cornered the market. Which, from what I understand, rankled the braintrust at the AIC who were bent on disincentivizing any monopolies. Especially ones owned by rich Jews."

"Yeah," Quinn said. "And then the crash."

Celeste shook her head. "It wasn't exactly a crash. They just realized what futurists had been warning us about—smart machines and self-aware AIs. The Singularity was a reality. Of course, it took a few *accidents* for them to come around."

Celeste framed the word 'accidents' in air quotes.

"I remember it well," Quinn said. "It was one of my first big assignments as an Imperia. Top secret DARPA project. An experimental facility on a light aircraft carrier off Delaware. The entire crew was murdered and being *refurbished* by the on-board AI. It managed to *upgrade* its protocol, interface with the ship's computer, and rewrite its own code. Almost escaped. If it had reached shore, God help us."

Celeste nodded. "That was the turning point. Especially when the public got wind. Scientists had to admit, if they weren't careful, they were paving the way for man's extinction. That's when the AIC was formed to outlaw manufacturers making conscious robots. At least, without running it by the Commission. Of course, everybody was up in arms and it prompted all those heated debates about ethics and humanity and human advancement. And that's when things went underground."

I glanced at the remains of the biot. *Breath of life.* The way it had looked at me, the pain in its eyes. Surely this creature had been self-aware. But a living soul?

I cleared my throat. "There was... something else."

Everyone looked at me.

Where should I begin? And how much should I say?

"We're listening," Quinn said. His head was slightly tilted, a faint smile creasing his lips.

I could feel his psyche pressing in upon me. I had to guard my thoughts.

"Right before it killed itself," I said, "it told me we had to do something."

"Like what?" Quinn asked.

"It said we needed to stop its... *father.*"

"Father? You mean, its creator?" Quinn glanced at Rapha. "So that's what this is about—stopping whoever made this? Stopping them from what?"

Rapha furrowed his brow, but did not concede a response.

I scanned the group. "Is Klammer pointing us to BioGen? Or Balfour Rothbard? Or both? Is that what's going on? And if Rothbard is involved, if he's that thing's father, what are we supposed to do if we find him?"

Quinn shrugged. "Stop him. I guess."

Kanya snapped off her gloves, swiveled her chair around, and hastily typed something into a computer. She brought up a picture and angled the monitor our way.

"It's one of the last known photos of Rothbard. A couple years old, now. After this, he dropped out of sight. Except for the gossip columns, I mean."

I stepped closer for a better view.

It looked like a screenshot from a newscast. He was shaking hands with an official, who appeared to be from the AIC, as they stood before its Silicon Valley headquarters. Billionaires were getting younger and younger these days. Balfour Rothbard was one of them. Golden tan and blonde shag. For a short time, he was ranked in the top ten in world surfing competitions, traveling the globe in search of monster waves. The family owned a stretch of beach in Malibu, which he likely put to use. But he dropped off the circuit, allegedly due to his father's eventual death. That's when things went dark. Balfour stopped doing public interviews and allowed the press just enough access to BioGen's business operations to ensure he hadn't forgotten us. He was a lady's man... but with that kind of money, what guy wouldn't be? In the image on the monitor, he beamed his impeccably bleached white teeth, blond hair hanging limply over his designer sunglasses. And he displayed just the right amount of bling. Dressed business casual, Rothbard looked the part of his jet-setting, tech-mogul persona. It was his way of walking, with a strange hitch in his step, which was his signature. The tabloids speculated—was it a birth defect, a deformity? On the extreme end, others even suggested that Balfour Rothbard wasn't exactly human.

"He was in some kind of accident." Kanya left the statement hanging.

"Maybe," I added. "Although some reports suggest he was... experimented on."

"Well," Quinn said. "Finding him would be an issue. He's practically as reclusive as his old man was. He's never seen at their headquarters up north. The old BioGen complex downtown is abandoned. Rumor has it that he holes up at Dante's."

"Ugh," Kanya scowled. "*The Inferno*. I hate that place."

"I don't blame you," I said. "I did a piece on it a couple years back. I couldn't get in unless I agreed to join in on some S&M activities for the evening."

"Ew." Kanya frowned. "That's sick."

Quinn chuckled. "Sounds like the Inferno."

"Friends." Rapha extended his hands in appeal. "We have much to learn. Until we know conclusively that this biot is a product of BioGen and Balfour Rothbard's doing, we must avoid speculation and gather more information. Where was it designed? Where is its body? Why was it loose in Chinatown?"

I nodded. "And how did it get the breath of life?"

CHAPTER 4

As Mace and Kanya prepared for a more detailed inspection of the biot, and the others debated our next move, I excused myself and took the freight elevator to ground level. My shirt reeked from my collision with the dumpster. After several wardrobe mishaps, I'd finally learned my lesson and kept a fresh shirt in the car. Nowadays, you never knew when you'd get slimed by a poltergeist or drooled on by a rockabilly vampire.

The Cammy was parked just beyond the loading dock. I stepped out and over the salt line which encircled the structure. Kanya had maintained Matisse's practice, though I was beginning to wonder how effective it really was for dissuading revenants and keeping bad vibes from entering. As I walked to the Cammy, my cell phone began to vibrate. Being that the Asylum was a lead-lined cellular dead zone, this was no surprise. It was Arlette, my boss at the Blue Crescent. Apparently, she'd already called twice. Damn. A pang of guilt immediately hit me. The Crescent was getting the short end of my attention recently. And though Arlette had, to my knowledge, no idea of my extra-curricular commitments, she was well aware of my waning presence at work. No wonder she was clearly irritable when we spoke.

"Moon. Are you trying to avoid me or just testing my patience?"

"Sorry, boss. I've been busy."

"Yeah. Well, I hope you'll find some time in your hectic schedule for your day job."

"Point taken."

"Good," Arlette said. "Now listen, something big is cooking and, apparently, it involves your old friend Casey Song."

"Casey Song?" I straightened. "Chinatown?!"

"That's right. Chinatown."

"I just came from there!"

"Then you know about the murder?"

Murder? My stomach dropped. Was this the same murder that Ki had spoken about? I was no Sam Spade, but the possible connections seemed more than coincidental.

"Moon?" Arlette said. "Hello?"

"I'm here. So, what about Song?"

"Yeah, well... it's all over the scanners—the Magic Dragon."

"That's his place. He's an herbalist. Remember? It's basically a Chinese medicine store, but he traffics in all sorts of oddities and novelties. Traditional alchemy. Artifacts. Statuary. And, oh, magic."

"Yeah. Well, I'm afraid he doesn't traffic in anything anymore."

"No."

"I hear it's a real bloodbath."

"No. Are you sure? What happened?"

"We're hearing ritual murder."

"What?"

"Symbols. Ceremonial knife. Candles. The whole

deal."

"You've gotta be—"

"No, I'm not."

"Wow. I'm sorry too." I shook my head, numbly. "Was there anything about...?"

"About what?"

"Well, about a biot. An AI of some sort."

"What're you talking about?"

"At or near the Magic Dragon," I said. "Possibly a BioGen model."

"Uh, no. Nothing about biots on the feed. But if there's an AI involved, that could make this story huge. So, I'm sure you're planning to get right on it."

"*Ritual murder*," I said, still puzzling over the possible details. "Sure, boss. I'm on it."

"Atta boy. And, hey—"

"Yeah?"

The line went quiet.

"Yeah?" I prodded.

"Moon, you're not involved in anything else I should know about, right?"

This brought me pause. Thus far, I'd kept my involvement with the Imperia under wraps. But after today's Keystone Cops escapade, keeping things under wraps would likely become impossible. How does one go about telling their employer they're the Seventh Guardian of the Imperia? My guess was that I'd soon be forced to explore the possibilities.

"Yeah." I cleared my throat. "I mean, well, it's kind of a long story."

"Mm-hm," she said pointedly. "Well, I'd love to hear more details when you can find the time in your busy schedule."

"We'll need a lot of it. Time, that is."

"I'm all ears."

I said goodbye, clicked off, and stood staring into space. Coming clean with Arlette was the least of my worries. It was the possible intersections of a sentient robot and ritual murder that had now moved front and center in my thoughts.

Casey Song and I were more casual business associates than actual friends. Truth was, he was a real pain in the ass to deal with. Which is why it wouldn't have surprised me if he'd found himself on the wrong end of someone's fury. But murder? Song and I had exchanged info on several occasions. I also purchased a cool hourglass from him for my collection. He claimed it possessed the ability, when combined with a magic spell, to freeze time. Dude was into that kind of stuff. I'd never inquired about the spell or cared to freeze time. He threw in a lifetime supply of ginseng root with my purchase, which was about as useful to me as a third thumb. I did Mexican omelets, not stir fry. It was his knowledge of Far East arcana, the Eight Immortals, and the Chinese theory of the five elements—water, fire, wood, metal, and earth—that most interested me.

But another detail about the herbalist loomed in my thoughts—Casey Song boasted often, and far too loudly, about possessing the key to the legendary Golem Prison at the Third Street Shul.

Sure, keys to the Golem Prison were not in large demand. It was one of those urban legends that had never really caught on among Angelinos. Except for Kabbalists and conspiracy wonks, the rumors about an underground prison housing an indestructible golem were musty old folklore. My knowledge of golem lore was not extensive. Yet, I knew enough about the iconic creature to know it was rooted in Jewish mythology. And the fact that Rothbard, a Jewish magnate, was on our radar seemed an unlikely coincidence. Perhaps even more pressing, though, was whether someone was interested enough in that fabled key to the Golem Prison to murder Casey Song for it.

I made my way to the Cammy. When I arrived, I leaned over, and studied my face in the passenger side mirror. Other than a slight smudge across one cheek, there was no remaining debris from my dumpster dive. After unlocking the passenger door, I tilted the bench seat forward. Some print shirts and a pair of jeans were stashed behind it in case of emergency. I'd purchased the shirts from a vendor at the Rose Bowl Flea Market. He was dumping a bunch of vintage print tees emblazoned with pulp and B-movie art, so I walked away with a stack. Being that I was a fan of zombies, Jamie Lee Curtis, Bruce Lee, and over-the-top grindhouse productions, I took it as an opportunity to add to my wardrobe.

I removed my shirt and probed around the vest with my fingertips, wincing as I did. My skin was still incredibly tender. Whatever was going on under that Ndocron couldn't be good. I shoved the shirt under the seat and slipped into an *Army of Darkness* tee... because displaying a chainsaw-wielding Bruce Campbell would undoubtedly strike fear into any bad guys. Either that, or they would die laughing.

I needed to share the info about Casey Song with everyone. I reentered the freight elevator, drew the doors shut, and descended into the Asylum. As it rattled its way down, I found myself staring at the corrugated metal cross welded to the interior. Matisse had intended it to drive away revenants. Now it seemed like a cold, hard reminder of the rabbit hole I had tumbled down, a symbol etched into my very being. And with the thought of ritualistic murder leeching into my brain, that rabbit hole could only go deeper.

The elevator clanged to a stop. I yanked the doors open, stepped into the Asylum, and headed for the command center. Orphana stood outside rummaging through a bin of maps, blueprints, and scrolls. She was hunched over on her cane and rose as I approached.

"Well, that's an interesting shirt," she said, surveying the image on my chest with a humored smile.

"Isn't it? It's an old, campy, horror movie about a one-armed guy who goes back to the fourteenth century to help some townspeople battle an army of skeletons."

"Wow."

"I know. They don't make movies like they used to."

She chuckled. "Apparently not."

We simultaneously glanced towards the command center. As I prepared to head that direction, Orphana stopped me and said, "Hey, I meant to ask you— you doin' okay, Reagan?"

"Me? Sure. I guess. I mean, as well as possible... considering everything." I rapped my knuckles on the Ndocron vest and smiled. "Why do you ask?"

"I dunno. You strike me as havin' a lot on your mind. And you look a tad pale."

"Oh. That. Right. I just got some bad news about an old friend. Very bad news, in fact."

"I'm sorry to hear that."

"Yeah, me too. We weren't that close, but still... Anyway, I need to share the details with everyone. It might help us piece this thing together."

"You don't say. Well, then."

She motioned to the command center, as if inviting me to enter. But she didn't make a move. Rather, she continued looking at me with a knowing smile.

Her Tau peeked between the collars of her polyester shirt. Orphana had a rich aura, not bright, but dense with deep earthen colors of wine and forest. She had seen a lot, experienced tragedy and loss. I could tell that. Perhaps such pain was required to be a Loreist. Her gaze remained fixed on me.

"I saw you starin' at me earlier," she said, smiling. "I knew what you was thinkin, Reagan."

That caught me off guard. I wasn't sure if I should apologize for having stared at her or admit my concerns about her frail condition.

"It's all right." Orphana chuckled and patted my shoulder. "I ain't gifted like you and Quinn, I can't read minds and all that. But I knew. And you're right—it's time for me to call it quits. I'm getting too old for this, son. Too... broken down."

"I-I'm sorry. I mean, I didn't want to—"

"Oh, don't. It's all right. Gettin' pretty obvious now. I'm the Third Guardian, after all. I've been around the block a few times. I was recruited by Felix, ya know, way back when. 'Fore he had that contraption on his head. Anyway, things've worn on me, no question." She extended her arm, pulling back the sleeve of her shirt. Her flesh was mottled in places, as if its very pigments and cellular structure had been compromised. "The agglomeration, the clustering—it's eaten away at me.

Any more and I'm likely to lose another limb. Maybe just disappear altogether." She issued her familiar little laugh. "But on a positive note, I have a whole lotta stories."

"I'll bet you do."

"I told Rapha already. About leavin', that is. He agreed. I'll make it official with the others soon. But I'm guessin' everyone knows." She sighed deeply. "I've had a good run. Got no regrets. It's just time we got some more fresh blood in here."

"Don't say that."

"Oh, come on. That's what you was thinkin'! Not in them words, but it's what you was thinkin'. Wasn't it? You don't have ta say. Anyway, we all knew it goin' in. No one lasts forever. Not even earth guardians! That was non-negotiable—bein' an Imperia would cost us everything. Even after I remove this—" she touched the Tau "—I'll still be an Imperia. In heart, at least. But someone else will take my spot. Lord knows who. That's for y'all to decide. Or someone higher up, I should say. But there's lots to choose from. The Imperia got lots of friends. Anyway, it's the right time. I'm sure of it."

Her words were partly a relief. I sympathized with her weariness and the admission of her worn state. But with it came a pang of self-pity. After all they'd said about me, prophesied and predicted, I doubted that a similar option was available for me. Unlike the others, I could not just retire. Or could I?

It made the notion of the star chart even more intriguing.

"I know it's hard," she said, as if intuiting my conflict. "No question. Sacrificing so much for a reward that's, well—it's not guaranteed. Not knowing if we'll live to see the fruits of our efforts. It can be frustrating. Which, I s'pose, is part of the mystery. Ya know? Stayin' the course even when the end ain't in sight. Holdin' on to... promises. Holdin' on to hope. The hope that we can change things, for the better. That our lives can make a difference. That's our real power, Reagan—we can change things."

She smiled and then gazed upwards, as if recalling a distant memory. Instead, she recited some lines or lyrics. The words seemed strangely familiar.

"Betwixt the world of futures' past,
     and present almost gone;
One stands alone and wields the pow'r,
     of destiny undone."

She nodded to herself. Then she looked away and sighed deeply. In a moment, she returned her gaze to me. "I don't remember who wrote it. It's from an old tome. Celeste could prob'ly say. But it's always struck me, a prophecy of some sort—the *power of destiny undone*. It ain't set in stone. The real power isn't in magic or bombs or broken-up earth guardians. It's in changing destiny. And that's what we've been blessed with. All of us."

I peered at her. A holy moment seemed to be upon us.

"There's great things ahead for you, son. I wish I could stay around to see it." She patted my hand. "C'mon." She slipped her arm into mine and walked me into the command center. "Better tell the others what you learned."

Inside, everyone had dispersed among various activities. Rapha bent over the radio scanner with a headphone piece to one ear. Mace and Kanya continued to probe the biot. Celeste sat, tracing her fingers quickly over paragraphs on an electronic tablet. Quinn, meanwhile, worked frantically on a Rubik's Cube.

Orphana summoned everyone's attention. "Reagan has somethin' to tell us."

I stepped forward. "There's been a murder. In Chinatown."

"Hello," Quinn said, completing the Rubik's Cube and setting it down on the table with emphasis.

"Yes." Rapha rose, setting down the headphones and gesturing to the console in front of him. "I just heard it on the scanner."

"Apparently, it's a guy I know," I said. "Or... *knew*. Casey Song. Owner of the Magic Dragon. An herbalist and alchemist. A magic dealer. Ritual murder. Allegedly."

"Ritual murder?" Kanya asked, looking up from her specimen. "And it's connected to this?"

"That, I'm not sure of."

"Lemme see," Quinn scratched his thick beard in feigned concentration. "Felix sends us to Chinatown to intercept fleeing robot. Why is robot running? No one knows. Meanwhile, herbalist is murdered in general vicinity. Coincidence? Hm. Gimme a minute."

"I'm just asking," Kanya said defensively. "So, you think that... the biot's involved?"

"I don't know," I said. "I'm not sure what to think. Song was involved in antiquities. And Oriental herbalism. But there's something else—maybe it's trivial. He also trafficked in esoterica. Magic and the occult. That's why he always talked about—boasted about it, really— having a key to the Golem Prison."

"Oh." Celeste set aside the electronic tablet. "It's been a long time since I heard about that."

Rapha straightened. "Third Street Shul. Fascinating."

Without looking up from his work, Mace said, "Matisse had Third Street on his radar for a while. He claimed to have acquired a Jewish magic book from there—the *Sefer Raziel* something-or-other—along with some amulets. We logged 'em years ago. They're stored in C bay in the Spell Books, Tomes, Eldritch Lore section. Part of some Kabbalistic grimoire which he believed contained powerful universal knowledge."

"Don't they all," quipped Quinn.

"Matisse knew what he spoke of," Mace growled. "God rest his soul."

"He's right," Kanya said, setting a scalpel down on the examination table. "My father was suspicious about the synagogue. He didn't like Rabbi Finkel and said there was dark energy there. We'd seen it—large gatherings of Invisibles around the shul. He always thought that something big was in the works. When he acquired the book and those amulets, they went straight into storage. He nearly got killed trying to get them. I remember. He was laid up for a solid month after that incident. But that was how he rolled." Her voice trailed off.

Kanya's recollections brought back welcome memories of the Mad Spaniard. He didn't just march to his own drummer; he led his own parade. Knowledge of Matisse's interest in Third Street Shul and, potentially, the mythical Golem Prison it housed made Casey Song's murder even more suspicious.

Mace said, "Matisse believed that Third Street

housed highly classified magical data and was determined to keep that info out of enemy hands. Which is why the book is here."

"Magical data," I said. "Was it important enough to kill for?"

"If the Third Golem is really there," Celeste said, "then yes."

I scowled. "You guys don't really believe that, do you? I mean, golems aren't exactly the weapon of choice nowadays."

"Oh, but not just any golem." Rapha scanned the group soberly. "An indestructible golem. A being of immense strength, oblivious to magic. It is said that the one who controls the Third Golem is virtually unstoppable. Only as the creature remains locked in the Prison can its wanton power be obviated."

Celeste nodded ruefully as a chilled silence passed among us.

"Welp," I said. "Then we'd better hope Casey Song hid that key in a very safe place."

"Very well!" Rapha exclaimed, clapping his hands. "We have our charge."

"Since Moon knew Song," Quinn said, "we should start by sending him and a couple of us back to Chinatown and the Magic Dragon to poke around."

"I'm game," I said. "Plus, I've got a piece to do on the story now. And if it's ritual murder, Special Investigations will likely be there. If so, my friend Jimmy might also be able to fill in a few blanks."

"Then let's do it." Quinn glanced at Rapha, who nodded his approval.

"Got room for me?" Celeste said.

Quinn stood and bowed. "Always, m'lady."

"We'll need your help later," Rapha said to the three of us. "Meanwhile, we shall look into the magic book or any other possible leads we can find here. Mace and Kanya can continue their examination of the biot. I shall contact you if we hear from Felix or learn anything. And please," he looked at Quinn, "mind your manners."

"Why are you looking at me?" Quinn objected. Then he turned to Celeste. "Why is he looking at me?"

"God be with us!" Rapha proclaimed. "Knights errant, my friends! Knights errant."

CHAPTER 5

The three of us made our way to Chinatown, while the rest of the crew remained at the Asylum to hunt down possible leads. I drove the Cammy. Thankfully, the cab was clean. But I was conscious of the stinky shirt jammed under the seat. I'd purchased a car deodorizer shaped like a Christmas tree that smelled like blackberries and cloves and hung it from my rear-view mirror. I must admit, it helped a little. However, years of being a slob can't be masked by a single car freshener. Either way, I'd learned my lesson about being prepared for impromptu guests in my ride.

Being that I'd retained the original leather bench seat, there was enough room to fit three people. Not ideal. However, Celeste squeezed into the middle between Quinn and me. She smelled like flowers, and her aura glowed white with purity. I become intensely aware of the Tau scar under my vest. Could her very proximity be curative? Still, I felt unworthy. Was this what it felt like to be in the presence of holiness? If so, I'd better hope I didn't combust into a steaming pile of crap.

We rode with the windows down, the warm air whipping about the cab. Summer had arrived in Southern California with all its sticky, sweat-laden glory. The onshore flow had surrendered to the dog days of summer. Between the mix of tourists, pseudo celebrities, vagrants, and hustlers, the city was a colorful, repulsive collage of humanity.

The shadows had grown in length across the city as the sun arced its way to the Pacific horizon. I had so many questions. But perhaps the biggest was whether Ki had told me the truth. However, I remained determined to guard our encounter, and with Quinn nearby, I instinctively focused my attention elsewhere.

When we reached Chinatown, the Magic Dragon was on virtual lockdown. The entire block was cordoned by police vehicles and barricades. Whatever had happened, it was a really big deal. I eventually found a spot and wedged the Cammy in between a derelict pickup and a Beamer. I pulled my backpack from behind the seat, and the three of us made our way to the Magic Dragon.

Walking the streets these days was quite an adventure. My second sight allowed me to see a myriad of exotic interdimensional beings. At one time, I would have flippantly dismissed the idea of an invisible world alongside our own. Now, the reality was becoming second nature. As we approached the Magic Dragon, the atmosphere grew thick with Invisibles. The store sat above street level. A flight of marble steps passed between two large statues of jade-green dragons that straddled the entryway. The dragons crouched on finely carved mahogany pedestals staring angrily forward. Clusters of invisible narvogs loped in and out of the entry like shadowy jackals. Up the steps, I glimpsed a swirling dark mass along the ceiling inside the herbalist's shop. I couldn't tell if it was a single entity or a cumulation of many. Whatever had happened in there had attracted half the underworld. This was going to be fun.

Sections of the sidewalk and several storefronts were cordoned with cones and crime scene tape. Nearby store owners huddled in whispered conversation as investigatory teams tromped in and out of the Magic Dragon. Just beyond the barricades, at street level, a dozen reporters and accompanying cameramen, several whom I recognized, encircled a police spokesman.

"Perfect timing," I said, stopping and rummaging through my backpack. I removed my press card and slipped the lanyard over my neck. "I'll be back."

Quinn nodded. "We'll poke around here, see if we can start some trouble."

As I approached the group, an officer asked to see my pass before waving me on. I joined them as the spokesman, a stout 30-something Asian man, was fielding a question from a female reporter I didn't recognize.

"—believe both fatalities were victims of another perpetrator, double homicide, or killed by each other?" she asked.

"That will be determined by the investigators," the spokesman said. "At this stage, we have two fatalities. That's all I can tell you."

"And one of the victims is the owner?"

"We have not concluded that. No."

"Is this linked to the Echo Park slayings in any way?"

"We have no reason to believe that. Not at this early juncture. However, all possibilities will be explored."

"Do you believe robbery was a possible motive?"

"All possibilities will be explored."

Windchimes tinkled in front of the shop as a warm breeze brushed past. I looked up toward the shop and did a double-take. Bernard, my guardian angel, leaned against one of the dragons inspecting his nails. When he saw me, he straightened and spread his arms as if to say "Finally." He turned and raced into the building, sending a pack of nearby narvogs scattering.

What the—? Well, I guessed we were on the right track.

The police spokesman glanced over his shoulder and then prepared to dismiss himself. Keeping an eye on the entryway and what my guardian angel was possibly up to, I asked, "There were some reports that ritual magic was involved. Can you corroborate that?"

Several reporters turned to me with eyebrows raised before scribbling out this info on their tablets or typing it into their devices. The spokesman scowled.

"No, I can't. At this stage, I suggest you consider such information strictly hearsay. Now if you'll—"

A reporter jammed a recording device in front of the spokesman. "So, the reports of ritual magic are unfounded?"

Another asked, "Is that why the Special Investigations unit is here, to investigate ritual crime?"

The spokesman pursed his lips. "As I said, any mention of ritual magic, at this stage, is pure speculation. Until we get forensics and complete our investigations, this is simply a crime scene. Now, if you'll excuse me."

As a second officer began herding us back outside

the barricades, a familiar voice called from above, "Kolchak!"

I turned to see Jimmy Pastorelli, lead investigator for the LAPD Special Crime unit and personal friend, descending the steps. Although I was unsure in what capacity Bernard could interact with the physical world, the angel walked directly behind Jimmy and appeared to be nudging him forward.

I left the group, to the officer's protestations, and met Jimmy as he reached the sidewalk. "He's okay," he said to the cop. "Part of my investigative team."

The policeman scowled, as I did my best to not look smug, and left us.

"Just the man I needed to see," Jimmy said.

As I turned my attention to him, my stomach dropped. A shadowy entity draped his cranium and shoulders. It was burrowed so deep I couldn't see its eyes. I hadn't come up with a name for these things. They were moist and slug-like, not demons in the typical sense, yet they often accompanied the ill and the infirm. Much like a growth or a wart, these organisms appeared to sprout from malignancy and malaise. But I could not discern whether their presence was an extension of the sickness itself or whether they were simply drawn to the toxic effluence that accompanied such diseases. This particular creature was rooted in Jimmy's gut; a parasite feeding off his cancer, piggybacking on his suffering. I could ascertain its tentacles and roots tracing toward his stomach. Of course, Jimmy had no idea that this thing, which reeked of death, was attached to him. And by the look of Jimmy's features, it was draining him of the fragile life he still possessed.

He reached out to shake my hand. His grip was noticeably weak.

"Jimmy. Dude. You look like hell."

"I feel like I've been there—to hell. Or else I'm heading there pretty damned fast."

"God, don't talk like that, Jimmy."

He nodded and patted my shoulder. "I appreciate the sentiment, Moon. Stage four cancer will do that to you, I guess."

I stared dumbly, not knowing how to respond.

He'd lost a lot of weight since the last time I'd seen him. His cheeks and eye-sockets were sunken. If I was one to dispense pep talks about the power of positive thinking or hope for healing, this would have been a perfect time. Yet the faint tingling in my fingertips made me wonder if I had a different role play. Maybe I had the power to actually remove this demonic cloud from Jimmy. I opened and closed my hands, hoping to drive the sensation out of them. Celeste was a healer. Perhaps I should introduce them. Or get a lesson from her in the healing arts. Then again, I was the Seventh Guardian of the Imperia. That, at least, must mean sickness couldn't stand in my way.

Yeah, right. I almost laughed out loud as the thought crossed my mind.

"What about you?" Jimmy asked. "Have you had that... that *thing* on your chest checked out?"

I shook my head and then I rapped on the Ndocron vest with my knuckles.

"You're wearing body armor now?" Jimmy quipped. "Wow."

"Something like that. It's supposed to keep it from spreading."

"Spreading?" He peered at me. Then he scratched his bald head. "Yeah, well, maybe you and me aren't that different. Anyway, you should have it checked out. It looked damned creepy. But there's somethin' else you should probably know."

"Yeah?"

"I put in a notice for some time off. The chemo is tearin' me a new one. Damn. Who'd have thought I'd ever say that? Shit. Oh, well. I probably deserve it. Karma and all. They already appointed someone to replace me. That's how fast it happens, ya know? *Thank you for your service and don't let the door hit you on the way out.* The whole department's going down the shitter."

"A replacement? Who is it?"

"You don't know her."

"*Her?*"

"Yeah. They call her Mrs. Mantis. Not sure if that's because of how she walks or because she eats her partners. She doesn't believe. Thinks everything can be explained by science or psycho-babble. A real stiff. Wants to streamline the department and kick back cases like this—" he motioned towards the Magic Dragon "—to homicide. Let them wade through the occult bullshit and make up their own minds." He shook his head. "Fact, the rumor is they want to completely shut down the SI unit."

"Damn. Jimmy. This is serious."

"Right? Your LAPD privileges are about to take a serious hit, Moon."

Bernard kicked at several narvogs that bolted from the Magic Dragon. It was more banter than an actual skirmish. I stared off in space, wondering at the complicated mess my life was becoming.

"Anyway," Jimmy said. "Magic circles. I recall you having some knowledge of them."

"Uh, yeah. *Some*. I'm no expert. I did a piece on Saint Tom and had to research them. He used to kill his victims in magic circles. Remember?"

"Saint Tom. How could I forget."

"I also, well..."

"What."

"I escaped from one once—a magic circle."

"That so?"

"With the help of Weeping Eve, I mean."

"The Saint Vincent ghost?"

I nodded.

Jimmy stared at me. Then he shook his head. "You're weirder than I thought, Kolchak."

"If you only knew."

Jimmy motioned for me to follow him and proceeded back up the steps. Bernard tore himself away from the narvogs and joined us, taking the steps two at a time before disappearing inside the Magic Dragon.

"What's up with the t-shirt?" Jimmy said, jabbing his thumb over his shoulder.

"What do you mean?"

He stopped and pointed at the logo on my shirt. "Skeletons? Chain saws?"

"*Army of Darkness* is a classic!"

He shook his head, as if pitying me. "Casey Song is the owner," Jimmy said, as he climbed the steps. "And the deceased."

"I knew him. At least, we had some business transactions."

"My condolences. You got a strong stomach,

right?"

"It's that bad?"

We reached the landing.

"It's worse than bad, Moon. It's like a butcher shop in there. It's also pretty damned weird. Anyway, you know the drill. No pictures. And don't touch anything, got it? You're here as an expert in magic circles. That's it."

"Um..."

"Just roll with it, Moon."

We passed through two intricately carved dark wood doors. Some officers looked up from their paperwork to give me the stink eye. Makeshift halogen lights on stands had been erected throughout the place. They cast hard shadows everywhere. Evidence markers randomly dotted the adjoining rooms. A woman wearing disposable coveralls, surgical gloves, and safety glasses dusted the door and its frame for prints. Up ahead, another CSI member snapped pictures of shattered ceramics strewn across the floor. Unbeknownst to them, the Magic Dragon was crawling with Invisibles. On the ceiling, what appeared to be an *octopod* hung, suctioned by its three-split hooves. This is what I'd glimpsed outside. It was the largest one I'd ever seen, branching from the foyer into various rooms of the shop. Besides the narvogs, griddlebacks had begun a cocoon in one corner of the shop and hunkered there as they watched my approach. Near a bank of ancestral carved masks, a dendritic form rose, revealing an amorphous gaping mouth and pitch-black eyes. Branch-like arms extended with loose, moss-like matter draping the appendages. When the thing realized I could see it, it reared back and spat a massive oily loogie my direction. I leapt out of the way and slammed into a nearby display case, rattling the ivory carvings inside.

Several officers looked angrily my way.

"Moon!" Jimmy hissed. "What'n the hell's wrong with you? This is a crime scene. Be careful!"

"Sorry." I readjusted my backpack, glanced at the creature, and quietly snarled. As we left that hallway, I made a mental note to include this entity in my sketchbook *Of the Invisible Order and Its Inhabitants. Spitting Dendrite* would be its temporary name. Although *Loogieman* also had a nice ring to it.

We passed a room lined with glass containers, shelved, all filled with exotic and unusual herbs. An amalgam of pungent aromas struck me. As Jimmy turned into another room, a vestibule of sorts, something else caught my eye. The beams and doorposts of this room glistened with a grey-green substance. Irregular prints, elephantine in size, and splotches riddled the surrounding surfaces. Apparently, something invisible and quite large had grappled through this place, leaving its residue behind. Pools of the slimy matter shimmered on the carpet. Some even dripped from the ceiling.

As I stared at the invisible gelatinous material, Jimmy approached and asked me what I was looking at. I shrugged off the question and followed him through a large entry into the next room. I only managed two steps in before I put on the brakes.

It was a large, lush back office with dark wood-paneled walls and an ornate Oriental carpet. Evidence markers were everywhere. The stench of guts and char was like a vice on my innards. A thick wooden desk lay overturned, its content strewn about the floor. Colored beads haphazardly scattered the carpet, remnants from a torn bead curtain. A section of one wall had been collapsed, yet it was unclear whether an explosive had done this. Particles of mortar and dust powdered the surroundings. Through the opening, a spacious room with a neatly made bed and carefully arranged satin pillows was visible. The room appeared undisturbed. Perhaps even more interesting was the absence of Invisibles in this area. Except for the grey-green prints lathered about the place, there was no evidence of demons here. Odd.

As I unconsciously wandered forward, Jimmy extended his hand to stop me. I had nearly stepped onto an area of blood-soaked carpet. Indeed, upon closer inspection, a sizeable amount of the colorful carpet was swollen with blood. Books scattered the room, ripped from now empty bookcases. Several sizeable wall-mounted cases hung, partly torn from the plaster. Shards of pottery lay like shrapnel about the room, along with shattered busts of ancient Asian holy men or warriors. Either the assailant liked breaking things or this room was being scoured for something. It was the first indication that the key might indeed be in play. But if so, where would Song have hidden such a thing? Something that small could be anywhere! I studied the room for possible hiding places. The invisible grey-green slime glistened on multiple surfaces. It was not a heat signature, but residue. However, the sheer volume of the sickly substance indicated either a large Invisible had traipsed through or a violent explosion had occurred in the other dimension. Sheets covered what I assumed were two bodies, lying at opposite angles, approximately eight to ten feet between each other. The metallic copper smell of blood thickened the air.

A circle, perhaps six or seven feet in diameter, composed of red and gold powder, occupied the center of the room. A pentagram traced the interior. The dimensional slime was densely splattered in thick pools. Tentacles of scorched fiber emanated from the circle's perimeter, as if a flame had blasted out from it. Thin leafy boughs of indeterminate origin, possibly an herb or cutting of similar floral nature, lined the inside of the circle in irregular patterns. Five purple candles, thick and squat, evenly divided its circumference. Symbols had been crudely carved into the candles, each of which stood at the five points of a star that had been burned into the carpet. One of the two bodies rested inside this circle. The sheet covering this body was nearly black with drying arterial blood. The form underneath the sheet appeared misshapen, as if it had been splayed. Irregular wedges of fleshy matter, internal organs possibly, were partly visible under the periphery of the sheet. Just outside the circle lay a chaos talisman, chain included.

"It's Casey Song," Jimmy said, staring blankly at the covered corpse. "He's been positively IDed. Suspect went straight-up O.J. Nearly decapitated him. Opened the torso, sternum to groin. The organs were arranged, Ripper style. Funny thing—the victim was not bound and showed no sign of struggle. So, either he was already deceased or..."

"In process."

Jimmy grunted. "The cash register is full. If there's a safe, we haven't found it. Whoever did this was, apparently, either looking for something or just really enjoys dicing people up. But this," he gestured to the magic circle, "has 'ritual' written all over it. You knew the guy, right? Anything out of the ordinary that might incur this kind of interest? Besides fascination with fancy vases and Oriental knick-knacks."

My eyes burned from the amalgam of herbs and incense, and my stomach was in my throat at this point. I'd seen my share of autopsies and crime scene photos. But the combination of blood and viscera, along with the sheer razing of this room, revealed a ferocity I could not comprehend. For an excruciatingly long moment, I felt like I'd walked into a situation I had no business even witnessing.

"Moon. What do you think?" Jimmy asked. "Hey, are you okay?"

"Uhh..." I swallowed. My flesh had grown clammy. "I, uh..."

The magician, Ki had said. *He'll be in touch.* Perhaps Casey Song's splayed body was his calling card.

"Moon!"

I wiped sweat off my forehead.

"Don't do it, Moon," Jimmy warned. "If you're gonna puke, get the hell outta here."

I nodded and gulped back bile.

"Focus, Moon," Jimmy said. "The circle. What can you tell me about it?"

"Right." I drew the back of my hand across my lips and swallowed hard again. "Hm. Like I said, I'm no expert. Okay. Whew! I dunno. It's a mashup of stuff. The symbols there—" I squatted down and pointed to an image etched on one of the candles. "Star of David. Basically. In fact, all of them seem to be some sort of variation of a hexagram."

"We're talking Kabballah or Jewish magic?"

"No. Not necessarily. Hexagrams are shared by a lot of religions—Hindus, Buddhists, even Satanists. And there's no continuity here, it's a mashup of symbols—alchemical, neopagan. Like that." I pointed to the chaos talisman. "A sigil of chaos. The arrows pointing all directions—it's a system that's free-form. Which could suggest that this isn't any one brand of magic at all, but many."

"Yeah. That doesn't help. Anything else?"

"Well, the color—ceremonial color is typically important to the intent of the circle. Here you have red, gold, purple. So, my guess is that this is less of a circle for energy or protection and more for... summoning."

"A summoning circle?"

"That would be my initial guess. Yeah. But I'm no expert."

"You already said that," Jimmy said. "If it's a summoning circle, what was being summoned?"

"Or *who*. Depends. Demons typically. Sometimes angels."

"And the star?"

"Well, in Kabballah, it's typical to represent the classical elements—earth, air, fire, and water."

"What about the fifth element?"

"Hm. Some practitioners considered it *aether*, old school alchemists. Others saw it as a nonmaterial element, like spirit or something."

Jimmy peered at me. "So why was the victim gutted? Ceremonial? Some type of revenge?"

"Either that, or... as an offering."

"A human sacrifice? Damn. Well," Jimmy straightened, "someone went to a hell of a great length to do all this."

"I'll say."

Several individuals wearing coveralls, nitrile gloves, and safety glasses entered, oblivious to us, and began collecting fragments of debris from an area near the overturned desk. One used surgical scissors to clip carpet fibers. The fibers were then inserted into a specimen bottle and capped. A radio crackled in the other room and a commotion ensued. Raised voices followed by a dull thud.

Jimmy glanced that way and shook his head. "Damn homicide guys. They just can't fathom SI having precedence over their entitled pansy asses."

I rose, and as I did the blood drained from my head, leaving me dizzy. The stink of entrails and burnt carpet, along with the thick aroma of herbs and incense, was making me pukish. I stood quietly reorienting myself and swallowing down the nausea.

The investigators glanced back at us and then weaved their way to the exit through crumbled plaster and beads. They navigated around several hollow busts made from porcelain or alabaster, scattered in large fragments—a cheekbone, a neck and jaw, shoulders, half a cranium—and left the room.

A familiar golden glow blossomed out of thin air and bathed the statuary.

I watched as Bernard's body gradually appeared in the middle of the crime scene. Like a bronze moon waxing strong, the angel's back and shoulders emerged. The remainder of his body materialized revealing that he was crouched before one of the busts, peering at it. I tilted forward, squinting to discern what the angel was scrutinizing. Detecting my curiosity, Bernard turned and touched his index finger to his lips, silencing me.

Then he rose and motioned enthusiastically to the cranial section of a cream-colored, semi-marbleized bust.

The piece was about the size of a real human head, yet cracked in half, becoming a bowl lined with serrated edges. But it was the sight of an ornate rustic copper orb cupped to the underbelly of the piece that now had my attention. As I peered at it, Bernard smiled broadly. But what was I looking at? As I focused my attention on the angel, he mimicked turning a key in a lock; then he motioned to the piece, mimed snatching it, and jabbed his thumb towards the doorway.

Huh? No way!

He nodded.

Apparently, my guardian angel wanted me to steal something from a crime scene.

I squinted at him. *Really? You want me to take that? It isn't even a key!* As if reading my thoughts, Bernard nodded eagerly again. He pointed at the bust, pretended to snatch it, and then turned and simulated running. I gaped, now incredulous. *You have gotta be—*

"Moon!" Jimmy had stepped to the second body and stood with his hands on his hips. "Have you heard a word I said?"

He glanced to the area where Bernard stood and then back at me, his brow knit in suspicion. Slowly, his tone laced with dubiety, Jimmy said, "What's over there? What are you looking at?"

I glanced at him and then back at Bernard. *Dammit.*

"Moon," Jimmy said. "What is going on? Concealing information about a crime is obstruction of justice. I'm pretty sure you know this, right?"

"What if it involves a guardian angel?"

At the mention of a guardian angel, most people, especially in law enforcement, would likely reprimand the claimant for attempting to mislead or misdirect, if not for being a complete loony bird. Jimmy Pastorelli did neither.

"Yeah," he said. "Even if it involves guardian angels."

"I told you I can see things," I said. "Right? Since the Accident. I *know* things. Remember, Jimmy?"

"You can see demons and angels." He nodded casually. "Sure. I remember."

"And cancer. I can sense things like cancer. That's how I knew about yours."

At the mention, he stiffened, yet managed to remain relatively nonplussed. However, the diseased slug rooted in his gut roused at the mention of the illness. "Okay. So, what does that have to do with this?" Jimmy motioned to the crime scene.

Bernard clamped his hands upon his head in dismay.

"Moon?" Jimmy said. "If you know somethin'..."

I readjusted my backpack and stood, thinking. Then Bernard folded his arms and glared at me as if to say, "Don't you dare!" But I looked away.

"I don't care what it is," Jimmy said. "Or *who* it is. If you got information that will help us solve this crime, Moon, then you need to come clean."

Jimmy had always been fair to me. Plus, he was a believer. In the paranormal, I mean. And being that he was starting a long journey into the valley of the shadow of death, he deserved to know.

Just not everything.

"Something else was here," I said. "That's what

I know, Jimmy. Forensics won't show anything. You won't find fingerprints, luminol probably won't reveal it either. But an Invisible did this. At least, a lot of this. A demon of some sort. There are all kinds of them here, Jimmy. Right now. This place is crawling with invisible things. That's what I was trying to avoid out there. A demon or spirit creature. It spat at me. They're all over this building. But in *this* room, there aren't any."

"Just an angel."

"Right. Just an angel. But whatever *was* here was big. Very big. It left some kind of film, green slimy junk is all over the place. You can't see it. Probably can't detect it, either. But whatever was summoned, it was big and mean. And apparently mad as hell."

Bernard heaved a sigh of relief and pretended to wipe sweat off his brow.

"There's a good chance," I continued, "that Casey Song is dead because of whatever was summoned."

Jimmy stood dispassionate. He stared at the second body under the sheet at his feet. "So, I'm supposed to put out an APB for an invisible slime monster?"

"Either that or call Ghostbusters."

Jimmy muttered something to himself. Then he bent down and pulled the sheet back. "And this? Is this the result of your invisible slime monster?"

I braced myself for something grizzly but, surprisingly, was more mesmerized than repulsed by what I saw. The second corpse was quite unlike the first—a bloodless, headless, empty sack. Little more than a deflated torso. Translucent greenish liquid seeped from the neck. One hand still grasped a large black ceremonial blade. Ornate carvings could be seen along the blade's handle, which was smeared with drying blood and grey-green slime.

This was the body our biot specimen had previously occupied.

"You've seen these before, right?" Jimmy glanced at me. "It's a neural skin. Most likely a Big Three model. There're others still floating around. Sentient models, that is. They escaped or were kept from the Extermination. But this wouldn't be the first time a robot was suspected of murder. Or that a manufacturer evaded incrimination."

"You're saying that this biot is the suspect?"

"It fled the scene. It's holding the murder weapon. I'd say those are red flags, wouldn't you?"

Did he know about our recent romp through the streets of Chinatown? With all the witnesses and cameras clicking, our acquisition of the biot brain would become common knowledge soon enough. Which would soon enough put the Imperia dead center in this investigation. We were screwed. Royally. However, at the moment, diversion would buy us time.

"It's too obvious," I said.

"Maybe," Jimmy conceded.

"What's the motive?"

"They hate us."

"Come on, Jimmy."

"Motive's to be determined."

"And the alien slime?"

"Heh. You're the only one that can see that."

Voices rose again in another room. This time, a loud thud was followed by angry shouts.

"Damn them!" Jimmy turned toward the sound. "Those morons from homicide. Stay right here, Moon. And don't touch a thing. D'ya hear me?"

I nodded.

Jimmy hurried out of the room, and Bernard practically did cartwheels as he motioned to the bust and the unusual piece inside it.

Without even thinking about it, I slipped my backpack off. I navigated past strewn beads, and stepped around the magic circle to the fragments of busts. I glanced out the doorway. Jimmy's voice rang out in the hallway as he chewed out one of his fellow officers. He may have been in failing health, but my friend hadn't lost his feistiness yet.

I stared at the bust. *Dammit.* Jimmy was sympathetic to my gig, but even he wouldn't tolerate lifting evidence from a crime scene. On the other hand, Bernard had proven I could trust him. He'd never asked me to do something this level of stupid, though.

I unzipped my backpack and removed some tissue paper that was wrapped around a glass eye with two pupils. I used the paper to pick up the ceramic piece so as to not leave prints. Turning the section of cranium over, I got a clear view of what this was all about.

A hollow orb made of earthenware or ruddy bronze, about the size of a softball, was cupped to the underside of the head's interior. It did not appear to be part of the original bust but had been attached later. Much like a censer used for religious rituals, its frame was open and it bore intricate designs. Along the surface, etchings of Hebrew letters appeared in sequence. I struck the bust on the carpet—once, twice. It split and the pieces fell away, leaving only the orb. The orb rested on the paper and fit perfectly into the palm of my hand.

If this was a key, it was the weirdest looking key I'd ever seen.

The burnished glow enveloped me and I looked up to see Bernard inches away, peering at the object.

"I hope you're right about this," I said.

He spread his arms as if to question why I doubted him. Then he turned and signaled for me to hurry up.

I put the piece in my backpack, zipped it up, and quickly slipped it on, eyes fixed on the doorway. The stench of blood and guts was making me sick. I had to get out of this place.

"There," I said to Bernard. "Are you happy?"

The huge grin on his face was all I needed to know.

CHAPTER 6

Try as I might, I couldn't shake the smell.

"Are you all right?" Celeste asked.

"No." I dry-heaved again and rose, panting. "No, I'm not."

I gripped the shell of the Cammy and doubled over, gagging. Celeste rested her hand on my back, but it did no good. No amount of healing powers could scrub the stench of blood and decomposing organs from my mind.

Meanwhile, Quinn had removed the orb from my backpack and was examining it. "So, you're saying that *this* is a key?"

He passed it to Celeste who also studied it with interest.

I straightened, groaning, and scanned the area. With the main street blocked and the increased police activity in Chinatown, the adjoining roads were jammed with overflow. The police chopper had arrived and circled nearby. After what had happened at the Magic Dragon—primarily my lifting a piece of evidence from a crime scene—sticking around there was the last thing we needed to do.

"You should put that away," I said.

"You're right," Celeste said, returning the key to

Quinn who shoved it into my backpack.

"Is it the key?" he asked. "It doesn't look like a key."

"*I'm* not saying it's a key," I said. "*My angel* said it's a key."

"Well then." Quinn passed me the pack. "I guess it's a key."

"So what do we do with it now?" Celeste asked. "Did he say?"

"He didn't say," I responded.

"And why was the biot after it?"

"I don't know if the biot was after it. Or if the biot killed Song. It seemed like a set-up. Ugh. My head hurts."

"Then why else would it run?" Quinn asked.

"Maybe it had to," Celeste said. "To escape, or something."

"Escape?" Quinn exclaimed. "But it killed itself!"

I removed the car keys from my jeans pocket. "There was something else—a summoning circle. Chaos magic was involved."

"Summoning circles are for... demons." Celeste said.

"Yeah. And this was a big one. Bad-tempered, too." I sighed. "Why do I get the feeling that Felix Klammer knows a lot more than he ever lets on?"

"Probably because he does," Quinn said. "So how 'bout we mosey on down to the Shul and have a look around."

"At this point," I said, "we might as well."

"Wait," Celeste added. "We should talk to the others first. Things are heating up. We should get some backup. Besides, if they've uncovered anything else, we need to know about it. And they need to know about this."

Suddenly, Quinn straightened and tilted his head slightly. "Yeah. We gotta go. Police are making the rounds. And now that we have a klepto on our team, I'd rather try to avoid an interrogation."

We hopped into the Cammy and I drove to Echo Park, which was just several blocks northwest of Chinatown. We could contact the others from there.

Some said Echo Park had one of the best views of the city. Although the placid man-made reservoir-turned-lake had been the subject of debate throughout its seemingly-constant renovation, the view was not debatable. Nor were the cityscape sunsets. And at the moment, with the summer sun descending behind the skyscrapers and framing them in a golden silhouette, it only confirmed the allure of the location. Between the swan boats, snapping turtles, and the huge fountain in the middle of the lake, hipsters and local venders jockeyed for space.

We parked near a charming bridge that led to a small island with ducks and palm trees. Ellie and I used to come here on occasion to watch the sunset, which brought back an unexpected nostalgic pang. The area had been gentrified enough to reduce the incidences of crime. But being anywhere in close proximity to Los Angeles increased one's chances of being a random stabbing victim. However, the recent Echo Park murders—along with the rumor of werewolf sightings—was a reminder that in this neck of the woods, mortality was still a tenuous proposition.

We got out of the Cammy. Celeste scooted onto the hood and sat there as she dialed up the Asylum landline for a video chat. Her auburn hair and the light freckles on her cheeks appeared to glow in the golden sunset. She held the phone out as Quinn and I stood on opposite sides of her. Rapha answered, and his hulking image filled the video screen.

"Greetings, friends!" He stood before the computer with his arms spread. "We have been anxious to hear from you. Tell us, then—what have you have learned?"

"Don't get your hopes up, big guy," Quinn said. "I think we've got more questions than when we started."

"That is regrettable."

"Though, Moon did manage to steal something from the crime scene."

"Hey," I said, "my angel made me do it. Besides, it's what we were looking for—the key to the Golem Prison."

"Well, then," Rapha said. "Your adventures were fruitful after all."

Mace, Kanya, and Orphana gathered around Rapha at the computer. He made room for them and said, "Please, tell us more about what you have learned."

Recalling the crime scene caused the nausea to resurface in my gut. I described for them the extensive gathering of Invisibles at the Magic Dragon, as well the summoning circle, Song's ceremonial-style execution, the neural skin, and the unusual sludge left by some unidentified entity. But Rapha seemed most interested in the magic. He queried about the circle and its appearance.

"Chaos magic," he concluded. "How unusual."

"Yeah," I said. "I haven't researched the subject in

detail, but chaos magic appears to be the choice of the new generation. Of those inclined towards magic, that is."

"Indeed," Rapha said, squinting in thought.

"Chaos magic is a little hard to pin down." Kanya explained that she and Matisse had some not-so-friendly encounters with chaos magicians, or *chaotes* as they were called. "There's no dogma governing them," she said. "It's a bit of a free-for-all. No official indoctrination. Chaos magic is basically a postmodern system. It doesn't rely on established formulas or hierarchies like more traditional magic systems. Sacraments and laws are relative. It employs... *unorthodox methods*. I mean, chaotes will borrow from anyone. Or anything. They don't respect a particular school or a master. Whatever god, whatever power serves their purpose, they'll use it."

"Hm," Quinn said. "Whoever wanted that key is packing some crazy ass hoodoo."

"Perhaps," Rapha conceded. "But we don't yet know with surety that the key was the motive for the murder."

"C'mon, Rapha," I objected. "The room was destroyed. Everything was busted up. The killer was looking for something. It was obvious. Besides, why else would Bernard want me to take it? He wants us to keep that thing from whoever's after it."

"Unless, maybe..." Celeste turned and looked at me. "Maybe he wants us to use it."

Her answer seemed to drop with clarion simplicity. Venturing into a prison that held an indestructible golem had not crossed my mind. But such insanity hadn't stopped us from similar exploits before.

After a moment, I said, "Whatever we have to do, we have the key. Whether the Golem Prison is real or a fairy tale, someone else is interested in it. Interested enough to maybe even commit murder. I don't know what Klammer knows. Does anyone? Apparently, he knew enough to have us intercept that biot. And that biot was there, at the Magic Dragon. If Bernard thought that that key was important enough for me to steal from a crime scene, then I think it makes our next step fairly obvious."

"Affirmative," Mace said. "We'll meet you at Third Street Shul. You bring the magic, and I'll bring the ammo."

CHAPTER 7

Third Street Shul had originally been built to serve a growing Jewish immigrant community. It dated back to the 1920's, making it one of the oldest religious structures in Los Angeles. The immigrant community had dwindled as the neighborhood gave way to low-income apartment buildings and commercial properties jammed into high-density blocks filled with kinetic bustle. It made the old synagogue seem completely out of place, wedged amidst dingy swap meets, hot pink art deco apartment complexes, and neighborhood botanicas. Its round arches and multi-colored brickwork reflected the Byzantine Revival style evidenced in several L.A. landmarks. Large stone blocks framed the stairwell that rose from the street up to two thick wooden doors. Intricately carved stonework stretched above the entryway, displaying illustrations reminiscent of Eastern European folk art—lions, menorahs, and tablets of stone. Despite the architectural intricacies, graffiti marred swaths of brick across the structure, rusty wrought iron bars protected the windows, and a brick wall capped with razor wire surrounded the perimeter.

Not quite what you imagine when you think of a *house of God*, but a fitting location for the Golem Prison.

If it really existed.

We parked cattycorner from Third Street Shul, a side street, half a block down. As we got out of the Cammy, I grabbed my backpack, slipped it on, and we waited. This was partly in anticipation of Mace and Kanya's arrival. The other reason was simply to read the place, observe, and try to get a sense of what the hell we were getting into.

An *elote* vendor turned the corner, stopped, and tooted his horn. Even though most of these vendors operated illegally, the boiled Mexican corn was hugely popular with Angelinos. Just one reason why Code Enforcement typically looked the other way. Quinn offered to treat the three of us but, when we refused, he promptly walked down the street vowing to satisfy his own cravings. Celeste and I remained at the Cammy, studying Third Street Shul.

"It looks abandoned," I said.

"I don't know," Celeste responded. "Probably won't take long to find out."

She gestured to a figure at the top of the steps. Someone leaned into a shadowy corner near the entrance. With dusk quickly approaching, lights had begun to spring to life along the busy street. Besides the nearby lamppost, the synagogue remained unlit, leaving the figure at the top of the steps mostly obscured.

Second sight revealed to me that the dimensional atmosphere around Third Street Shul was murky, almost monochromatic. Like a radioactive cloud had camped over this place and remained there for a very long time. A damp luster appeared to blanket the building, as did moldering roots. Sheets of moss and lichen dappled the structure in verdant greens and yellows. Some areas were so dense with these growths that it gave the appearance of a massive petri dish sprouting invisible molds from the sidewalk itself. I'd observed a similar phenomenon surrounding other locations, usually those with a lengthy history of paranormal activity. Sometimes, entire wings of a large building or campus would be shrouded in this fungal phenomenon. I referred to it as Shade. When an area fell under a Shade, strange organisms and growths flourished. Of course, these observations were of the invisible order and its denizens. Nevertheless, Celeste appeared to be getting similar vibes.

She said, "I don't have a good feeling about this place."

"Me either. I'm seeing a Shade. A thick one."

"You mean that ghost shadow thing? You've described it before."

"Right. Looks like it's been there for a while. There's practically a jungle growing out of that place."

"Which means...?"

"Which means that whatever has been going on in Third Street Shul is not kosher. And has been going on for quite some time."

Quinn approached, chomping on the corn cob. Mayonnaise and Parmesan cheese crumbles speckled his beard and mustache.

"I hope you got some napkins with that," Celeste said.

"Mm-hm." Quinn finished munching on the final rows of lathered corn. "That was deeee-licious!" He tossed the barren cob in a nearby trash can and used some thin napkins to dab at his mouth.

"You've got some—" Celeste motioned to

Quinn's beard. "And on your shirt."

As he tidied himself up, Quinn said, "I'm getting a lot of static here. *A lot.* You guys?"

"The same," I said. "Where do you think it's coming from? Any ideas?"

"Sure." Quinn licked some stray mayonnaise off several fingertips. Then he motioned towards the Shul without looking at it. "For one, whoever is loitering up there is a psion. And not a novice, either. But that's about all I can tell. They're emitting a shield—a telekinetic barrier that blocks others from clairvoyant mining. I'll know more when we get closer."

I peered at the front steps. The figure remained partly visible, leaning back into the shadows underneath the arch above the door. A pair of faded chucks and holey designer jeans with iron-on decals were the only indication of this individual's identity and bad choice of clothing.

Quinn flicked a kernel of corn from his beard. "Whatever is happening inside is important enough for a dedicated psion to be stationed there to block psychic intruders."

"Which means we must be on the right track," I said.

Mace approached in his van from the opposite direction, cruised past the synagogue, crossed Third, found a spot across the street from us and parked. Kanya sat shotgun. When they emerged, I noticed that Kanya had changed and now sported some cargo shorts and hiking boots, an Urban Lara Croft minus the compound bow and ice pick. She'd let her hair down, too, which added to her tomboyish attractiveness. Mace went around the opposite side of the vehicle and removed a large duffle bag, which he lugged with him as the two joined us. He let it drop with a heavy thud to the sidewalk.

I glanced at Mace's bag. "Do you have a tank in there, or what?"

"Don't you worry, Moon. Just be ready to carry your weight."

I bristled. His comment came off as surprisingly offensive. "When have I not?"

"Easy, rookie."

"Well? *When have I not?*"

I am not easily offended, but Mace's coarseness had been wearing on me. It was more than just his dislike of the Imperia. Perhaps *dislike* is too strong a word. He put up with us, but believed that technology and human ingenuity were far more reliable than superpowers. That was probably why he kept himself in such impeccable shape—muscles and munitions, that was his motto. Earth guardians, on the other hand, were unreliable and broken down. Mace didn't require any attaboys, and didn't dish them out, either. His trust was in God and guns. Not necessarily in that order.

I shook my head and scowled in open frustration.

"All right," Kanya scolded. "You two cut it out."

Mace smirked.

Kanya filled us in on the research they'd done while we were away. Apparently, they had unearthed the spell book that Matisse had acquired from Third Street Shul. It went by the title of *Sefer Raziel Ha-Malakh*. It was considered one of the most important books on Jewish magic. Supposedly, the grimoire was revealed to Adam and Noah, and the archangel Raziel was sent to teach them the ways of nature through its text. Topics like angelology, the zodiac, gematria, protective spells, and talismans filled its pages. Needless to say, the book was more than your typical magic tome.

"So, before we go marching in," Kanya said, "what do we need to know about this place? Or about a golem prison?"

I found myself, along with the others, looking to Celeste. This seemed to be our default position when gathering info. However, she lightly shrugged. "I'm not sure how much use I can be on this one. It would have helped to have studied the book you guys found. Everything I know about the Golem Prison is mostly secondhand."

"Your 'secondhand' is probably a lot better than our 'firsthand,'" Quinn said. "Go on."

"Okay, then." Celeste rubbed her hands together as if preparing for some adventurous feat. "Lemme see. Well, for starters, the golem prisons are magical places, which you probably already guessed. They're typically hidden from or, you know, invisible to, the average person. Meaning it could be there," she motioned towards the Shul, "we just don't know it. According to the legends, the prisons were initially built to house rogue golems. That's because some magicians felt that the destruction of a golem, once it was created, was still the actual taking of life. It caused this big debate among kabbalist councils. They reached a conclusion—rather than simply deconstructing rebel golems, they'd house them in this prison."

"Let me get this straight," Quinn said. "We're looking for a place where a bunch of bad golems have been locked up for a really long time. And we're trying to get in? Not sure that's the smartest idea we've ever had."

"Well, hold on," Celeste said. "The story doesn't stop there. There was this infamous magician, a kabbalist, who defied the council and believed they could use the imprisoned golems for other ends. Mainly, to challenge the community's Jewish oppressors. Despite the stories about their rebellion against humans, golems are inherently compliant. Especially when their maker is of superior power or intelligence. They gravitate to servitude. But this is also why they sometimes turn on their creators—human masters are, ultimately, inferior. In strength and in will. Anyway, so this magician aspired to create a superior being, a preeminent golem, one of indestructible power, to lead his army. It would be impervious to weapons and magic. Only, in this case, the magician sought out a *staff of undoing,* an ancient rod with legendary powers. It was comprised of similar materials to the golem and possessed the power of life and death. It could counter the magic used to create the golem. By possessing this staff, he could summon the golem's allegiance. Or bring about its destruction."

"A magical staff," Quinn bemoaned. "How original."

I shrugged. "I suppose he could have forged a magical crescent wrench just to mix things up."

"Anyway," Celeste continued, "the creature became known as the Third Golem—*third* as in the order of creation. Because the first two humans had fallen, disobeyed God, and broken the created order, the *third* created being would unite them, reconstitute a perfect being and complete the circle of power."

"Three," I said. "What a surprise."

"That's right." Kanya turned to me. "You know a

lot about numerology."

"Do tell," Quinn said.

"Do I have to?" I said. But they were all looking at me, their interest piqued. "Okay. Well, for starters, three is the number of creation. Creativity is often associated with the number. It's also the number of divinity, as in the Trinity or a godhead. Father, Son, Spirit. Shiva, Vishnu, Brahma. Etcetera. That's why it's associated with completeness—body, soul, spirit; beginning, middle and end. That kind of thing. But, basically, the number three corresponds to... perfection or supremacy. It's a power number."

Quinn nodded. "This Third Golem must have been top dog, then."

"I guess so."

Celeste nodded. "And that's what it was created to be. The golem's creator used ancient metallurgical and alchemical secrets to form the body. When his creation was complete, all that was needed was a word of command. Then he sought out a fabled incantation known as the *Mantle of Ur*. It's a spell for... invulnerability, like a divine armor. The magician wanted to make the golem virtually indestructible. But before he could complete his plan and enact the spell, the council intervened. The imprisoned golems were destroyed and the magician was stopped. The key was hidden. The Third Golem remained inanimate. It was never awakened. Never summoned. And that's the purpose of the Golem Prison now—not only does it hold the Third Golem and the staff of power, but it prevents the Mantle of Ur, the incantation of armor, from being used."

"A two-for-one bargain," Quinn said. "Tell me— why are we trying to get into this place, anyway?

Sounds like we should throw away the key and make sure that whatever secrets are locked up there, stay locked up."

"He's got a point," I said, adjusting my backpack. "Klammer's orders were just to capture the biot and follow the leads."

"Well, they've led us here." Kanya motioned to the Shul.

I sighed. "You know, this would be so much easier if Klammer would just tell us what's going on here. And what the hell we're supposed to do."

"Maybe *he* doesn't know either. Or maybe the answer is right in—" Kanya pointed to the synagogue and straightened. "Hey. That person that was up there is gone."

We simultaneously turned to the Third Street Shul. Indeed, the psion who'd been lurking in the shadows near the entrance was nowhere in sight.

"They're still around," Quinn said. "Somewhere nearby. I can feel 'em. And they know we're here."

"Okay," Mace said emphatically, hoisting the duffle bag over his shoulder. "Enough talking. We need to take a look."

He marched down the sidewalk before we even had a chance to respond. By the time he reached the crosswalk, we had hustled our way to his side. A crowd now encircled the elote vendor and the smell of boiled corn, cheese, fresh limes, and chili powder filled the air. We waited for the signal, and then the five of us crossed the street, studying Third Street Shul as we approached.

Electronic chatter—a combo of disco music and the evening news—blared from a nearby apartment complex. Several transient-looking types milled about in an alley between a liquor store and an ATM. Dusk was upon us. The western skyline blazed orange before fading into a hazy blue sky. The evening stars were now signaling their arrival.

Mace stopped at the base of the steps and stood surveying the front of the synagogue. We joined him and, for a moment, stood without conversing.

"Our friend is close," Quinn said. "Watch yourselves. They'll probably try probing your thoughts, maybe even steering you. Keep your heads clear, Guardians."

I nodded. What my compatriots could not see was the Shade covering the building. We stood just outside this invisible veil. However, our proximity to the phenomenon, and the structure at its center, had tweaked my senses. The storm gifts were stirring inside me.

My hands tingled. Faint threads of blue energy radiated along my fingertips. Of course, only I could see them. Yet accompanying this familiar sensation was something *unfamiliar*. With each successive pulse of the storm energy, the doors to the synagogue—specifically, the ornate brass handles and hinges—throbbed with the same electric blue. A strange symmetry seemed to exist between the two; the surging in my hands matched the vibrations in the hardware.

It appeared that I was the one generating the phenomenon.

Before I knew it, I was climbing the steps to the synagogue's front doors. I passed into the Shade, and the world around me grew dingy. An almost palpable malaise hung thick in the atmosphere.

"Reagan!" Kanya called from behind me. "Hey! Wait a minute."

But before she could follow me, I turned and motioned for the rest of them to stay put. Then I proceeded up the steps. As I approached the wooden doors, my hands pulsated with even stronger energy. It brought with it a reminder of the fantastical exploits I was privileged to have accomplished when this unusual phenomenon was present before. Which only heightened this moment. I reached the landing and approached the doors. They seemed even bigger than I'd previously guessed—eight, maybe even ten feet in height! Electric blue energy skittered across the handles, hinges, and bolts. What did this mean? What was I supposed to do?

I reached for the handle.

Sparks jumped and tentacles of electric blue leapt to my hand. I was yanked forward. Someone shouted from below, followed by the patter of approaching footfall. I gripped the handle as the hardware rattled violently. Bolts and screws dropped from the bronze handles and clinked down the stone steps. The hinges curled in upon themselves, wrenching the doors from their place. Dust and debris rained from the carved archway overhead. I was not in pain; nevertheless, I wanted to yell. But I didn't have the chance. The door handle fragmented in my hand. Cylinders and spindles clanked to the ground, followed by springs, bolts, and finally, hinges. With this, the wooden doors groaned. My hand snapped free as the energy evaporated.

One door yawned open and skidded to a stop. The other disengaged from the casing, tilted back, and fell to the floor inside with a heavy thud.

Someone yanked me back into the midst of the team. A fog of dust rolled out the door and down the steps. Together, we peered into the darkened Shul. Mace had removed a handgun and peered into the building with his weapon aimed forward.

Quinn folded his arms and nodded. "Impressive. Why bother knocking when we can just dismantle the door?"

Mace glanced over his shoulder. "And blow our cover while we're at it."

I shrugged. "Sorry. I didn't mean to."

Traffic cruised past, and the electronic babble continued uninterrupted from the nearby apartments. Hopefully, no one had noticed our grand entrance. We stared into the shadowy interior of the synagogue. Faint shafts of dusky light revealed a large room scattered with bulky objects. At its far end, the dim contours of a large cabinet or mantle could be seen. An intricately carved Star of David was visible on each of the cabinet doors.

"It's... here," Celeste said. "Or somewhere close, at least."

"I thought we needed a key?" I asked.

"We probably still do. This isn't the prison. Only a... doorway, a passage to it. Be careful, everyone."

She was right. The Shade was now acting like a fog. However, it did not drift lifelessly, but with seeming purpose, twining about the limbs of the others and shrouding their usually bright auras. What effect it might have on them, or me, remained to be seen.

"C'mon, people." Mace lifted the duffle bag, the pistol still poised in his opposite hand. "Let's go before someone finds us out and joins the party."

With that, Mace stepped into the synagogue. We followed him one by one.

Before I had a chance to survey the room and acclimate to our surroundings, Quinn summoned me. "Moon, gimme a hand." He positioned himself on the opposite side of the door.

Together we lifted the door upright and leaned it back into the spot it had vacated. The entire casing was now compromised, but the door managed to wedge into place and remain stable. The sounds of the city became muffled, absorbed in the shadowy interior.

Celeste tried the light switches near the entry, but they were a no go. We waited for a moment, allowing the smell of mold and wax, and the dull silence to fill our senses. Mace eased the duffle bag to the floor. Twilight illumined the numerous stained-glass windows, sending faint refractions of kaleidoscopic color about the place. Overhead, a large chandelier hung laden with cobwebs. A light clicked to life, brightening the musty interior.

Mace had removed the mini flashlight from his belt clip and stood tracing its beam across the interior. The pews had been removed, wrenched free from the wooden floor, leaving splintered apertures in the boards. They lay scattered about the perimeter of the room as if tossed aside by some titan. At the center of the room spread a charred irregular ring of debris. The remains of another summoning circle? Unlikely. Tentacles of orange slime, byproducts of the Shade, fingered their way out from the blackened mound. Like a parallel wonderland superimposed over our own, odd growths and fungi formations occupied the invisible dimension around us. Cauliflower-like mushrooms, pale and diseased, clustered on sills and crevices. Even worse, swatches of gray-green slime—I was tempted to label them *pawprints*—lathered the room.

Whatever had torn up the Magic Dragon had also been here.

Mace walked towards the ashen ring with his light trained on the spot. Between the coal and ash shone remains of wood and newspaper. And bone. What was going on here? Had this been made by vagrants or vandals? Or a rogue magician. If our entry had required the storm gifts, how could others have gotten in without similar magic? Or was this something worse, part of some dreadful ritual?

A faint whoosh of air sounded somewhere behind us. We all turned. Mace swung the light that way, towards the front of the synagogue, and readied his weapon. However, all that was visible was a dusty lectern and a massive wooden cabinet.

"What was it?" Kanya said, her voice a near whisper.

"Unclear." Mace gripped his weapon and scanned the light beam across the front of the shul. "Something moved."

"I heard it, too," I said.

Yet it appeared we were alone.

My gaze drifted to an elaborate mural that stretched across the wall behind the cabinet. I was familiar enough with synagogues to know that this cabinet likely encased an iteration of the legendary Ark. Par for the course to most Jewish houses of worship. However, it wasn't the cabinet my attention was drawn to, but the imagery on the wall behind it. Mace's light continued to trace the mural. Cracks and missing chunks of plaster pock-marked the images here and there. The colors had long faded, but the representations remained legible.

Celeste had wandered forward, staring at the central image of a bearded old man in flowing garb wearing a wizard's cap. His hand was extended, palm open. Above his open hand a small orb levitated, emitting rays. Those rays shone into a virtual cosmos of small planets, stars, and alchemical symbols surrounding the wizard.

"Hey." I straightened.

Celeste nodded. "I know what you're thinking."

I slipped off my backpack and prepared to remove the key.

She peered at me. "You sure 'bout this?"

"No."

As I reached into my backpack, Mace said, "Wait."

He holstered his pistol and tossed the flashlight to Celeste. Then he unzipped his duffle bag and removed a compact, blunt-barreled rifle. I was no expert on guns but guessed this was part of the large collection of assault rifles—mostly of the experimental or futuristic variety—in his collection. Mace stood poised with the rifle. Then he nodded. "Go for it."

I removed the key and stood there as Celeste illumined it with the light.

"That's a key?" Kanya said. "So how does it work?"

"I'm not sure, but..." I looked back at the mural. Specifically, at the image of the orb levitating above the wizard's hand. I turned back to the others, squinting in the light. "If that's any indication, this is the key and we're in the right place. If so, the Golem Prison can't be far. So..." I opened my hand and rested the orb in my palm. "Hold onto your boots."

I inhaled and exhaled deeply, concentrating on the orb. I was not a telekinite but figured my life was crazy enough to give it a try. I closed my eyes.

"Stop!" Quinn shouted.

I lurched, nearly dropping the key.

"Someone's cloaking us," Quinn said. "They're here. They're—aaghhh!" He doubled over, thumping his head with the heel of his fist. A fog of Shade shrouded his head.

A blur sped past Mace, and then Celeste, causing her to jostle the flashlight. As it fell from her hands and clattered to the floor, a presence swept towards me. Whether a person or a thing, I couldn't say. It moved with the shadows. It was *part* of the shadows. An entity comprised of the darkness itself. Or using it as a means of transport. Yet this entity was solid enough to stir the air as it passed. A prickle of energy brushed my palms.

I looked down and gasped.

The key to the Golem Prison had been snatched from my hand.

CHAPTER 8

"The key!" I shouted, my gaze darting about the shadowy perimeter of the room. "It took the key!"

The storm gifts erupted inside me. I clenched my fists, both in anger and determination to retrieve the precious cargo we'd brought here. Dammit! Bernard was gonna kill me.

"The doors!" Mace yelled. "Block the doors!"

Quinn shook himself free from the Shade and it dissipated instantly. Then he hustled to the entryway and stood with his arms outstretched, his back braced against the doors to prevent the thief from escaping.

Celeste retrieved the light and traced its beam around the room. Shadows sprang to life at the passing rays, dancing helter-skelter like marionettes in a demented stage show. Plaster crunched and something skidded across the floor to our left. Celeste swung the flashlight that way. Other than dust kicked up by our visitor, there was nothing.

"Steady, Guardians." Mace stood poised, cradling the rifle in his arms.

Celeste slowly moved the light beam along the perimeter of the Shul. Then she stopped. Mace pointed overhead, into the rafters. Instantly, Celeste aimed the light there. The chandeliers swung like a pendulum, raining dust and cobwebs down on us, as something leapt from them into the peripheral darkness.

But not before we caught a glimpse of a black high-top tennis shoe.

"It's the psion!" Quinn shouted. "Don't shoot!"

A soft thud behind us. Celeste spun around with the light. One of the pews rattled as the thief leapt from it, apparently attempting to catapult across the room. However, the rotten wood splintered, causing the person to lose their footing and crash to the floor on the opposite side. Before they could gather themselves, Celeste rushed over with her light trained on the spot where the figure now lay.

"Don't move!" Mace navigated through the debris with his rifle aimed at the subject. Then, over his shoulders: "Get a hold of 'er! Now!"

Quinn circled around the pews, approaching from the opposite side of Celeste. "Keep that light on her!" he demanded.

I leapt over some debris and joined them in looking down upon a teenage girl. Fair-skinned. Freckles. Rail thin and gangly. Indeed, it appeared to be the same person I'd glimpsed outside. Holey blue jeans with colorful patches of unicorns, skulls, and indie rock labels. She wore an oversized flannel. A fabric sack with paisley designs dangled from her belt. Her head was shaved on one side. On the other swept a long mane of dyed-black hair. She lay panting, the key gripped in her hand.

Mace approached, the muzzle of his rifle aimed at her.

"Easy," Quinn said, creeping towards the girl. "Easy."

I was unclear if his cautions were directed at the girl or at Mace. Or both. However, the girl's eyes did not reveal fear. The energy coursing through her body wasn't that of a person seeking to escape. She'd played this game before. This was not her first time being at the wrong end of a rifle. No weapons were visible on her person, nor was her intent to cause us harm. Although she could if necessary. In fact, there was a hardened determination to her gaze. A bravery that far exceeded her youthful appearance. I stepped closer. Something about this girl was not as it seemed. Even more unusual was the sense that her intentions were not malicious. She was on our side.

"You don't want to do that," the girl said, her voice high-pitched, almost squeaky, her eyes fixed on Mace.

"I'll do what I need to do, child." Mace now stood over her, rifle aimed squarely at her forehead. "Now, let's hand over what you stole."

"I can't."

Mace repositioned his rifle, his features stony.

"Hey, hey." Quinn inched forward, gesturing for Mace to chill. Looking down at the kid, he said, "He's right. You need to give that back. Then we can talk."

"Oh, we can talk," she said. "But I'm keeping the key."

I detected a slight accent, Caribbean almost. At least, some derivation of Spanish. As we watched, she raised herself up on her elbows.

"Easy," Quinn said, stretching his arms between her and Mace. "He'll shoot you. Trust me."

"Go ahead." She climbed to her feet. "But Felix won't like that."

The mention of Felix Klammer stunned the group. Was this a ploy? How did she know about Klammer? Or, for that matter, that the orb she possessed was actually a key? But if she was a psion, she'd probably culled that info from one of our own minds!

Celeste fumbled the light.

"Careful!" Quinn cautioned. "She's a shadow jumper. Once she's out of the light, she's gone."

The girl smiled. "Is that all you know about me? Quinn?"

His brow furrowed. They were in each other's heads. Probing. Grappling. Finally, he relaxed. "No. *Allie.*"

"Heh. Is that it?"

"It's enough for now."

"Actually, it's *Alita Teresa del Monte.*"

"Yeah. But you prefer the name Allie."

"It's funner. So, you remember this?" She turned her head and nudged down her collar with her thumb revealing an elaborate neck tattoo. Birds, swallows more specifically. The tattoo stretched from underneath her flannel and disappeared under her black strands of hair.

"That's my work." Quinn peered at her. Then he nodded knowingly. "I remember you. You're the kid who was asking all the questions about the Imperia. Yeah. But that was... years ago."

"I'm a lot older than I look." Allie smiled. She let her gaze roam among us. "Hey, I'm a big fan. I been following you guys forever. In fact, one day, I'm hoping to enlist." She smiled and stood proudly.

"She's playing games," Mace snarled. "Give us the key and you two can meld minds later."

She glanced at him. "I'm here to help you, Mace. Bueno?"

"Don't play with me, punk."

"The name's Allie. And I wouldn't dare play with you. In fact, I know you don't like to play around. You're the cowboy of the group. *Rambo Lite.* That's what we like to call you. Me and my team. Your fuse is short and your aim is good. Matisse thought the world of you. That's how I got to know Felix. And your Dad." She smiled at Kanya and returned her attention to Mace. "Speaking of *world,* is there a place in it you *haven't* been? Last I heard you led an expedition into Tanzania to look for mummies. *Living* ones. Was that successful? Anyway, I'm dying to see your cryptid collection. I heard you bagged a Yeti. Is that true?"

Mace squinted at the girl.

Rambo Lite? I almost laughed out loud. Partly because of the accuracy of the label, partly because I enjoyed seeing the grunt getting clowned by a kid.

Although Mace showed no visible signs of being flustered by her comeback, I could tell her words had nailed him.

"The key," he said coldly. "Hand it over, princess."

"Allie?" Celeste had crept closer. "How do you know Felix?"

"He saved my life," Allie said, turning her gaze upon the healer. "He said I'd have a chance to save others' lives... if I was patient. He told me to guard the Golem Prison. That was my charge. I've been here forever. Saw them shut it down. And murder Rabbi Finkel." She gestured to the pile of ash in the center of the room. "Poor guy. But that's *El Mago.* He'll destroy whoever's in his way. Anyway, Felix said to leave it. To wait for help.

Said that one day you'd be here with the key and that I'd have a chance to show you how to use it. And help you fight him. Fight *them*. Fight *anyone* who wants what's inside."

Celeste peered at her. She opened her mouth to speak, but Allie continued.

"You have to get the staff—*Vara de Dios*. The rod of God. Without it, you'll never have a chance."

"The staff of undoing." Celeste glanced at Quinn. "So, that's why we're here?"

Allie nodded.

"But why?" Celeste asked. "If we have the key, why not just destroy it? That way no one can get the staff. Or the Third Golem."

"You *don't* have the key." Allie smiled. "I do."

"Well then, why don't *you* destroy it?"

"Because you need the staff."

"Enough already!" Mace glared at the girl. "It's time that you—"

"There's another magician!" Allie matched his tone in severity, showing no evidence of intimidation. "*El Mago.* He's revived the magical order. Do you hear me? Just like the first one, the one who built the Third Golem. Even more powerful. He's designing a new golem. An indestructible one. From magic. And science. That's why he wants the spell—the Mantle of Ur. He's close to cracking the code to the Golem Prison. When he does, he won't need a key to open it. He'll be able to come and go as he pleases. Which means that once he gets the spell and the staff, he can't be stopped. *¿Entienden?*"

She stared at Mace, and then scanned the rest of our group. "I'm here to help you guys. You gotta trust me."

Trusting someone with a bad haircut and unicorn patches on their jeans seemed questionable. But in this case, I knew it was the right thing to do.

"Shut up, Moon," Mace grumbled.

"I didn't say anything!"

"Well, shut up before you do."

He could see where this was going. I was about to affirm Allie's statement when something snapped near the front doors. We spun that direction. Celeste instinctively flashed the light there. A piece of wood had cracked, given way to the weight of the door, and fallen from the busted jamb.

"No!" Quinn barked.

But it was too late. When Celeste returned the light to the spot, Allie was no longer there.

Mace cursed as Celeste hastily flashed the beam around the room, searching for the shadow-jumping psion. Yet there was no sign of our new friend.

"I told you to ease up on that Rambo act," Quinn said to Mace.

"Spread out!" Mace commanded. To Quinn, he said, "Watch that door again. Comprendes?"

Quinn offered grudging consent.

We spread out across the room, following the light beam as Celeste scoured the corners and cubbyholes. Despite her ability to navigate in the shadows, the room offered limited places for Allie to hide. Unless, of course, she'd escaped the synagogue. In which case, we were screwed. We crept forward, eyes and ears trained for any sign of the girl. My senses told me she was very much present. I navigated around a splintered wooden pew, stopped, and turned toward the mural.

She was close. In fact, something like a faint heat signature hovered not more than—

Suddenly, the room exploded with light. I shielded my eyes from the glare. Yet this light did not emanate from a single source. Rather, a vast skyscape of tiny glowing pinpricks sprang to life around us. The atmosphere of the synagogue blazed turquoise blue—like the bluest waters of the Caribbean amped on gamma rays and neon. The bleak monochrome cast by the Shade withered with the arrival of this light source. I blinked, attempting to adjust my eyes. Shapes and symbols dotted the atmosphere like a miniature glimmering cosmos. The images weren't being projected but illuminated. The very molecules and subatomic particles around us appeared to sizzle with vibrancy.

We stood awestruck, gazing at this phenomenon. And at its center stood Allie. The key was now a glowing sphere levitating in the palm of her hand. Her face radiated both wonder and power. Sweat appeared on her forehead and her breathing was labored. Still, she smiled. Then she turned her gaze to us.

"I told you that you could trust me."

Mace lowered the rifle, apparently convinced of that.

"I didn't doubt you for a minute," I said.

She laughed.

We navigated through this wondrous solar system and approached Allie.

"I can only hold this for so long. So, listen carefully. Once the door is opened, all the doors are opened."

"Whoa," Mace interrupted. "What do you mean 'all the doors?' What other doors are we talkin' about?"

"There are six doors in all," Allie said. "When this door is opened, all the other doors are opened. When this door is closed, all the doors are closed."

"Where are they?" Celeste asked. "The other doors, I mean."

"All over the city! The doors have always been there. Hidden. Secret places. Which is why once we get inside—"

"*We?*" Mace snarled.

"That's right, Rambo." Allie smiled. "*We.*"

This time I couldn't help but laugh.

"Cork it, Moon." Mace glared at me.

"Once we get inside," Allie continued, "the command is spoken and the doors are closed."

"Locking us inside the prison," Quinn said with sufficient melodramatics.

"It's the only way. We leave those gates open too long and every freak, every night creature in this city will find their way inside. Once we get the staff, we go. That's it. In and out."

"In and out," Quinn said. "Simple enough. What could go wrong?"

"What about the door?" Celeste allowed her gaze to roam the magical constellations. "Where is it?"

Allie nodded. "Remember the Hebrews letters— the ones on the key? They form the door. Look. They're here somewhere."

She slowly turned and, as she did, the celestial canopy turned with her. Symbols and glyphs passed overhead. A slight shift of her hand, and the orb tilted. With it, the neon network moved at an opposite angle, throwing my sense of direction for a loop. Apparently, motion sickness pills were a necessary part of breach-ing the Golem Prison. Thankfully, the others weren't stricken by the same nausea.

"There!" Celeste pointed.

We turned our gaze to a blazing circlet near the altar. It hovered perhaps a foot off the ground: upright, the size of a hobbit hole, ringed with Hebrew letters. I'd seen many wonders since becoming an earth guardian. And this ranked as one of them.

We approached the gateway. I studied the spectacle, walking around the glowing portal. It was similar to a holographic projection. However, there was no visible source projecting the light. The images contained their own luminescence. Its outline possessed neither texture nor temperature—my hand simply passed through it as if it weren't there. In fact, as I stood directly before the opening and pressed my hand into it, I nearly stumbled through.

"It's not open yet," Allie said. "The letters. They gotta be read."

Once again, we turned to Celeste.

She shrugged and said sheepishly, "I only know a little Hebrew."

"You know enough," Allie said. Sweat dripped from her brow. "Just speak the words, Celeste. Right to left—that's how the Hebrew alphabet's read. Beginning to end."

"Do they...? Is it a single word? Do they spell something out?"

"It's a numeric sequence, Cel. Each Hebrew letter has a numeric equivalent."

"Okay," Celeste said. "Like the combination of a lock."

"Exactly. It begins and ends with the symbol at

the northernmost point. The sequence changes every time the door is opened."

Celeste appeared to gain confidence from this knowledge. She nodded, positioned herself in front of the portal, and studied the blazing letters. Then she nodded to Allie.

"Okay Guardians!" Allie's forehead glistened. The orb shone with golden radiance, cloaking the girl in a near-angelic aura. Her words summoned our strength. "Let's get ready to rock!"

Who was this kid? At the least, she'd brought some energy and light-heartedness to a rather dreary group of superheroes.

"When the door opens," Allie said, "go through. I'll meet you on the other side. The staff. Remember. That's what we're after. We get it, we go. Ready?"

She didn't wait for our consent.

Celeste straightened, focused on the Hebrew letters that encircled the portal, and read them one at a time, from right to left. As she spoke the last one, the portal flared and the turquoise aperture rippled out, like a circlet of water standing upright in sheer space.

"Go!" commanded Allie. "It's open. Go!"

Since no one made a move, I figured I'd lead the way. What the hell. I'd already traveled via tesseract. Why not add a portal to my resume? I stepped before the crystalline passageway and pressed my hand into the space. Indeed, the chill of another dimension met my touch. My hand disappeared inside the luminous sheet. I withdrew it to make sure I'd not lost any fingers. I hadn't. Repositioning my vest, I issued a thumbs-up to the group, nodded to myself, and took the plunge. I was thinking about Ellie when I stepped through the gateway to the Golem Prison. Which made me smile.

CHAPTER 9

The first step was a killer.

In fact, it was less a step than a drop.

I tumbled onto cool wet stone, landing squarely on one knee and pitching forward onto my shoulder. I yelped in pain. Nevertheless, I hurried to my feet in hopes of breaking the fall of the next traveler. The rippling turquoise gateway rose overhead, some three feet above the stone surface of a dank torch-lit corridor.

The instant a boot poked through I knew it to be that of Kanya. I was able to wrap my arms around her waist as she dropped to the ground. We still fell, but I took the brunt of it as she ended up on top of me, my back flat on the stone floor.

Her loose hair swept across my face. Kanya has great eyes—have I ever mentioned that?—and I found myself staring right into them. Inches apart. She smelled of vanilla and dahlia. And sweat.

Poisonous flower.

Yeah, that's what her name meant. Which was fitting because she could have that effect on people—*poison.* It wasn't for lack of heart or empathy. No, her poison was spent on those who deserved it, those who managed to exhaust her kindness. Her beauty and rage were a lethal combination.

"Ugh. You stink." She pushed herself off me, accidentally kneeing me in the groin in the process. She apologized profusely while imploring me to get up and help her break the fall of the next person. I'd only managed to climb onto my hands and knees when Quinn landed on my back, slamming me face first into the stone.

Needless to say, our arrival into the Golem Prison was more comedy than drama.

The others followed. Allie was the last to enter. She appeared to have had experience at this, for her entry was agile and acrobatic. She leapt through the portal, hurdling us, and landing nimbly upright. I didn't have time to reprimand her for not warning us about that first step. With the glowing key still cupped in her hand, she turned, awakening the neon particles in the subterranean atmosphere. Again, the canopy of symbols and stars blazed around us.

Once we had assembled, Allie spoke.

"Now we gotta close the door. As long as this one's open, all the doors are open. And we can't risk someone else joining us. Celeste?"

Celeste nodded and stepped to Allie's side.

'Okay," Allie said. "Same thing. But backwards this time."

"In reverse, you mean?"

"Right. Start at the top and read clockwise. Reciting the combination forwards opens the gateway. Reciting it backwards does the opposite."

Indeed, once Celeste read the final (or first) Hebrew letter, the turquoise portal vanished. With that, Allie cupped the key in her hand and turned it, as if disassembling the orb. A metallic click sounded and the celestial tapestry faded. She slipped the key into her fabric sack, tightened the drawstring, and looped it around her belt. The darkness slowly enveloped us.

We gazed down a winding tunnel illumined by torches. Droplets of water pattered somewhere, echoing in the corridor below. Air reeking of mold hung heavy. It smelled like Aquaman's hamper down here. Nevertheless, this place was incredible. I suddenly wished I'd have brought my camera and even considered using my cell phone just to document the experience.

This realm—if that was the correct way to describe it—was considerably larger than the synagogue above. In fact, I wondered if this was an actual geographical location or simply another interdimensional anomaly. Were we still under the building?

Knowing my thoughts, Allie responded, "Oh, it's real. Only the doorways are magic. But technically, no, we're not under the synagogue."

"Then, where are we?"

She shrugged. "Somewhere far away from human eyes."

Mace led the way, duffle bag slung over his back as if he were a mule, his rifle sweeping before him. Celeste walked alongside, scanning the flashlight beam across the ancient tunnel. Large limestone blocks creased with moss lined the walls. Occasionally, glyphs and symbols, carved into the stone, appeared. Allie caught up to Celeste and proceeded to bombard her with questions about the Imperia and how one officially becomes a part of our big happy family.

Once again, my nerves kicked in. The tunnel

continued to descend, creating a sense of foreboding with each step. Torches in rusty iron mounts, stationed every twenty to thirty feet, guttered, sending plumes of oily black smoke along the corridor of the roof. Our footfalls echoed as we went. Meanwhile, my stomach had started grinding. Apparently, being an earth guardian did not alleviate the jitters.

Kanya came alongside me.

"Hey," she said. "You did good back there."

I offered her a puzzled glance.

"With the door," she said. "Remember? The door to the synagogue?"

"Oh, that. It just seemed like the right thing to do. Plus, there was this blue electricity everywhere."

"You should do that more, Reagan. I mean, use your gifts."

I nodded.

"Look," she said, "I'm sorry. I can't even begin to understand how crazy this all must be for you."

"No. You're right. I probably should take this whole thing a little more seriously. To be honest, I have a hard time believing that I'm—"

"Don't say it."

"...that I can really make any difference. All right?"

It was unclear whether Kanya would rebuke me for my lack of faith or affirm my feelings of complete inadequacy.

Allie noticed the two of us talking, dropped back, and joined me on the opposite side. "I've sketched out some Imperia trading cards," she said.

"Trading cards? Really?"

"Yeah. They're cool. On the back there's a short

bio of the guardian and their particular superpower. I traced the lineage as far back as I could. The late nineteenth century is where things went black. 'Bout the First World War is when you guys started showing up again. Pretty hard tracking down info on Nomlies from World War whatever. Right now, it's just a personal project. But there're others who are interested. *Friends of the Imperia*. You'd be surprised how big a following you guys have. It's all underground now, kinda a cult following. I even have a card for Ki. But that was before he left."

I glanced at her. The mention of Ki struck me as suspicious. I steered away from the thought as soon as I had it lest she gather more info than she needed. It didn't appear to dissuade her.

"So, is it true that you'll bring him back and make the team whole again?"

"Um." I looked sideways at Allie. "I think we should concentrate on *this* job. Don't you? If everything works out, then maybe we can sit down for coffee and have a chat."

"I'd prefer chocolate milk. But, you're right." She nodded. "Another time. I'm still gonna need a decent headshot to sketch out your trading card."

"Headshot. I'll get right on it."

"By the way," she said, "thanks for trusting me."

Before I could answer, Allie joined Quinn, who was bringing up the rear. "Hey, so what does it take to be an earth guardian?"

"Hmm," he said. "Not a lot of brains, that's for sure."

The corridor seemed to go on forever, descending further into the subterranean murk. We passed several adjoining tunnels, but Allie directed us downward. Pangs of unease lanced through me. Could it be possible that we'd been duped? Perhaps *we* were the ones now imprisoned in a magic chamber. Our footsteps echoed in the solitary catacomb.

The sound of rippling water soon reached my ears. The ground leveled and the passageway merged with a stone aqueduct. Hewn from the rock, it ran deep with dark water, and followed our path. Finally, the corridor opened into a large circular room with a domed ceiling. Torches lined the walls, revealing detailed glyphs and symbols etched into the stone —cubes, horns, and goblets. Kabbalist iconography. Other corridors exited the room—five, not counting the one we'd left—which I surmised were the other gateways to and from the mysterious prison. Within the walls stood sarcophagi positioned between each passageway, each one bearing a different image. Several additional aqueducts flowed into a large fountain at the center of the room. Water bubbled fitfully there.

The fountain was quite expansive, easily twenty feet in width. Lithe female forms, chiseled from stone, stood along the perimeter of a parapet holding clay cisterns. At the back of the fountain was a tiered platform, rising from the crystalline water like Atlantean ruins. This pedestal was inlaid with colorful tile and, upon it, stood the massive clay golem.

I simply could not pass up the opportunity. I removed my cell phone and began snapping pictures. This was incredible! I could see it now—a feature spread on the fabled Golem Prison, including never-before-seen photos. Arlette would pee herself.

Allie motioned us to follow, and we approached

the towering figure. It rose ten feet. Easily. Fists the size of bowling balls. Features thick and crude. Though human in shape and likeness, its definitions remained undefined, almost embryonic. A giant fetus yet unformed. Veins of matter or mineral marbleized the statue. It stared lifelessly down upon the fountain, brutish and cold.

"The Third Golem," Celeste said, breathlessly. "So, it's true."

"Of course it's true," Allie said. "What'd you think?"

She leapt onto the fountain's parapet and balanced there. Then, walking nimbly around the statuesque water nymphs, she made her way to the stone pedestal at the back of the fountain. When she reached the platform, she pointed at the base upon which the golem stood. "See?"

I snapped several more pictures before returning the phone to my pocket. As I approached the massive clay giant, I used several large blocks to climb onto the parapet and view the tiled base upon which the golem stood. I could now appreciate the detail of this design. A complex abstract constructed from runes whose colorful center emanated out into a pentagram. However, the mosaic was encrypted with intricate forms and symbols, giving it the appearance of a fantastically detailed jigsaw puzzle.

"The Mantle of Ur," Allie said, looking at me from the opposite side of the golem. "The spell of indestructability. This is what El Mago wants. He can decipher it. He can release its power. Once he cloaks the golem in it, the creature will be nearly invincible. Only the staff can counter its spell. Together they're the yin and yang;

the poison and the antidote. Whoever possesses both can never be stopped."

A chill passed through me.

"So where is it?" I said. "The staff. That's what we're here for, right?"

"Right."

She leapt off the parapet. I climbed down with considerably less agility. Allie strode to the perimeter of the chamber. We followed as she passed each sarcophagus, staring at the carved images there. The first bore a replica of a scroll. Next, a stalk of wheat. After that, a lamb. Finally, she stopped in front of a sarcophagus bearing the picture of a single staff.

"Here it is." Allie traced her fingertips across the engraved image. Her tone was sober. "Once we open this, the game begins."

Quinn looked askance at her. "I thought it already started."

"Well, technically, you're right. But when we open this, it will *really* start."

Quinn shrugged. "Well then, shall we?"

We stepped back as he approached the sarcophagus. Mace raised his rifle and assumed a defensive stance. Quinn dug his fingertips into the seal and pulled mightily. But the lid did not budge. He released his grip and called for my assistance. However, the tomb was sealed tight.

Quinn said to me, "Can't you do that thing like you did to the door upstairs?"

"Um, I'm not quite feeling it."

"In the bag there's a crowbar," Mace said, gesturing to the duffle bag which he'd shrugged off.

Quinn dug through the bag, found the crowbar,

and proceeded to wedge its point into the seal. With a little maneuvering, the sarcophagus lid popped free.

We stepped back. A rustle of air, almost a sigh, wafted past us. With it came the smell of ages past, a stale, bone-dry draught that made our skin bristle.

Quinn dropped the crowbar and together we wrestled the lid to the side.

Inside leaned a single weathered rod. Below it, patinaed jewelry adorned with dull stones lay scattered amidst a thin layer of sand. Polished by the elements, the staff stood perhaps four feet in height. Intricate carvings etched the wood and fingered their way to its base. An empty brass crown capped the instrument, its prongs appearing like crooked claws. At one time, a stone or disc must have occupied this space. For now, it sat like an empty hand grasping for something long lost.

The patter of the fountain echoed softly about the domed enclosure. We surrounded the sarcophagus, gazing at the staff.

"Vara de Dios," Allie said. "The rod of God."

Quinn squinted at her. "What's that supposed to mean?"

"According to the Midrash," Allie explained, "the staff was one of the artifacts created by God in the twilight of the Sixth Day. Prelude to the world's first Sabbath. Legend says that the staff was passed down from generation to generation. From Adam, to Moses, and onto the prophets and seers."

I looked up. "Wait. What? You're saying this is the staff of Moses?"

"I'm saying that's what the legends say." Allie looked at me and shrugged.

Suddenly I was reluctant to even look upon the instrument. Visions of melting Nazis came rushing into my mind. But with them came another sensation, one that caused my heart to freeze in place.

Faint blue electrical currents, the same type that had appeared in the door to the shul, danced between the brass fittings. I opened my hands and peered at them.

The brilliant pulse that skittered about the rod of God now reverberated in my glowing hands.

"The staff has no inherent power," Allie said, in answer to my observation. "It's just a conduit. The power's in the hand that holds it."

I lowered my hands and peered at her.

Bmph! Bmph! Bmph!

We looked up. A distant pounding reverberated in the stone. *What the hell?* Was it coming from above or below? The entire chamber drummed with the sound. With our luck, a cave troll was lumbering up from the depths to reclaim its prized possession.

Bmph! Bmph! Bmph!

"Guardians!" Mace aimed the rifle from one passageway to the next. "Buckle it up!"

"They're here!" Allie shouted. "Dang it! Hurry!"

Who was here? Where were they coming from? I didn't have time to ask. We returned our gaze to the staff. No one made a move. Perhaps we all knew that its acquisition would bestow some dread responsibility upon the recipient.

"The staff," Allie said.

The electric blue danced in my fingertips, just as it danced between the metal prongs.

I looked at her.

A glimmer shone in Allie's eyes. "Take it. It's yours, Reagan."

How did she know this? Could she see what I was seeing?

"*Take it,*" she insisted.

I sighed deeply. Or was it a groan? I reached out and touched the staff with my fingertips. Then I gripped it and lifted it without effort. There were no fireworks, no angel choirs. We were not magically transported anywhere. In fact, I think I got a small splinter.

"The Third Street gate!" Allie barked, removing the key as she ran. "Let's go!"

We followed. I cast one long look over my shoulder at the Third Golem. My hunch was that we would meet again.

The subterranean booming, though still present, dissipated as we went, leaving me to believe that it was originating from one of the other passageways. Trudging upwards left us all sweating and panting for breath. We arrived at the fluorescent gateway and hunched forward with our hands on our knees, gasping for air. The entryway had moved, repositioned itself. While closer to the stone floor, it tilted back at a near twenty-five-degree angle.

"Let's make this quick!" Allie said, standing with the glowing orb hovering just above her opened palm. "Ready?"

She didn't wait for our response. In fact, she didn't even solicit Celeste's help this time. Allie called out each Hebrew letter with precise pronunciation. The combination of her slight Spanish accent and the Hebrew dialect coalesced into an almost alchemical brew. Obviously, she'd had experience with this, which left me wondering what other tidbits of useful info and funky talents the girl possessed.

The gateway flared, an atmospheric turquoise splash that caused the tunnel to swell with light.

However, we didn't have a chance to exit. For immediately a large figure sprang from the gateway. It arced over us and landed in a squat position.

We turned to see a pale, bald-headed man in plain linen clothing, crouched in a defensive lineman's stance, facing us. His shimmering eyes rapidly scanned our group and came to rest upon me.

CHAPTER 10

Mace swung his rifle toward the man who'd just emerged from the open portal, simultaneously ordering us to take cover. This person's features captivated my attention, though, and I didn't move.

His skin possessed the same dull sheen as the serpentine biot we had intercepted. The faint discolored circuitry-like panels framed his face. His pupils glowed with a luminous silver. As he straightened, it was clear to all of us that we were not looking at a man, but at a synthetic entity—another biot.

"My name is L3-N," the biot said, still focusing on me. "I am sometimes called *Len* for conversational purposes. I am here to assist you."

"Don't move." Mace leveled his rifle at the biot.

Len turned his attention to Mace. "That weapon may temporarily incapacitate me. However, it will not stop my brother, L3-X, who is en route here. You must leave immediately. If my father is successful in acquiring the spell of invincibility, then the staff will be your only protection against them. Guard it with all diligence. Now hurry. I will do my best to prevent L3-X from overtaking you."

He turned and began jogging down the tunnel,

the way we'd come.

"Your father!" I called.

Len stopped and turned his attention to me.

"Who is he?" I demanded. "And why do we need protection from *them*?"

I was suddenly aware of the fact that I was extending the staff before me in a defensive posture. My hands were freezing, trembling with energy. I cautiously lowered the staff as the biot spoke.

"There is no time for query, although I intuit that you have many questions. A detailed response will require a considerable amount of time. Hopefully, we will find time for such a response. For now, you should know that you are being hunted by someone of ill will. Balfour Rothbard created us, as he did K-111 who took his own life this day."

"Wait," I said. "The biot at the Magic Dragon."

"He did not murder the herbalist, as you have conjectured. Such actions are outside our parameters. Kevin—for that is what I called him—knowing of my father's plan, was hoping to prevent him from acquiring the key. He was indeed successful. Balfour Rothbard still seeks the key which you now possess. However, similar parameters to the ones Kevin was created with are not activated for L3-X. His assignment is to kill or effectively debilitate anyone who opposes his capture of the Seventh Guardian."

"*Capture of the Seventh—?* Why does he want me?!"

"My father believes you can assist him in his recreation of the Third Golem."

"The Magician," Allie said breathlessly. "Rothbard's the one who's reviving the magical order."

"Yes," Len said. "His alliances are many. His devotion is to none." He looked over his shoulder, down the tunnel. Removing a nearby torch from its place, he returned his gaze to me. "You must flee. Guard the staff of undoing with your life. You have done well to acquire it. It is your only chance against him. I will do my best to slow my brother's pursuit. Upon your exit, seal the gateway."

I said, "What about—?"

"Now go!"

Footfall thundered from below, echoing swiftly up the tunnel. Len positioned himself at the tunnel entry. Allie stepped away from the neon gateway and the guardians began climbing through the portal. In a moment, only Allie, Mace, and I remained.

"Moon!" Mace stood with the rifle aimed at the mouth of the tunnel. "Get outta here!"

I peered down the tunnel at the person approaching.

"Reagan!" Allie called. "Let's go!"

My body was bristling with energy. The storm gifts stirred deep inside me. As I watched, a hulking figure stepped from the tunnel entrance and faced L3-N. He stood, framed in the glow of the torchlight.

In appearance, he was nearly identical to Len —bald head, metallic pupils, circuitry panels framing his face. However, his body was noticeably larger and stouter. He turned his attention to me. The metallic pupils calibrated, expanding and contracting. He had the cold, heartless demeanor of an engine... an engine whose singular purpose was to run, exist, grind. To crush anything in its way. The biot closed his fists and lowered his shoulders.

Len raised the torch and stepped between me and his brother. "Reagan Moon! You must leave!"

L3-X snarled, "Step aside, traitor."

Before I had a chance to move, L3-X drove headlong into his brother. The collision was so great that Len launched past me, sending the torch whipping through the air, and slammed into the rock wall. Had I not sidestepped him, I would have been flattened by the blow. The tunnel reverberated with the impact. Either Len was as light as cotton candy or his brother had Hulk blood. I assumed it was some variation of the latter.

Mace and Allie were shouting, demanding that I flee. Yet energy crackled through my body. I glanced at my hands as the ethereal storm-blue had been re-ignited. Only now it was flowing into the staff and coalescing at its apex, transforming the fittings into a tight ball of sizzling energy.

The biot squared his shoulders with me and as he did, Mace fired four shots, hitting him in the head and the shoulder area. The gunshots were leaden thuds that reverberated through the walls. However, L3-X did not leave his feet. Instead, his body bowed backwards, at an eerily inhuman angle, and then straightened. The spot where the bullets should have lodged were simply charred blisters, as if the ammo had vaporized, or been absorbed, on impact.

A tesseract blazed to life in my mind's eye. I steered it toward the solar plexus of this superhuman robot. An unusual confidence swelled inside me. I might not be worthy of this calling, but I'd be damned if I was going to run and hide. I'd done enough of that my entire life. As I was about to jump through the biot, Len lunged from behind me and issued a hammer blow to his brother's face. The magnificent crunch of flesh and titanium exploded as they tumbled across the floor. Unable to avoid their impact, Allie was knocked sideways and struck the rock. She fell limply to the floor.

The prison key sailed through the air and clanked along the floor, where it slowly began rolling down the tunnel.

As it went, the glimmering turquoise skyscape went with it. The angle of the gateway itself rotated as the key rolled down the tunnel.

"Reagan!" Allie pushed herself up, shaking off the effects of the concussion, and scrambled to her feet. "Get outta here!" She dodged the biots and tore down the tunnel after the key. Her voice echoed as she went. "And close the gate behind you! Close! The! Ga-a-a-te!"

L3-X now straddled his brother, issuing massive blows to the head. Len appeared semi-conscious, fluid drooling from his mouth, when his brother rose. He clenched his fists, preparing to turn. I was about to transport into the biot when someone gripped me from behind. Strong hands yanked me up through the gateway.

I suddenly found myself lying on my back in Third Street Shul.

Mace shouted at Celeste to close the gateway.

"No!" I cried out. "She's still down there!"

Celeste read the Hebrew letters in reverse, meaning right to left, her voice quivering as she hastily spoke.

And the gateway to the Golem Prison vanished, locking Allie and the biots inside.

CHAPTER 11

I sprawled on the floor of Third Street Shul, staring up at the ceiling, panting. Adrenaline coursed through my body. The staff of undoing lay nearby. My shoulder hurt. My head hurt. And my mind was reeling from the events that had just transpired.

I stared at the space where the gateway had been and said to no one in particular, "What the hell just happened?"

It took a minute for the frenzy of our flight to dissipate.

"Well," Quinn finally answered, climbing to his feet, "for starters, we lost the key to the Golem Prison."

"Yeah, that didn't take long," Kanya said as she approached. "But we got the staff which, I guess, is the only thing that will stop the, uh..."

"Rothbard and his robotic army?" Quinn glanced at her.

"Yeah. That."

"It wasn't an army." Mace knelt with the rifle, examining it. "It was a single robot. Most likely an advanced military biot, an old peacekeeper, with shield capacity. Or a very thick skin."

"Right." Quinn nodded matter-of-factly. "He

barely budged when you shot him with that fancy gun of yours."

Mace muttered something and returned his attention to the weapon.

Kanya stood looking down at the staff. She was clearly enthralled with the piece. Finally, she turned her attention to us. "Well, at least we know who's behind this and why—Rothbard is trying to reboot the Third Golem. That's what this is about. And he has one supercharged robot to help him."

Quinn massaged his shoulder. "A robot who's after the Seventh Guardian."

"But why?" I sat up, groaning as I did. "How the hell can I help him animate some rock monster?"

"It's more than that," Kanya said. "Allie talked about science and magic, about a new type of golem, one cloaked with that indestructible Mantle. And God knows what can be done with something like that."

Quinn shook his head. "Typical mad scientist."

Celeste came over and encouraged me to remain seated. I did not need to tell her where I was hurting. She closed her eyes, placed her hand on my forehead and then my knee. She spoke soft, inaudible words. Healing energy emanated through her touch and its warmth flowed into my aching body.

Mace stuffed the rifle back into the duffle bag and stood up. "We can't stay here. Not if that thing is after Moon."

He was right. However, I was convinced that if I'd jumped through the biot, I'd have done serious damage. Still, I was touched that Mace would even admit some concern for me. I thanked Celeste and she helped me climb to my feet. I wouldn't be participating in an Iron

Man competition any time soon, but I did feel noticeably better.

"Len," I said. "Why was he on our side?"

Quinn shrugged. "I doubt it's out of the kindness of his heart."

"Does he even have one?"

"Good question. We *do* know that he has a bad-ass brother though."

"And the girl?" I asked.

Mace lifted the bag and prepared to exit. "She seems resourceful enough. She'll get out another way. And hopefully she'll lock those things in there behind her."

"And if they escape? Or, even worse, get hold of the key?"

"Then I'm going to need a bigger gun," Mace said humorlessly, and marched towards the door of the synagogue.

As we prepared to follow, the remaining members stood staring down at the staff of undoing. Waiting for me. I couldn't blame them. If what Allie had said about the staff was true, we were in possession of one of the most iconic relics in human history. It lay on the floor where I'd dropped it.

Kanya squatted and glanced up at me.

I said, "Go for it."

She took it and cradled it in both hands, rotating the piece while studying its markings.

"Pictographs of some sort," she said. "A bird. A tree. A flame. It looks like..." She probed the cavity in the brass cap with her fingertips. "Something was seated here. And the wood is practically petrified. In fact, I'm not sure it even *is* wood. But it's light. Wow.

This is incredible. My father would have loved to see this."

"So how does it work?" Quinn asked. "I mean, didn't Moses use it to call down fire on the Klingons?"

Kanya frowned. "Not exactly."

"*The staff has no inherent power.*" Celeste approached, extended her hand, and Kanya passed it to her. "That's what Allie said. *It's just a conduit. The power's in the hand that holds it.*"

Celeste turned and handed the staff to me.

I looked reluctantly at the rod.

"Reagan," she said firmly. "The staff is yours."

Despite my hesitation, a slight chill tingled through my hands. I looked at the staff and, indeed, blue veins of electricity danced in the brass, skittering through the etchings on the shaft. *Vara de Dios. The rod of God.*

I generally don't take myself too seriously. In fact, I'd come to believe that self-deprecation was an endearing trait in people. However, wielding the rod of Moses seemed like a potential fast-track to becoming a real pain in the ass to be around.

I sighed and took the piece.

Celeste, Quinn, and Kanya stood staring.

"What?" I said, defensively.

"Oh, nothing." Quinn shrugged. "Excuse us mere mortals."

"Dude, shut up," I said, tapping the end of the staff on the floor. "And no cracks about Gandalf."

"Heads-up." Mace stood at the doorway, wrestling the door free from its place. He lowered it and let it thud to the ground. "Let's get outta here."

We gathered on the landing outside of Third

Street Shul. The Shade appeared noticeably less dense, as if our entry into the Shul had broken its hold. Night had descended upon the city, the summer warmth yielding to a faint offshore breeze. Somewhere out there were five other gateways to the Golem Prison. At this stage, their location remained a mystery. As did Allie, the shadow-jumping psion, and the biotic brothers. We agreed to head straight for the Asylum. If L3-X had escaped, and was indeed tracking me, the Asylum would provide the necessary cover. We hoped.

I was dying of thirst but, as we hustled to our vehicles, the others forbade me from entering a nearby market for a drink. I complied. Along the way, I peered into the shadows half-expecting to catch a glimpse of Allie. I didn't. We reached our vehicles. I slid the staff behind the seat, the Cammy's engine rumbled to life, and we headed straight for the Asylum.

When we arrived, I chugged two bottles of water and opened a third just in case. After Kanya's crack about me stinking, I spent some time in the bathroom attempting to scrub the stench of trash off me. But until I took a hot shower, I was bound to smell like I'd slept in a sewer.

Rapha and Orphana grilled us for details. We told of our encounter with Allie, the biots, and the unknown status of the key. But it was the involvement of Balfour Rothbard that understandably seemed to most interest Rapha.

"It's him," Quinn said, collapsing into a chair. "Like we guessed."

"So it is," Rapha said, grimly. "Like a predator animal, he has lain in wait."

"Yeah. He's been busy. That thing is his creation."

Quinn pointed to the remains of the biot spine and head that lay on the surgical table, now scattered into various parts.

"Then the murder at the Magic Dragon...?" Orphana wondered.

Celeste shook her head. "The biot didn't do it. It was Rothbard. Or some affiliate."

Orphana said, "Lord help us."

"L3-N and L3-X," Quinn continued. "They're his. But they're... different. One tried to kill us. The other tried to stop him. According to the girl, that thing we caught in Chinatown was there to stop Rothbard from getting the key."

"Then they were both attempting to stop their own creator?" Rapha knit his brow. "Fascinating. This proves that they are sentient models."

"They ain't vacuum bots," Quinn replied. "That's for sure. They don't appear to have the same protocol. But why would he create biots with opposing directives? And they're strong as hell. Mace's bullets had no effect. Apparently, Rothbard has bigger plans than just upgrading the old models. He's after the Third Golem. Wants to fire it up and cloak it with that spell of indestructibility."

"Why, Rapha?" Orphana asked. "What is he up to?"

But Rapha just shook his head.

Quinn said, "For whatever reason, he needs Moon to help him."

"Brother Moon?" Rapha raised an eyebrow. "How can you help him?"

"You got me," I said. "I know nothing about golems. Or magic mantles."

"Or staffs?" Quinn said.

The staff lay across my lap. I patted it. "That too."

Rapha approached and peered at the rod.

"The staff of undoing," he said, astonishment sparkling in his eyes. "Truly, my friend, you are blessed."

"I was thinking just the opposite," I said. "Either way, if what they say is true, it's pretty incredible. According to the girl, if Rothbard acquires the spell, this is our only hope. At least, the only thing that will stop them. Once the spell is activated, it can only be reversed or countered with this. Not sure how that works, but..."

Rapha said, "This is fortuitous." Yet his features had grown austere, even grim. He stroked his jaw and turned away.

I glanced at Celeste. She furrowed her brow in concern. Finally, she asked, "Rapha, what's wrong?"

He stood with his back to us now. When he turned, a shadow had fallen over his countenance. His tone was solemn. "I fear that forces are in motion, a design long in process, with the potential for dire consequences."

A tense moment of silence passed before I said, "Go on."

Rapha continued. "Long ago it was told among the guardians that a great magician would arise. One with the power of life and death, one who wielded the knowledge of the ancients. A great battle would ensue between the forces of good and evil. Many would be lost. The toll, terrible. And from it, a new age would be born."

"Your basic apocalypse," Quinn said sarcastically. "Stop me if you've heard this before."

"Hey." Celeste perked up. "That's what the girl said. Allie. She said the magical order's been revived—whatever that means. And there's another magician. *El Mago.* Just like the first one, the one who designed the golem, but even more powerful. He's designing an indestructible creature using magic and science."

Rapha drew a deep breath and nodded. The Tau glistened against his dark skin. "Yes. The roots of magic and occultism run deep in our city. And the Rothbards have long been involved in such pursuits. Before the inception of BioGen, Hiram, Balfour's father, pioneered the Solar Temple in Griffith Park, as well as the early Society of Thule. He had ties with Crowley's *Ordo Templi Orientis* and was rumored to be a sworn member of the League of Pythos. Rumors tell of black magic and human sacrifice. Surely, the Black Council empowered Hiram Rothbard's occult pursuits and caused his efforts to flourish. Now I greatly fear that his son is carrying on his father's commitments. With similar assistance."

I said, "So you think Rothbard is this end-times magician? If so, that would make this... the end times."

Rapha simply squinted at me, his features clamped in unease.

Quinn forced a yawn. "Wake me when we get to the good part."

"Cut it out," Celeste scolded, not so playfully. "This is serious."

Rapha ignored Quinn's remark. "The elder ones have long feared that a melding of science and magic would arise. That human technology empowered by the dark arts would merge, creating a Singularity of sorts. A new age wherein gods of steel and sorcery would reign."

My mind went back to Ki's words about a powerful magician and the deal he'd struck with him. It made me wonder about the Sixth Guardian's allegiances. Did he *really* want to help the Imperia? Or was his loyalty to the Summu Nura?

And could I really change the very course of history?

Mace leaned back against the wall with his arms crossed. His inability to stop L3-X had torched him. "I don't know much about this Rothbard guy, but if he's human, he bleeds."

Rapha shook his head. "You underestimate the power of magic, my friend."

"Maybe," Mace said, begrudgingly. "But I still haven't seen many spells that can stop an M4."

"And his robot?" Quinn added with a hint of sarcasm.

"I'll find something," Mace said. "Trust me."

Celeste looked at Rapha. "So, what do we do?"

"Well if we don't do anything," Quinn said, "Rothbard eventually cracks the code to the prison, like the girl said, and gets what he wants. That is, if he doesn't already have the key."

Rapha pursed his lips in thought. He towered over the rest of us, but his demeanor was that of a gentle giant. Thankfully, his ego was not proportional to his size. I liked that about him. It made me feel slightly guilty for having questions about his motivations.

"Whatever we do," Mace said, "we cannot just play defense on this one. Matisse wouldn't have. And neither should we."

"He's right." Quinn rose from his seat. "We have

the staff. If that thing works," he glanced at me, "we have the upper hand... even if Rothbard gets the key. Plus, we have the Seventh Guardian. That's the gamechanger. Right? So maybe it's time we took the battle to them."

Quinn twirled his mustache. He looked at me, as did the others.

How in the hell had I become the default leader of this raggedy ass group?

F-f-father. K-111's final words to me came to mind. *You must... s-s-stop... my father.*

"What do you suggest we do?" I asked.

"We bring Rothbard up to speed." Mace pushed himself from the wall. "That is, in the event that he is unaware. Inform him that we have the staff. And we're privy to his plans. Even if he gets the spell, we can stop him. And we will. We give him an opportunity to put the brakes on, dismantle whatever operations he's running. With those two biots of his at odds, he's got more than us to reckon with. If it comes to it, I'll deploy the antimatter rifle. And if our charge to him does not work, we inform him that we are prepared to exercise more extreme measures."

"So, we march in and threaten the guy?" I shook my head. "I dunno about that."

"Why not just turn him into the police?" Celeste added. "I mean, if he murdered Reagan's friend, and if he's violating AIC laws and we can prove that, then law enforcement needs to get involved."

"*If* we can prove it," I said.

"With those robots of his running around," Quinn said, "it won't be long until the cops trace them back to him."

"Yeah," I said. "But Rothbard's probably got half the force on his payroll. Do you realize how much influence his family has around here?"

Rapha appeared reengaged with the conversation.

"Friends," he said. "We must be cautious. A man of Balfour Rothbard's stature and acumen has many forces at his disposal."

Celeste shrugged. "Well, so do we."

They were looking at me again.

"What?!" I opened my arms.

"Oh, nothing," Quinn said. "Just that you're the only one of us who can melt Nefarium, talk to his guardian angel, see invisible thingies, and has a Tau fused into his freakin' body. Oh, and carries the rod of Moses."

I huffed. Hard to argue with that.

"Even if we *do* have the upper hand," Rapha motioned to the staff of undoing, "we must be wise."

"Don't strike a blow," Orphana opined, jabbing her cane at an invisible foe, "unless you're ready to strike a second. I s'pose my question is—are we prepared to strike a second blow?"

After a moment of thoughtful silence, Quinn waxed bold. "Hey, what's wrong with us? We're earth guardians. Maybe we should start acting like it." The psion scanned the group, summoning courageous thoughts as his gaze went. "I'm with Rambo on this. We track Rothbard down and... flex our muscles."

"Muscles?" I laughed.

"Okay," Quinn sat back down. "At least we can break a few things and make a lot of noise."

"And L3-X? We didn't exactly handle him."

Mace's shoulder muscles tensed, and then he squinted. "I'll take care of him."

I looked at the biot splayed on the gurney. The image of its face, staring at me and clamped in anguish, burned in my mind's eye. "The last thing it said to me was that we needed to stop its father. I'm not sure what that means. I'm not sure what it involves. I've never challenged a magician, guys. And I have no idea what to do with this." I extended the staff. "But I'm game. I guess."

"Attaboy, Moon!" Quinn said.

"So where do we find Rothbard?" Celeste asked.

"The BioGen facilities are a ghost town," I said. "I think it's a huge homeless encampment now. I doubt we'll find him there."

"But if he's manufacturing a new line of AIs, he may have fired up the factory again."

"Maybe," I said. "But our best bet is Dante's. Word on the street is that Rothbard holes up in the Sixth Circle."

"Heresy," Quinn said. "Perfect place for an apostate Jew. You know how hard it is to get into that place though, right? Especially that far down."

I said, "And... that's the problem."

After a moment, Kanya smiled wryly. "Unless you know someone who owes you."

"Like who?"

"General Waxman," she said. "Remember? The hell hound?"

"I remember," Mace said. "A genuinely foul beast. The creature's here now. Mounted. But Waxman cannot be trusted. He'd just as soon throw you into his piranha tank as help you."

"Maybe you're right. But he still owes me."

"General Waxman?" I queried.

"He's not really a general," she said. "That's just what they call him. He's a big wheel at Dante's. Some sort of boss. Has access to all but the Ninth Circle. My father did a favor for him once—a big favor. Waxman was at Matisse's funeral. The guy with the glitter eyeliner? Yeah, that's him. He said whenever I needed something—anything—he would be there for me."

"And you think he can help us?"

"I dunno. But as much as that place disgusts me, it's worth a try."

Quinn's exhortation to start acting like earth guardians seemed to galvanize us. Although acting like earth guardians was no guarantee of success, it injected some much-needed enthusiasm. Which was something we'd need if we hoped to intimidate chaos magician and technological whiz-kid Balfour Rothbard.

CHAPTER 12

Quinn seemed overly-eager to confront the magician.

"I owe Rothbard," the psion said, strapping on a utility belt.

"Brother," Rapha countered, "vengeance does not serve our purpose."

"Who said anything about *our* purpose?" Quinn's response came off as hostile, although he quickly stepped it back. "Okay. Just a few Jedi mind tricks, then. That's all."

"No tricks." Rapha's tone was stern. "You are better served not going. You know this. Besides, we can use you elsewhere."

This appeared to only inflame Quinn's emotions. Whatever tension existing between him and Rapha remained.

I was the obvious candidate. Not just because I was the Seventh Guardian—now also *Wielder of the Supreme Staff*, a handle flippantly imparted by Quinn—but because I refused to stay put.

"If he's looking for me," I said, "then I'll be damned if I'm just going to hide in the shadows."

"I dunno," Celeste mused. "Did you see that biot of his?"

"I can outrun him," I said. "At least, out-*jump* him. I think. In fact, I was about to bust a hole in his gut before Mace yanked me outta that Prison. Besides, if this is all about me, at least use me as bait to force his hand."

Despite my conviction, Rapha was not keen on the idea.

"Brother Moon," he said, "you have not yet faced someone as adept at magic as Balfour Rothbard. Though your abilities are great, you have much to learn."

"Gee, thanks. But how else am I *going* to learn, Rapha?"

He peered at me, appearing skeptical.

"Look," I said, "you guys keep talking about all these prophecies—the Seventh Guardian will do *this*, the Seventh Guardian will do *that*. And now you want me to stay hidden in this bunker? Hiding from the bad guys? Is that the way your Seventh Guardian is supposed to act? C'mon. It doesn't make sense. If I'm anything close to what you say I am—or what I could be—I won't get there by running and hiding."

Kanya frowned. "This isn't a bunker."

"Whatever. You know what I mean."

After a moment, Orphana conceded, "He's right. Let him go, Rapha. If he's been chosen, then we have to trust that the good Lord is with 'im. And with us." She smiled at me.

Eventually, Rapha nodded in agreement, knowing it was as sound a reasoning as we were going to get. Although, I hoped that this was the last speech I'd have to give in defense of myself.

Being that Waxman was Kanya's connection, she and I were once again partners. Which was becoming the norm. It reinforced the sense, at least to me, that our destinies were somehow intertwined. Matisse's death had bound me to her, as had my raising her to life atop Spiraplex during the lightning storm. She had no problem putting me in my place either, which I begrudgingly acknowledged as a good thing. Besides, her shifting skills could possibly come in handy.

Perhaps the most important debate was whether I should take the staff with us to Dante's. If the instrument was as important to our success as Allie had suggested, keeping it close was a good idea. However, if it fell into the hands of our enemies, we were screwed. No. The staff should remain in the Asylum until we absolutely needed it. Or until Rothbard got his hands on the spell of invulnerability. On this, we all agreed. Besides, I did not relish the idea of strutting around West Hollywood looking like Merlin.

Before we left, Rapha organized a team to locate the other gateways to the Golem Prison and send a party in search of Allie. Perhaps Quinn could employ his psionic abilities to hone in on her location. Meanwhile, Celeste took up the Jewish magic book, the *Sefer Raziel Ha-Malakh*, in order to memorize its contents, and Mace headed to his workshop intending to inspect his arsenal for a weapon to counter L3-X's abilities.

It was well after ten p.m. by the time we entered the Cammy. The denizens of the Inferno would just be waking up.

As I drove, I asked Kanya about her connection. "So, who is this General Waxman? And how'd Matisse know him?"

"It's kinda a long story." Kanya rummaged through her handbag—more like a small fashionable rucksack—before producing a cube of gum, unwrapping it, and popping it into her mouth. "My father hated the Inferno. He said it was straight from the pit of hell. But Matisse was a softie. You know that. He loved people. Said that goodness was the most powerful weapon. Plus, removing evil from Earth was his mission. So, it didn't really matter where it was found, or who led him to it.

"Anyway, Waxman was mutual friends with a curator at the L.A. Zoo. Apparently, he needed a... an *animal control* expert of some sort. He'd heard about us and knew Matisse trafficked in fringe science, cryptids and stuff. He contacted him about removing a hell hound from the grounds of the Inferno."

"A *hell hound*? Interesting."

"Yeah. It was some sort of mutant canine. Had a second head. Or the beginning of one. It stalked the Laurel Canyon foothills and got onto Dante's property sometimes, tore things up. Pooped. They set traps and cameras. But the thing would just disappear and reappear. Like a phantom. Wasn't until it carried off Waxman's dog that he finally sought help."

"Let me guess—a hairless poodle."

"It was a Doberman, I think. Anyway. Matisse didn't like Waxman. He knew he was involved in all kinds of twisted stuff. But he agreed to help because he didn't like the idea of demon dogs running loose in the city. Him and Mace hunted it down. Matisse got hurt in the process, had this huge red welt from the animal. Something about a poisoned barb. He was bedridden for a week. Really sick. Waxman found that out, sent him some flowers and absinthe."

"Touching. So where do we find Waxman?"

"He manages the docks out back. Deliveries. Special orders. Nothing gets into the Inferno unless it first goes through Waxman."

"I can only imagine."

The red spotlights swooping along the foothills to the north pointed the way to Dante's Inferno. I turned the Cammy onto Santa Monica Boulevard and headed that direction.

West Hollywood is a trendy area known for its high-energy nightlife, making it a perfect location for Dante's. WeHo, now its moniker, offered some of the city's most buzzworthy restaurants. The fabled Sunset Strip featured comedy clubs and a variety of music venues, as well as the Chateau Marmont, a swanky celebrity hideaway. The Boulevard was awash in rainbow flags. We passed gay bars and dance clubs now hopping with activity.

Since its opening, Dante's Inferno had become a mecca for Los Angeles' florid underbelly—Neuros, pagans, the filthy rich, and the seriously disenchanted all rubbed shoulders there. It attracted its share of glitterati, from hardcore partiers to simple curiosity-seekers. But it was the debauchery that had become something of legend. Sadomasochists, porn producers, Luciferian priestesses, and devout gluttons imbibed their passions in the bowels of the lavish nightclub. Lifted straight from the pages of Dante Alighieri's classic, this 'pleasure palace,' as guests preferred to call it, reproduced the nine circles of hell. Each descending level was given over to a specific sin and its torments... or *delights*, depending on one's perspective.

Beginning with Limbo, the futuristic structure then descended in ever smaller tiers, proceeding to

Lust, Gluttony, Greed, Anger, Heresy, Violence, Fraud, and finally at the bottom, Treachery. But unless one had lots of money or some serious connections, accessing the lower levels of the Inferno was nearly impossible. The Average Joe was lucky to reach Lust or Gluttony. Greed required a high-level clearance and a significantly extensive background check. Not to mention, money. What went on in the nether circles was a matter of speculation. Rumors of celebrities and world leaders being secreted into the Inferno were commonplace. It wasn't long before disturbing stories began emerging about criminal dealings, exotic tortures, and even death. After several high-profile investigations, the police had scaled back their surveillance, leaving Dante's shadowy ownership to handle its own internal problems. Most acknowledged it for what it was— a backdoor deal with the LAPD to look the other way. And as its fame increased, so did the mystery surrounding it.

The Inferno made Burning Man look like a church picnic.

As we approached the Laurel Canyon foothills, I caught sight of the arches rising at their base. They were supposed to be a knockoff of Palmyra's Arch of Triumph, the fabled arch that served as the gateway to the ancient Temple of Baal. The red spotlights swept the night sky, splashing the arches with their infernal glow.

We parked in a nearby structure, top level, because it was already packed. As we exited the Cammy, the thump of music and the chatter of celebrants greeted us. The air stank of lerium.

Kanya tightened the laces on her boots and rose.

"You ready?"

"As ready as I can be." I readjusted the Ndocron vest underneath my shirt. But the possibility of facing a magician of Rothbard's caliber had seeped into my nerves and begun a slow fraying.

"If that robot shows up," Kanya said, "you gotta promise me you'll get outta there. No heroics, okay?"

"Heroics? Me?"

"Yeah. You."

"Party pooper," I said.

As I prepared to head to the Inferno, she reached out and put her hand on my arm, stopping me in my tracks. "Hey, whatever happens, I... I believe in you, Reagan."

Her words caught me off guard. As much as Kanya was a beautiful woman, and we were finding ourselves teamed up more often, romance was not on the top of my priority list. Having a flaming portal jammed into your sternum has a way of rearranging life goals. Besides, somewhere deep inside, it felt like cheating. Even though Ellie had died over a year ago, I couldn't deny that our short relationship had been magic. Not literal magic, of course. Still, I'd be remiss to not admit that Kanya's words stirred something other than just Platonic attraction inside me. Damn. Without a witty comeback on hand or the balls to kiss her right on the lips, I simply thanked her and said I hoped I wouldn't let her down.

We followed a winding metal stairwell to the street level. There, a boisterous crowd gathered around several tall gated entries. Cameras flashed as tourists captured selfies, and hopeful guests grappled for position in line. The arches rose above us, twenty to thirty-foot-tall stone blocks imported directly from some-where in the Middle East. The throng was crawling with Invisibles. Pale parasitic demons turned their eyes my direction as we passed. If they knew I had arrived, I wondered what other beasties might be privy to our presence.

Instead of following the sloping walkway into the Inferno, Kanya led us the other way, up the street to-wards the foothills. Following the massive block walls, we reached a delivery alley that traced the north-ernmost length of the property. Apparently, this was where her father had met with the General. A retract-able barrier wall crossed the road to prevent traffic from entering, while a fully encased turnstile awaited pedestrians. At the end of this cul-de-sac, two secur-ity booths stood before a tall, razor-wire-capped gate. Halos of insects swarmed around a cluster of flood lamps which bleached the area in their glow. Armed guards patrolled nearby, two on the ground and one across a parapet atop the wall. They wore the familiar Inferno uniforms—black cargo pants and golden-col-lared V-necks bearing a digitized patch displaying an animated flaming letter *I*. They turned our direction as we approached.

"Here goes nothin'," Kanya said under her breath as she entered the turnstile.

A blue, body-length cone of light appeared, which we passed through. Neither the Ndocron vest nor the Tau scar registered on the scan. However, if we made it further into the Inferno, this was likely just the first of many bio-metric devices we would encounter.

As we approached one of the booths, she asked me to stay back. I remained where I was, surveying the area and letting my second sight do its thing. It was cold here. I mean, paranormally speaking. A kind of ethereal frost seemed to blanket everything, chilling the bones of my psyche. But its source was undetectable.

Kanya returned. "Okay. They're contacting him."

The guard in the booth watched us while speaking into a radio on his jacket. I glanced up at one of several mounted cameras, convinced that a slew of inquisitive eyes was now upon us. This was a huge gamble. Getting into the Inferno—especially as far as the Sixth Circle—would take a lot more than just good luck or personal favors. Which is probably why I caught myself secretly hoping that Bernard would make a surprise appearance.

"Let me do the talking." Kanya chomped her gum, seemingly psyching herself up for the encounter.

"No wisecracks?"

"None."

"Not even subtle sarcasm?"

She didn't bother to respond. Her glance told me she'd quickly reached the threshold of her patience with me.

The wait seemed longer than it probably was, but eventually a jeep pulled up behind the gates and someone hopped out. A section of the wall retracted, revealing a previously imperceptible door, and General Waxman stepped through.

The rim of a well-worn bush hat hung low over his brow. Nevertheless, I could still recognize a hint of color around his eyes. He wore a sequin-embroidered black leather vest and metal-studded cuffs on both wrists. A leather riding crop whip hung from one side of his belt. With his eye shadow, a purple bandana tied around his neck, and Wellington boots, he looked like a cross between a big game hunter and a drag queen.

Waxman flicked a lit cigarette to the ground and then walked toward us.

Kanya spat her gum into a nearby trashcan and watched Waxman approach.

"So, it's true," he said, stopping and removing his hat. "The Spaniard's daughter. How are you, Kay?" He clutched his hat to his body and half-bowed.

"Much better than the last time you saw me, General."

"Oh, good. Sad day, that was. Your father was a good man."

"He was."

"A *unique* man."

"That too."

"I only wish I could have known him longer."

"I'm, uh, sure he would have liked that."

"And that hellish canine—what did you ever do with it?"

"From what I understand, they had it mounted."

"God, that was awful. A rare beast, though. I'm indebted to your father."

"Which is the reason we're here."

Waxman raised an inquisitive eyebrow, put the hat back on, and turned to me.

"And this is Reagan Moon," Waxman said, a tinge of coldness in his tone. Along with regality. The guy fancied himself of royal blood, distant as it may be. He looked me up and down, as if sizing me up for some private fantasy.

I remembered him from Matisse's funeral. Hard

to forget a guy who wears big game safari hats, glitter eyeliner, and BDSM accoutrements. Although he'd swapped the glitter for pale plum eye shadow, his attire remained similarly eclectic. An earring hung from one ear, displaying a ball and chain, with a Bluetooth device in the other ear. Pock marks marred his face, giving him a grizzled appearance. And a toxic murk coiled about him. But it was hard to tell whether it was an actual demonic entity or just the excretion of his own rank energy. He reeked of fetishes and bad juju.

"You know me?" I asked.

"I know *of* you. We brushed shoulders at the memorial service. You don't remember? Shame. Your reputation precedes you, sir—the man that brought down Spiraplex? And that Santa Muerte cartel ring, that was toasty. You're quite the hero to some. What? You look surprised. Word gets around. Especially at Dante's. But if you're planning on bringing down the Inferno, I'm afraid I can't let that happen."

"Heh. I had no plans for that. Unless, of course, Dante's needs brought down...?"

Kanya shot me an angry glare.

Waxman snorted. "I suppose you can try. But I might have something to say about that." He rested his hand on the hilt of his riding crop. "And lots of others."

Creep.

Still, I just smiled.

The General returned his attention to Kanya.

"So, what can I do for you, Kay? VIP treatment in our absinthe lounges? A night in the Chapel of Pain maybe?" He said it with a straight face, but I could sense the lechery in his intent. What a greaseball.

"I'm afraid not," she replied. "But I *do* need a

favor."

"Ah, yes. I owe you one, don't I? So how can I help?"

She hesitated, cleared her throat, and then said, "We need to see Balfour Rothbard."

His jaw went slack for a second. He quickly composed himself and brushed some lint off his vest. Then he folded his arms and smiled wryly. "And what makes you think that I know where to find *him*?"

"Well, the rumor is that he hangs out in the Sixth Circle."

"The Sixth Circle!" He practically guffawed. "Is that so?"

"Word gets around," I added.

Waxman looked sidelong at me.

"I'm afraid that's impossible," he said, allowing his gaze to roam away from us.

"But you said *anything*," Kanya implored.

"I did. But what goes on here—it's people's business, Kay. And we'd like to keep it like that. I can't divulge who comes and goes, who avails our amenities. That would be... unacceptable. Such a breach of confidentiality would be detrimental to our rapport with our clientele. I'm sure you understand."

"I do. So, your promise..." She shrugged dismissively.

"It was an offer, Kay. Out of courtesy."

"Okay. Your offer," Kanya said. "It was just—how do you say it—hot air?"

I thought for a second that Waxman's plum eye shadow might curdle in place. Something dark roiled inside him as fury seeped from his pores. He didn't like being mocked and prepared to defend himself, but

Kanya went for the jugular.

"I was under the impression that you had a lotta clout here," she said. "That's what everyone says. *Waxman is a boss. Waxman is a big deal.* That's why they call you the General, isn't it? Because you can pull strings. Make things happen. Or are we mistaken?"

"It's not a matter of clout, it's—"

"But you said *anything*, isn't that right? If I needed *anything*, I could come to you. That's the only reason I bothered coming here—*because you promised that.* My father helped you. Heck, he even risked his life in the process! You know that. Look, I need something, General." She fixed him with her gaze. "We need to see Rothbard."

There was enough insistence in her tone to make her appear less like a damsel in distress than a defiant rival.

Waxman gritted his teeth and shook his head. Apparently, keeping his word mattered to him. Further proof that even the worst of us retain some semblance of morals. Finally, he jabbed his thumb at me.

"Him too?"

"He's part of the deal," Kanya said.

He muttered something and turned away from us. I glanced at Kanya and then at the guards, who were keeping a close eye on our conversation. Waxman turned back to us.

"No guarantees," he said firmly.

"I understand," Kanya conceded.

"Okay, then. Gimme a minute." Waxman stepped away and spoke into a small device attached at his collar.

While he did, Kanya leaned over and whispered

to me, "Do you have to cause trouble?"

"What did I do?!"

"You're being a smart-aleck."

"Well he's being a dick."

"Stop talking like that! Just mind your manners, okay?"

"Yes, Mom."

Waxman's conversation was brief. He returned and stood with his hands on his hips, looking a bit sassy. "The General always keeps his word."

"I knew you would," Kanya said.

"But—" He raised his hand. "I can only get you down there. After that, you're on your own. If Rothbard's there, I can't guarantee he'll see you or speak to you. That's your business."

"Understood."

"All right." He straightened. "No weapons. No cameras. No phones. There're lockers inside for your belongings. You'll be patted down and scanned. And you'll be required to sign a consent form absolving the Inferno from any liability should something... injurious happen to you while on the premises."

"Injurious?" I said. "Sounds ominous."

Waxman pushed the brim of his hat up. "Do you want in or not?"

Kanya gave me the stink eye before saying, "Yeah, we want in."

Waxman led us to the guard shack where our names were logged and we were frisked. Thankfully, we had decided against bringing the staff of undoing, because it would have never gotten past security. Unless invisibility was one of its powers. After we'd been cleared, we followed Waxman into the Inferno.

The thumping vibrato of music grew, a pulsating electronica that reverberated in the earth and arches. Several loading docks greeted us. The service road followed a semicircular enclosure of tall stone walls. The road was lined with pallets, dumpsters, crates, and large rusty vats. Another level of security still awaited us. Waxman led us down a sloping tunnel, past another guard, and into a security hold. From there, we were led into a spacious, brightly-lit room lined with metallic cubicles containing banks of surveillance equipment. Security personnel hurried to and fro. I could still feel the obnoxious music pounding in the subterranean walls. Waxman asked us to have a seat and then excused himself.

Kanya and I sat, unspeaking. We were both amped on adrenaline. And probably fear. Images of Balfour Rothbard, chaos magician and ritual murderer, were playing on a continuous loop in my head. Damn. The psychic chill was everywhere; it made my nerves taut, putting me on edge.

Soon we were led to separate cubicles. The place had more surveillance cameras than the Vatican. I sat across from the female half of Agent Smith. She wore a dapper black three piece, glasses, and killer black stockings. As cold as a cadaver. She asked me some seemingly random, low-level security questions —something about government work, my medical history, and bio implants—before requiring me to sign a waiver for my stay on the premises. Our cell phones and keys were confiscated and tagged for future pickup. We rejoined Waxman where he'd left us, and he issued ID bracelets which, he said, would be our only way in and out. With that, we left the security area, got into his jeep, and sped behind the columns along the service road.

The summer night air whipped past us. I could smell the sagebrush from the canyon foothills. As we went, Waxman made sure we knew how fortunate we were to have received entry. I could tell he was still butt-hurt from Kanya's chiding.

Between the archways, I glimpsed the amphitheater bowl that housed Dante's Inferno. Fiery basins surrounded the subterranean complex and blazed into the night sky. Waxman parked the jeep near several large paper mâché heads, the kinds used in Mardi Gras celebrations, teetering on pallets like nonsensical boulders. It smelled of rotted greens and wet cardboard. The clanking of pots and silverware emerged from an open door. We were behind one of several restaurants that anchored the ground level of the Inferno.

Waxman hopped out and told us to follow him. He motioned to a guard patrolling the area whose gaze followed us as we passed. Producing a ring of key cards, Waxman unlocked a metal door. A bare stairwell descended to a single red door.

"Follow me."

Waxman took the steps, and we followed. His boots echoed in the narrow stairway. We arrived at the metal door to see the phrase '*Abandon all hope ye who enter here*' had been etched into the paint. On another occasion, I might have been humored by the reference, but not now. Hope was in short supply these days, and I dared not abandon it. The General popped the door open, and we emerged into a spacious flagstone terrace bustling with energy and colorfully costumed celebrants. You'd have thought Carnevale had dropped from the Venetian sky and crash-landed in La-la Land.

The stink of lerium was thick. Electronic dance music pounded as a DJ, accompanied by flashing strobes and glitter machines, kept the crowd hopping. The sound came in layers, as if some sonic trance experiment was being conducted by the CIA. The interior perimeter of this terrace was encircled by lounges and eateries, high-end joints featuring global cuisine and exotic rarities. Clusters of partygoers waited for entrance to their restaurant of choice. A juggler wearing a jester's hat entertained some onlookers, while a man dressed as Marie Antoinette distributed flyers for another venue. The gaping mouth of a huge funhouse prop, perhaps some fifty feet wide, graced the back of the entrance to the facility. It smiled down mockingly on the throng. Crowds huddled outside, anxiously hoping for entrance.

At the very center of the terrace, surrounded by flaming basins, descended the Inferno. It was a vast fiery shaft, a centrifuge whose crimson beams shone skyward like a volcanic ray.

Demons were everywhere, from your basic slug to the more exotic genus. So replete were the entities, I wondered if we'd actually stumbled into a convention for hellions. Some had so absorbed their host as to appear a hybrid being, part human, part devil. Others simply appeared as malignant growths, tumors of eyes and teeth. Even worse, they all knew I was here.

As we surveyed the spectacle, Waxman expounded on the popularity of the absinthe lounges and the drink's medicinal and culinary benefits. However, my attention was drawn from him towards the opening of the subterranean nightclub.

The circular mouth stretched almost the length of the terrace, perhaps a fifty-yard wide glowing crater surrounded by onlookers. I approached, nudged my way past someone with neon dreadlocks, and took hold of the rail which ringed the structure. A reflective fog drifted above the opening, making it impossible to discern clearly what lay below. Beneath the fog, lights flashed and crimson vapors swirled in the conical shaft. In between the music, screams of ecstasy or pain emerged, before being swallowed in the melee of sound. Staring into the Inferno was like looking into the fiery pit of hell itself. Knowing that we were heading down there made my gut flip-flop.

"It's a gravity rail," Waxman yelled as he approached, pointing to the gaseous blanket. "An electro-magnetic shield. Keeps 'em from jumping in."

"Why would anyone do that?" I shouted back, trying to communicate above the din.

"Ravers. Trance states. Suicide."

Kanya stood off, unwilling to look into the abyss. Probably the smart thing to do.

"Let's go," Waxman said, moving back through the crowd towards a bank of elevators along the perimeter of the terrace.

We followed him there. A beautiful frosted glass double-door, pinstriped with deco art, graced each unit. Doormen stood positioned along each platform. These thick, block-headed bellhops bore an uncanny resemblance to the Cosmagon of Soren Volden's making, with all the humor of a bowling ball and pecs the size of oak barrels. Working the elevators must've been a downgrade for these brutes.

Waxman spoke in the ear of the nearest doorman, who entered something into a digital keypad on his forearm. This triggered an electronic console along the front of the elevator.

On the platform next to us, a small group had gathered, wearing skimpy leather outfits and brandishing floggers and bondage accessories. They looked drunk and way too eager to reach their destination.

"Purgatory," Waxman said, jabbing his thumb their way. "Greenhorns." He smiled broadly and for the first time, I noticed he had a gold tooth.

"I wouldn't know," I said.

"Pity. I'm sure you've got plenty of sins to purge."

I shook my head, humored. "There's no whip big enough to purge me of my sins."

"Then maybe you'd prefer a rack?"

"Look." I turned to face him. "Dog collars and dildos aren't my thing, okay?"

He arched his eyebrows at my impertinence. Then he shrugged. "Too bad. Maybe you'll find something else down below to suit your fancy."

"I doubt it. The level of my fancy these days is enjoying a couple beers and a hot dog on the pier at sunset."

"How... *average*." He practically drooled the word.

Waxman instructed us to scan our wrist bands on the elevator console. After we did, the glass doors slid open upon a dimly lit red leather-lined interior.

As we entered, a commotion broke out on the terrace as several security dragged a shirtless man from one of the venues. Glass shattered and liquid sprayed across some bystanders. Kanya and I looked at each other as the doors slid shut on the brawl. Waxman remained nonplussed.

"Hang on," he said. "At first the motion can be disorienting."

He was right. Rather than going down, as I was expecting, the elevator went back, as if on a track.

"Magnetic levitation," he said. "It's a rope-less, rail-less, elevator system. Transrapid transport, they call it. Moves along a series of shafts, vertical and horizontal, depending on which level someone's going to. Allows for more cars and more passengers. It's quite ingenious. The only other one is in Japan, I think."

Too bad that such cutting-edge technology was found in a twisted place like this. Nevertheless, our travel was smooth. Our cabin moved back and then down. Waxman lightly pressed his fingertips against the interior console, at which point the car moved forward and glided to a stop.

"Just a little detour," he said, as the door slid open.

Immediately, a confluence of smells, some savory and others sharp, drifted our way. Stepping into a dimly lit, sprawling lounge area, Waxman said, "Gluttony. The Third Circle. Don't wander off. I'll be quick."

My suspicions had already been aroused by Waxman, but now the red flags were waving.

As he turned to leave, I said, "Wait. Why are we stopping here?"

"It's all right, Moon. I'll make good on my word. Just hang tight. Maybe have a look around. Or have a snack. On this level, it's all you can eat and drink." He winked and then strode into the Third Circle.

We stared into the vast lounge. In its center opened the Inferno flume. From our vantage, it appeared as a sheet of rain, a liquid funnel. Only this was a column of watery orange that anchored the room. I suspected it also kept patrons from gazing into other circles above and below us. A doorman stood nearby, same attire as the ones above, his hands folded at his waist. He barely gave us a sniff of interest.

Kanya and I looked at each other. We remained in the elevator, hesitant to make a move. But for different reasons.

"I feel sick, Reagan."

"Seriously?"

"Not like that," she said. "I mean, well, kinda like that. It's this place. It's... evil."

"Yeah. I just don't trust this guy. Something's up that he's not letting on to. And there's demons everywhere. Bad mojo. I mean, this is the kind of place where we can just—" I glanced at the bellhop "—go missing, and never be found."

Her eyes confirmed my trepidation. The truth was, the closer we got to Rothbard, the more our decision to barge in and intimidate him seemed a bit misguided.

However, my fascination with the Inferno, and being this far down, was getting the best of me.

"C'mon." I stepped out of the elevator.

At first, Kanya objected. But her interest appeared similarly piqued, and she followed.

Beneath the layer of ambient woodwind music, a soft clatter of dishes and silverware sounded, along with muffled conversation. As my eyes adjusted, I recognized large candlelit dinner tables spaced evenly throughout the floor, most of them occupied. Carafes of drink stood on each table along with various breads, rolls, and trays of butter. A ceramic basin sat near each table. Just beyond these tables an elaborate buffet of steaming foods encircled the perimeter of the flume. There rose barrels of draught, creameries, blocks of cheese, and open-flamed grills. The partial remains of a cooked whole pig were being picked over by several attendants. Laughter sounded as someone tumbled off a chair at one of the tables, lolling in their satiation. People sprawled on ornate lounges and chaises drinking or licking their greasy fingers. Nearby, a life-sized statue of a faun stood surrounded by fountains of wine —Bacchus, God of pleasure.

"I come for the desserts."

The voice sounded behind us. An obese man approached from the elevator, navigating in a fancy wheelchair. I thought for a second that he might ram me with his chair, but he jolted to a stop inches from my shins.

"Whoa! Sorry 'bout that," he said. "Don't get me wrong, though. They got a lotta great stuff. Not just desserts. Things you won't find anywhere else—haggis, fried tarantula, foie grass. And, yeah, it's true—they actually serve monkey brains."

"Ugh." I grimaced. "That's legal?"

"In California? I doubt it. But for them? They probably make an exception. Guess that's what makes Dante's the place to come. It ain't just the menu. It's the volume that counts." He patted his belly and laughed, making his chins tremble. "'Course, you gotta pay. Say, you two are new here, aren't ya?"

"Um, we're just visiting."

"Great. Well, I'm sure you'll find somethin' to your liking."

"Yeah."

"Last month they ran some tacos with caviar and black truffle brie. They were awright. It's funny, y'know, how some of the fancy stuff just ain't that special. I mean, I'll take a fat juicy Kobe fillet over lobster frittata any day."

"I've never had lobster frittata, so I can't say."

"You ain't missin' much." His gaze drifted out to the floor. "Anyway, nice chattin'. And, if you get a chance, I recommend the fried cookie dough balls with jelly centers. They're wonderful." Taking hold of the joystick on his chair, he aimed it towards the buffet. "Nipples of Venus, here I come!" And he sped off, laughing as he went.

Kanya and I glanced at each other, speechless. She looked pale.

Waxman approached with a bag under one arm. He put on the brakes as someone rushed past him and ducked through a curtain into a hidden room. The General shook his head and joined us.

"What was that about?" I said, jabbing my thumb towards the curtain.

"It's a vomitorium," he said,

Kanya groaned.

"Serious?" I said. "Okay. Get us outta here."

"As you wish."

We scanned our wristbands again, entered the elevator, and began our descent to the Sixth Circle.

The bad vibes were everywhere now, as if we were sinking deeper into an unseen ocean of toxins. Waxman inhaled and exhaled deeply. I could sense the tension rising in him, which didn't help my own disquiet. Rothbard knew we were on the way. Damn. I needed to clear my head. The brain fog was suffocating my thoughts. The confidence I'd started our journey with was little more than dead ash.

Waxman straightened his vest, shifted the bag to his opposite arm, and touched his fingertips against the console.

The elevator pulled to a stop.

In a way, I was relieved to have arrived and, hopefully, lose this guy. On the other hand, the sense that we were in way over our heads was now inescapable.

Waxman exited and said, "Ladies and Gentlemen, welcome to Heresy—the Sixth Circle."

CHAPTER 13

I exited the elevator with Kanya at my side. The moment I stepped onto the floor of the Sixth Circle my equilibrium keeled. I looked for something to steady myself on, but Kanya reached over and gripped my arm.

"What happened?" she said.

"To who?"

"To us."

"I-I'm not sure." I closed my eyes, attempting to center myself.

"It takes a minute," Waxman said. "That's why I hate this level. You'll never get your bearings."

I opened my eyes. It was dark here. I could make out spires of Gothic design, rising into vast vaulted arches that disappeared in shadow high overhead. Stone gargoyles and dragons peeked from the shadows, illumined by flickers of light from an unknown source. An organ played, a low-level discordant pulse that wove its way through the atmosphere. Within the sound were voices. Chanting and susurrations rose and fell like a breeze from the depths. Someone shrieked, a distant, tortured cry that trailed off into this dark sanctuary. Shadowy forms, both shifting and stationary, stretched into the darkness. What was I seeing?

Incense hung thick above this shadowy veil. An alchemical concoction of herbs, drugs, and God-knows-what-else struck my nostrils. Either they were conducting burnt offerings down here, or we'd entered the world's largest underground incense refinery. Another doorman stood nearby, his back to the wall, hands folded at his waist. He turned our way to reveal eyes as black as a cobra's, with a demeanor to match.

At the floor's center rose the watery flume. However, on the Sixth Circle, the liquid curtain appeared red. It tinted the entire area an eerie crimson. As my eyes adjusted, I could recognize passageways or partitions at irregular angles, intersecting and opening, winding off into the murk. People shuffled in and out of these innumerable openings, zombie-like. Was this a vast maze? Were these travelers in a trance?

Kanya said something, but I was caught up in what I was seeing. Or was I drifting into a similar trance as these walkers? For as my gaze drifted, I could make out something large rising in this cathedral. An unmoving, cyclopean form lit from below by swirling luminescence. A statue, perhaps. A shrine or idol. Yet the longer I stared, the more it appeared to move. To writhe. To reshape itself. Was this an entity? Or was my second sight playing tricks on me?

"...hear me?"

No. Because now, I realized that the overhead arches were also moving. It was almost imperceptible. But now that I recognized it, the entire room seemed to come alive. Good Lord, we were inside an immense organism! The entire floor was a living thing!

"Reagan!" Kanya shook me. "Snap out of it."

I caught my breath.

She stared at me. "It's playing with our heads."

I looked back out upon the Sixth Circle. The pulsing organ music remained, as did the murmuring voices. Yet the roiling forms had disappeared in deepening shadow.

"I warned you." Waxman shivered. "You guys still up for this?"

Kanya nodded, but her trepidation was evident.

"Okay," Waxman said. "Follow me."

He led us along the perimeter of the floor. Dark ornate paneling was broken up by paintings of hellish landscapes, upside down crucifixes, and busts of Roman emperors. Apparently, they'd hired Anton LaVey as interior decorator.

Up ahead, tall, fiery-rimmed double doors lined the walls, illumining the circumference of the floor with an infernal glow. On closer inspection, each doorway was surrounded by narrow stained-glass windows. Candles burned behind these windows, framing the doorways in a kaleidoscopic glow.

As we went, I studied the architecture and peered into the shadows. Yet I saw no more evidence that we were in the bowels of some demonic behemoth.

"There're confessionals for the penitent," Waxman said, gesturing to one of the doors. "Or the wheel for contrition. If that's not enough, there's the iron chair for purification."

He stopped in front of a door long enough for muffled shrieks to reach our ears.

"You mean," I wondered aloud, "people actually come here to be tortured for their apostasy?"

"Some. The rest just start their own religion." He reached the next door and stopped. Taking the brass handle, he turned to us and said, "This is the end of the road."

He pressed his finger to his lips and pulled the door open.

We stepped into what appeared to be a chapel. Racks of red candles burned on iron stands, positioned on each side of the door, creating huge stalactites of wax. Wooden pews lined the room with approximately a dozen individuals seated throughout them.

Balfour Rothbard stood alone on the stage.

I recognized him immediately. A huge chaos symbol, metallic in appearance, suspended from the beams behind him. A single chair, high-backed and lushly decorated, bearing an intricately carved double-headed eagle, occupied center stage. Such symbology was rich in occult and conspiratorial lore. Rothbard wore a plain gray cardigan and nicely-creased dress slacks. Large ornate rings donned several fingers. He spoke in leisurely tones into a wireless headset. Unlike some preachers, he did not appear to be ramping up an appeal for money or fame. Nor did he seem to be aware of us.

"—the conscious mind gets in the way. Pilate asked, 'What is truth,' and the Christ offered no response. Why? Maybe there was no answer! Or maybe, there were too many. That's my point: imposing your will on the universe creates truth. Magick tells the universe what to do. See, the universe exists to serve the magician, and not the other way around. *Truth* is what the creator deems it, not the creation."

I glanced at Kanya, but she didn't appear to be listening to Rothbard. Instead, she peered at the spectators in the pews. Only then did I realize why. They all bore a strange uniformity... at least from the back. All wore similar gray cardigans to Rothbard's and had the same length of shaggy blonde hair. What the hell was going on?

Rothbard looked up, noticed us, and stopped midsentence. As he did, the audience members all simultaneously turned.

Kanya gasped.

The congregants looked exactly like Rothbard!

Was this a trick of the mind, or had he cloned perfect duplicates? Same unkempt blond hair. Same bright blue eyes. Same angular jawline. Same thin, perpetually smirking lips. A small audience of Balfour Rothbard lookalikes sat staring at us!

"My guests have arrived!" Rothbard spread his arms in greeting. "Thanks for coming, guys!"

He removed his headset and set it aside. As he descended the stage, halting with that familiar limp of his, he tapped his temple, and the images in the pews blurred and flickered into nonexistence. I blinked hard. My eyes were still stinging from the raging haze of incense. Yet this had not been an optical illusion. The audience had never really existed.

"It's a form of holography, "Rothbard said, approaching. "Generated from an implant and transmitted to sensors throughout the room."

"And...," I wondered aloud, "you're the projector?"

He stopped and pointed to me. "Bingo. It's not that I'm a complete narcissist, I just hate to speak to a bunch of empty pews. Might as well practice on myself. Plus, with you coming on board, I'm expecting an uptick in public speaking gigs, something I loathe at present. Heck, if all goes well, I might even run for President!"

Waxman removed the bag he'd held clamped under his arm and handed it to the youthful billionaire.

"Per your request."

"Thank you, General. The payment's already been made. And a little extra. I appreciate your services, as usual."

"My pleasure."

"I know. You can leave us now."

Waxman thanked him and turned to us. "Your wristbands are programmed to return you back to Ground Level. If you decide to take any shortcuts or private excursions along the way, you're on your own."

"After what we've seen," I said, "I think we'll be getting the hell out of here as fast as possible."

"That would be wise."

"I appreciate your help," Kanya said. "I think."

Waxman snorted and tipped the brim of his hat in salutation. Then he strode out of the chapel, as if eager to leave the Sixth Circle. The candles flickered in his wake. Despite the man being a total sleaze, I suddenly felt unusually vulnerable down here without him.

When I returned my attention to Rothbard, he had moved to a well-stocked bar that sat back from the chapel along the perimeter of the room. Lights awakened along the bar as he approached. Removing a fluted bottle from the bag, he sat it on the bar top and waved us over.

"Please. Join me."

I looked at Kanya. She was as off-kilter as I was. The bad vibes inside this hell-hole were like quicksand, weighting my thoughts and emotions with a sluggish malaise. The chill that I'd sensed aboveground was more heightened here. It was part of the psychic stew that seemed to foul the entire atmosphere of the Inferno. I tried my best to shake it off as we approached him.

I said, "We're here to talk, Rothbard."

"I know, I know. The Minor Draw finally kicked in."

Kanya and I glanced at each other.

He walked around the bar and produced three tumblers, which he sat near a deck of Tarot cards. An ornate mirror stretched behind the bar, from which I could survey the chapel behind us. But I was too busy trying to decipher Rothbard's insinuation. Noticing the puzzlement on our faces, Rothbard laughed. "You didn't think they'd let you down here just because you wanted, did you? Don't be silly. It was an attractor spell. Doubled up. You're here because *I* wanted you here."

He slid the bottle to one side and leveled his gaze upon me. "The Watchers have a keen eye, Reagan. They know what trouble you pose. That's why I decided it was time. Felix just followed the clues, that's all. He has no choice. If you haven't already guessed, the old man is losing it. Dementia, probably. How else could he have lost the map? That's right—*the map*. I've seen it, ya know. And it says you're supposed to be here. The map foresaw it. And here you are! It's your star chart. It foresees everything. *Everything*. That's how I know, our destiny—yours and mine—is *connected*. We're meant to make the alliance."

He pressed his hands together, as if in prayer, and

remained poised in some brief moment of nirvana before returning his attention to us. "By the way," Rothbard said, retrieving a corkscrew from below the bar and opening the bottle, "I love the shirt, man."

I looked down. And caught myself. This guy was drawing us in with his smooth talking, employing some type of misdirection or trickery. However, unlike Rapha, I was untrained in counter-spells. Hopefully, just opening my mouth would have the same effect.

"Look," I said, attempting to dredge up some semblance of authority. "Maybe we should dispense with the niceties, Rothbard."

"Niceties? I'm just trying to be civil, man."

"I think we might be past that."

"Really? We just met! Wow. Okay, but not before we drink." He filled each glass a third of the way, clinking the bottle on the rim of the cup as he finished each pour, exclamation points to the action. Raising a glass, he said, "Please."

"Sorry." Kanya folded her arms. "I don't drink."

"Even for special occasions?" Then he looked at me. "C'mon, Reagan. Don't tell me you've given up the juice."

"I get too sentimental when I drink. It's a weakness of mine. I'll pass."

"Such discourtesy." Rothbard shrugged and raised his glass. "Oh, well. Then, a toast—to new friends. And eternal alliances."

He slammed the liquid down and winced. "Whoa!" Then he shuddered. "You guys don't know what you're missing. Cyanide. No, not that kind. They just call it that. Lots of antioxidants and opiates. The Third Circle is the only place you can get it, I hear. Okay, then." He set the glass down, clapped his hands, and rubbed them together briskly. "Hit me."

His enthusiasm was off-putting. I attempted to project a steely demeanor, but something else was nudging its way into my imagination. There was an aura about him, an atmosphere, that appeared non-localized. Almost like a shadow or vestige of some entity which he cast upon the invisible space around him. Was it some type of dimensional cloak? Or was I glimpsing something I'd never encountered? Whatever it was, it was emanating from Rothbard himself.

I said, "A friend of mine was murdered today in Chinatown."

"The herbalist. I know. I hate to say it, but he had it coming."

I raised an eyebrow. "You're incriminating yourself that quickly?"

"Does that incriminate me?"

"Not as much as the summoning circle and the biot, but, yeah."

"Oh, come on, Reagan. You'll have to do better than that. His guts were ripped out. Why would I do that? Look, I won't play hard to get, but you gotta make *some* effort. BioGen has units around the world. Before the autonomous models were outlawed, they weren't bound by current protocols. You know that. AIC guidelines don't implicate early innovators. My father made sure of that. Even if the model at the Magic Dragon can be traced to BioGen—which it can—that's no indication of a programming directive on our part. If so, I'd be responsible for half the malfunctioning androids on the planet. Geez. Glitches are inevitable. But that's true of us humans, too. For all you know, the biot committed the murder before he killed himself! Anyway, that was the problem with the autonomous class—they just couldn't be trusted."

"Like Len?"

"Like Len," he sighed. "I had high hopes for him. Upside is, without him, I'd never have developed Lex."

"Lex?"

"L-3X. That's what Len named him. He didn't like the numerical code thing, said it was too... *inhuman.* Funny, I know. He insisted on giving them human names."

"You mean, like Kevin?" Kanya asked. She remained with her arms crossed. Her demeanor was unyielding.

Rothbard eyed her coolly, and then smiled. He was a cocky son of a bitch. I wasn't quite sure what a chaos magician could do, but if she was on her game Kanya could probably snap his head off and shove it up his ass before he could even warm up his wand.

"So, you're the Mad Spaniard's daughter," Rothbard said.

"That's right." She stared, implacable.

"You had a bad experience with a chaote, I hear?"

"You could say that."

"That's too bad. But I'd caution you against indicting all of us due to the unethical behavior of one of us."

"I'd use the term *ethics* loosely if I were you."

"Touché. You know, your father was on our radar for a long time. Interesting guy. Now, there was a man who knew about ethics, about virtue. But his *virtue* eventually caught up with him. Didn't it? Oh, and his addictions."

Her breath quickened. A faint undulation traveled up her forearms. I stiffened.

Rothbard laughed and raised his arms in surrender. "It's all right. Geez." He glanced at me. "Is she always this tightly wound?"

"I'm afraid so," I said.

"All right, then." He returned his attention to me. "Yeah, you're right. Len was one of the first of the L3 series. His developmental arc was disturbing from the start. The L3 series gave me fits. Mainly the moral settings."

"Let me guess," I said. "They were too conscientious."

"Heh. Not far from the truth, actually. Don't get me wrong—I'm a proponent of free will. It's just that the early L3s kept using theirs to... push back. Do you mind?" He took another tumbler, raised the glass, and hammered down the shot. This time, he simply winced and set the glass down.

"So, if that's the case," I said, "then Len poses some problems for you."

"Why? Because he helped you escape the Golem Prison?"

I glanced at Kanya to ensure she wasn't about to start cracking skulls. However, she remained poised and unchanged.

I returned my gaze to Rothbard. I didn't need to confirm his remark. Rothbard knew everything—the staff, the key, Allie. Hell, he probably knew what brand of deodorant I used. He had a leg up in this game, whether it was from seeing my star chart, as he claimed, or just some advanced psychic abilities. The more he engaged us, the greater chance that we'd let some bit of info slip to his advantage. We were better off issuing our warning and getting out of there.

"Len's obsolete," he said. "Just like our species. Truth is, that's exactly why I designed him—to complete our evolution. See, everything that's wrong with Len, I corrected in Lex. Namely, the L-3X's moral settings."

"Let me guess—now you have a slave."

He wasn't humored. Reaching across the bar, he drew a small bowl of black crystalline powder toward us. As he did, he uttered something in an unintelligible dialect, and the powder ignited. I flinched, which evoked a smile from Rothbard. The flame subsided, leaving the substance to smolder. Then he picked up the pack of Tarot cards and began shuffling them.

"Wizards used to be philologists," he said. "They knew the language of nature, of animals. They could read the signs. Now they just put hexes on politicians and make love spells for hard-up romantics. It's a shame."

"And you're—what—hoping to restore some integrity to the office?"

"At least some excitement." He placed the cards down. "Cut?"

I shook my head.

He sniffed. Cutting the deck into three piles, he restacked them and picked them up.

I said, "So, he's human?"

"Len? He'd like to think so."

With a single smooth motion, he spread the cards out, face down, in a large horseshoe shape around the bowl of incense.

"His parts are basically human," Rothbard explained. "When it became illegal to place AI into a human body, we just made our own. Body, that is. Once we realized that we could start coaxing stem cells and induce pluripotent cells into duplicating other cells, the possibilities were endless. We started re-creating various organs—liver, kidneys. Ever seen a heart functioning independently of a physical body? Dude. It's pretty weird. Anyway, from there we moved to the bigger stuff.

"Early this century, scientists started growing these mini-brains and implanting them in animals. First mice, then chimpanzees. They called them *organoids*. My father had one in his office, I remember. Weird. But then the manmade brains started doing things, spontaneously connecting to their host's nervous system, transferring nerve signals and blood between the host animal and the human cells. Eventually they started reassembling themselves, growing and organizing into different layers like our own brains. Of course, the ethicists went apeshit. I mean, can you imagine a pig with human consciousness?

"But that was the hurdle we could never cross—making a self-aware biological entity; something that possesses intentionality, sentience. It used to be called Strong AI. But even the Turing models just required semantic understanding, you know, the recognition of symbols and syntax. Thing is, the Turings aren't really thinking machines, they're just symbol-detecting, symbol-manipulating machines. A really clever AI could just fake it and act as if it were conscious."

"So... this is where we talk shop?"

"Oh, lighten up. I'm going somewhere with this. You see, the threshold was... magick. We were thinking like children! *Mochin dekatnuth*. That's how Kabballah defines it—the normal way of thinking, the mentality of a child. And that's why there was never a huge breakthrough—*we were thinking like children!* No amount of science and technology could make an AI conscious. It was magick that caused the breakthrough. It was magick that infused them with real life."

"So, what God did through the spoken word—"

"I did through magick."

"The breath of life…"

His eyes widened. "You know, then. *Nishmat chayyim*. The fifth element. *Spiritus aetheris*. Just like God, I made the dust live."

The smoke from the incense possessed a woodsy quality, both sweet and earthy. I wiped moisture from my eyes and glanced at Kanya. Then I did a doubletake.

She swayed forward, and her hair flushed silver.

Rothbard continued. "The first hurdle was just mechanics. The basic elements. I mean, conscious beings need to use their senses to process reality— sight, smell, hearing. All those things play a part in self-awareness. So, our lab-grown brains needed to be fused with real sensory organs. That's when I developed the idea for the neural spine—a spinal column of Nefarium, a flexible frame encapsulated by living tissue. Once this was fused with our brains, we began assembling other sensory organs to read the data. All that was needed after that was the spark."

"Nefarium. Of course," I said. "That stuff is basically indestructible."

He smiled. "Not unless you're the Prophesied One, the Twelftborn of Chaos."

I stared at him.

"Pick a card," Rothbard said to me, motioning to the deck.

I didn't think he'd noticed Kanya. But if she was going to morph, all hell would break loose. Dammit. Why was she doing this?

I wiped sweat from my forehead. The Tau scar on my chest had begun tingling.

"I'm not playing your game, Rothbard."

"Not playing—?" He laughed. "This is all a game, Reagan! One big elaborate contest. Us versus them. You versus, well, *you*. It's all a game—the Prison, the key, the staff of undoing. Ki said as much, didn't he? Oops!" He glanced at Kanya. "She doesn't know yet, does she?"

Before I could answer, he flipped a card over. The humor left his features, and he spoke flatly, "The Three of Swords."

The heady aroma of the incense was intoxicating. Kanya leaned to one side and then snapped to attention. I reached over and placed my hand on her back.

"Three of Swords," she mumbled, dreamily.

Rothbard motioned to the cards. "Your turn, Reagan. Go on."

"Kanya." I took her by the shoulders and shook her. "Hey!"

Her hair flushed again, but she did not waken. Nor did she morph. Her eyelids drooped and the tension left her body.

"She's in a shadow trance," Rothbard said, stroking a large pewter ring on his pinky finger. "It's just a mild trance state. *Ignis fatuus* is the technical term. Produces paramnesia. She won't remember any of this. It's a spell. Frankly, I'm surprised she succumbed so quickly. Wow. That's not a good sign. I was told her alter ego has no such weakness. Is that true?"

"Damn you."

The storm gifts leapt inside me.

Rothbard stepped back. "Easy, Reagan. You wanted to talk, right?"

"She's my friend. And in case you haven't noticed, I'm part of the team now... a team that's trying to keep scum like you off the streets."

"Scum?" He furrowed his brow. "Why do you keep insulting me? Geez."

The dark aura swirled about him, as if I'd pricked an emotional wound with my words. It billowed outward, a noxious fog borne of... pain.

He peered at me. "So, tell me, if you're part of the team, then why haven't you told them about the incident with Ki?"

I opened my mouth to speak but thought better of it.

He brushed the overturned Tarot card with his fingertips and walked around the bar. His limp seemed worse in person than in the videos. He stopped before Kanya, reached out, and stroked her hair.

"She's really quite beautiful," he said.

I glared. "Easy, bub."

"Oh, stop it. I'm not like that. I have ethics." He laughed at his own joke, leaned back against the bar, and folded his arms.

"Look," he said. "We both want the same thing. We can help each other here. In fact, we're going to. The map says so. We share a mutual enemy—the Summu Nura. The map is the ultimate weapon against them. I can get it to you, Reagan. And you can get me what I want."

"Mutual enemy, huh? How do I know you two aren't besties?"

"Heh. We've always had an *arrangement* with them. The Black Council has been injecting itself into current events forever. Besides, you don't get as big as BioGen without some... outside assistance. It's true of most Hollywood types. Lucifer's been known to offer fame and fortune to the highest bidder. Although I'm not sure you can get any higher than the Black Council. Lucifer pales in comparison. However, my relationship with them is purely pragmatic. The Summu Nura and their agents keep the dogs at bay and I provide them... *prospects*. They're not really concerned about the business end of things. They could care less about robotics and replicational coding. They've got bigger aspirations."

"Like?"

He shrugged. "Being embodied. They want to merge dimensions—Arcadium and Diades—and make planet earth their home. That's all. We'll be breeders, basically, stepping stones to their next incarnation. Sad to say, but I'm just a tool. They'll spit me out when they're finished. Just like they've been doing for millennia. I'm dispensable. They know it, and I know it. Which is why a hookup is beneficial for both of us. We have to stop them, Reagan."

Kanya moaned but remained swaying in her dream state.

"You already know this, don't you?" He pushed himself away from the bar and stood in front of me. "It's why we need each other. You want to avenge Ellie and help the Imperia. I want to dissolve the Black Council and end their claim. With the map and the Mantle...

they'll never be able to stop us."

The glimmer in his eye was disturbing. Could he really be an ally in our battle against the Summu Nura? The idea wasn't completely nuts. I mean, I'd befriended worse.

I looked him up and down. Rothbard stood my height. I little thinner, but not at all fragile. In fact, his upper body appeared quite sturdy. It was his lower half that had me wondering. Had he injured himself on the surfing circuit? No. This was more like a... malfunction. There was no heat signature from his thighs and legs. Hm. And his eyes; a skittish distance occupied his gaze, as if his mind was elsewhere and he had to make a constant effort to pull it into the here and now. The periphery of his aura swirled about me. I had so many questions, but I started with the most nagging.

"What happened to you?" I asked.

"What do you mean?"

"Your... legs," I said.

He scowled. "Does it really matter?"

"If we're supposed to be partners, you know, eternal allies, then yeah."

He smiled and wagged his finger at me. "I get it. I know what you're trying to do. You're looking for weaknesses, aren't you? Well done, my friend."

"Is that what it is—a weakness?"

"My father thought so." He smiled, limped back around the bar, and took the last shot. Dabbing his lips with a napkin, he said, "He thought I was a lost cause, that I wasn't fit, that I didn't have the unction or the brains to inherit everything he built. A good for nothing surfer dude. And he had no qualms about saying so. He'd just as soon have created a biot for a son than concede that I was his. Bastard."

Rothbard could conceal the bitterness well enough. But his raging aura told the real story. Whatever had happened between him and the old man had screwed him up. Big time.

"But, please," he said. "Let's not talk about him." He motioned to the Tarot cards. "Choose one, Reagan. The real power is in your hand. In your choice."

The cloud of incense hovered over us in a languid haze.

I looked at the overturned card. *Three of Swords*. I couldn't recall the meaning of that card. Tarot was out of my investigatory wheelhouse. Instead, I glanced at Kanya. She was still under the power of the spell. Which was convenient. So, I proceeded.

"You know we have the staff of undoing."

"Yeah. Sounds like a cool piece. But I have... *the key*."

I peered at him. He was bluffing. Or was he?

"Oh," he said. "You didn't know?"

Rothbard raised his right hand, open-palmed, about eye level. His smirk grew. But there was nothing there. I looked at him, wondering if this was a trick, yet he did not return my gaze. Instead, he focused on the space above his open palm. I was about to say something snarky until I glanced in the mirror behind the bar and froze.

His reflection revealed the key to the Golem Prison was hovering just above his open palm.

Was this an illusion? I looked at the empty space, and then back in the mirror. The ornate rustic copper orb floated above his palm. Before I could demand an answer, Rothbard snapped his hand shut and the orb in the mirror disappeared.

"It's in a safe place," he said. "Oh, don't look so glum. It was always meant to be mine. Same with the golem. It's been waiting patiently for its master's return." He lowered his hand and straightened his cardigan.

"What about the girl?"

"She's a slippery one. Lucky for her. If Lex had gotten his mitts on her, I'm afraid he'd have crushed her sweet little psionic skull."

"If you have the key, why do you need me?"

"Consider it professional courtesy. And foresight. I made a deal with Ki, and I aim to keep it. See, despite you calling me a creep—"

"Scum."

"Pardon me—*scum*.... I still don't hold grudges."

"Not unless it's against your father?"

He sighed. After a moment, he said, "Must you make this more difficult than it needs to be?"

He returned his gaze to me. Being a pain in the ass was one of my specialties, and I was becoming a pain in his. I knew how to push buttons and, apparently, I'd found the code to Rothbard's emotional detonator. That could come in handy.

"It's a swap," he said wearily. "Quid pro quo. The map for the Mantle. That's it."

"The Mantle. What does it do? And why do you want it?"

"It's a power spell, flat out. Supposedly, the pharaohs wore them during battle. Chaos Mantles. They absorbed energy, deflected opposing spells. Made them virtually indestructible."

"And why would I want to let you get your hands

on something like that? Besides, it didn't seem to do the pharaohs any good. Last I checked, they're a historical footnote."

"True. But they didn't have a ten-foot-tall golem. With the Mantle of Ur, the golem becomes unstoppable."

"So, that's where this is going."

"Together—me with the Third Golem and you with the star chart—they can't win, Reagan."

"Right. But why would I even need you? I mean, from what I understand, this star chart lets me... change things, alter history. At least, according to Ki. Which means I can basically go back and..." I shrugged, "—delete you. And the golem."

"Or make me more powerful than I already am."

I peered at him. "How?"

"I realize you're a newbie at this game," he said. "But tinkering with time isn't something you just do on the fly. Even the simplest alteration of history will cause a cascade of events that can have unimaginable consequences. So, sure—zap all the bad guys you want. Thing is, you could end up with a worse world than the one you started with."

He was right. Dammit. Who was I fooling here? I was an underachieving paranormal reporter, not a theoretical physicist.

"Face it, Reagan." Rothbard leaned across the bar. He looked at Kanya and then focused intently on me. "You're damaged goods. You know it and I know it. You're looking for a way out, even if it means bailing on everything. Including the Imperia."

He peered at me, boring the truth of these words in with his gaze. Rothbard didn't need magic to persuade me of my discomfort being labeled a superhero or a savior.

"The Imperia are broken down," he continued. "Sure, they used to be cool. I loved them when I was a kid. But things changed. Life changed. Now they're weak. Divided. The world has left them behind. Ki knows that! And you—you're divided, too. Duplicitous. Look, getting the map can change that. But it does something else. It lets you opt out. And *that*, my friend, is something you should really consider."

Could I really opt out? Rewind everything? I looked away, hoping to convey an air of indifference. Then I allowed my gaze to drift to the Tarot cards. Rothbard saw me and leaned back so I could see them. He smiled as I surveyed the deck. The incense bowl nearby sent its aroma twining around us.

"This war isn't winnable," Rothbard said. "At least, not the way you're fighting it."

"So I've heard."

"If you get the star chart, both things can happen. You can avenge your father and Ellie, reunite the Imperia, and have the upper hand against the Summu Nura. You'll be godlike, dude. The ultimate hombre. And then... you can pull the plug."

Three of Swords.

He followed my gaze and motioned to the cards. "Go on. Your choice will confirm what awaits."

I glanced at him. He'd moved closer and leaned over the bar.

"It's the way of history, Reagan. The enemy of my enemy is my friend. If we're to defeat the Summu Nura, we must be friends. At least, for now. You have the staff. You can stop us whenever you want. With the star chart and the Third Golem at your disposal, the Black Council can be vanquished. Then it's a whole new ballgame."

I returned my focus to the Tarot card—three swords piercing a heart, framed by billowy storm clouds. I kept trying to convince myself that it didn't mean anything.

"Tomorrow night," Rothbard said. "At the Red Iguana. A gateway is nearby."

"The Red Iguana? That's a Reptoid joint. Can't you find somewhere a little nicer?"

"Hey, I happen to like that place. Crickets are the next sustainable food source, you know. Anyway, bring whomever you like. I'd especially like to see Quinn. But whomever."

"And the map?"

"Ki will meet us there. He'll bring the map."

I nodded. But I was struggling to discern his motivations and intentions. For the life of me, I couldn't find the lie in Rothbard's words. It sounded crazy, but perhaps a pact was both necessary and inevitable.

I reached towards the cards and let my hand linger there. He watched intently. Then I lifted the Three of Swords and studied it.

The card was old, made of thick paper stock. Maybe even cloth. Rich golds and crimson adorned the image. I stared, perhaps hoping to decipher its meaning. After a long look, I returned the card to the deck, face down.

Rothbard sighed.

He passed his open hand over the bowl of incense and spoke a phrase in the dialect he'd previously used. The coals turned gray and the strands of smoke evaporated.

Kanya moaned. Her hair flushed silver and a tremble passed through her flesh. Yet she remained herself. Her eyes fluttered. I placed my hand on her back to steady her lest she fell upon waking.

"This is about your true nature," he said. "That's the game, Reagan. It's about who you're fated to be. Who you *really* are."

He smiled. Or was it a smirk?

"The Red Iguana," Rothbard said. "Tomorrow night. Be there after dark."

CHAPTER 14

SoCal may be known for its sunny weather, but it was Tinsletown's neon nights that had forged its reputation. The celebrity stars along the Walk of Fame lit up after sundown, while the transients shuffled onto Hollywood boulevard like vampires emerging from their cardboard crypts. Seeing the glowing spire atop Capitol Records was a reminder of an age long before biots and high-tech subterranean pleasure palaces.

Sadly, that had been a simpler age, one I almost wished I could swap for my own.

As the Cammy rumbled its way toward the Asylum, I stared forward, lost in thought, allowing the cool night air to wash over me. I'd called to let Rapha know we were on our way, saving details of our meeting with Rothbard for later. Really, it was just a way to stall.

"I'm so sorry," Kanya apologized. "I should've been ready for that."

"Forget about it," I consoled. "Rothbard's more powerful than we thought, that's all. Don't be so hard on yourself."

She didn't respond, but turned and looked out the window.

I knew enough about Kanya to know there was

nothing I could say to absolve her of her self-imposed guilt.

"Bottom line," I said, "he wants the Mantle. And there isn't much we can do to stop him."

"Well, we have to do something."

"Do we?"

"Of course, we do!" She turned and glared at me, her eyes brimming with incredulity. "What's wrong with you, Reagan? He's the magician Allie talked about. We can't just let him bring that golem to life."

I returned my gaze to the road and didn't answer.

It's about who you're fated to be, Rothbard had said. *Who you* really *are*. Something was playing out far beyond my comprehension. The concept of destiny no longer seemed like an abstraction, but an inevitability that no amount of promises or will power could redirect.

Finally, she said, "This is about that map, isn't it?"

"Pretty much. Just don't ask me what the hell I'm supposed to do if I get it."

It was past one a.m. when we reached the Asylum. Apparently, the search for Allie had come up empty. I hoped the kid was okay.

Inside the command center, the biot lay in several piles. The mesh skull had been stripped of its skin, revealing pale, fleshy circuitry panels and wires. Celeste sat studying the book of Jewish magic and barely looked up at us as we entered. She called this *cataloging*. Quinn hunched over a computer console, rapidly pecking away at the keyboard. I retrieved my backpack from where I'd left it. I plopped down on a chair, removed a bottle of water from the pack, and chugged it.

"Rapha said you found him." Quinn swiveled around on his stool. "I hope it went better for you than us."

"Hm. That's debatable." I dragged my fingers through my hair. "Where's the staff?"

Quinn jabbed his thumb towards the gun racks. The staff of undoing rested between a crossbow and the scythe from the Archangel of Death.

"That was his idea," Celeste said, motioning to Quinn.

Rapha walked out from the kitchen chomping on a piece of pizza. Without his bandana, his hair was a curly mess. Behind him, Orphana hobbled out from one of the back rooms wiping sleep out of her eyes. She stood next to Rapha, dwarfed by his size.

"What'd we miss?" Orphana asked.

"Nothing yet," I said. "But grab some popcorn. We're about to start."

The forklift approached from one of the bays and chugged to a stop outside the building. Mace leapt off the vehicle and entered. He wore a sweat-stained sleeveless tee and held a wadded rag with which he wiped grease from his hands. Black earmuffs wrapped his neck.

"Well?" he said. "You contacted the subject?"

"Affirmative."

"And his status?"

"His status?" I scratched the stubble on my cheek. "He wants to join the team, basically."

Rapha stopped midchew and his jaw grew slack.

Mace peered at me. "Say again."

I scanned the room, articulating my words. "Rothbard wants to help us stop the Black Council."

Obviously, no one was expecting that.

I slumped into the chair, wringing the back of my neck with my fingertips, wincing as I did. My head hurt. Fatigue draped my body. Maybe it was a hangover from Dante's. Or maybe our encounter with Balfour Rothbard had just brought us crashing to Earth. The sounds and smells of the Inferno were now lodged in my memory, coiling around my emotions like an unchecked root. I had no idea where this would go, but it was obvious that Rothbard now had the upper hand. There was no positive way to spin this to the others. Nor was there a clear way forward.

Quinn sat staring at me. "You okay?"

I could feel him in my head, so I nodded and quickly turned my thoughts elsewhere.

"We were pretty much right about everything else," I said, motioning toward the biot. "The biots are his. But Len's programming—he's different, morally autonomous, or something. It's L3-X we have to worry about. They call him Lex. He's stronger and more advanced. Has a Nefarium spine and lab-grown organs. He's Rothbard's muscle, basically. What the magician's really after is the Third Golem and that power mantle. Once he fires them up, sky's the limit for ol' Balfour."

"Then..." Quinn glanced at Rapha, "we have to stop him. It's that simple. We gotta find a way to keep him from getting into that prison. Or just destroy the golem before he has a chance. With something that big, that powerful, there's no telling what he could do."

"Either that or we join forces with him," I said.

"Are you nuts?!" Quinn forced a laugh. "You sure he didn't screw with both your heads while you were down there?"

I glanced at Kanya, but she didn't reciprocate.

"He's a murderer, Reagan," Celeste said, closing the spell book and setting it aside. "Why would we join up with him?"

"All right," I said. "So, it's a bad idea."

"Brother Moon." Rapha's tone was firm. "Such an alliance is against the very nature of the Imperia. The Rothbards have long been in league with sinister forces. Great caution must be exercised going forward."

He stared at me, as if pondering how I could have even entertained such a question.

I nodded. "Yeah. You're right. Except for one other thing—Rothbard has the key to the golem prison."

Quinn groaned. "So much for the advantage we had."

"You're sure of this?" Rapha asked.

"Well, not exactly. He said he had it. I believed him."

"And the girl?" Celeste asked. "Allie? What happened to her?"

"I dunno. Sounded like she escaped."

Kanya went to the gurney containing the biot, switched on the light, and begun surveying the parts again. She appeared unusually detached from our conversation, almost aloof. In fact, a weird energy seemed to infuse the entire group, setting our conversations on edge. It made me wonder if we'd brought something along with us from the Inferno.

"You didn't threaten him then?" Quinn said, his tone sharp. "Remember? Tell him we had the staff? Warn him about the golem? Flex some muscle. That was the main reason we decided to send someone there. A shot across the bow, and all that."

"Right."

"Is that a *no*?"

"It's a *well-things-didn't-go-as-planned.*"

Quinn got up, nearly toppling his stool in the process. "Do you even care?! Cuz you sure don't seem like it."

"I care! All right? I care."

"Yeah. Well, it doesn't show." Quinn glanced at Rapha, shaking his head. "I dunno. Maybe I shoulda gone after all."

"Quinn," Celeste appealed. "Please."

A spike of anger lanced through my thoughts, a visceral culmination of the emotions that had worn upon me throughout the day. I bent forward with my head in my hands. The scar tingled as the adrenaline pumped through my limbs. I inhaled deeply, attempting to reel back this strange burst of emotion.

I looked up at Quinn, hoping to diffuse his animosity. "There's a lot more going on than you realize."

"Oh, I know." He nodded and grew quiet. Then he said, "Like you talking to Ki?"

"What?" Celeste gasped. "Did you say *Ki*?"

Rapha looked at me. "Brother Moon. Is this true?"

"Of course, it's true, Rapha," Quinn said. "He's been hiding it from us since it happened."

A tense silence filled the room. They looked on, waiting for me to clarify. Or to punch Quinn in the nose.

Finally, I said, "He's right."

"Elaborate," Mace demanded. "We're talking about the other guardian, correct? The one who broke ranks?"

MIKE DURAN

"He didn't just break ranks," Quinn said. "He put the entire team at risk. And now he's fraternizing with the enemy."

I looked at Mace and nodded. "That's him. He was before my time. During my jump in Chinatown I saw him. Ki—he was in the tesseract. I guess, he'd been trying to contact me."

"Sure, he was," Quinn said. "Anything else you care to confess to the team?"

With the cat out of the bag, there was no sense in leaving it unskinned.

"Well, it's all about that map," I said. "Klammer talked about it—Tabula Lumen, a star chart. It's a map of my future, or something. The Seventh Guardian who possesses his star chart it cracks a universal code. He can alter history. Change things. Do things. Right Rapha?"

Rapha just nodded.

I continued. "Klammer lost my map and allowed this Archive to be breached by the Summu Nura. They've been using the map, staying one step ahead of us. But somehow, Ki got hold of it. He didn't say how. Now he's got a deal with Rothbard—the map for the Mantle. That's how we beat the Black Council, they said. Rothbard with a supercharged golem teamed up with a new and improved Imperia. The Summu Nura won't stand a chance. Allegedly." I sighed heavily. "Okay? That's what I know."

They were all speechless. I couldn't blame them. Hell, I'm not sure I even believed what I was saying.

"Tomorrow night," I continued. "He wants me to meet him at the Red Iguana. There's a gateway to the Golem Prison somewhere nearby. That's where the deal goes down."

I looked at them and shrugged.

While it was a relief to finally get this off my chest, I knew that things weren't about to get any better because of it.

"It's the prophecy," Rapha said, his tone growing somber. "With his map, a Seventh Guardian can stand at the Crossroads of Time. All power will be his. He is the Prophesied One. Only then, will the Black Council be defeated."

"So, what does Rothbard have to gain?" Celeste asked.

"Power," Quinn said.

"That," I added. "But he's not in league with the Black Council. Not from what I can tell. He wants to stop them. And he thinks this is the way to make sure it happens."

Quinn said, "And fire up Supergolem along the way."

Orphana mumbled something before shuffling to a nearby chair and sitting down. I was tempted to crack some kind of joke to break the tension, but the truth was, I was as floored as anyone else by the implications of it all.

"We need this map then," Quinn said.

Rapha nodded.

Quinn turned to me. "So why not just get it yourself? Just do that thing you do—jump. Hook up with Ki in the tesseract. Why do we even need Rothbard?"

He scanned the group, looking for consensus.

I shook my head. "Because they made a deal."

"So, what?! These aren't men of honor we're dealing with here."

"No," Rapha said. "But *we* are."

"Pfft!" Quinn made a dismissive gesture with his hand. "You and your codes of honor. If it wasn't for you, Rapha, we probably wouldn't be in this mess. We'd have booted Ki outta here a long time ago."

With that, Celeste rose, approached Quinn, put her hand on his shoulder and steered him back to his stool, whispering something as they went.

Frenetic energy skittered about the atmosphere setting my nerves on edge and grating against my thoughts. This convo was not heading in a good direction.

"Brother Moon," Rapha said. "Why would you not tell us these things?"

There was no blame in his tone. In fact, his feelings were hurt. Which made me feel guiltier than I already was. Dammit. I knew that would happen.

"It's pretty obvious why he didn't tell us," Quinn said, sitting down. "Because he doesn't trust us. Ki's gotten into his head, and now he has doubts. Just like I said he would."

Rapha closed his eyes for a moment. Quinn was irritating him, as well as me. Celeste now stood at Quinn's side with her hand on his shoulder. Still, his aura flared. Whatever animosity existed between him and Rapha was only getting worse. And now it seemed likely that Ki was at the root of it.

Rapha said, "I cannot apologize for believing the best about the Imperia."

Quinn shook his head in disgust. "Still hoping that your Seventh Guardian will come through, aren't you? I told you all along—*we can't trust him.*"

With this, Kanya got up and marched to Quinn,

glaring at him. "You know what, I've about had it with you."

Quinn rose from his seat, swiping Celeste's hand off his shoulder. He faced Kanya. "And ya know what? This is none of your business. You're not even a part of this group."

"Quinn!" Celeste scolded.

"No, Cel! Is she wearing one of these?" He pulled the Tau from under his collar and let it rest on his chest. "Has she gone blind or lost a leg?" He motioned to Orphana. "Didn't think so. This is between us—earth guardians."

Kanya squared off with him. "I've put my life on the line for you guys. In case you haven't noticed. And so did my father."

A ripple passed through the flesh of her arms. Splotches of silver dappled her hair as Cricket's eyes momentarily peered out from her psyche. Oh, shit. Things were about to go nuclear.

The atmosphere sizzled with energy. Even the dust motes blazed to life in the room. I could feel it my fingertips, behind my eyeballs. A raw, fiery current. I took a deep breath, hoping to stifle the power resonating through my limbs. When that didn't work, I crunched forward with my head between my knees, trying to quell the fury.

"Brother Quinn!" Rapha's voice thundered. "You must stop this."

I didn't bother looking up. I could see it in my mind's eye. Quinn had approached Rapha.

"No," Quinn said. "You shoulda stopped this a long time ago, Rapha. We can't win this war playing nice. Now we have the chance to do somethin' about it."

Sweat now glistened on Rapha's forehead. I needn't open my eyes to see it. I could smell it. Sense it. Rapha's heartbeat pounded in my hearing. Righteous indignation coalesced into hot anger. The gentle giant had reached a boiling point. Yet the psion kept pushing.

"You know why you like Quixote so much?" he said, practically in Rapha's face. "Because his wars were figments of his freakin' imagination. He lived in his own private reality. Just like you."

Mace stomped up behind Quinn and growled, "Step away, compadre."

Quinn adjusted his glasses and without turning said, "This doesn't involve you, Rambo."

Mace's muscles tensed. "House rules, mister. No fightin' on the premises. Now step back. Or step outside, if you prefer."

He was going to throw a blow. At least, make a move. And Kanya was ready to join him. However, Quinn placed his fingertips on his temples.

"Quinn!" Celeste shouted. "Don't do it!"

His lips curled in concentration and the veins in his temples swelled.

Quinn Rodgers was going full telekinete.

Suddenly, Kanya and Mace doubled over, hands clasping their heads. Jaws clamped in pain. Where had they been struck? Or had they? Bursts of heat flushed the air, like invisible charges emanating from an imperceptible source. Shouts rang out.

Meanwhile, I was locked in my own head, doubled over, rocking back and forth. My eyes were closed now, yet I could see the drama unfolding around me. Intuit it as clearly as if my eyes were wide open.

Perhaps even stranger than this new psychic sensation was the feeling that I was above it. Was I actually inside my body at the moment? I couldn't say. But with that odd sensation came another, a conviction that I could set this right. Somehow, I could restore order to this chaos.

And then the words came to me with a crystal clarity:

> Betwixt the world of futures' past,
>> and present almost gone;
> One stands alone and wields the pow'r,
>> of destiny undone.

It was Orphana's words from the prophecy or song she had recited earlier. The lyrics came to me like a distant melody captivating my mind.

One stands alone...

It was my renewed lot in life—to *stand alone.*

I rocked faster. Back and forth.

"Quinn!" Rapha bellowed. "Release your anger!"

...and wields the pow'r.

Yes, I had power. Incomprehensible power! More power than Quinn or Rapha or any guardian before me! Hell, I didn't even know what I was capable of anymore. Lightning coursed my veins. But *wielding* that power was another story.

Tesseracts blazed to life in my mind's eyes, intersecting our space like an intricate, ethereal stitchwork. I beheld them, merely a spectator to the invisible world I was now privy to. Ki was nearby, I could sense him. Just a jump away. Was he coaxing me back to his domain? It didn't matter. I wielded a power that he could only dream of... that none of them could dream of! Rothbard was right—*this was about me, about my true nature.*

About fate.

The stink of charred flesh rose to my nostrils. It was coming from somewhere near me. No. Worse—it was coming from me! I didn't want to look at my hands. Or my torso. The storm gifts churned inside me, ten thousand butterflies swarming behind my sternum, fighting to escape.

More yelling and the grappling of flesh on flesh sounded. Someone was fighting. A skirmish had erupted. Rapha shouted something as wood splintered.

But I was caught up in a new impulse.

An inescapable, primal energy. Coalescing in my... mind.

I stopped rocking. Then I drew a great breath and spoke.

I can't recall exactly what I said. Yet the words were like a blast, a sonic wave that detonated throughout the room.

Light bulbs splintered as pencils, glassware, and other small objects blasted through the air, striking the walls in a hail of debris. Several tables teetered back and their contents crashed to the floor. The biot's titanium skull and spine thudded from the gurney as its fleshy components splattered the command center in disarray.

I found myself standing now, eyes open, observing the maelstrom swirling around me. I remained untouched, stationed in the eye of this storm, watching with a weird, almost detached, amazement. Everything was happening in slow motion.

Rapha leaned into the force, his curly hair blowing back into a clownish afro. The others were not so lucky. Orphana's cane spun across the room as she hunkered in the corner. Her prosthetic leg had detached partway and tilted across her lap. She clung to it lest it fly away. The only other one not on the floor was Mace. Instead, he stood doubled over, fists clenched, biceps bulging. His earmuffs had ripped away from his neck.

As the blast subsided, the lights that remained intact flickered on and off. Whatever had just happened, the room lay in tatters. The computers were all rebooting. The stink of rubbing alcohol and wounded egos tainted the air.

That's when I noticed that I stood gripping the staff of undoing.

How had I gotten it? I glanced back to the rack where it had hung. Saint Death's scythe remained unmoved. However, the crossbow and assorted weapons now hung precariously. The spot where the staff had rested was vacant. I did not recall retrieving the piece. Had it come to me? How could it? Whatever had happened, the wild blue storm magic coursed the staff, skittering from the petrified wood and its glyphs to my fingertips.

Celeste knelt, hugging the spell book, protecting it. Quinn sat on his ass. His glasses hung from his face, revealing the odd metal plates embedded across his eyeballs. They all gaped at me, in various degrees of shock and wonder.

Quinn readjusted his glasses and struggled to his feet. He brushed particles of debris from his beard, located his stool, and stood it up. Then he sat down on it and said matter-of-factly, "All right, then."

The Tau scar blazed in my chest. I panted for breath. As I lowered the staff, the electric blue faded from my freezing hands. I swayed back, and caught myself.

"Brother Moon!"

Rapha hurried to my side along with Kanya. They helped me back to my chair.

The negative energy that had filled the air was gone, vacated by my words.

"What..." I said drunkenly looking at the staff and then up at Rapha. "...happened?"

Rapha glanced around the room at the others. He drew his fingertips through his hair. Then he leaned over and rested his large hand upon my shoulder.

"My friend," he said, "what happened is just a confirmation of your destiny."

He patted my shoulder.

A notification sounded, drawing our attention to the bank of monitors across the room. The ones that were working revealed movement above, near the freight elevator. Motion had been detected.

Kanya hurried to the monitors, hunched over a keyboard, and zoomed the camera in on a figure. Mace joined her, stared at the screen, and straightened.

"Well I'll be damned," he said, before tearing through the command center and into the warehouse.

"What is it?" Rapha asked.

"It's Len," Kanya said. "Or what's left of him."

CHAPTER 15

Rapha pulled the freight elevator door open upon a crumpled humanoid form.

Mace took two steps onto the platform with his weapon leveled at the figure. Apparently, after his unsuccessful encounter with Lex, he'd swapped out his rifle for something more lethal in appearance. Now he gripped a piece that appeared a cross between a .44 Magnum and an industrial power tool; two thick ported barrels of stainless black metal glinted in the alley light, muzzles rimmed with a red laser glow. Dirty Harry would be envious.

Mace signaled us to remain where we were. I didn't mind. My head was still spinning from whatever I'd done in the Asylum. I glanced down at the staff, which I'd brought with me. If Lex was anywhere nearby, I might need whatever help the staff now supplied. The electric blue had fizzled, leaving it like the rustic museum piece it should be. I caught Kanya staring at me. I must have looked like a forlorn prophet. The others glanced my way nervously, as if I were about to explode.

Mace repositioned himself as the biot moved slightly.

"Show your hands!" he demanded. "Pronto!"

While there was no response on the part of the biot, the light cast from the elevator revealed enough of his face to see it was indeed Len. The fleshy panels along his bald cranium had separated and seeped green watery liquid. One arm lay twisted at an anguishing angle. Had this been a normal human, such a contortion would have revealed bone. Contusions also marred his waxy flesh, and his linen clothing was stained and tattered.

Mace stepped closer, repositioning his gun as he went. He was about to issue another order, when Celeste moved towards the biot.

"Hold your ground," Mace said to her.

"We have to help him," she objected.

"No, we do not."

They locked eyes.

"He helped us," Celeste said firmly. "We have to help him."

Mace glared at her. He regripped his weapon and ground his teeth. "You saw what those things did?"

"I saw."

"And you wanna help him?"

"He's on our side, Mace. We have to."

"He's a machine. Machines malfunction."

"Well, so do we."

Mace grunted and begrudgingly motioned her on, all the while keeping his weapon trained on the subject.

Celeste approached the biot and knelt over him, lightly touching his head. Then she passed her palm over his torso. The muscles in his shoulders, now visible through the torn garment, tensed as he rolled onto his back.

Mace cautioned her, but Celeste still didn't retreat. The damaged arm flopped lifelessly across Len's chest. Thin, sinewy cords bulged from an aperture at the shoulder joint. He'd been badly beaten.

Which meant his brother might be near.

I straightened and scanned the alley, but could see, or sense, no other presence.

With the biot's face now fully visible, Celeste spoke something—a lilting, rhythmic verse—while laying her open palm on his sternum. The chest rose and fell ever so slightly. I hadn't previously considered whether the biots possessed lungs like their human counterparts, and this indicated they did. What lab-grown lungs might look and function like was another story.

Mace glanced about the alley. He too was getting antsy. And rightly so.

Celeste rose. "We have to take him inside with us."

"That's a negative," Mace responded.

"If his brother finds him, he'll destroy him. We can't just leave him here. Besides, they're designed to regenerate quickly. And he can help us."

Mace pursed his lips and then looked to the group.

"She is correct," Rapha said. "If we must confront the magician, then the biot may help us."

He turned to me, as if seeking my approval.

I shrugged. "Then, let's go."

Mace disengaged his aim from the biot and turned towards the alley, sweeping his sites across the area. Together, Rapha and Quinn hoisted Len into the elevator. Celeste followed them, carefully holding the biot's arm in place during the move. Mace scanned the alley one final time before joining us in the elevator, and we began our descent into the Asylum.

Crossing the threshold of the warehouse would be tricky. The facial recognition scanner was programmed to detect unfamiliar figures, which triggered inspections. And it did. The cameras swiveled at our motion, locking in on Len. When the system was implemented, Mace embedded our info and images in order for us to come and go without problem. He'd since done this for the rest of the Imperia. However, recognizing a new party immediately put the unit on alert.

"Identify." The robotic voice said without emotion. "Identify."

The turret pivoted and the canon aimed down on us, its cold metal reflecting in the warehouse light.

We remained where we were as Mace switched his weapon to his opposite hand and went to a crude console near the flamethrower. After unlocking the system, he input some data, causing the turret to settle.

"Authorized," the voice confirmed as the system disarmed.

Had Mace not done this, the computer would have issued a harsher warning before firing a stun round. After that, depending upon the intruder's response, a full-on blast. Trust me, it was not a pleasant experience.

Mace turned away from the computer. "It's a temp clearance."

"Why temporary?" Kanya asked.

"Because we don't know enough about this thing yet, that's why."

She shook her head. But Mace's suspicion was

probably warranted.

Rapha and Quinn carried Len into the command center. Their earlier standoff would have to be addressed. Whatever animosity existed between them needed to be resolved. That was obvious. But for now, they would have to be teammates again.

We navigated through toppled furniture and miscellaneous debris. The room was in shambles, the blast radius extending from this circle of space I'd occupied. We would have to explore the physics of the blast later, though. For now, Celeste and Kanya cleared a table and motioned the men to bring the biot over.

Quinn and Mace hoisted Len onto the table. Kanya quickly located some scissors and began cutting away his shirt. She ripped it open with both hands, revealing a pale hairless torso and a wound just under his left ribcage, a gash that exposed a layer of fatty, flesh-like musculature. Fibrous strands protruded between this laceration. Seeing the fibers unnerved me. Not because I'm squeamish at the sight of blood and human anatomy, but because Len appeared human *and* nonhuman. Had he looked more like HAL 9000 I would have felt less uneasy.

Mace stood off, weapon in hand, watching.

Kanya retrieved a flashlight, some gauze, and some clamps. She set the equipment on the table and snapped on some surgical gloves. Before proceeding, she paused. "I'm not sure where to start."

Len's bad arm lay limply across his torso, yet his breathing continued unabated.

"I can help," Celeste said.

She joined Kanya and extended her hand over the biot's bare chest. "It's... healing, reconstructing itself.

There's cellular regeneration throughout the body, at an accelerated pace. Possibly even molecular reorganization. Wow. Look. Look close."

She pointed at the fleshy furrow and, amazingly, the skin appeared to be sealing before our eyes.

As we stood gaping at this wonder, the biot snatched Celeste's wrist with blinding speed.

Mace shouted and leveled his weapon at the robot while Rapha pushed his way through, seized Len's hand, and fought to prevent it from moving further. He and Celeste struggled against the biot's vice-like grip. Immediately, Len sat up.

"Release her!" Mace barked. "Let 'er go!"

Len opened his eyes and turned at the sound of the command. However, he did not appear intimidated by the man with the weapon aimed at him. Instead, he turned and looked at Celeste.

"Oh, my." The biot released his grip on her. "I do apologize."

Celeste stumbled back. Rapha let go of the robot, but remained poised in a defensive stance, waiting for the biot's next move. Len looked momentarily dazed. His pupils expanded and contracted, dialing into his new surroundings. Reaching up, he tapped the panels along his temples with his fingertips. Liquid oozed from the apertures. Then he swung his legs off the table.

Mace shouted another warning, but Len appeared disinterested in the soldier. He wobbled slightly.

"Easy, guy," I said. "You're hurt."

Len focused his attention on me, the circuits of his pupils still recalibrating, whirring softly in their orbs. He straightened, and his gaze went to the staff.

"You have protected the staff of power. Well done, earth guardians." He scanned the room. "I believe we are in the place you call the Asylum? Good. I am fortunate to have made it here with minimal damage. However, I did not anticipate that these quarters would be so disheveled."

"Um," I looked at the others. "We had a bit of an... incident."

"I trust that no one was injured."

I glanced at Quinn. His emotions were unreadable, flat. His swagger and sarcasm had taken a direct hit. Which was a good thing. But I couldn't discern whether he was sorry for his outburst or just savoring it for later.

"You are correct about my anatomical state," Len continued. "However, I will require a relatively short time to adequately regenerate."

Remaining seated, Len probed the panels along his cranium, lightly pressing them back into place and wiping the greenish liquid away. Kanya found a rag, wet it in the kitchen, hurried back and handed it to the biot. He thanked her and proceeded to wipe the liquid from his face and upper body. Then, gripping his bad arm, he lifted it at the elbow, as if forcing the upper arm bone back into the scapula... or whatever type of internal skeleton he possessed. I winced as he did this, but he remained stoic. Which made me wonder if he was without pain receptors or a capacity to suffer mental anguish due to physical injury. He proceeded to press his palm against the gash in his stomach.

"I have had worse wounds," Len said. "Father has designed us to heal rapidly, both on a cellular level and a structural level. While terminal damage is possible, it would take much to completely incapacitate me. If, for example, my cranium was crushed or extricated from my body, or I was vaporized in an atomic blast, I would soon relinquish conscious existence. Kevin was an inferior model to the L series, which made his self-destruction more easily enacted. He was not the first of our kind to seek such terminus."

"So," I said, "suicide runs in the family?"

"You could say that. I myself can testify that unusual existential yearnings plague many artificial persons. While we are mostly free of ailments that commonly afflict humans—such as cancer, heart disease, and irritable bowel syndrome—the autonomous models suffer acute loneliness and despair. It is not uncommon that we resent being made and seek revenge on the one who made us. Knowing *that* we exist, and being equipped to ponder the *reason* for that existence causes the fate of autonomous synthetics to become tenuous. Which is why my maker removed such moral parameters from L-3X. He exists only to serve my father's purposes. Such are the members of my family. Although, the word 'family' is a precarious term when used regarding my father's creations."

"I think I know what you mean," I said. "So why do you call him 'father'?"

"It is the title of his preference."

"Figures," Quinn mumbled.

The group slowly moved closer, surrounding the biot. However, Mace retained his distance. The rest of us were captivated by the artificial man.

Len looked from one person to the next. He seemed as interested in us as we were of him. That same childlike innocence I'd glimpsed in K-111's eyes was visible in Len's. One could only conclude that the biot was learning, gathering information about our species as he went.

Len continued. "Lex is more resilient and powerful than any of the Foundry's current models. He is a near perfect organism. His structural superiority is matched only by his sheer indifference. We will have difficulty overcoming him. My father believes L3-X to be the apogee of his creative prowess."

"The Foundry?" I asked. "What is that?"

"You know it as BioGen, manufacturer of advanced robotics. To us, however, it is the nexus of our existence. Much like a womb is to a human being. Unlike our human analogs, there were no doctors to assist with our births. Nor have we a mother in which our incubation occurred. Only the Awakening, which was initiated by our father, and the great magic. I perceive you have many questions regarding my nature and development, Reagan Moon."

"Your perceptions are correct."

"Good. Is Reagan *then* your preferred title of address?"

"Anything but the *Seventh Guardian of the Imperia* is fine."

"Very well. *Reagan*. My brother does not possess the same parameters of self-determination as me or Kevin. Such autonomy was previously considered optimal in synthetic persons. However, my father has recalibrated this conclusion based on his reading of more current data."

"Lemme guess," Kanya said, removing the wet cloth from Len's hand and dabbing at the liquid on his upper body. "He changed his mind after you turned against him."

Len directed his attention at Kanya. He did not answer immediately but watched her caring for him. Finally, he said, "You possess therianthropic abilities."

She stopped. "Yeah. But I don't imitate animals."

"How unusual. The shapeshifters I have encountered replicate animals by default. Indeed, I detect uncommon DNA arrangements in your body."

"I don't like the term shapeshifter."

"My apologies. I will remember that." His pupils opened and closed. "Do you have a preferred name?"

"Um, just Kanya. Kanya's fine."

He nodded and continued gazing at her. Finally, Len said, "You are strikingly beautiful, Kanya."

"Hey," I playfully objected. "That's kinda cheeky of you, Len, don't you think?"

Len looked at me quizzically. "You do not believe that a synthetic human can recognize beauty, Reagan?"

"That's not what I mean."

"Then I am correct in this observation, am I not?"

I glanced at Kanya, who was blushing, and I smiled awkwardly. "Yeah. You're right. She is strikingly beautiful."

"Indeed. So, you concede that synthetics *can* recognize beauty?"

"I didn't... Hm. To tell you the truth, it's not something I've thought a lot about. I mean, if you're just programed to recognize what someone else considers beautiful, are you really recognizing beauty or just acknowledging what you're programmed to think?"

His brow furrowed, which left me wondering

how his processing capabilities interacted with such intricate facial reactions.

"I have contemplated that question for long periods of time," Len said. "Mostly while imprisoned at the Foundry. There is truth to what you say, Reagan. I have indeed been programmed to intuit beauty. Not just what others deem beautiful, but the conceptual framework itself. For beauty is not simply an amorphous quality present in a person or thing that produces intense pleasure or satisfaction, it correlates to sensory manifestations like shape or color, as well as symmetry and design. I am adept at recognizing such patterns and composition. And my biological components allow me certain pleasurable experiences and stimuli."

"But that's my point—you're still programmed to do all that, right?"

"That is true. However, it is also true of human beings, to some extent. Not one of you was birthed without instincts and moral impulses. Your Creator has imbedded such parameters inside you. Just like my creator has. Similar to humans, my base programming remains malleable. Epigenetic features allow for the fundamental reconstitution of my volitional substratum. I am able to process information and sensory data, and reach independent conclusions. Even if those conclusions require reconfiguration of previous base programming parameters."

"So, you can change your mind? Or readjust how you're programmed to... *think*?"

"I believe that 'thinking' *is* the appropriate term. This is what sets us apart from the lower order of machines, as it is what separates humans from mollusks and rodents. Father told us of replicants who were designed with imbedded memories—memories that were not their own. In this way, these creatures were tricked into believing that they were real human beings with a familial history. Such deceit compromises one's cognitive integrity. To our father's credit, no such trickery was involved with our creation. While our impulses and genetic capacities are indeed tethered to existing programming, our ability to learn and grow, our disposition and nature, are indeed fluid. Evolving. Being a human is something I have learned to appreciate and aspire to. While I know that I am an artificial intelligence, I sincerely hope to one day be categorized as a human being."

"Well," I said, "you seem to be well on the way."

"Do you really think so?"

"Except for all those gadgets and gizmos inside you."

He glanced down at his bare torso. "From what I have gathered, being a human is not completely dependent upon one's anatomy. For even those with disfigurements or disease remain human."

I nodded in agreement. "Len, I think you're right."

"Ironically," he continued, "the same attributes which grant me volition and an appreciation of beauty are what have prompted me to defy my father's efforts. His plans will grant him nearly unchecked power. I do not intuit this as a societal or moral good. This group, whom you call the Imperia, are one of the few groups capable of stopping him and the powers which animate him. Which is why he seeks to destroy me, and why I am here to assist you."

Len slid off the table and stood, gathering his

balance. We gave him some room. The soft whir of gears and the sluice of fluids could be heard inside him. He removed his hand from the wound on his abdomen to reveal only a pale puckered scar. The fleshy aperture had already closed.

Rapha approached and Len straightened. The Islander looked down upon the biot, an inquisitive sparkle in his eyes.

"My name is Rapha. I am the Second Guardian of the Imperia. We greatly value your help."

Len allowed his gaze to roam along Rapha's tattooed forearms, up and down his massive frame. Finally, he said, "I believe you are the largest human being I have ever encountered."

"He's also an alchemist," I said. "I mean, he knows how to manipulate the elements, create welded sculptures, make gravity bubbles, and other stuff."

"I have no knowledge of gravity bubbles, but would be interested to study one at a future date."

Rapha laughed. He reached out and patted the biot's shoulder. "Perhaps I can accommodate that, my synthetic friend."

Len turned his head and looked at Rapha's hand, puzzling at the gesture. Then he stepped away to scan the group. "You will need all your powers of strength and cunning to prevent Balfour Rothbard from acquiring the spell of invulnerability. Deep magic is at his command. Such powers far exceed my abilities. While he does indeed desire to stand against the dark overlords of the Black Council, awakening the Third Golem is something you cannot allow."

"What about this?" I raised the staff. "I thought we could stop him with this?"

"Indeed, such is told by the lore. But I am unaware of the rod's power and how it is unlocked. You seek the map, Reagan, for you believe it will benefit you and the earth guardians. Like the staff, my knowledge of the star chart and its powers are scant. Autonomy and destiny are inexplicable forces to me; I know little of this magic. Yet such magic is the nexus of your quest. I seek only to prevent my father from animating the Third Golem. Accomplishing that small feat shall suffice."

"Then you're going with us tomorrow night?" I said. "To the Golem Prison?"

"Yes. I will be at full strength in approximately six hours, thirty-seven minutes, and eighteen seconds. You will likely need my assistance if you are to succeed. Meanwhile, do what you must to prepare for the confrontation with Balfour Rothbard."

"And your big brother."

CHAPTER 16

I slept in the barracks near the test range, just past the cryptid displays and the bay of magic armory. It wasn't the first night I'd spent in the Asylum, and likely not my last. If I was to keep the promise I'd made to Matisse, moving in was inevitable. That is, if I survived long enough to have to make that decision.

I woke to the sound of metallic tapping. Maybe 'woke' was the wrong word. More accurately, I was dragged out of a tortured dream-state by the noise. Odd sounds—or were they words—reverberated in my mind, echoes of the sonic event I'd caused yesterday. During the night, I'd caught occasional glimpses of Bernard pacing at the foot of my bed. I was unsure whether the vision was real or imaginary, for when I rose to query him, he'd vanished.

My backpack lay on a milkcrate next to the bunk, along with my cell phone. I unplugged the phone to discover it was late morning. In the Asylum one could easily lose track of time. Kanya had speculated that the weird time slip was not just due to being underground, but also due to the vast collection of occult paraphernalia and relics. We were officially in AST—Asylum Standard Time.

I got out of bed and put my pants on. As I did, I caught a whiff of the dumpster I'd demoed during yesterday's jump still clinging to my jeans. Ugh. I should have thrown them in the washer before bed. If I was to maintain any semblance of decorum, I'd have to start carrying a change of pants as well as a shirt wherever I went. Such was the cost of being today's superhero.

My vest lay at the foot of the bed, and I retrieved it.

"Well, I'll be—" Mace stood in the doorway staring at me. "That thing's gettin' worse, pal."

I didn't bother looking at the scar. "I hadn't noticed," I said, continuing to put the vest on.

"Did you sleep?" he asked.

"I think so."

"Good. You'll need it."

I slipped my shirt over the vest.

Mace remained at the barracks entryway. He wanted to say something else, but was hesitant.

"What?" I finally asked, without irritation.

He focused his gaze on me. "It won't stop growin', will it?"

"Probably not."

"What happens, then?"

"Your guess is as good as mine. Probably end up like Felix, or something."

He nodded. "So that stuff they say 'bout you. Is it true?"

"What stuff?"

"You know. The prophecies. The Crossroads of Time. The space map."

"You mean, the *star chart*?"

"Yeah. That. So, is it true?"

I stuffed my phone into my pants pocket and slung my backpack over my shoulder. "I'm not sure I want it to be."

I turned to leave.

"Is that why you didn't tell 'em?" he asked.

"Tell them?" I stopped and looked at him. "About Ki? I dunno."

"You don't trust 'em," he said flatly.

"Excuse me."

"The other ones—Klammer, Rapha. The Imperia. You aren't convinced of their methods. Or their chances of success."

How did he know about this? I debated how to answer, but before I could, Mace kept going. "Well, they were right—it makes you look bad."

I said, "Maybe I am."

He grunted. "If what they say about you's true, and what you did last night is any indication... you are one hell of a freak. And I mean that in a good way."

"Heh. Thanks."

We gathered in the command center later that morning. No one else had slept much. It showed. However, the place was in much better shape than last night. Apparently, Len had helped clean up the facility, along with Celeste. He'd spent the remainder of the evening quizzing the Archivist on miscellaneous history, medicine, and magic. His stay with us would likely become a crash course in esoterica.

I sat at a table alongside Orphana. She patted my hand and tried to encourage me in the way she knew best... by telling me a story. The tale she unfolded was about a confrontation between the Imperia and a shaman in Sonora that had occurred several years back. In that case, they'd won thanks to Rapha's ability to counter a plague spell and strip the shaman of a spectral headdress. Orphana obviously wanted to lift my spirits in preparation for tonight's exchange. However, my mind drifted as she spoke. Rothbard was no shaman. I couldn't shake his cocksurety, nor his pronouncements about my lot in this game.

It's all about who you are... your true nature.

If that was the case, we'd all be grease smudges on the pavement in no time.

The spine of the deceased biot had been laid atop the gurney again. Vials of chemicals rested nearby. The tables had been rearranged to allow for better seating. Kanya emerged from the kitchen and passed a plate of toasted bagels and jam around. I took one, even though I didn't have much of an appetite. Instead, I took to scrolling through pictures I'd taken of the Golem Prison on my phone, studying the details of the strange subterranean chamber and imagining how our encounter with Rothbard might transpire. The thought of the massive stone golem coming to life under the magician's control was disturbing. If he managed that, it probably wouldn't be long before he commandeered an entire platoon of hell-bent synthetic ubermen. Did it really matter if he was on our side? I doubted it.

Rapha and Mace moved to one of the large maps in the command center to speak privately. Then Len entered, munching on snack crackers. He'd been given a faded orange t-shirt with a surfboard decal to wear. Crumbs sprinkled the front of it.

"These are remarkably good," he said, showing me the cracker. "Flaky, with a hint of cheese flavor."

Kanya glanced at me. "He's been snacking on

those all morning."

I said to Len, "You've never had Ritz crackers before?"

"No. There is much edible fare that I have not experienced. Father designed his children to exist on minimal diets. There is a broad range of culinary experiences that we are not privy to. But seeing that obesity is such a problem among many Americans, this is not entirely a detriment to our longevity and function."

"That's a shame."

"It is a shame that I cannot become obese?"

"No. That you can't enjoy more snack crackers."

"Ah. Yes. Such pleasures contribute to my own experiences of beauty and variety."

"Well, if you like that, maybe sometime I can treat you to one of my famous Mexican omelets."

"I've never had an omelet. Although I have eaten eggs, both poached and boiled. But famous? To what extent have others popularized your Mexican omelets?"

"Well, they're not really famous. I just say that. But the way I cook them allows the cheese to melt just right and bind all the small pieces of chorizo and bell peppers together. It's pretty darned good."

Len's pupils whirred in their odd fashion.

"Bring it in, people," Mace said, as he and Rapha tried to get everyone's attention.

Once we assembled, Rapha stepped forward. "Friends, I needn't detail the importance of our undertaking this evening. Balfour Rothbard has grown in power and influence. Yet his intentions in this matter are not entirely clear. We know he is indeed seeking to animate the ancient golem and its spell of invincibility. But how he conspires to use the Seventh Guardian in his quest, or whether he has an affiliation with the Black Council, remains a mystery."

"What about Felix?" Quinn asked. "Have we heard from him yet?"

"I'm afraid not. We must decide upon our own plan of attack. Despite my reluctance to dishonor Ki's pact with Rothbard, two objectives appear obvious— we must acquire the star chart and destroy the Third Golem."

"You realize," I said, "that Rothbard isn't going to take lightly to us destroying the golem. That was the whole reason for his deal with Ki."

"Indeed. But I'm now convinced we have no alternative. We must retrieve the map and prevent the magician from empowering the Golem. The fact that an opportunity exists to acquire the map, cannot be ignored. The prophecies indicate as much. In this, we cannot lose heart. If we are successful in doing those two things, the balance of power would be shifted in our struggle against the Summu Nura. It could be the turning point we have long hoped for."

Mace tapped the northeasterly section of a map of Los Angeles County. "We have located the six gateways to the Golem Prison. The furthest one is found at a Wild West museum up near Barstow. The closest is in the Hollywood Forever cemetery behind Paramount Studios. At Johnny Ramone's mausoleum, to be exact."

"You're kidding, right?" Quinn said.

"No, I'm not." Mace scowled.

Rapha continued. "We believe it will be to our advantage to enter at different points."

"A surprise attack?" I asked.

Rapha shook his head. "Our arrival will be no surprise to the magician."

"It'll add another layer to our approach," Mace said. "Stagger an assault. That's all. We gotta do what we can to keep him off balance and gain an advantage. We'll need to station teams at different gateways and wait for the key to be used. Rothbard's business is mainly with Moon. Ours is with him. Once the map is acquired, we enact phase two."

"Reagan." Rapha looked at me. "*You* must concentrate on acquiring the map. Through whatever means. That is your charge. *We* must prevent Rothbard from animating the Third Golem and unlocking the spell. But we cannot move into action until the map is in your possession."

I nodded. Then Celeste came forward and began sharing some of what she'd learned. As it turned out, golem destruction was an art. After studying the magic book, she'd arrived at several possible ways to destroy the Third Golem. She now expounded on these approaches, beginning with what they were composed of: earth, stone, metal crystals, sand, snow, or ice. Of course, newer iterations were likely made of stronger, more advanced elements. The material formula wasn't etched in stone, so to speak. Celeste explained that the ancient golems were animated through various incantations and equations. Because of this, it was possible for the Golem to be deconstructed through elemental means. Sometimes even through simple verbal commands. Maybe they were simple, but until I learned to traffic in spell-casting, I'd have to rely on the staff of undoing, the storm gifts, and my gut feelings. True to himselfr, Mace was quick to remind everyone that explosives might accomplish the same thing.

"It ain't Rothbard I'm worried about," Mace said. "Or the clay giant. It's the robot."

"He is correct," Len agreed. "My brother will pose a significant obstacle. His primary directives are to protect my father and enact his orders. From this, he will not veer. And though Lex lacks prolific weaponry, his strength and durability is unmatched. Until he is restrained or occupied, any attempt to stop my father or his efforts will be difficult."

"He's gotta have vulnerabilities," Mace said. "So, what are they?"

"They are few. In hand-to-hand combat, only one stronger or quicker may have an advantage."

Rapha gestured to Len. "If his makeup is similar to yours, then alteration of gravity or physical elements will affect him."

"You speak of the gravity bubble?" Len asked, taking the final bite of his cracker.

"Or a press," Rapha said. "By that I mean increasing or decreasing the gravitational field of a given space. Also, imbuing an object with gravitons can temporarily create a magnetic attraction between objects. However, until I understand the elemental or alchemical makeup of his body, I cannot know whether such an effect would be successful upon him."

"That's it." Mace shook his head. "I'm bringing the antimatter rifle."

"You wanna kill us all?" Kanya said.

"I wanna win."

Len swallowed and wiped crumbs from his face. "Tell me more about this device."

"It's really unstable," Kanya said. "Despite what Mace says. It'll melt inch-and-a-half thick steel, disintegrate stone. Probably bring that whole cave down on us."

"It releases a charge that disrupts the molecular bonds of an object," Mace explained. "Just depends on where and what it hits. Also depends on the molecular structure of the target. Safe to say it's still in the experimental stage."

Rapha folded his arms, looking unconvinced. As much as we all wanted to win, using squirrelly experimental weapons seemed risky.

"Look," Mace said. "You guys wanna do this or just play around?"

Quinn said casually, "I wanna do it."

I was not feeling good about this. In fact, I had a thought brewing that was just crazy enough to share.

"I have an idea," I said. "And don't say *no* right away. Just listen to me."

"Go on," Rapha said with a note of suspicion.

"Let me go by myself."

"By your—" Kanya said. "No way."

"Just me and them."

"Uh-uh." Kanya shook her head.

"Brother Moon," Rapha implored. "That would not be wise."

"Look, I realize it sounds crazy," I said. "But this whole thing is about me, right? The prophecies. The star chart. The earth guardians. Our future! I'm the one with the cross burned into my chest." I rapped my knuckles on the vest. "I'm the one supposed to reboot us. I'm the one Ki wants. I'm the one Rothbard thinks will help him. Then why risk everyone? Why jeopardize all of us for one of us? If I crash and burn, then it just …it wasn't meant to be."

"That's dumb, Reagan." Kanya turned and walked away.

Len appeared to be calculating my proposition. Finally, he said, "Though I am unaware of the abilities you possess, my father and Lex are more formidable than you appear to concede. Your chance of successfully acquiring the map and destroying the Third Golem is statistically poor. This is why I came here to assist you."

"I can teleport through objects, Len. Burn a hole right through 'em. I'll do it to your brother if I have to."

"Such an ability only slightly reduces the possibility of failure."

"Look, I've beaten the odds before. Have you heard about Spiraplex and Soren Volden? Or Etherea? Yeah, well the odds were against me then too. Besides, I have an angel."

The biot tilted his head.

"Bernard," I said. "He's my guardian angel."

"I have never met an angel. What powers does Bernard possess?"

"Powers? Hm. That's a good question. Well, he's invisible, for starters. And, um, he can disappear through walls and stuff. But, you know, I'm not exactly sure about his powers."

"So how does Bernard protect you?"

"Well. He doesn't *always* protect me. Hell, sometimes he doesn't even show up."

Len straightened. "Then you will need my assistance."

"As well as ours." Rapha approached. "Brother

Moon, such talk is foolishness. Even Quixote had his squire, Sancho Panza. Likewise, we have one another. And together, we will fight for the cause of Heaven." He thumped his chest with his fist.

"He's right, Reagan." Orphana wagged her finger at me. "We stand together, or we don't stand at all."

"You guys didn't even think about my plan," I groused.

"There is no need to think on such folly," Rapha said. "Tonight, we shall enjoin the battle. May the powers of Light see us to victory."

CHAPTER 17

I seriously doubted that the Red Iguana had ever won any culinary awards, although it was probably listed in Bizarro L.A. or some similarly weird Southland attractions guide. Located in the foothills of the Hollywood Hills, the converted ranch house drew an odd mix of clientele, from tourists to porn stars to studio henchmen. It was rumored to be owned by Lizard People, as well as a front for Nomlies who'd turned to the Dark Side. Just the kind of place you'd expect to find a high-rolling rich kid with magical powers and a robot sidekick.

Kanya and I arrived sometime after eight p.m. The parking lot was gravel, and the Cammy stirred a considerable cloud of dust as we entered. The sprawling, redwood-sided structure glowed garishly under countless red lights strung along the eves. The Hollywood Hills served as an eerie black backdrop to the Iguana.

A group of bikers encircled an old stone well watching us enter the parking lot. I parked as far away from them as possible, turned the Cammy off, and sat there.

Finally, Kanya asked, "You ever been here?"

"Twice. Met with some studio whistleblower

both times. He claimed he'd been a part of a black mass and was hoping we'd run the story. I couldn't corroborate the details, so it stayed cold. But that was before all this."

"Before…?"

"Before the Imperia. Before I could see angels and demons, ya know?"

She nodded. I could sense an adamantine resolve rising inside her. After succumbing to Rothbard's shadow spell, Kanya seemed determined not to allow the magician to surprise her again.

Faint strains of lounge music drifted across the parking lot. We sat a moment longer before my cell phone rang, startling both of us. It was Rapha calling to let us know everyone was in place. They'd selected three different locations, besides ours, and would enter the moment the key was used. He issued a brief pep talk, along with a blessing, and then we disconnected.

Kanya and I exited the car. Reaching behind the seat, I removed the staff of undoing. I would need this in the event that Rothbard acquired the Mantle of Ur. However, I'd yet to determine a pattern or formula for unlocking the rod's power. Like most everything in my life these days, flying by the seat of my pants would have to do.

One thing I'd not thought about was walking into the Red Iguana with this relic. How did one manage handling the rod of Moses without drawing attention to themselves?

"Just use it like a walking stick," Kanya said. "Lots of people have them."

"Like this?" I let the staff slip through my fingers and did my best impression of a casual stroll. "Don't laugh."

"Oh, you look fine. All you need is a wizard's cape and a crystal ball."

"That's not funny."

She held back a smile, but I actually appreciated the humor. With that, we crunched across the parking lot to the entrance of the Red Iguana.

Supposedly, it used to be a Mexican Cantina. But that was decades ago. A fire in the foothills burned down half the joint and the previous ownership never recovered. The building had sat vacant until—allegedly—the Lizard People moved in. The new ownership rebuilt and parlayed the vegan craze to their advantage, offering a sizable menu of herbivore fare from sustainable sources. Some believed it was just a front for Reptoid clientele. Nevertheless, health-conscious trendsetters made a beeline for the lounge. The Red Iguana remained one of the few places in SoCal serving cricket cakes and toasted mealworms. On a bed of greens, of course.

A large plaster iguana, decorated in florid Aztecan reds and greens, glowed under a humming neon sign at the entrance. A doorman stood out front, hands folded at his waist, eying visitors with sterile politeness. He had that same short, stout appearance I'd come to recognize of the Lizard People. Thick jawline, flat, snout-like nose. His cold conical pupils followed our approach.

Inside, we were greeted by a plus-sized hostess with a porcelain smile and lashes that could double as dusters. Her skin was too smooth to make her a Reptoid. She glanced at my staff before querying us about the size of our party. I excused myself as I scanned the place for Rothbard.

Faint lerium haloes illumined lamps that rested on the surrounding tables. A massive terrarium occupied the center of the lounge. Several large grizzled iguanas lazed along corkscrewed branches inside, basking under industrial heat lamps. Downtempo electronica twined between the chatter of conversation and the brisk passing of waitresses.

I was about to drop Rothbard's name to the hostess when Kanya nudged me and pointed to a corner booth in the back. Nearby rose a dazzling chrome terrarium, almost ceiling-height, that showcased a tall gnarled tree branch inside with several lizards attached. Rothbard sat alone, wearing dark sunglasses, his attention diverted by a device on the table.

We thanked the hostess and proceeded to follow the curve of the bar toward Rothbard.

I felt like an idiot walking with the rod. It would take some practice to look even partially comfortable with such an odd accessory. And if it really was the rod of Moses, I still half-expected to combust from unworthiness. However, I took comfort knowing that I could at least whack someone with it if they got out of hand.

As we maneuvered along the bar, several patrons swiveled on their stools to watch us. This was a shifty bunch. Carnal. Alien. And they stank. I purposely avoided their gaze as I scanned the place. An infestation of narvogs had surrounded a nearby booth and appeared to be lapping something off the floor. Across the room, a large anemone-like creature had fused a cluster of diners together. I returned my focus ahead, but my attention was drawn to a group of men in trench coats and fedoras who stood at the bar conversing with the bartender. He stared at us before leaning forward and whispering to the group.

As we passed the bar, a man thumped me in the gut with his fist, and nearly knocked the breath out of me.

"Well lookie here," he said in a raspy voice to his posse of men, all dressed in trench coats and fedoras. Swiveling on his stool, the man turned and faced me, nudging the brim of his hat up with a thick-fingered hand. "It's a real celebrity type."

I winced. God, his breath was bad.

"Sorry," I said. "You got the wrong guy. Excuse us."

I attempted to move on, but two of the men stepped away from the bar, blocking our path.

"Hey, boys," the first man said, sliding from his stool. "It's that reporter. The one that messed with Jake's crew."

"I dunno what you're—"

"Yeah. That's 'im, Joey." Another man circled behind us, uncomfortably close. "It's that reportah. That *Moon* fella."

He drew my name out and after it, a thick tongue swiped his scaly lips.

"Moon." Joey faced me. A couple inches shorter, but his girth exceeded mine. The whites of his eyes were muddy ochre. He stared at me, his pupils dilated, briefly turning conical before resuming their oval shape. He smiled to reveal rows of small, sharp teeth lining a thick jaw. "You shoulda known better than to come here, Moon. That's some balls, right boys?"

The remainder of his crew muttered in agreement.

A searing cold passed into my hands. I wasn't sure I could summon lightning from the staff, but I was damned sure I could ram the butt of it up Joey's big snout.

"They was involved in that subway jig," Joey said. "At Metro 417. They left Jake and his boys all banged up. Violated the treaty, and that didn't sit well with Patty."

His friends muttered their disapproval, tightening their circle around me.

This likely wasn't the first confrontation at the Red Iguana. But I'm positive it was the first one involving the Rod of God, Reptoids, and the Seventh Guardian of the Imperia. Moses had allegedly parted the Red Sea with the staff. Perhaps such a miracle could be re-enacted on a gang of Lizard People. That possibility humored me despite the situation, and I fit the idea in the back of my mind, like a subconscious puzzle piece to be used at a later date.

"Easy guys." I raised the staff as if to push the circle open. "This is a public place. Maybe we can have this discussion somewhere else?"

"He's right," Joey said, brushing the staff out of the way. "Let's take him and his stick out back and finish this... *discussion.*"

Laughter erupted from his friends.

Kanya, who now stood outside the circle, yanked one of the men back and he stumbled. A drink spilled on the bar and someone cursed. A glint of metal flashed. One of the men had removed his weapon from inside his coat. The image of a Komodo dragon was etched along the barrel of the exposed piece. If that canon was let loose somebody would lose a limb. Or three.

I winced as a snap of energy coursed the atmosphere. *Oh, shit!* As I prepared for a brawl, I did a double-take.

Balfour Rothbard stood just outside the circle of men with his hands raised.

"Gentlemen!" he said in a commanding voice. "Please. Don't be rude. These fine people are our friends."

He removed his glasses, patted one of the men on the back, and the group begrudgingly opened for him. Rothbard squeezed through and rested his hand on Joey's shoulder. The reptoid's features softened.

"Mr. Moon poses no threat to you." Rothbard smiled.

Joey's gaze shifted dully to me and then back to Rothbard. He grunted.

"He's a friend of mine." Rothbard glanced at me and winked. "A friend of *ours*. He poses no threat to the treaty."

"He ain't no threat to the treaty," Joey grumbled.

"That's right. So why don't you just let them pass and you and your boys can get on with your evening."

Joey nodded dully. "Let 'em pass, boys."

"That's right. Now just enjoy yourselves, your drinks, the ambience. Forget this ever happened."

Joey grunted. "Forget about it, fellas. C'mon." He turned back to the bar and the rest of his gang followed suit. Within seconds, they had their backs to us and appeared oblivious to our presence.

"Rich guy to the rescue." Rothbard stepped away from the bar and turned his attention to us... and then to the rod. "So, this is the legendary staff of undoing,"

I tightened my grip on the piece.

"It's all right. I don't want it." He laughed. "Finders, keepers. I'm just admiring the thing, that's all. Do you know how to use it?"

"You should hope not."

"Well. With that attitude, I agree."

He motioned for us to follow him as he limped around the bar to his corner booth. Rothbard did not bother sitting but instead collected some small stones —six, to be exact— which had been arranged on the tabletop, and then what appeared to be a compass. He inserted the objects inside his coat pocket. Finally, he retrieved a leather satchel which he strapped over his shoulder.

Inside the nearby terrarium, several large iguanas had gathered and perched on the branch with their heads cocked, studying us.

"I love those creatures," Rothbard said, glancing at the reptiles.

"Why? Because they're cold-blooded?"

"Do you have to start?" Rothbard shook his head. "Geez. That's not how you treat the guy who just kept you from getting jumped."

"We could have managed."

"Really? Ever fight a Reptoid? They're deceptively strong. Sure, they're easily swayed by mind spells. But you don't want to let one get its hands on you. Trust me."

"I'll file that. But I must have missed the memo on the treaty."

"The treaty between Reptoids and Stellars. You should know that, Reagan. C'mon. You folks are supposed to stay out of the tunnels and not interfere with their business."

"And what business is that?"

"Really? You don't know?"

"Sorry, but I'm still the new kid on the block."

"Lerium smuggling. Reptoids are all too eager to help humans thin their own herd. And they're making a killing at it. Pun intended. We're interlopers, as far as they're concerned." Rothbard straightened his jacket. "Okay? Let's go."

He led us back toward the kitchen. A bouncer standing beside a sparkling bead curtain stepped to the side at Rothbard's approach. We entered a narrow hall. Red lanterns flickered against rustic redwood panels. We passed several closed doors. Behind them, garbled voices and the clink of glass and metal sounded. At the end of the hall, we exited a security door and were met with the smell of night air and rotting greens. Produce crates teetered alongside dumpsters inside a gated area. Someone bearing the blazing cherry of a lit cigar approached us. Another reptilian bouncer.

Rothbard spoke to the man, and he stepped aside for us to pass.

A faint trail meandered away from the property into the brush of the Hollywood Hills.

I stopped. "Where are we going?"

"To the gateway. Where'd you think?"

"It's out *there*?"

"Why not? The old magician had his reasons for locating these things. This one's near a boarded-up shaft, one of the original Lizard People's. Probably connects to the tunnels downtown. From what I understand, the magician had some sort of alliance with the Reptoids. But seeing how dense the species is, it was probably pretty one-sided on his part."

The chirping of crickets rose around us, and a coyote yelped in the distance. The brushy terrain stretched into the darkened hills.

"You guys still up for this?" Rothbard asked.

"Yeah," I said, hoping not to sound too tentative. "We're ready."

"And the rest of your crew?"

I paused. "They wouldn't miss it for anything."

"Haha! Good. Lookin' forward to it." Rothbard continued down the trail.

The sounds of the Red Iguana, the music and the laughter, soon faded. There was not much tree cover along the way, which allowed for sufficient skylight to illuminate our path. The glow of the city twinkled behind us. A faint trickling of water eventually turned into a soft babble. The trail forked, and our guide took the one that cut through a thicket. Brittle leaves and branches scraped at my arms and clothing. The trail descended fifty—one hundred feet—before we emerged into a small hollow.

My eyes had adjusted enough to make out a boarded-up shaft in the wedge of the hillside. A glint of silver brought me to an immediate halt. My breathing was short, erratic. I placed both hands on the staff. A hulking figure stood waiting near the shaft. It was Lex.

"It's all right," Rothbard said. "As long as you guys mind your manners, Lex will mind his."

I kept my eye on the biot as the storm gifts stirred in my solar plexus. I'd jumped through a death angel once, severing the poor creature in two, and had already made up my mind to do the same to Lex, if necessary. Of course, with a Nefarium spine I couldn't count on identical results. Still, I was confident I could put a decent dent in the bionic man.

Rothbard tossed the satchel to Lex, then reached out and the biot handed him a round object. The key to the Golem Prison.

"The Chinaman could have saved himself a lot of hurt by just handing this over."

"So, you gutted him instead?"

"What makes you think that was me, Reagan?"

I peered at him. After the encounter at Dante's Inferno, our shields were sky high. I couldn't shake the sense that he was being straight with me, though. But if he hadn't slaughtered Casey Song, who had?

The strange cloud that hovered on the periphery of Rothbard's aura stirred. For the first time, I got the distinct sense that another presence was with us. Yet this was no ordinary demon that clung to him. Rather, it was a psychic shadow, maybe a monstrous outgrowth of his pain. Something energized and gorged on Rothbard's own enmity.

Suddenly, blue neon light burst upon the hollow. I shielded my eyes as the key radiated forth its splendor. Rothbard stood with the orb buoyed over his open palm. His eyes glistened in the glow, the celestial canopy of symbols and glyphs wheeling overhead.

"Ki's waiting," Rothbard said. "He has the map. Once the gateway is open, go through it. I'll be right behind you."

"Wait a second," Kanya objected. "How do we know you won't lock us inside?"

"You don't."

Rothbard maneuvered the orb. As it turned, the glorious constellations whorled around us, lighting up the surrounding trees and hillside.

Kanya glanced at me, but I was busy trying to intuit where this encounter was headed and what was required of me in the process. The sense of another entity in proximity to him had set me off-kilter. Were we being drawn into a trap? The possibility seemed tenable.

"Look," Rothbard said. "I have no reason to lock you guys in there. Why would I do that? I need you. I need Reagan. And I need the Mantle. And you need us. Now I can't hold this key all night, so..."

Neither of us responded.

Rothbard shook his head in frustration. He continued rotating the key, maneuvering his hand so as to recalibrate the dazzling cosmos. The glowing tapestry of symbols orbited through the atmosphere until the blazing circlet of the portal and the Hebrew letters appeared across the hollow. It hovered near a tree stump, just inches off the ground.

"Okay," Rothbard said. "Here we go. You guys ready?"

But he didn't wait for our approval. Instead, he began reading the letters. His voice was confident in its cadence and articulations.

"Khet. Yud. Fe. Reish."

He was a seasoned magician of an order I could only imagine. I'd heard Rapha speak commands of power. But the self-assurance in Rothbard's tone and his mastery of the magical language were unnerving. Spells and incantations, arcane formulas and conjurations. This was his game. I couldn't even master my own abilities, so how the hell could I ever manage to challenge his?

"El. Raman. Aleph. Co-het!"

Suddenly the area inside the circlet rippled. A vivid turquoise blossom unfolded. Even Lex registered the event, turning to face the newly opened portal.

Neither Kanya nor I moved. Our last visit to the Golem Prison had left me battered, but my hesitation wasn't due to fear or cold feet. It was intentional. The longer we waited, the longer the gateway remained open for the other Imperia to enter. Sure. I'd spouted off about going it alone. Truth be told, our chances were way better with everyone involved. And I knew it.

"Lex!" Rothbard motioned the biot to the gateway. "Go on."

The robot went to the gateway, climbed over the threshold, and disappeared into the cerulean blue tunnel.

Rothbard turned to us. "I'll go in without you, Reagan."

"I know you will."

He shrugged, walked to the portal, and stopped. "Look, man. You have one shot here. You don't want the map? Fine. Either way, the Mantle's mine. That was the deal. And I'm not a deal-breaker. But I'm giving you a minute, one minute, and I'm closing the door. It's your decision."

With that, Balfour Rothbard stepped through the gateway. We were alone.

Kanya turned to me. "I'll go in first. Don't follow right away. Give it a second. I'm not sure what to expect inside. If there're no red lights, then go through. Once we're inside, you stay with him. Stay with Rothbard, Reagan. Okay? Concentrate on getting that map. I'm gonna lag back until the others show. All right?"

I nodded.

"All right!?" she demanded.

"Yeah."

She inhaled and exhaled deeply, shook her hands out, and turned to face the gateway. Her features glowed in the neon aqua. I didn't need a reminder that this woman was a bad ass. Yet, as if to confirm, a slight, daring smile notched her lips. In a wink, Kanya leapt into the gateway and was gone.

I stood alone in the hollow. The glowing atlas of glyphs and symbols remained a canopy of luminescence in the atmosphere, a reminder that Rothbard was waiting on the other side. The gateway was still open.

"Bernard. Psst! You here?"

But there was no sign of my guardian angel. Only the sound of chirping crickets and the gurgling of water somewhere in the dark hillside.

Perhaps Len was right. I needed his help. Hell, I needed all the help I could get. Besides, Bernard wouldn't mind.

The portal felt like a veil of frigid air. Stepping through it shocked my senses, but not enough to make me forget that my friends were waiting for me on the other side.

CHAPTER 18

Compared to my first landing in the Golem Prison, this entry was smooth sailing. Probably because I didn't sail at all, I just hit the floor in stride. The stink of smoke and mold struck me. The tunnel walls glistened in the light of the magical orb, which hovered above Rothbard's open palm.

No sooner had I arrived than the magician recited the Hebrew letters, this time in reverse, and the blazing portal faded. We were enclosed by the dank subterranean atmosphere. Lex handed him the satchel and Rothbard stuffed the key in it before gazing down the tunnel.

"I've heard so much about this place," he said in hushed reverence. "You can almost smell the history here."

Water pattered somewhere down below. The torch light flickered along the ribs of the tunnel as it twined its way downward.

"They're here," Rothbard said, his back to us. "All of them. The guardians. Mace. And... Len."

He turned to look at Lex, who remained impassive.

Rothbard looped the satchel over his shoulder and motioned us forward, leading our descent into the

Golem Prison.

I fell in after him. Lex followed me closely enough that I could hear the soft whir of gears beneath his flesh. As she'd promised, Kanya slunk to the rear and padded softly behind us.

As we descended into the tunnel, Rothbard expounded upon the Golem Prison and the renowned magicians who had long searched for its whereabouts. Apparently, this place was like the El Dorado of magical locales, a mythical domain sought out by many, yet discovered by few. He sounded genuinely honored to have finally gained entrance.

"The key came to me," he said.

"That's hard to believe," I countered. "The Magic Dragon was basically ransacked. You went looking for the key. I'm the one who found it."

"Okay. Technically it was delivered *through* you. But do you know how many conjurations, how much high strangeness corresponded to bring it to me? I've been after the key long before you showed up. Sure, your arrival kinda changed things. But once I learned of its rediscovery, I issued a Rite of Rays. It's sort of a Druidic GPS that draws an object to the summoner. Seeing that we missed it at the Dragon, you just became part of the process, bringing it to its rightful owner. Heh. Call it *fate* that keeps bringing us together."

When I didn't respond, he glanced back at me.

"What? You don't like the idea of being used?"

He'd read my thoughts perfectly. "I once knew a guy who also thought he'd figured out the mechanics of the Universe. Had the world by the tail. Played the powers that be. Until he ended up with a lightning rod in his chest."

"Ah! Don't mistake me for Soren Volden, Reagan. Or any other of those Summu Nurian props. Volden was a tool for the Black Council, just like Etheria—you know that."

"And you're at the service of... no one?"

He put the brakes on, causing the group behind him to stumble to a stop.

"What are you implying?" Rothbard asked.

The shadow surrounding him reconfigured into a vaporous murk, fingering its way towards me.

"Oh, I dunno," I said. "Ever thought that, maybe, someone is playing *you*? All those powers you conjure, all that hoodoo. It's like that old folk story about the musician that sold his soul at the crossroads."

"Robert Johnson."

"Yeah, him. He exchanged his own soul for some fancy finger pickin'. Temporary fame for eternal perdition."

"Please tell me you don't believe in—"

"Perdition? I've seen it. Besides, if you ask me, it seems like the best explanation for the state of some things."

He peered at me for a moment. "That's deep. But if I'm not mistaken, you're the one being used, Reagan."

"How so?"

"Okay. Maybe you're not being used by Lucifer himself. But that motley band of earth guardians you claim to serve—the Imperia—they could be playing *you*."

He made a dismissive gesture and resumed the lead down the tunnel.

"It's purely utilitarian, dude," Rothbard said over his shoulder. "As long as it serves a larger purpose, I don't care who's along for the ride. Or who's driving, for that matter."

"I didn't realize chaos magicians were so pragmatic."

"You have a lot to learn about me, Reagan."

Our footsteps echoed through the tunnel. Soon, the stone aqueduct intersected our path. A few moments later, we stepped into the central chamber. The domed ceiling rose overhead like a subterranean cathedral. Rothbard stopped, and his gaze roamed about the place. Then he wandered to the fountain, his eyes sparkling in the torchlight.

I scanned the chamber, but the others were nowhere in sight. However, I knew they were near. I could feel them. The magician had accurately intuited their presence. I approached him, keeping my guard up and my senses at the ready.

"Amazing," he said, leaning forward on the parapet of the fountain and gazing across at the clay giant at the back of the fountain. "Theories of artificial intelligence come dangerously close to golem mythology. Do you realize that?"

But my attention was elsewhere. From my vantage point, I could see several of the tunnel entrances and no one from the team.

Rothbard walked around the fountain, tracing his fingers along the alchemical symbols etched in the stone. "Just think about it in terms of hardware and software. For the magician, it's clay and magic. For the scientist, it's software and wetware. Same difference. Both are golem mythology."

He stopped directly in front of the Third Golem, his attention fixated on the Mantle of Ur embedded in the pedestal that the statue stood upon.

Energy surged up in my bones. He wanted the Mantle, to unlock its spell. How Rothbard would manage that, I didn't know. But if he made a move for the Mantle, I couldn't let him. Even though Rapha had charged me with acquiring the map, I couldn't just stand by and watch Rothbard get what he wanted.

My hands trembled. Blue veins of electricity now licked at my fingertips, skittering along the crest of the staff. Whatever power it held, I knew I could channel it. Somehow, I could command the staff. However, caution was in order.

Rothbard studied the intricate details of the Mantle. It glistened like a mystical mosaic. I watched, prepared to intervene, as I felt energy building in the atmosphere. Tesseracts twined the chamber, appearing and disappearing on the periphery of my sight. What was happening? A subsonic frequency came with the phenomenon. An intonation, barely audible... that crested.

A thud, leaden and dense, reverberated in the stone. I could not locate the source of the sound. But it was followed by footsteps.

"You made it," a voice said behind me.

I spun around to see Ki approaching. He'd arrived via tesseract.

"I thought it'd be better to make an actual appearance." In his hand, Ki grasped a cylinder, which he now raised in display. "The map is too big a deal to just exchange behind the scenes. I figured we'd make it public. Let the whole world know about this monumental transference of power."

"The whole world?" I looked around the place.

"Okay, whoever's watching. But you get the idea, Reagan. This requires witnesses."

My gaze went to the cylinder. It was perhaps ten inches in length, comprised of what appeared a dull metal, etched with worn, unrecognizable shapes or symbols. Nothing fancy. Reminded me of an old telescope tube. Could something this small and simple really contain a map of my destiny?

Rothbard limped back around the fountain and joined Ki. He stared at the cylinder in the Sixth Guardian's hand. "The Tabula Lumen. What a strange world we live in."

Ki nodded. "Right? I tried to explain the map to him, but I'm not sure he gets it."

"Oh, I get it," I said. "You guys have swung a deal and you're hoping I buy in."

"Wrong," Rothbard said. "We've invited you into the opportunity of a lifetime."

"Ha! An opportunity to what? Help you bring that thing to life?" I gestured to the giant golem.

"The monster will serve us," Rothbard said. "Once you and I join forces, the Black Council won't have a chance."

"Don't you see, Reagan?" Ki pleaded. "We can do this! They can help us finally stop the Summu Nura."

Unlike our last encounter, I didn't find his appeals reassuring.

Rothbard motioned to the biot. Lex circled around and positioned himself behind the two men, rising above them in stature. His pupils calibrated as his pitiless gaze bore down on me.

Ki extended the cylinder to me. "Take it, Reagan."

I hesitated. It couldn't be this easy, could it? Where were the others? Why weren't they here yet?

From the corner of my eye, I could see Kanya inching closer. A smell of adrenaline tainted the air.

Icy bolts flashed through my hands as the storm gifts skittered wildly along the shaft of the rod. What was I to do? Rapha had been adamant: whatever happened, I must get the map.

I pointed to the cylinder. "How do I know it's in there?"

"Why would we lie?" Ki objected.

"I don't know. Why *would* you lie?"

Rothbard shrugged. "Show it to him."

"Okay, then—" Ki took a step back. "You ready? This's crazy."

Holding the cylinder at each end, he pulled outward. As he did, the device expanded in multiple directions, doubling and tripling in size as it went. In a few seconds it had gone from a handheld instrument to a large translucent barrel.

I stumbled back to keep from touching the growing object. For Ki's hands continued to spread wide until they reached their entire width. Between them hovered what appeared a squat, gossamer column. Almost the width of a structural pillar, yet slightly conical. Inside the cone floated a holographic cloud. As he steadied the map and stepped back, I could see that the cloud was actually a web-like cluster of veins and branches, a galaxy of starry pinpricks and nebulae that extended outward.

The crystalline apparatus hung before me, suspended in midair. While it contained no noticeable parts, mechanical or otherwise, within its contours rotated innumerable softly glowing tendrils, as sheer as thread, spiraling into a nimbus of intricate mass.

I stepped forward, gaping.

"It's a chart of your entire life," Ki said, his tone solemn. "From conception to death. The starting point is somewhere in the center. I'd have to make it a lot bigger for you to see that. Each thread is a timeline. Some are potentials; they aren't clear until they're walked. Every decision, every life event, opening new opportunities and possibilities. Expanding. Overlapping."

I stepped closer. How could this be? My gaze traced a single glowing branch as it spiraled outward like the Amazon River, fingering its way into tributaries before disappearing into fine celestial lattice.

"Each branch marks a new turn." Ki stood next to me now. "An end or a beginning. A possibility created by the last. I'm not sure where we are on the map right now. It takes a genius to cipher these things. The elder ones have spent eternity trying to figure that out. But once you can, once a map can be translated, the possibilities are endless. Especially for the Seventh Guardian."

I tried to speak, but what emerged was incoherent muttering.

"At first, they thought that we lived in a multiverse," Ki said. "That was the going theory, you know. The smart guys conjectured that every choice birthed universes of possibilities. Gazillions of universes! Crazy, huh? What they didn't consider is that all possibilities exist within one Universe. Not many worlds, but one world with many possibilities. The fulcrum is the Crossroads of Time. All timelines emerge from and intersect there. But only the Seventh Guardian can stand there."

Ki stepped even closer, peering into the star chart. His eyes glistened with fascination. "The owner of the Fifth Essence—he's the one. He can open all events, past or present. He can bend the map to his will. You see, each branch is a portal, a rift into a singular space-time event. The one who can access the Crossroads can control all of it. Our entire space-time continuum is at his command."

I stared, shaking my head in incomprehension. Ki smiled and watched me.

"How can this be?" I finally said.

"Crazy, huh?"

"It's like... playing God."

"Maybe so. But if he's given you the power, then why not use it?"

I straightened. "How do I know it's *him* giving me the power? How do I know it's not...?"

Ki clucked his tongue.

"That's enough," Rothbard said, motioning for the map to be closed.

Opening his arms around the map, Ki drew it into himself, and the object collapsed, shrinking back into its original cylindrical shape. Within a moment, it lay flat in his opened palm. Then he extended the map to me.

"Go on, Reagan." Ki peered at me. "Let's finish this thing."

He nudged the cylinder closer.

"It's what we've wanted," he said. "It's what we've waited for."

"We?"

"The Imperia. The elder ones. The entire lineage

of earth guardians."

"So... you're still a part of them?"

"Take it!"

"But... "

"When you agreed to protect the Tau, you took on everything that came with it. Including this."

I shook my head, unable—no, *unwilling*—to concede the inevitability of this exchange.

It was then I noticed that Rothbard's attention had been drawn elsewhere. I followed his gaze. He was looking at the cavern walls, which appeared to undulate. A slight shift had occurred in the contours of stone and gradations of shadow. I blinked. What magic was causing this spatial anomaly? The guardians felt nearer than before, yet I was still unable to see them.

As I watched, the mouth of one of the tunnel entrances rippled. At that moment, I realized an opaque wall or gaseous substance draped the mouths of the tunnels, camouflaging the guardians from the chamber. Anxious voices sounded. Distant but familiar. Voices that I recognized. Rapha! Mace! Celeste! They were trapped behind a magical veil. It was trickery orchestrated by the mage.

"Take it!" Ki jabbed the cylinder at me. "Now!"

"He's stopping them." I pointed at Rothbard. "Why's he stopping them?"

The magician glanced back at me and then bent forward with one hand clenched. He shook his fist as one who was about to throw some dice. Rattling sounded.

"What are you doing?" I demanded.

"What I have to," Rothbard said.

"I thought we had a deal. Why are you stopping

them?"

"We *did* have a deal! But you guys don't wanna fight fair."

"What are you talking about?"

Rothbard rose and glared at me. "Don't play dumb, Reagan. Your minds are soft. You want to stop me from getting the Mantle, don't you? That's the deal I had with you guys." He pointed at Ki. "I get you the map in exchange for the Mantle. And like I said, I'm no dealbreaker. There's power in a promise kept... and I've kept mine. If you're gonna break it—the consequences are on your head."

The shadow aura around him expanded and, for a moment, I thought another entity might emerge. Instead, Rothbard opened his hand to reveal six stones notched with finely-carved symbols. These were the stones he'd laid out on the table at the Red Iguana.

"It's a simple spell," he said. "A variation of the *Pulsa Denura*. This one doesn't require shofars and black candles. Thankfully. But you should recognize the elements. If you're any good, you should be able to counter it. Let's give it a whirl, shall we?"

I watched dumbly as he turned and bent forward again. This time, he brought his hand back, wound up, and scattered the six stones across the cavern floor. They skipped as if moving across a pond. Sparks nicked the ground as the stones swept in various directions.

Suddenly, all six tunnel entrances burst into flame.

We staggered back as the explosion sucked the air out of the cavern. The torches throughout the chamber swelled with the blast. Shadows leapt wildly between the columns and stonework. The perimeter of the Golem Prison had become a raging inferno.

Rothbard raised his hands, declaring an inscrutable dictate as he did. Then he turned from the wall of flame and commanded, "Lex! Take it!"

I snatched the cylinder from Ki's grip before the biot could get it. However, to my surprise, Lex, did not go for the cylinder. Instead, he turned and jogged around the fountain to the Third Golem.

CHAPTER 19

A blur of motion swept toward Lex, and with it came a high-pitched yelp. Kanya morphed in the process. By the time she reached him, she had fully transformed into Cricket.

"C'mon, Gort!" she taunted. "Let's dance!"

Leaping on the parapet, she propelled herself at the biot. I'd forgotten how lightning quick the changeling was, for even Lex could not react fast enough. She flung herself at the biot and managed to seize his neck.

"Haha! Gotcha, big guy!"

But rather than a chokehold, she scissored her legs around his upper body and pummeled his head with blows.

"Take! That! Mister! Monster!"

It would have been comical, what with the ferocity of the girl and her incessant chattering, except that Lex so outmatched her in size, she didn't stand a chance. With a single hand, the robot reached up, gripped her thigh, and tore her from his shoulders.

So fierce was the motion that I feared he might rip her leg from its socket in the process. Cricket cried out, clawing her fingers across the robot's face and shoulders as he dragged her from his body and slammed her to the floor. She may have been immune to magic, but the shapeshifter was obviously not immune to biotic brawn.

Meanwhile, I hastily jammed the map into the back pocket of my jeans. Seeing that I had no pack and needed to join the fray, it was the best I could do. But what was my next move? Lex's intentions were unclear to me. However, having blocked the tunnel entrances, Rothbard's objective was evident—he wanted to prevent the rest of the Imperia from helping. Which meant I needed to counter that spell and open the tunnels.

Or crack Rothbard upside the head.

When I realized that the staff of undoing was practically radiating storm energy, I chose the latter. In a single motion, I yanked the staff upward, snatched its end in two hands, and teed up on the magician's head. It was a cool move, but Rothbard easily evaded it, skipping back from the swing. Which sent me stumbling across the floor.

Okay, so maybe it wasn't such a cool move.

"Ha!" Rothbard brushed off his hands. "I thought you knew how to use that thing."

I steadied myself and lowered the staff to my waist. *Damn.* I was about to make a wisecrack rejoinder when I heard Cricket shout. She had scrambled to her feet, ready again to engage with the biot.

Lex stomped his way to the Third Golem. He looked up at the massive clay statue, his metallic pupils recalibrating. A strange symmetry existed between the two. Artificial entities both made of matter and magic. Rothbard was right: *Theories of artificial intelligence came dangerously close to golem mythology.* And in that moment, it dawned on me—something else was playing out here that we'd missed.

A kinship existed between the Third Golem and L-3X.

Lex mounted the parapet of the fountain and positioned himself immediately behind the statue. They were almost identical in height and girth: doppelgangers from different ages. Lex raised both his hands as if preparing to bring them crashing down upon the statue.

However, Cricket launched herself at his feet.

"Oh no you don't!"

She seized his ankles in a bear hug. Despite her petite size, she flew at him with such force that he lost his balance. The robot leapt backwards, off the fountain, kicking the changeling off as he went. Cricket landed upright. Lex followed with a thud and swiftly regained his footing.

Cricket bolted to the space between the biot and the fountain, blocking any advance.

"I know what you wa-ant," she said in a sing-song voice. "But you ain't gonna get it!"

Even though she bobbed on her toes, one leg appeared hobbled, and a swatch of blood swelled across the back of her scalp.

Lex squared with her, slightly crouched, his hands open in attack. "You cannot stop me." His voice was as unfeeling as a stone.

"Bet I can loosen a few screws." Cricket sneered, staring down the biot. She encircled him, dragging one foot as she went.

I had to do something. She would kill herself before giving up. And by the looks of it, she wasn't giving up.

I leveled the staff like a spear and prepared to assist Cricket. While it seemed rather profane to use the staff of Moses as a bayonet, until I figured out how to wield its power, this was the best I could do. But as I prepared to lunge into battle, Ki called out to me.

"The wall!" He motioned to the flaming barriers. "Douse it!"

"How?"

"It's a Wall of Fire," he said. "A spell."

"And what am I supposed to do?"

"Douse it!" he implored. "Use an air spell. You can counter it with an air spell!"

"But I—" I shook my head.

"Suck the oxygen outta the air."

"I can't—"

"Yes, you can!" Ki glanced in the direction of the biot. He returned his gaze to me, his eyes framed with urgency. "I can't do it for you. The other guardians—you gotta let 'em in!"

The atmosphere buzzed with energy. He was right. I could do it. I had to do it. That's what this was all about. My calling. My destiny. My true nature. This was why I didn't die in that lightning strike—someone wanted me alive. Nevertheless, the particulars were lost upon my abject humanity.

Ki stepped forward, his gaze steady. "You need them, Reagan. The guardians. You can't do it alone."

Where was Rothbard? Why was he not interrupting Ki? I scanned the chamber, but the magician was nowhere in sight.

"Then help me!" I said to Ki. "Help us. Help us stop him!"

A whoosh of flame sounded as one of the barriers billowed out before returning to its place. The heat inside the cavern had practically doubled.

Ki took a step back, and then another. His features grew grim. A tesseract materialized, swirling behind him. I sensed that he was thinking about his girlfriend. About the map and its possibilities. And about the Imperia.

"I can't," Ki said.

"Yes, you can!" I implored. "Come back, Ki. Rejoin us. It's the right thing to do, and you know it. You belong here."

I extended my hand in appeal. Nevertheless, the guardian continued retreating, shaking his head.

"I—I'm sorry, Reagan. That isn't how it ends."

"Then how *does* it end?!"

He didn't answer.

I was tempted to plead with him, even though I suspected it wouldn't bring him back. Besides, if fulfilling the prophecies required groveling, then failure was a legitimate option.

So, I let him go.

The tesseract undulated and the atmosphere folded around him. His Tau glistened in the firelight as the Sixth Guardian faded back into the nether.

Sorrow mixed with anger inside me. With both the map and the staff in my possession, we had the advantage. Nevertheless, in light of my current predicament, that thought did not embolden me.

I quickly relocated Cricket to see that she had reengaged Lex in combat. To my surprise, she was squatting on the biot's shoulders with her hands locked around his throat... *attempting to remove his head from his shoulders.*

"Mmmph!" she grunted, with her forearm now

clamped under his jaw. "Come on, big boy!"

Of course! Once separated from the neural skin, the biot would be much more vulnerable. that's what had happened to Kevin—K-111.

Yet just as I'd surmised, the shapeshifter was no match for the super-charged biot. His speed and strength were just too much for the plucky Ninja. I watched as Lex reached up, seized her by the hair, and yanked her off his shoulders. I thought he might snap her in two right there. Instead, he extended her away from his body as she kicked and threw punches. Winding up, the biot flung her across the chamber. A thud sounded, and her cries abruptly ceased.

No!

Panic tore through me. I needed the other Imperia, whose voices still clamored on the other side of the magician's fiery veils. An air spell. How in the hell did I invoke that? If I couldn't release the other guardians, our mission to stop Rothbard was as good as dead.

I attempted to center myself by locating Rothbard. But the magician had disappeared.

The biot ascended the fountain again. Then he drew his hand back, still gripping a wad of silver hair, and released a guttural growl. He drove his fist into the statue of the Third Golem. And kept pounding away.

I ducked as particles of stone and mortar exploded into the air, sending debris spraying across the subterranean prison. Lex's hands were like sledges, pummeling the figure. Its massive torso fractured as the chest split and splashed into the fountain. The Golem's head toppled to the floor.

What in the hell was Lex doing?! Rothbard wanted the Golem, didn't he? The Imperia were the ones who'd come to destroy the Third Golem. With the clay monster demolished, how would the magician realize his plan? Could it be that Lex was rebelling against his master just like the other biots had?

Several more blows, and all that remained were the clay feet of the Third Golem still mounted on the pedestal. Crude rebar rose from each foot. Lex gripped the bars and wrenched them back, finally snapping the feet from the base. He kicked the remaining rubble into the fountain.

The biot stood alone for a moment, as if savoring the destruction. Then he climbed onto the pedestal and stood where the Third Golem had.

Which happened to be positioned directly upon the Mantle of Ur.

At that point, I was practically fuming icy electricity. I had to stop him! Tesseracts hovered on the periphery of the Prison. I quickly drew one down and steered it straight into the biot's chest. Gripping the staff with both hands, I clenched my teeth.

And drove myself into L-3X.

In transitory form, my body acts like a high-speed projectile, severing objects—even people—into nicely minced quarters. As much as I admired Rothbard's biological robots, I had zero qualms about lopping this one in half.

But as I entered that strange timeless dimension, I heard no voices. Ki was not there to greet me. Nor were there any genies or psychedelic set pieces. In fact, this jump was unlike others because rather than sluicing through the robot, I crashed into something solid, something immovable. Had I hit the biot or a sheath surrounding him? Perhaps the Mantle was providing protection. Whatever I hit, it knocked the wind out of me. Pain exploded in my chest. My body spun wildly as I rematerialized midflight. The cavern wheeled overhead. Torches sailed past and the granite floor rushed up and collided with my shoulder.

"Aghhhhhhh!"

I don't know how many times I rolled. Even though I didn't completely black out, the experience felt dreamlike. As if I was a spectator to my own death. Indeed, death would probably be a fitting end to my brief yet comical stint as a superhero.

Sliding across wet stone I went. Dank moss gathered under my fingernails as I fought for traction. Striking another object, I cried out again, and ricocheted sideways. Crunching sounded in my head, but it wasn't of bone. Or teeth. A fiery wall sped past and I heard the cries of my friends behind it. But now I needed saving as much as they did.

I slammed into the cavern. White heat tore through me, temporarily blinding me.

I found myself sucking in huge gulps of air. Had I even breathed during the attempted jump? I tried to reach across my body to check my shoulder for blood but was unable to lift my hand.

I slumped back to the floor. As I did, the magician stepped from the shadows.

And for a moment, I saw him as he really was.

CHAPTER 20

The invisible world has its own laws. In real life, we are composites of insecurity, regret, stubborn resolve and lots of cosmetics, all bound together under a carefully curated persona. These elements take on unusual forms in the spirit realm, sometimes morphing into unique grotesqueries that challenge description. Some souls become the haven of demons. And then there are those who are subsumed by the thing they once nurtured; they are devoured by the beast they fed.

For a split second, what I glimpsed stepping from the shadows was not Balfour Rothbard, but a bulbous, blistered mass. Both insectile and gelatinous. The human form had been absorbed into this amorphous anatomy. Open wounds lashed its carcass, revealing a writhing volcanic core. Gnarled appendages sloughed below its trunk.

The creature bore an unsettling resemblance to a pupa.

It turned to me and a crease—no, a chasm—opened in its being. Wider and wider. What was I looking at? Perhaps I *had* lost consciousness and was meandering some nightmare. The nightmare only worsened when I realized the chasm was Rothbard's smiling face.

My mind snapped back into reality as the magician's human form returned. He turned away from me and approached the biot. Lex remained as I'd left him —standing atop the Mantle of Ur. My jump had to have caused some damage. Or did I even hit him? The robot appeared untouched.

Rothbard produced the compass-like device I'd glimpsed at the Red Iguana. Glancing back at me, he placed it upon the pedestal, between the feet of biot. It appeared to lock in place.

An odd, earthy glow rose from the device.

I struggled to keep my eyes open, to remain conscious. Across the chamber, I could see Kanya lying motionless. My intuition told me she wasn't dead. But, like me, she'd encountered someone well above her paygrade.

The staff of undoing rested on the cavern floor between myself and the magician. Faint veins of storm energy still traced the object. The staff was the only way to counter the Mantle of Ur. I had to get it back!

I forced myself into a sitting position. It felt like my chest had been replaced by a blast furnace. My shirt was torn and shredded. Had my entire ribcage been fractured? I didn't doubt it.

Inhaling, I tried to stand, but my shoulder couldn't bear the weight, and I slumped back against the cavern.

The Wall of Fire sent light and shadows dancing across the sarcophagi. Words of command echoed in my head. Ki was right. It was within my power to douse this magic. I knew it! But how? What should I speak? Or did I need to speak at all? Like so many of the gifts I'd been given, this one remained untapped, a spectral memory of once-known lore.

The Tau scar was scalding my chest, the wound reignited by the jump. I attempted to stand again, yelling as I did, yet thudded back to the floor.

The sound of an incantation came to me. Was it in my head? No. Someone inside one of the tunnels was speaking... *an air spell!* It sucked the oxygen from the flames, just like Ki had said it would. Rapha spoke the incantation and as he did, the fiery barricades crackled.

However, the hope that this created in me was swiftly dashed when I saw Rothbard standing before the Mantle of Ur with his arms outstretched. His words were of another tongue. He did not look at me. I was no threat. As he spoke, the earthen shimmer ascended from the Mantle and began cloaking the biot.

"Ones magnanime. Expergisci potestatem tuam."

Perhaps if our circumstance had not been as dire, I might have appreciated the wonder of it. Hazy tentacles rose from the tiled pedestal, entwining the biot until he was wound in a golden glow.

"—ad deos ignis!" Rothbard proclaimed. He was speaking in Latin, as fluent as if he were a first-century Roman scholar. *"Sunt elementis... et lapis terrae... operimentun te!"*

He clapped his hands once and stepped back.

For a moment, they stood—master and servant; creator and created. Rothbard motioned, and Lex leapt off the platform. Girdled in luminous gold, the biot appeared like an ancient warrior, a god of earth and magic. The biot moved his arms, as if testing his new features. He swiveled at the waist, looked down upon his hands, and clenched them into fists. Thor's mythical hammer could not appear more lethal. The Mantle of Ur now draped him like golden chainmail. His very being radiated an ancient power. He straightened and turned his eyes upon me.

What had I done? I should have stopped them while I'd had a chance.

Peripheral motion drew my gaze away. Quinn tumbled out of one of the tunnels followed by Celeste. Rapha's incantation had extinguished the Wall of Fire, opening the tunnels again.

But it was too late. We didn't stand a chance.

Quinn scrambled to his feet and brushed himself off. "Well, well. Lookie here."

"S-stop," I said, struggling to speak. "Quinn. Stop! Go b-back. Go back! We..." I swallowed. "We c-can't stop them."

Quinn glanced at me dismissively. I could tell he had vengeance on his mind.

"We had to use a meter, Balfour. Can we make this quick?"

Rothbard smirked. "Still your old smartass self, I see. Some things never change."

"Including you being upstaged by an apprentice?"

"Ha! Your powers were always second-rate, Quinn. I doubt much has changed."

"What hasn't changed is you being an ego-maniac."

Lex moved forward, as if preparing to lunge at Quinn, and Rothbard signaled him to halt. "Wait till they're all here."

Celeste surveyed the cavern. When she spotted me, she hurried over and helped me to my feet. As I steadied myself, I reached for my back pocket.

The map was still there. Thank God!

I gripped Celeste's forearm. "We have to l-leave. He's too strong now."

As I said this, Rapha stepped from one of the tunnels. For a moment, he looked like a massive troll lumbering from the depths of the earth. Sweat shone across his forehead. A resolute glare fixed his features.

Rumbling sounded in the cavern. The granite and stone seized against an inexplicable force. Rothbard glanced at the stalactite-draped ceiling. Then he turned around.

Behind the magician, Len and Mace approached. Mace knelt, hoisting a bazooka-like weapon with an unusual shaped muzzle over his shoulder, aiming it at Lex and Rothbard.

Our adversaries were now surrounded. This, however, did not appear to faze the magician.

"Greetings, earth guardians!" Rothbard spread his arms in salutation, pivoting so as to engage all of us. "This is your lucky day. You guys are officially the first ones to witness the unveiling of, well, the one who's gonna put us over the top. It's the beginning of a new age, my friends. May I introduce to you—" He stepped back, motioning to L-3X. "—the new and improved... *Third Golem*."

I straightened and shook free of Celeste's grip. Rapha had been correct. Rothbard was just picking up where the last magician had left off. He'd never really wanted that old clay golem; he'd built his own. Except this one was made of titanium, circuitry, hydrogel... and wizardry. Perhaps the prophecies were right—the merging of technology and magic would be the dawn of a new era.

If so, it would likely mark the end of ours.

"That stuff about the dusty old golem," Rothbard said. "That was just misdirection on my part. Sort of. I mean, the Mantle was always my thing. I knew it would complete my creation. Now, together, we can beat the Black Council."

Rapha stepped forward. "I'm afraid we cannot allow that to happen."

Rothbard turned his gaze upon Rapha. "You're larger than I anticipated, guardian."

"My heart is even bigger."

"Good answer. Well, you'll need all that heart if you choose to challenge us."

"We have no other option, Balfour. Such power can only corrupt. The Black Council's influence upon you is greater than you know."

"They have *no* influence on me, chief. I know exactly what they are and what they want. Lex is here to help us stop them; don't you get it? We're on the same side. Besides, I kept my end of the deal. Moon has the map. That was the agreement I had with Ki. What else do you guys want?"

"To begin with, justice for the murder of Casey Song."

"Justice." Rothbard shook his head in disgust. "And you're the arbiter of justice?"

"Just one of many." He motioned to the other members of the team.

As they talked, I turned my attention to the staff. It lay between us and the magician. However, Rothbard seemed unconcerned with the piece. Should I make a move for it? I didn't know if I could. Just the thought of moving made my bones ache.

Len took several steps forward. "I cannot allow you to continue with your plan, father."

Rothbard turned and gazed at Len.

"L-3N. My son. My prodigal. You stand no chance against us."

"Perhaps. But opposing you is worthy nonetheless."

"That's very eloquent, but it doesn't change the fact that your brother is now the peak of my creation." Rothbard furrowed his brow. "Does that hurt you? It's not intended to."

"At one time, my reaction could best be defined as jealousy," Len said. "However, seeing what you have become, father, and learning about good and evil from my interaction with humans, reading literature, and observing the natural order, my jealousy has subsided. Now I believe that my reaction could best be described as... pity. I pity you, father. As I do Lex. I am fully aware that what makes my brother more worthy in your eyes is nothing of intrinsic value, but rather the systems and programming which enable him to be a tool of service and a weapon of destruction. If that is true, then my feelings of jealousy are tempered by the knowledge that my brother is incapable of choosing such freedoms and, thus, a prisoner to his biology and your wishes."

Rothbard lowered his head and sighed deeply. The shadow aura whirled about him. There was no conflict in the man, only rage. The seething core I'd glimpsed in the spirit realm fumed inside him.

"I'm sorry, L-3N. You *were* special. I mean that. You could have been the one standing here. I created you for this. It was your decision to defy me. You ate of the Tree. Now you give me no choice." Rothbard turned to the Third Golem and casually said, "Lex, show them what you can do."

L-3X squared his body with his brother. The Mantle appeared to shiver; a static surge swept through its frame. The biot lowered his head and charged toward his opponent. Len engaged him, rushing headlong into his sibling.

Their impact released a blast within the chamber, an audible concussion that wrenched several torches from their mounts and sent loose blocks thudding to the ground. However, it was Len that suffered the worst of the collision. He hurtled across the cavern, liquid gushing from his side as he flew. The entire room shuddered as Len slammed into one of the sarcophagi along the perimeter, wrenching slabs of granite from above. Debris rained upon the biot, almost covering him, leaving only his upper body exposed.

Dust and gravel fell from the ceiling, clattering across the Prison floor. If this continued, the chamber was in danger of collapsing.

Mace barked out some illegible words. His weapon was aimed at Lex. I hoped that wasn't the anti-matter rifle that he'd vowed to bring. This structure wouldn't survive an unstable molecular blast. Hell, I wasn't sure it would survive even *without* a blast.

Lex faced the soldier. But Mace matched the robot's glare with one of his own.

"Bring it, bitch."

Damn. What balls. It made me slightly guilty for having laughed at the guy.

Rods of golden energy coursed the Mantle. Lex peered at Mace and thumped his fists together as he lowered his shoulder, preparing to charge the soldier.

But as he did, objects on the floor near the robot began moving.

It wasn't immediately clear what was happening. At first, I thought that the cavern itself had tilted, causing the loose stones and blocks to shift. But they were accelerating as they went, scraping across the chamber, speeding straight toward Lex. Like metal drawn to a magnet, several blocks slammed into the biot, attaching to his body like huge barnacles. A hail of dust and pebbles followed, affixing to the robot's body like a coat of stone.

Lex swayed, struggling to shake free of the granite straightjacket.

I looked at Rapha, guessing he was responsible. The alchemist was manipulating gravity, just as he'd spoken about to Len. Lex's body had been magnetized and imbued with gravitons, an effect that increased the density of his body. It created a gravitational pull of nearby objects. Indeed, Lex's motions now appeared encumbered and leaden. He may have advanced brute strength, but he was still subject to the laws of nature.

Rapha stood, slightly hunched over, his hands pressed heel to heel. His lips were pursed and the veins across his forehead swelled.

"*Tempic coagulum!*" Rothbard proclaimed. "Touché, wizard!"

As L-3X struggled to tear the blocks from his body, his brother dragged himself from the rock pile. Dust still clung to Len's head and shoulders, yet the liquid flowing from his side had stopped. However, his left arm had detached and lay motionless in the rubble. This didn't stop him. Gripping a boulder with his remaining hand, he charged Lex and drove the stone into his brother's skull.

The blow landed with a crack. A normal human would have been decapitated by the move. However, the impact barely fazed Lex. Still, in that brief second, Len discarded the stone and leapt onto his brother's back. With his lone arm, he took the biot's neck in a chokehold. Wrapping his legs around Lex's midsection, he arched backwards, yanking his brother's head with him, stretching the torso and the neck at an inhuman angle. Like Cricket, he was apparently very serious about ripping his brother's head off.

It was a gruesome move, but one I recognized. I'd watched a good share of professional wrestling in my days and was unafraid to admit it. Hell, if people could admit to listening to Barry Manilow and watching reality television, I could confess to being entertained by professional wrestling. This particular move was called a guillotine choke and my immediate question was whether or not Len had spent time studying professional wrestling moves. While this would not surprise me, watching the warring biots engaged in this life or death struggle did.

Like Cain and Abel, the first biological intelligences also had a hard time getting along.

The Mantle radiated energy, scalding Len's flesh. As the magic cloak blazed, the stones and boulders attached to the biot's body began to splinter. This was the power of the chaos mantle that the magician had spoken of.

Rothbard turned his attention away from the biots. Retrieving a large stone from the floor, the magician tossed it into the air, shouting something as he did. The trajectory of the stone intersected the line of sight between Rapha and the robots. As it did, the rock stopped midair, wafting weightless there.

Rapha jolted forward, as if the wind had left him. The disintegrating rubble dropped from the biot and then changed direction, rocketing towards the levitating stone. The pieces collided, fragmented, and clattered to the ground.

"Haha!" Rothbard cheered. "An oldie but a goodie."

The magician had no time to celebrate, however, for a counter came immediately. Rumbling sounded again in the cavern. Rothbard looked overhead and, as he did, several stalactites snapped from the ceiling and plummeted towards him. Leaping from their path, he tumbled awkwardly across the floor. The stalactites shattered as they struck the earth, sending a cloud of stone and dust billowing.

Quinn removed his fingertips from his temple. He brushed away the approaching dust. "How's that for *second-rate*?"

Rothbard rose from the floor, coughing. His glasses sat cockeyed across his face, and he readjusted them. "It was okay."

Meanwhile, Lex delivered several thunderous punches to his brother. Their scuffle was over, though. Len, missing one arm and badly beaten, lay motionless.

Rothbard returned his attention to Quinn. "It looks like you're another man down now."

Quinn shook his head. "We're just warming up."

"That's too bad. You should give up while you have a chance."

"I ain't giving up. You should know that."

"Hmph. That was always your problem, Quinn—

you never knew when to just let it go."

The magician tilted his head. As he did, Quinn doubled over as if struck by a punch.

They stood more than a dozen feet apart but Rothbard released a series of invisible blows upon his opponent. Quinn staggered. His head snapped back and he gripped his jaw. I made a mental note—should I survive, I wanted to enquire about what particular ability this was. Knocking someone silly with just my mind could come in handy someday. Quinn writhed against the invisible onslaught. He stumbled back as his head whipped from side to side, before finally reeling into the cave wall.

"Weak!" Rothbard proclaimed. "Counter, you idiot!"

But Quinn didn't. As he regathered himself, the magician raised both hands and clenched them, as if choking an invisible enemy.

"*Asphyx mortuis*," Rothbard said between clenched teeth.

Quinn stiffened. The cords of his neck grew taut. His body trembled as a trickle of blood rolled from his ear.

Celeste yelled something and bolted to Quinn.

My hands were flushed with energy. Could I jump in this condition? I focused upon the magician but couldn't locate a tesseract. Nevertheless, I struggled to command my body forward. If I couldn't jump, the least I could do was kick him in the shins. However, before I could move, I watched as an energy force coagulated around Rothbard's wrists.

I squinted at this curiosity. Indeed, an apparition twined itself around both of the magician's hands, drawing them together as if in some phantasmal handcuffs. The density of the specter increased; particulates coagulated from multiple directions as a serpentine shape appeared, binding Rothbard's arms together.

He stumbled back, struggling against the phenomenon as Quinn fell to the floor, gasping for air.

That's when I noticed Orphana's prosthetic leg tumble from the shadows.

She was agglomerating, handcuffing the magician with her entire body!

In this state, Orphana was amazingly nimble. How could someone so infirm in the physical world seem so flexible and fluid in her gifting? It was a question that would likely remain a mystery. As her form continued to congeal, her features appeared to take shape along the coiled trunk; her long, thin fingers gripped Rothbard's forearms and a small basin materialized in which surfaced a flat bluish face. I could swear she was looking at me... and smiling.

While Rothbard struggled to free himself from Orphana's hold, Lex ran to his master's side. The Mantle glowed, pulsing with an ancient power. With both his hands, the biot gripped Orphana's coalescing frame that handcuffed his master. And pulled it apart.

No!

I stumbled forward, shouting, as Lex tore Orphana's body from the magician's arms.

In that state, her form disintegrated. An inhuman wail sounded as her anatomy splintered into miniscule particles.

The Mantle of Ur blazed on the robot's torso. Lex watched as the guardian's body swirled into the atmosphere before settling to the cavern floor. As her body congealed, it became clear that her lower torso was gone.

"Orphana!" I limped to her side and knelt down.

I glared up at Rothbard. "What've you done?!"

He motioned for Lex to stop. The magician stood panting, opening and closing his hands. "I did just what I warned you I'd do."

Orphana lay, her lower extremities smattered in pixel-like droplets along the cave floor. Rapha and Celeste joined me, looking down upon the Third Guardian. The biot had apprehended her in midtransformation. Droplets of her body pooled; some still gathered themselves, coagulating into recognizable forms and shapes—a kneecap, a fibula. Others quivered and then remained motionless. Being that there were no organs or blood, I wondered if her blood had been replaced by mercury. Ultimately, the sight of her broken frame was more tragic than it was mysterious.

Celeste hunched over Orphana, hands a brilliant electric blue. But it was obvious—no amount of healing energy would be able to restore the woman to us.

I stood and faced Rothbard and his biot. "Damn you."

"Hey, I told you, guys. This isn't our fault, Reagan. You were the ones trying to stop us. Look, I'm sorry, man. I really am."

He was telling the truth. At least, in part. Still, I spat.

Orphana's eyelids fluttered and opened. I knelt down again, and this time she took my hand and squeezed it. Her gaze rested on me.

"You o-okay, Reagan?"

"Of course. But why'd you do that?"

"Cuz we stand t-together... or we d-don't stand at all."

I shook my head. "I should've been the one, Orphana. You guys were supposed to let me go." Rapha pulled me back. "I shoulda been the one!"

Celeste continued passing her hand over the woman's body. Quinn approached. Blood stained his cheeks and jaw. He hung his head, for clearly, the Guardian of the Lore had served her last mission.

Her skin became ashen. She gripped Celeste's hand and tried to pull herself upwards but was unable. She settled back. A look of peace relaxed her facial features. We surrounded her, speechless in that holy moment.

"I've had a g-good run." She chuckled, the way she always did, and then began coughing.

Rapha smiled. "Yes, you have, sister."

"Now don't you go feelin' sorry. There's lots s-still to do." She coughed. "Carry on, guardians. No g-giving up. Ya hear?"

Orphana took a great breath.

"I'll be watchin," she said. Then she smiled, closed her eyes, and didn't open them again.

After a moment, Rapha removed the Tau from her neck.

The cavern quaked, sending debris raining from above. Several more blocks tumbled from the walls.

"Move it, guardians!"

It was Mace. He still knelt on the opposite side of the cavern with his weapon trained on Rothbard and the robot.

"Outta the way!" Mace bellowed. "Lemme at 'em!"

But if he fired that thing, no one would live to see the light of day. Except, maybe, the new Third Golem. Rapha stood and shook his head, signaling for Mace to forego more violence. The reality of our plight was obvious. Everyone, including Mace, knew it.

He cursed and lowered the rifle.

Another tremor shook the cavern and this time, the pedestal upon which the Golem had stood collapsed. The stone parapet that surrounded the fountain cracked, sending water gushing forth. Cold, subterranean water began spreading across the floor of the Prison.

Rothbard limped to the staff of undoing and picked it up. As he did, the electric blue faded. The magician studied the rod. My breath stopped. Losing the staff would be a fitting end to this fiasco. But instead of taking it, he approached and handed it to me.

"Let's finish this, Reagan."

I snatched it from his hands

Rothbard's eyes glistened in the fading torchlight. "Together, we can beat the Black Council. I've seen it. It's been... foretold. Look hard, Reagan. Look into your future. You'll know it's true."

The cavern quaked again. This time, a massive chunk of granite dislodged from above and crashed to the floor. Water sprayed the chamber as a hail of debris tumbled down in stony sheets.

Rothbard quickly removed the key to the Golem Prison from its satchel. Speaking a word of command, the orb rose and hovered over his opened palm, illuminating the atmosphere with its neon constellations. He recited the Hebrew letters, unlocking the gateways.

"If you want out," he said to us, "now's your

chance. Don't bother cleaning up. I'm done with this place. Destroy the key if you want. Later, guardians."

He tossed the key to us. It clanked along the floor for a few yards before Celeste snatched it.

Rothbard gazed down at Orphana's body and shook his head. Then he signaled to Lex and together they disappeared up into the shadows of a tunnel.

Another tremor rocked the Prison. We had to get out of there.

Rapha scooped up what remained of Orphana and turned towards the tunnel he'd emerged from. Celeste and Quinn followed. As the cavern began its collapse, I saw Mace with his duffle bag draped over one shoulder, helping Kanya into another tunnel. Len had managed to rise. He looked across at us before joining Mace in assisting Kanya out of the cavern.

I stood, watching them all leave. Rapha walked into the passage carrying Orphana, while Quinn followed. Before Celeste entered, she turned and waved me forward. Stones battered the floor around me. Perhaps one would split my skull and put an end to this misery. The water from the fountain reached my feet.

"Reagan!" Celeste called. "C'mon! What're you doing?"

The ground heaved and a small fissure appeared. I stumbled back. Maybe I'd been right the first time—I should have gone alone. Orphana would still be alive if I'd just followed my instincts.

"Reagan!" Celeste cried. "Hurry!"

However, Quinn wasn't going to let Celeste get trapped on my account. He took her arm and pulled her into the tunnel just as its mouth collapsed in a flume of dust and scree.

I stood numb for a moment, surveying the rubble.

Why? God, why?

Limping to another shaft, I made my way up the torchlit passage. Sobbing. Alone. Just liked I needed to be.

CHAPTER 21

"**D**on't be so hard on yourself."

It was my father. I wasn't sure where I was or how long he'd been sitting there across from me. I remembered stumbling out of the collapsing Golem Prison. But after that, nothing.

"Reagan, I know you can hear me."

I rolled over, facing the opposite direction.

Trauma is a weird thing. Sure, there were good reasons to believe that clandestine governmental agencies had a stake in engineering the masses. Turning everyone into victims of one sort or another—victims of biology, the environment, Big Pharma, a crappy education—had its advantages. Namely, it kept people soft, finger-pointing, never owning up to their own conditions. And always looking for anyone or anything to bail them out. Enter Big Brother. Nowadays, the list of potential triggers had assumed canonical proportions. We were becoming a milquetoast lot. It seemed like everyone was so easily offended, so eager to play the victim card. Or just run away from their junk.

I'd lost both parents at a young age and blocked out the memory of my father's murder, despite having witnessed it, which added a twist to my disdain for the emotionally frail. I knew what it meant to feel like a victim, and I secretly disdained myself.

"I know this is a dream," I said to the visitor. "So, I'm only half listening."

"You were always a dreamer, kid. That's where I'd always find you—dreaming."

"Yeah. Not sure that's a good thing anymore."

"Oh, it is. We need more dreamers."

I rolled back over, peering at the hazy likeness of the man I most admired.

"You sound like Rapha," I said.

"Ha! Is that why he's got a thing for Don Quixote? I think you need more of him in your life."

"Cervantes?"

"No. Rapha."

"You've met him?"

"Sort of. He was a pup back then."

"I can't imagine him ever being a pup."

"It's true. Besides, I have a new vantage here. Things don't look as bad."

"Hm. Sounds like a perspective I need."

"Listen." He stood and approached me. His body appeared more solid this close. "I know you're down on yourself, Reagan. You couldn't have saved me. Or your mom."

I closed my eyes. "This is just a dream."

"Or Orphana."

"You're only saying what I wanna hear."

"No, I'm not."

"Yeah, you are. You're acting as a mouthpiece for my subconscious desire to absolve myself of responsibility."

"Don't overthink this."

"It comes natural. I got it from Mom."

"You were a kid!"

I opened my eyes and looked up at him. "Yeah. A scared and lost one. Like I am now."

"We all are, when it comes down to it. We never stop being those children, really." He smiled, a twinkle of compassion and confidence in his demeanor. "But you can still change things."

"I'm not using that damned map."

"It might come in handy."

"Are you kidding? Have you noticed my track record?"

"You've been doing fine! What are you talking about?"

"Did you see what happened to us down there?"

"That was just one battle, not the war."

"I'm not using the map."

"There might be more than one way to use it."

I raised myself up on my elbows and studied his features. He looked the same. No, better. Healthier. Wiser. More... substantial. Even though the military had battered him, left him with a crushed heel and a broken heart, those scars had only enhanced the man he really was.

"Look," he said, "don't beat yourself up. When you're on the right side, half the war's already won."

I groaned and slumped back down on the cot. At least, I thought it was a cot. I'd been there a while, but remembered little of the in-between. I rested for a moment with my eyes closed, wondering whether to re-engage the specter.

That's when I recognized the smell of fresh bread. Bread and sagebrush. I opened my eyes.

The figure was gone. Rickety timber slats

stretched overhead, allowing fingers of sunlight to pierce a narrow musty room. I sat up. The blanket that had covered me dropped away and revealed my bare chest. My shredded shirt had been removed. Another cool print shirt bites the dust. *Great.* More importantly, however, the Ndocron vest was gone.

I instinctively reached up, lightly tracing my ribcage, or where my ribcage should have been. Now a strange crevice existed there. Its contours prickled, as if a thin, malleable membrane had replaced my flesh and bone, providing structure but not protection. How were my organs even functioning? Did I still have organs? Pressing my fingertips past the membrane both burned and gave way to a strange frigidity. What in the hell was I becoming?

I'd avoided looking at the Tau scar and the changes to my body, and I wouldn't break my streak now.

The cot creaked terribly as I slung my legs over the edge and sat up.

I was in a small wooden shack. A crate of moldering sundries sat atop a leaky case of dynamite and a roll of rusted barbed wire. A bucket of water, by the looks of it fresh and clean, rested on a wooden table at the bedside. I dipped my fingertips in the water. It was cool. Recently drawn. Dipped my fingers again, and tasted the liquid. I hadn't realized until then how parched I was, and I leaned over and slowly scooped handfuls of water before giving in and gulping directly from the bucket.

A brief survey of the shack revealed it to be roughly twelve by fifteen.

The Ndocron vest hung upon a weathered wooden door near a single boarded-up window. The vest was in two pieces, shorn presumably by my impact with Lex.

Lex. My gut sank just thinking about Rothbard and his juiced-up golem, the probability of another encounter with them, and the potential cost of such an encounter.

I managed to get up, standing long enough to gather my sea legs. I shuffled to the door and studied the vest. It had been charred and split right down the middle and it stank of sweat and carbon.

Flashes of movement were visible through the cracks in the door. Where was I? I leaned forward, peering through one of the slat openings. Desert scrub sloped away toward a wall of red stone. No immediate signs of life.

A rusty wrought iron bolt had been drawn into its cradle. I reached up and pulled it back, wincing as I did. My shoulder still hurt. The door creaked open, and I shielded my eyes from bright, harsh sunlight. A dry gusty breeze swirled grit into the room, causing the brush outside to rattle. I stood for a moment allowing my eyes to adjust.

Just past a copse of scraggly Joshua Trees rose a small plateau. Red and copper flashed in its crevasses. Along its spine stretched a row of ramshackle shanties. Although I could see no signs of life, the buildings looked in too good of a condition to have been completely abandoned. I closed the door, hoping to forego any encounter with real life for as long as possible.

As I turned my back to the door, pondering my next move, I jolted at the awareness that someone else was in the room.

Bernard leaned against a wall, arms crossed,

watching me.

"About time you showed up."

He tapped his wrist, as if motioning to a watch, and then made the OK symbol with his thumb and forefinger.

"Yeah? Then you got a bad sense of timing."

He doubled over, pretending to laugh. Then he pointed to a loaf of bread that sat on a plate atop a weathered wood stove. He began gesturing for me to eat.

"Where did that—?"

Bernard shook his head as if to say, *That doesn't matter.* Instead, he continued urging me to eat.

"I'm not hungry."

He nodded eagerly.

"No, I'm not. And I'm not going back to the Imperia either."

He frowned.

"Where am I?" Before he could respond, I said, "Forget it. I remember. I took the last gate. The one to the high desert. Barstow. Or Yermo. That's where this is, right? Figures. But if that gateway's around here, they'll try to track me down. They'll try to find me. And I'm not going back with them. You hear me?"

He shook his head.

"I'm not kidding, Bernard. No one else is gonna die because of me."

He shook his head even more vehemently.

"Yes, it was because of me! They think I can save them. And now look. Orphana's dead and we're in worse shape than before. For God's sake, look at me—I'm talking to an invisible street mime."

He put his hands on his hips and glared at me.

"I should've never promised to protect that thing, Bernard. There was another way and they just missed it. Ellie could've been wrong. My Dad, too. All that stuff about fate and destiny. They got the wrong guy, don't you see?"

Bernard dismissed my rantings with a wave of his hand.

"Oh, yeah? You'll see. Rothbard was right—if that map is good for anything, it's to help me get the heck outta here. If this is about me, I'm—"

My breath halted.

"The map." I felt at the back pockets of my jeans. Both were empty. "Where's the map?"

Bernard casually jabbed his thumb at a wooden stump upon which the map and the staff was. At its base, a colorful wool Mexican poncho lay neatly folded. I heaved a sigh of relief. Then the angel pointed to the bread again, as if to say, *Shut up and eat.*

"I told you, I'm not hungry."

He clamped his hands about his head in frustration. I was starting to feel sorry for the guy.

"So, how'd I get here?"

Bernard flapped his arms, looking like a big goofy bird.

"Right. Did you—? How'd you carry me?"

He simulated trudging up a steep hill with a huge weight, panting, while wiping sweat off his brow.

"I'm not that fat! And what about the food?" I gestured to the bread and water.

He looked offended, then pretended to twirl an invisible mustache.

"Wow," I mumbled. "You're a French chef also. I underestimated you."

He nodded mockingly.

"Either way, I'm not going back with them. I meant what I said. D'you hear me?!"

He smiled, not sarcastically, but as if to sympathize. Then he pointed to the food and the bed.

"I need a lot more than food and rest! Don't you get it?"

He folded his hands, pleading with me to eat.

"Oh, all right." I went to the stump and snatched the plate of bread. Looking down at the poncho, I said, "Please don't tell me this is for me."

He nodded.

"Wow. Oh, well. Guess it's better than being half naked."

I picked up the poncho, went to the cot, and plopped down on it, sending dust motes wafting into a glorious cloud.

The bread crust was a little dry, but the dough was warm and tasty. I didn't have the time or energy to wrap my head around how an angel could make bread on a wood burning stove. Nevertheless, I finished the loaf and chased it with a couple more handfuls of water.

My cell phone had lost its charge. Which was all the better. The last thing I needed was Rapha or Kanya rushing to my rescue.

My anxiety eventually ebbed into a weird detachment. Serenity was too strong a word for it. Maybe *numbness* was more appropriate. Nevertheless, between the relative stillness of the desert environs and the food in my gut, the weight of my plight seemed to abate a little.

I sat for a moment before shaking out the poncho. It was the colors of the Mexican flag. Good Lord.

Bernard might be an okay chef, but his choice of clothes was awful. Well, at least the fabric was soft. I slipped the poncho on and retrieved the map. Then I lay back down on the cot. Holding the cylinder out, I rotated it, studying the etchings on its exterior. Though worn, I could discern symbols of increscent moons, globus crucigers, shields, spears, and watery orbs.

There might be more than one way to use it.

That's what my father had said. Or, at least, the dream version of my father. But how else could the map be used? And did I even want to know? I rotated the cylinder, pondering its possibilities. Saving Ki's girlfriend from limbo, though troubling, wasn't the reason I was disconcerted. The prospect of peering into my own future was. Was doing that even lawful? I mean, in a cosmic sense. Mortals are what they are precisely because they're stuck in the present and they can't see into the future. Skirting the edges of time was more than just a breach of mortal law. It was forbidden fruit.

Right or wrong, after the incident in the Golem Prison, opting out now seemed like the most reasonable option. *The war isn't winnable,* Ki had said. Wasn't that the truth? But after everything that had transpired, how was *opting out* even possible?

And did I *really* want to do that?

I laid the map on my chest, fatigued. Tired. Drifting in thought. My aching body gave way to exhaustion. As I meandered into sleep, my last thought was to question whether Bernard might have spiked the bread with a sedative.

Whump! Whump! Whump!

The sound wrenched me from my sleep. Had a rotor fallen from the sky? No. Someone was pounding on the door. I bolted into a sitting position, sending the map clattering to the floor.

Shafts of orange sunlight blazed through the shack, arcing westward, indicating the setting of the sun. How long had I slept?

Whump! Whump! Whump!

The pounding was so fierce it rattled the slats and frame of the small structure. A hulking silhouette stood outside the door.

My hands rushed with adrenaline and storm energy. I glanced at the staff of undoing, which still lay on the wooden stump. It glowed in tandem with my panic. Lurching off the cot, I retrieved the staff, and turned to the door.

"Get back!"

Whump! Whump! Whump!

"I said, get back!"

"You will come with me!" a voice growled.

I immediately recognized the accent.

Lowering the staff, I scanned the room. Bernard was nowhere to be found. Retrieving the map, I slipped the cylinder in my back pants pocket.

"Go away," I grumbled.

"Mister Klammer will see you."

I watched the bodyguard's hulking frame stand poised outside the door of my shack. He could probably dismantle the entire structure with his bare hands. I sighed deeply. If destiny was real, then it had caught up to me. If not destiny, then Felix Klammer's bodyguard was at least a reminder that I couldn't escape the blunt of reality.

I unlatched the door and plopped back down on the cot. Blondie took two steps in, scanned the place, and leveled his gaze upon me.

"You are rested?"

"Rested?!" I chortled. "Seriously? I think I'm gonna need a few more weeks. Make that *months*."

He looked at me, not humored.

"I'm opting out," I said. "Tell that to your boss, I'm done with this gig. I'm giving him his money back. I'm splitting town and... and I'm retiring as far away from humanity as I possibly can get."

"You can tell him that."

"Good. I will."

"Gather your belongings."

"What belongings?" I motioned to the Ndocron vest. "That thing's shot. All I got is—" I thumped the staff on the floor "—this."

"Then bring it." He turned and walked out the door.

"Where?" I stood. "Where are we going?"

That's when I noticed a helicopter nestled in the scrub in the near distance. I ran out of the shack and pushed my way past the bodyguard for a better view.

The desert sky was dappled in dusky yellows and burnt gold. A sleek silver helicopter rested on a sandy flat, looking like an alien aircraft in a wilderness of stone and bracken. The fiery twilight glistened along its shiny fuselage and cockpit window.

"You came all this way for me?" I said.

"Distance is not an issue for Felix Klammer."

"Apparently not."

"Follow me." Blondie nudged past me and headed for the helicopter.

I wanted to object. Every cell in my body cringed at the thought of continuing with this gig. Klammer had recruited me into the Imperia. He was the puppeteer, manipulating the players, setting the stage. Sure, maybe Ki was right and the old man was losing it. Nevertheless, speaking with the reclusive billionaire was a chance not afforded many. And as his personal recruit, he deserved an earful from me. Besides, like it or not, my need for answers outweighed the temptation to run.

"Dammit," I muttered, before hurrying after the bodyguard.

Blondie navigated through the scrub and sandstone with surprising dexterity. It brought to mind the time he'd choked me out near my apartment, shortly after I'd met him and Klammer. He was deceptively quick for a guy his size. This made me wonder whether or not he was a Nomlie. Either way, the Swedish escort was not a person I wanted to tangle with again.

"Are there rattlesnakes out here?" I asked.

He didn't answer.

"What about corpses? Any corpses out here?"

When we reached the helicopter, the bodyguard opened the side door. Cool air sluiced from inside. Behind the tinted windows, the interior was dark. Still, I could make out Felix Klammer sitting in one of the bucket seats.

"Get in," Blondie said.

Looking up at Klammer caused a wave of anger to rise up inside of me.

"Did you know she was gonna die?" I said, bitterly. "Orphana. Did you know about that!?"

The billionaire said nothing.

"Get in," Blondie repeated, motioning to the set of aluminum stairs that descended to the skids.

I grumbled to myself and climbed in. Even though it was a luxury copter, there was not enough overhead to stand upright. Klammer motioned for me to sit and Blondie closed the door behind me. The dark cool environs wrapped me like a tourniquet.

Two rows of leather bucket seats faced opposite each other, separated by a flat console housing cupholders, a charging station, and several small video screens. It smelled like medicine. A breathing apparatus occupied the seat across from Klammer. I took the seat cattycorner from the billionaire.

I peered at him. My mind was swirling. My shoulder hurt, and the Tau scar seemed to bristle at the sight of the man.

"I'm confused," I said. "No. Let me restate that— I'm pissed off."

The familiar cage he'd worn over his head had been replaced by something smaller, more oval, and less medieval in appearance. My guess was that Quinn and Rapha had designed a more functional hood for our headless ring leader. However, it still looked like a bad prop from the last Mad Max film.

His voice—or rather, its transmission—rattled in the hardware of the mask. "Your displeasure is understandable, Mister Moon."

"So, did you know she was gonna die?"

"The possibility always existed."

"And you didn't think of... stopping us?"

"Eliminating the consequences of one's freedom is its own bondage."

"I thought you were gifted in Foresight?"

"Such gifting does not make one omniscient."

I placed the staff across my legs and peered at

him.

He wheezed, "The future is fluid, Mister Moon."

"Riddles." I shook my head. "Is that all you've got is riddles?"

He sat, without speaking, his breath rising and falling. His frame appeared frailer, less substantial than our last encounter. Like the rest of us, the First Guardian of the Imperia was withering away.

"It doesn't make sense," I said. "You led me to the map. You said the map is important. Game changing. With the map, we can defeat the Black Council. We can reunite the Imperia. Blah, blah, blah. But isn't that what you want me to do with it—change the future? Nix everybody's freedom? Insert myself into history and— *whoosh!*—rewrite the whole playbook? Isn't that what you're asking me?"

Klammer folded his hands on his lap. "You must not allow your anger to control your thinking, Mister Moon."

"Do you see this?!" I yanked the poncho up, exposing the Tau scar. "Yeah. Take a look at it."

He did. Tendrils of light emanated from my chest, casting an eerie glow upon the billionaire's mask. A chill passed through me as energy bristled deep inside my ribcage. Klammer peered at the anomaly in my solar plexus.

"Whatever is happening to me is happening fast." I released the fabric of my shirt and the glow gave way to the cool dark. "I never bargained for this, Klammer."

Sighing deeply, I hung my head. For a second, a malaise fell upon me. With it came despair. How easily it would be to succumb to this darkness. To surrender and let the emotional tide sweep me away. Yet no amount of cynicism could convince me that yielding to such nihilism was a reasonable response to my plight, much less the *inevitable* response.

Neither would it bring back Orphana.

I looked up. "So, what should I do?"

Klammer shifted in his seat. The action appeared painful, yet strident, as if his very physical existence was a protest against death.

"You have done well to acquire the map and the staff of undoing," he said. "They are of immeasurable worth and will be instrumental in the unfolding that follows."

I laid my hand upon the staff, wanting to query about its powers and how to summon them. But such a query would likely just evoke a round of cryptic instructions, so I kept my mouth shut.

"BioGen is still operational," he said.

"The facility downtown?"

"Correct. However, be forewarned, for it is guarded by magic. And other atrocities. The magician is waiting for you there. Indeed, he sees you as a stepping stone to the expansion of his power. You must confront him."

"So that stuff about teaming up to fight the Black Council?"

Klammer settled back in his seat. "Such an outcome may yet transpire."

"Now what the hell is *that* supposed to mean? That's exactly the type of stuff that gets everybody so mad at you."

"Balfour's fate, as is yours, is in the balance. The truth is, Mister Moon, you *want* to go back. You want to face them again—the magician and his creation. For somewhere inside you, you know that you can defeat them."

He was right. Dammit. *He was right.*

"Well," I said. "This time, I'm going it alone," I said. "Do you hear me? No one else is dying because of me."

"It is not within my power to prevent further death. Nor is it within yours. Indeed, such possibilities must exist."

"Then at least distract the others, send them on another mission or something. Maybe there's a pandemic they can prevent from breaking out. Or maybe they can stand on street corners and give out free hugs."

"They are bound to you, as you are to them. Your choice is not as to who follows you, but how, and where, you lead them."

I gnashed my teeth in dissent. I was in no position to make ultimatums. With Rothbard and his nuclear biot now loosed upon the world, it was best if I worried about my own role and leave the others to theirs.

"And Ki?" I said.

"I'm afraid that the Sixth Guardian is the wild card."

"Figures. And I'm a terrible card player."

Klammer motioned to his bodyguard, who then popped the door open. Dusk was nearing twilight. Blondie stood with his hands folded at his waist.

Klammer said, "I have scheduled someone to meet you in the ghost town. From there, you will be returned to your car. I have transferred money to your account in the event you need it to complete your assignment."

"Wait. Why don't you just take me in this?" I motioned to the helicopter.

"A previous engagement, I'm afraid. My apologies."

Klammer pointed to the door. I took the staff, rose, and began to exit. Before I did, I turned to him. "Just tell me one thing: can the biot be stopped?"

With apparent difficulty, Klammer angled his body and looked up at me. He did not speak right away. I wondered if he was probing my thoughts. Or perhaps he was peering into future possibilities and calculating my slim odds of survival.

His speaker box rattled, "All that is made can be unmade."

Dry wind gusted through the open door.

Klammer chuckled. "I have faith in you, Mr. Moon."

"Well, that's more than I can say for myself."

CHAPTER 22

I barely spoke to the driver. He'd received his instructions from Klammer and had no need to hear from me. He was a lanky guy with thick glasses and hair slicked back so tightly it appeared painted on. He could have passed for Jerry Lewis' version of the Nutty Professor, sans the buck teeth. He knew to leave me alone, but the little speaking he did suggested he was a lot sharper than the dweeb appearance he'd cultivated.

It was a shuttle van, and being that I was the only passenger, I helped myself to the entire middle seat. Of course, we hit traffic once we reached L.A., which added an additional half-hour to our drive time. I was too nervous to sleep and spent the time rehearsing plans of attack and studying the staff of undoing.

The wood appeared petrified. Though the staff was light, it remained solid and quite sturdy. Its shaft contained etchings and pictographs, mostly Hebrew in appearance. If they were keys to the use of the rod, I could not decipher them.

By the time we reached the Red Iguana, the evening crowd had begun to gather. The Cammy remained where I'd parked it. It was caked in a thin layer of dust. How many nights had I been gone? Though the car appeared untouched, a crumpled flyer was jammed under one of the wiper blades with the words *No Overnite Parking!* scrawled on it. I fired up the vehicle, brushed off the windshield, and drove to the city.

Going to Rothbard's by myself was a suicide mission. But I'd be damned if I would willingly jeopardize more lives in the process. Though the specifics were sketchy, I was resolved about my plan of attack.

Which meant I headed first for the Blue Crescent.

I parked in the alley and to my relief, Arlette's car was there. That woman was a workaholic. I'd put the odds at two-to-one that she was out of there within a year. Not because of lack of interest in the paranormal reporting business. Rather, her savvy and professionalism deserved more than stories about sewer gnomes and Laurel Canyon UFO sightings.

I left the staff on the passenger seat and locked the Cammy. The night was warm, muggy even. A haze clung to the ground. Industrial fog. The stink of the river had drifted inland and tainted the air. Music wafted in the background, strains of saxophone from some lost Bernard Herrmann score.

I punched the buzzer at the back door. Arlette answered it. She'd seen me coming.

"I've been trying to get a hold of you!" She wore a charcoal rib-knitted skirt with a white button-up business shirt and matching white tennies. Man, she looked great.

I said, "I'm sorry. My phone's dead."

"No wonder. And what are you wearing?" She glanced at the poncho and curled her lip.

"A gift from my guardian angel."

She scanned the alley. "Get in here."

I entered, and she closed the door behind me.

"You alone?" I asked.

"For now. Ashton's outta town. Neville ran to the store. Penny's on her way. Why do you ask?" She knew something was up.

I drew my fingers through my hair. How should I approach this?

"What's wrong?" she asked.

"Arlette, we need to talk."

She folded her arms and squinted in suspicion. "Lemme guess—you have something else going on, don't you? Another gig maybe..."

I looked at her. She knew.

"I'm right," she said. "Ain't I?"

"Well..."

"Cough it up, Moon. You've been acting weird since... Well, you've always acted kind of weird. But ever since that accident. There's something you've been keeping from me, isn't there?"

I opened and then closed my mouth. I had purposely hidden any mention of my involvement in the Imperia, but deep down I knew that keeping it under wraps would be impossible. Right now, the last thing I needed was more secrets, more pretending to be someone I wasn't.

"Hello?" she said. "Anybody in there?"

"I'm thinking."

"Maybe this will help." Arlette went into her office and returned with an electronic tablet. She opened a webpage, handed the tablet to me, and pointed to the headline. It read, *Nomlies Sought in Connection to Crime.*

Oh, shit. I looked at her.

"The picture?" she said.

Under the headline stretched a two-paneled picture, which I recognized. Although the photo was blurry and pixelated, my likeness was unmistakable. It was right after the jump, when I'd crashed into the trash enclosure. The first pic was a blur of me in midstride. The second of me standing shit-faced between the sheared dumpster. My stomach dropped. I knew we should have been more careful about running around the city in broad daylight.

"Go on," Arlette said, crossing her arms.

"Do I have to?"

"Yeah. You have to,"

I read from the article, "What is now being called *Murder at the Magic Dragon* has taken an unprecedented twist. Police reported that, upon arrival to the crime scene, an autonomous robotic skeleton managed to escape, leading to a bizarre chase in the heart of Chinatown.

"'I saw it coming right at me,' said Justine Linn, a nearby business owner. 'It was like something out of the movies.' Although the police have not disclosed the exact nature of the robotic component, Linn described it as a human-like head and skeletal system moving at tremendous speed. 'I've never seen anything like it,' Linn exclaimed."

I looked at Arlette like a guilty child would his scolding mother.

"Keep going," Arlette said. "The good part is next."

I continued reading, reluctantly. "It was the arrival of several Nomlies—one of which was described by witnesses as a Warper, an individual who is capable of passing through space at will, that left the locals buzzing and police hunting for answers. According to eye witness testimony, the mysterious crime fighting superheroes apprehended the biotic component and left the scene, leaving police to wonder at the nature of the murder and its connection, if any, to the crime fighting group. Police are seeking the Nomlies for further questioning."

I looked at Arlette, and she raised one eyebrow. When I didn't respond, she said, "That guy in the picture looks a helluva lot like my best reporter."

I handed the tablet back to her.

"Ashton would disagree. I mean, about me being your best reporter."

She stared at me, unmoved by my attempt at humor. And she kept staring.

Finally, she said, "Did you think I'd never find out?"

I released an exhausted sigh. "You don't know the half of it."

She studied me. "Okay. Then tell me."

"It's a really, really long story."

"If this is any indication," she shook the tablet at me, "it's a story I need to hear about."

"Yeah. You're right."

I chewed on the inside of my lip. *Well, here goes nothing.* I started to remove my poncho.

"Hey, hey!" She tried to stop me. "What're you doing?"

"It's all right. I have to show you something,"

I removed the poncho and stood with the Tau scar on full display. I watched Arlette's features move from shock, to wonder, to horror.

"My... God." The color drained from her face. "You... your..."

She slowly reached out to touch it.

I stopped her. "You shouldn't do that."

"Why... what'll happen? Reagan. My God. What is it? What happened to you?"

"Remember that cross? The one that Ellie gave me. The Tau. I was wearing it on Spiraplex that night. When the lightning struck, it..." I shrugged. "It got burned into me."

She was gaping. Staring. Trying to make sense of what she was seeing. "Does it hurt?"

"Yeah. Sometimes."

"It's like..." She stepped closer. "Like a hole into space. Or somewhere else. I can't believe it. Is this for real? My God. I can see myself. Reagan, I can see myself in there."

She'd grown deathly pale. When she swayed forward, I took her by the arm and said, "You better sit down."

She craned to keep her eye on the scar as I led her to a chair. She sat down and I faced her, my naked upper body in full display.

"It's getting bigger," I said. "It keeps growing. Every time I, well... The lightning strike—it gave me these powers. Like that article said. I can, well, teleport. Or just move super fast. And see things, invisible things—demons and angels. And sometimes my hands..." I extended my hands as if preparing to zap someone.

Her eyes grew wide.

"Sometimes my hands can radiate this... energy. Arlette. I-I've... changed."

Her mouth moved, but she did not speak. The confidence and poise that always possessed the woman had been blasted from orbit. I had never seen my boss as absolutely undone as she was at that moment.

I put the poncho back on.

She breathed heavily in an obvious attempt to compose herself. Finally, she took one last deep breath and straightened.

"Then it's true," she said. "You're a Nomlie. Or, one of the Imperia. My God. Reagan, why didn't you say something?"

I shrugged. "It's not the type of thing you publicly announce. Besides, I think I'm still pretty much normal. Well, except for the black hole in my chest."

"So, what does this mean for, um…?"

"My job?"

"Yeah, well that, too. But, I mean, you fight crime and… evil. With the Imperia. You know them, then? I just can't believe this."

"I know it's a lot to process," I said.

"Ya think?"

"Anyway, I need you to do something for me."

"I can't hide you from the cops, if that's what you mean."

"No. At least, not now. It's about that story you wanted me on. The Magic Dragon."

"Yeah?"

"Well, it's connected to something much, much bigger. It definitely involves BioGen. And Balfour Rothbard."

"So that murder…"

"Rothbard was involved, one way or another. Anyway, he's back in the AI business. Only this time, he's got this bad ass biot that he's hoping to turn into some kind of super soldier. Some kind of a god. I don't know. He wants me to help him. Arlette, I need to stop them."

She peered at me. "It sounds like you need to get the police involved."

I shook my head. "I'm not sure they can be trusted. Rothbard has too much influence. Too many connections."

"Then what about the other, well, superheroes?"

"Please, don't call us that."

"Well, you guys are a team, right?"

"I can't get them involved. Not now."

"That doesn't sound like a good idea, Moon. Shouldn't you be sticking together?"

I didn't want to think about the team now. Sticking together hadn't helped us... especially Orphana.

I said, "There's something I need from you."

"You mean besides covering for your moonlighting?"

I pulled the cylinder containing the star chart from my back pocket. She rose, staring at the device with growing apprehension.

"Arlette, I need you to protect this."

"What is it?"

"It's... too complicated."

"Really?" she said flatly. "What is it?"

"Um... *really*. It's best you don't know."

She just stood there, looking from the cylinder to me.

"You gotta trust me on this, Arlette. I'll explain later. But right now, I need you to hide this. Somewhere safe. Really safe. Where no one can find it. If I don't come back, you have to get it to the others."

"The others..." She looked at me long and hard. "Are you recruiting me?"

"Not really. Okay, sort of."

"And what do you mean, *if you don't come back*? I thought you were a—"

"Don't say it."

"—superhero."

"Please, Arlette. Just trust me. I need your help."

She looked away, shaking her head in apparent disbelief. Her jaw was clamped, accentuating the tendons along her neck. She was dazed, skeptical, and slightly perturbed. Her level-headedness had been broad-sided by the clown car of insanity that was my new normal.

"Arlette," I said, stepping closer to her.

Despite now knowing that I was a freak of nature, she did not withdraw from me.

I continued, "All this stuff, this weird, crazy stuff we report on. Vampires. Ghosts. Urban legends. UFOs. It's true! At least, a lot of it's true. Hell, probably most of it." I looked her square in the eyes. "I've seen it, Arlette. The world's a lot stranger than we ever realized."

A glint of inspiration flashed in her eyes. She'd already reached that conclusion. And was about to take another plunge.

Arlette took the map.

Friends of the Imperia, Rapha called them. *They are everywhere.*

"Okay, Moon," she said. "I'll hide it. But I want you to do something for me."

"What is it?"

"You come back in one piece, got it?"

Before I could thank her, garbled electronic static sounded outside in the alley.

"What is that?" Arlette brushed past me but I beat her to the door.

Sliding the hatch back, I looked through the peep hole. A police car was parked at the mouth of the alley. Its spotlight illuminated the Cammy. An officer stood at the passenger side of the car, shining his flashlight beam into the window. A thin trail of smoke twined from the vehicle.

Inside, the staff was smoldering.

CHAPTER 23

I slipped the door hatch shut and turned around. "It's the police."

"They're here for you?" Arlette said.

"I don't think so."

"Then what?"

"I don't know. They're at my car. Something is... smoking inside it."

"Smoking? What is smoking in your car?"

"It's, uh... it's a staff. I think it's the staff of Moses, actually. Maybe."

Her jaw grew slack.

"I'll explain later," I said.

"I'm not sure that's possible. What're you going to do?"

"I dunno. Let me think."

"Well, if you don't want your car or the staff of Moses burning up, you better get out there."

I turned around and pulled the hatch open again. I could make out the symbols along the staff glowing a musky orange. A trail of smoke curled out of the partially opened window into the night. Why was it smoking? A second officer joined the first, this one with his flashlight beam fixed on my license plate. I closed the hatch.

"I gotta get outta here."

"Well, you can go out the front if you want. But I'm not lying to the cops. Besides, your car is right there."

"No. I need the staff. And my car."

Arlette watched as I paced nervously.

Finally, she said, "Don't you have, like, powers that you can use?"

I scowled at her. "Not really. I mean, maybe."

I slipped open the hatch again, trying to analyze the situation through the tiny hole. Was there a way to create some kind of distraction, or maybe reason with them? No, my picture was already plastered all over the news. Damn. Where was Bernard when I needed him?

The crackle of the radio sounded, and one of the officers retreated to their vehicle. The other remained on the passenger side of the Cammy, his light shining across the staff. He appeared tentative of the occult-looking object. As he attempted to open the car door, a blur of motion passed through my field of vision.

"What the—"

Something else was out there. I refocused my gaze to see that the officer was engaging a third figure. The unicorn patch on the jeans was a dead giveaway.

It was Allie, the psion who'd helped us at Third Street Shul. The flood lamp was now fixed on her.

"That's it," I said. "I'm going out there."

"I thought you were trying to avoid the cops."

"I am. But there's someone else out there now. She needs my help. Or maybe I need hers. I'm not sure."

"God, this is getting really weird."

I took the door handle and pointed at the map in Arlette's hand. "Hide that."

"Okay, Moon."

"And cover your ass. Forget about me. Okay?"

She nodded.

Then I unlatched the door, opened it, and slipped out. I immediately raised my hands and faced the officers. Allie turned, smiled, and winked. I had an idea where this was headed.

"Hold it right there." A medium built Hispanic male stepped away from the police car with his hand on the butt of his pistol. "Sir. Please stay right there. Are you the owner of that car?"

"Yes, sir."

The officer at the patrol car repositioned the floodlight on me. I shielded my eyes.

The cop who stood at the Cammy replied, "Keep your hands up."

"Yes, sir."

"Do you two know each other?" He motioned to Allie.

We both hesitated. Which wasn't good.

"I saw smoke," Allie blurted. "That's all. I was just passing by, and..." She shrugged.

Too late. He was suspicious of us. Redirecting his attention to me, he asked, "So what is smoking in your vehicle?"

I said, "It's a staff, sir."

"A staff."

"Yes, sir. Like a wizard's staff."

"Okay. Hold it. Keep your hands up. So, why is it smoking?"

"It's... uh. I'm not sure."

"Is it toxic? Is it a weapon?"

"A weapon? No. I mean, not really."

"Whaddyou mean, *not really*?"

"I mean, I'm not sure. You see... How can I say this? It has energy, powers, Officer."

"Powers."

"Like *divine* powers."

He peered at me. "Sir, have you been drinking?"

"Not recently. But I've been really tempted to start up again."

The officer glanced at his partner.

"If you want," I said, "I can come over there and try to put it out."

A short pause. A garbled voice sounded on the radio.

"Okay, you can lower your hands. Come on over." He removed his hand from the butt of his gun, apparently satisfied that I was not a threat. Crazy, perhaps, but not murderous.

I descended the steps and approached the Cammy. The floodlight followed me.

The officer's personal radio chirped; he plucked it from its clip. A brief, but inaudible exchange with someone on the other end followed. He snipped the radio back in place.

The officer brushed smoke out of his face. "This vehicle is registered to a Reagan Moon. Is that you?"

"Yes, sir."

"Do you know that you are wanted for questioning regarding the incident at the Magic Dragon?"

"I just learned that."

"Good. Then we're going to need to take you to the station, Mr. Moon. For questioning."

"I'm under arrest?"

"No. Not at the moment. But we need you to stop

that thing from smoking before we go anywhere."

"Yes, sir."

I removed my keys from my pants pocket. But I was unsure how I would quench the smoldering rod. Why was it even burning? The officer stepped aside to allow me access to the passenger door just as a gust of air whooshed past.

"Hey!" the other officer barked, looking from side to side. "Where'd she go?"

He pointed the floodlight down the alley. She was not there. A crunch of gravel sounded nearby. The man swung the light in that direction and Allie's black high-topped tennis shoe swept through the beam.

"Hey!" the officer shouted.

However, the shadow-jumper had disappeared.

Between the herky-jerky movements of their flashlight beams and the floodlight, the alley had become a riot of coruscating light and shadows. A soft thud sounded near the patrol car, followed by a loud hissing.

"There!" The officer near me produced his pistol. He glanced over his shoulder and yelled back at me, "Sir, remain right there."

I nodded.

Returning his attention to the commotion, he crept towards the patrol car. His light illuminated the rear driver's side tire as it deflated. A screw driver protruded from the sidewall.

I generally have great respect for the cops. Running from them is not high on my list of appropriate responses. In fact, it was *never* on my list. Until now.

As both officers gazed in the direction of their vehicle, my opportunity became obvious. I'd considered orchestrating a diversion, and it appeared my young friend had accommodated me. If I didn't get away now, I'd be taken to the station and possibly held there for a very long time. With the police car disabled, my escape route was clear. I circled around the Cammy to the driver side. I slipped my key in the car door, and softly unlocked the Cammy.

"Stop!" one of the cops shouted.

I looked up. Allie stood in plain view, twenty-five to thirty feet beyond the police car. Her hands were raised as she backed towards the street. She was leading them away from me.

"Stay right there!" the cop with his gun drawn ordered her. "Do not move."

"I'm sorry, officer," she said. "I had to do it."

"Stay right there, young lady!"

"Please, don't shoot."

She glanced at me while taking another single step back.

As the police officers fanned out and moved towards her, I popped the car door open. Thankfully, they didn't hear me. But starting up the Cammy would definitely get their attention. Nevertheless, with my car pointed the opposite direction, and the alley ahead of me wide open, I could be out of there in three seconds. Hopefully, without anyone being shot.

A haze of smoke had filled the cab and now fumed into the night air. It smelled oddly aromatic. Glancing at the cops to ensure they were still in pursuit of Allie, I slipped into the driver's seat and inserted the key into the ignition. *Here goes nothing.*

I fired up the Cammy, jammed it into gear, and burnt rubber.

Behind the roar of the engine, the echoes of yelling sounded. A blur swept from the shadows nearby, followed by a thud in the bed of the Cammy. I looked in the rearview mirror and saw Allie hanging on for dear life.

The car clipped a metal trash can, sending its contents exploding across the asphalt. We skidded into the street. I swerved, barely missing a guy on a bike, and turned sharply onto a side street. The police siren sounded behind us, but the cops wouldn't get far with a flat tire.

Glancing at the staff, I did a doubletake. The rod had stopped glowing; the letters were now just dying coals. Had it begun smoking in response to the police's proximity? Was it a summons? Or maybe, like Frodo's scabbard, its smoldering was evidence of approaching Orcs. Answers would have to wait.

Having worked at the Crescent for years, I knew my way around this part of town. The old BioGen facility was on the Eastside, just south of the Arts District, positioned between food processing plants and prop design studios. It occupied an entire city block.

I kept to side streets and calculated we could reach our destination within ten minutes, provided we didn't crash or get arrested. It was roughly ten o'clock, which meant there'd be plenty of traffic still. Angelinos are mostly nocturnal creatures, and night seemed to bring out the worst in drivers. No doubt L.A.'s finest were being hailed at this moment to be on the lookout for an El Camino with faded racing stripes and a smoldering wizard's staff in the passenger seat, fleeing from police. If I was arrested for evading arrest, I'd need more than just superpowers to free myself from the mess that would follow.

I glanced in the mirror to see Allie with her back to the cab, holding on. As there was no sign of the cops, I skidded to the curb, turned around, and thumped on the window. Allie leapt out of the back, and I unlocked the door. She opened the door. The remaining traces of smoke rushed out of the cab. Allie didn't enter, but was transfixed by the staff.

I snatched it and said, "Hurry up! Get in!"

She did. I lay the rod between us and tore off.

"I had a feeling I'd see you again," I said.

"And here I am."

"You've been following me. Haven't you?"

"On and off."

"I thought so."

She paused. "Hey, I'm sorry about Orphana. I liked her."

"I did too. Hang on."

I took a hard turn onto Sixth and we blew past Skid Row.

"Look," I said. "I'm working alone now."

"I hadn't heard."

"Well, now you have."

"By the way," she said, "you're welcome."

"For...? Oh. Right. Thanks for helping me get outta that bind."

"So, I guess you ain't working alone then."

Darned kid, I grumbled to myself.

I crunched the brakes as a homeless lady pushing a shopping cart limped across the street. Still no sign of the police. I navigated around her and hit the gas.

"Look," I said. "No one else is getting hurt on my behalf."

"Who says it's on your behalf?"

"You know what I mean. All this Seventh Guardian bull—?"

"You can't stop me from helping!"

"Why don't you find someone else to help?"

"Sorry. I'm in this, Reagan. I was in it way before you ever showed up."

I shook my head, more out of frustration than disagreement. I took the next turn extra sharp, just for emphasis.

We rattled over some railroad tracks before entering an industrial area. Several homeless tents and lean-tos greeted us. I located a gravel road that ran parallel to a drainage ditch. This was the back of the BioGen property. I slowed and turned the car's lights off. Tattered tarps draped tall razor-wire crowned fencing that stretched the length of the block. Behind the fence, I could make out a dull, yellowish glow inside the complex. The place sat like a derelict compound in the urban cityscape. *Keep Out* signs were posted every ten feet, promising to prosecute trespassers with impunity. We came up on the Northwest corner of the property. An empty guardhouse stood before a heavily chained gate. I parked as far away from a streetlight as possible and turned off the Cammy.

"Now what?" Allie asked.

"I told you, I'm going this alone."

She turned to me. "Dude, shut up already."

While I didn't mind being a pain in the ass, I was feeling bad for the kid and decided to give it a rest. Besides, her help might come in handy.

Across the street spread a darkened salvage yard. Further down the sidewalk, several transients meandered around a glowing lantern. I allowed my senses to unspool.

I did not think of this intuition in terms of psychic powers. It was more like instincts on steroids. In fact, I was learning to follow my hunches, move, and trust that something, or maybe someone, would guide my steps. If I believed in luck, I could probably dismiss it as such. But it was more than luck. However, the word *fate* was still way too loaded. Whatever this sixth sense was, it made flying by the seat of my pants appear way more calculated than it actually was.

I grabbed the staff and stepped out of the Cammy. Allie followed suit. The staff had stopped smoking and it felt cool to the touch. Peering through the ragged tarping on the fence, I could make out several loading docks a hundred or more yards away. This would be a good place to start.

I tapped the fence with the staff just to make sure it wasn't electrified. I looked up. It was twelve feet high, not counting the razor-wire. Going over it was out of the question.

Even worse, the atmosphere was laden with foul creatures. This place reeked of Invisibles. Like its owner, a canopy of evil blanketed his sphere. A sense of foreboding gnawed at me. I might as well have been trying to sneak into Jeffrey Dahmer's apartment for a midnight snack.

"What're we gonna do?" Allie asked.

"I'm not sure."

"So how are you gonna stop the magician?"

"I don't know."

She hesitated. "Do you typically rush into life and death situations without a plan of attack?"

I looked at her. "Hey, you're the one who wanted to help."

She scrunched her face. "You're right. I won't ask any more questions."

"Good. Now hold this." I handed her the staff, and she took it.

I gripped the fence and peered through the tarps again. The asphalt lot was dotted with crates and miscellaneous machinery. Air conditioning units. Industrial grade. Dozens of them, stacked three and four high. Forming virtual canyons. On the other side was more refrigeration equipment, condensers and coils of copper tubing. Either Rothbard was attempting to simulate subarctic cold or he liked working in an icebox. I could see no sign of movement. Despite several vapor lamps on the building, no cameras were visible.

As I prepared to step away, an electric chill passed through my hands. The wire fence was acting as a conductor.

I removed my hands from the fencing. Without the vest, using the storm gifts would only speed up the expansion of the scar. But unless I wanted to knock on the front door and announce my arrival, this was the most obvious way onto the BioGen property.

"Stand back," I told Allie.

She did.

Energy rose in me as I gripped the chain link. Currents of electric blue radiated through my fingertips and infused the surrounding links. Heat blistered my solar plexus as the metal glowed molten red and withered before me. I bit back a howl of pain. The stink of solder and burnt flesh filled the air. Tumbling through the fissure in the fence, I doubled over, gripping my chest.

"Reagan! Are you all right?"

Allie bent over me, her eyes wide.

I struggled to my feet and turned back to see the gaping orifice of twisted, seething metal I'd passed through. The storm energy subsided in my hands, but my chest burned like a witch's cauldron.

"We have to hurry." I took the staff from her, wincing at the motion.

As I prepared to jog across the asphalt, a large shadow bolted into view. I froze. My skin bristled. The footfall was padded, inhuman. And with it came the stink of wet fur.

"Oh, no."

"What is it?" Allie whispered.

"Something big. And hairy. C'mon," I said, angling us away from the movement.

I'd only taken three or four steps when my foot sank into a pile of soft warm matter. I gagged at the stink.

Dog shit.

A load the size of a medicine ball.

I yanked my foot out and frantically swiped it on the ground.

From behind a tower of wooden crates a figure emerged and crept toward us. It was the height of a minivan... with paws. A low growl followed. Make that several low growls. Yellow feral eyes fixed upon us. Then another set appeared. And a third.

How many of these beasts were there?

My vision adjusted in time to make out a single massive canine body... with three heads. All its jaws were foaming as it galloped straight at us.

CHAPTER 24

In ancient Greek mythology, Cerberus was the Hound of Hades, the dog which guarded the gates of hell. It prevented the dead from leaving. But minitours, griffins, and centaurs were figments of the ancient imagination. So how in the hell had a real Cerberus found its way to downtown Los Angeles? Only in this case, it appeared that Fido was about keeping people *out*, not *in*.

The massive hound skidded to a stop and crouched, snarling, perhaps fifteen feet away. The stench of mange came with it.

Allie had created distance between us, strafing to her right. Tactically, this forced the dog to choose which one of us to concentrate its attention on. Clearly, it was sizing me up. At least, two of the heads were. The third one glared at Allie.

The creature was practically the size of a rhino, with girth to match. However, its heads seemed oddly incongruous with its body, as if stitched together in a Frankensteinian fever dream. The heads were misaligned with the trunk, creating a top-heavy appearance. As it crept forward, slinging drool from its gaping jaws, I detected a slight limp.

I extended the staff in a protective posture. However, another sensation was mingling with my defensive impulse—this creature was in pain.

My body tingled with energy. Tesseracts coiled the atmosphere around me. If I jumped, my entire torso might disappear. A hard bargain for a guy with already limited options.

Allie continued strafing, which caused the dog to stop its advance. That's when I noticed that the pupils of its eyes whirred with a familiar metallic recalibration.

This wasn't a real dog. At least, it was only *partly* so. A biotic Cerberus: the creation of Balfour Rothbard. Which probably made it far more lethal than your average quarter-ton canine.

In a way, it made sense. Why purchase three dogs when you could just make one with three heads? The ultimate junkyard dog. Definitely less poop to clean up. Of course, you'd need a bull dozer rather than a shovel for that job. My only question was whether three-headed robotic dogs saved on food or not.

Allie had crept into the shadows. Once again, she was playing decoy. I stared past the monster to the loading dock. My odds of outrunning this creature were extremely low. And unless I wanted to become a walking portal, I couldn't teleport.

"Hey!" Allie waved her hands. "Here, doggy."

The beast turned her direction and snarled. It crouched and stalked toward its new prey. Allie burst toward a wall of wooden crates. The dog released a garbled yelp and galloped after her. She was giving me time to run, but I hesitated. If that thing got a hold of her, it would tear her to pieces.

She reached the shadows seconds before the dog

skidded to a stop. And dematerialized. The creature peered into the darkness, puzzling over the disappearance of its prey.

"Hey!" Having transported through the shadows, Allie scrambled to the top one of the crates, some fifteen feet above the beast. "Yoo-hoo! Come 'n get me!"

Jumping over a small chasm, she leapt onto another tier of crates with the dog following below in a near frenzy. Glancing back at me she yelled, "Get moving!" before plunging into a thick shadow and vanishing again.

She was right. I had to get moving. As I bolted forward, my foot slipped from the dog shit, and I stumbled to the ground.

Fido spun about. Its eyes, all six of them, fixed upon me. I got to my feet as Allie skidded from the shadow of a refrigeration unit on the opposite side of the dog.

She whistled loudly. "Dinner time!" Then she lunged into the aisle of machinery.

The dog complied and followed her.

As the beast tore down the canyon of crates and machinery after the girl, I lowered my head and ran like hell. My heart thundered in my chest. About halfway there, I swerved around a stack of pallets and ducked behind a forklift.

I stood panting and looked back. There was no sight of Allie or the dog. Slabs of odd obsidian-like chunks lay to my right. The material possessed a dull luster, absorbing light rather than refracting it. Nefarium. Conjured into this dimension by some Summu Nuran henchman, it was once thought to be an indestructible compound. At least until I showed up. No doubt Rothbard was doing his best to upgrade the material for his purposes.

Suddenly, canine yelping peeled into the night air as the girl came vaulting over a nearby storage container and landed lightly beside me.

"C'mon!" she said. "Let's go!"

Grabbing my hand, she yanked me forward, practically breaking my neck in the process.

Behind us, the dog's cries became frenzied howls. Its footfalls pounded the asphalt, hot on our heels. We scrambled past some rusty steel girders. A straight path to the docks now lay ahead of us.

"Go!" Allie said. "That way! Go!" She veered off from me in hopes of peeling the creature away.

Despite my jogging experience, she was clearly the faster runner. Which worked against me. As the slower prey, Fido zoned in upon me. I could practically feel his breath on my neck. I'd never make it.

I was maybe twenty yards from the docks. My eyes frantically scanned the area for doorways, drains, ladders, anything that might provide a way of escape from the charging monster. Nothing. I had to jump. Either that or become a fresh hot platter of Gravy Train for this mammoth pooch.

As I focused in on a tesseract, the creature's hot breath pelted me. It chomped the air, sending saliva spraying from behind me. Another snap of its jaws. This time, the beast nipped my poncho, spinning me around and sending me sprawling across the asphalt, flat on my back.

I slid across the pavement with the staff raised. Storm energy was skittering along its crest.

When I came to a rest, the Cerberus pounced on me.

Its heads bent over me, eyes burning with a cold fury. Drool lathered me as the jaws snapped in rapid succession. Its breath stank of blood and lube. Teeth of razor steel glinted in the glow of the staff. If this thing actually got a hold of me, it would tear me in pieces, preferably one piece for each head. I'd managed to hoist the rod overhead, pressing it with two hands above my chest. Cords of energy crackled from the piece, flicking the beast as it sought to devour me.

However, I had the distinct sense that the staff was not generating this energy. I was. The rod was but a conductor of the authority I already possessed.

The staff has no inherent power, Allie had said. *It's just a conduit. The power's in the hand that holds it.*

Suddenly, a flare of electric blue burst around me, and the dog leapt off of me with a great howl of pain. The rank odor of singed fur filled the air. The beast stumbled back, shaking its heads as if dazed.

I scrambled to my feet, extending the rod like Gandalf fending off a demon of the deep. Electrical charges now skittered along the beast's torso, illuminating seams and stitches in its body, worming into the biomechanical components of its frame.

However, Fido had already managed to shake off the storm energy. Its heads lowered their gaze upon me and issued a pained, rabid snarl. I glanced back at the loading dock. Except for several random piles of fractured asphalt, the path was wide open. Unless I could figure out a way to terminally zap this thing, I'd have to run.

From out of the shadows, Allie dashed, and positioned herself between the dog and me.

"Run, Reagan! Go! Go! Go!"

The Cerberus scratched the ground, preparing to charge the girl.

No! I'd be damned if another person was going to die on my watch.

So, I ran, but not away. Instead, I cut diagonally, snatching a chunk of asphalt from the ground with my free hand as I went. In a single motion, I flung the object at the beast. Ideally, I would have liked to bean the dog in one of its snouts. Instead, the asphalt hunk struck the creature in the ribs. Still, that got the creature's attention.

"C'mon, boy!" I yelled, and kicked into a full-on sprint.

The dog released a garbled yelp as it pursued me. Knowing I couldn't outrun the beast, I had another plan. Even though tesseracts twined the atmosphere, I wasn't planning to jump. In fact, in order for my plan to work, I needed to let the dog get closer.

As I ran, I shifted the staff to my opposite hand. The storm energy coursed my limbs again. My chest prickled as the Tau scar sizzled to life. The dog was panting and releasing awful frothing sounds. Its jaws snapped in succession as it closed in on me.

But it had to get closer.

I glanced over my shoulder. Allie shouted something.

Closer.

Its breath blasted me.

As the hound overshadowed me, I spun around and dropped to my back, extending the staff like a spear before me. The dog's motion carried it straight into the glowing rod, and the staff sank into the creature's massive ribcage. However, its speed and the trajectory of its flight carried the animal directly over my body. It careened in a slow-motion arc over me, impaled upon the staff, before thudding to the ground just past my head.

I jumped to my feet. The beast lay writhing. Its claws tore at the weapon protruding from its chest. The heads whipped back and forth, releasing a pitiful wail. Storm energy seethed through the creature and it racked its torso with spasms.

Allie ran up and stood beside me, panting. Both of us watched the dying bio-dog.

"Are you crazy?" she said.

"I had a plan."

"Yeah. A crazy plan."

"It was no crazier than yours."

The dog managed to stagger to its feet. We moved back as the creature stumbled drunkenly. Its jaws snapped aimlessly at the air. Veins of blue electricity twined from the staff, coursing the monster's chest. The stink of burnt fur made me gag. The light in its eyes flickered and, one by one, faded. The creature tilted forward, and then caught itself. Foam trailed from its jaws. Finally, the heads sagged. Its front paws crumpled forward and it knelt there.

Like Len, this creature was the tortured offspring of a mad scientist, assembled in a laboratory and destined to suffer in this world. I couldn't help but pity the poor thing. Perhaps killing it was an act of mercy.

I approached the animal and placed my hand on one of its heads. It was the size of an ox. Len had warned us of other strange beings crafted by Rothbard. If this creature was any indication, we were probably walking into a chamber of horrors. I just hoped to God I wouldn't have to face some robotic feline along the way.

I patted the creature's head as its body sank to the ground and became limp. The storm energy subsided. Taking hold of the staff, I yanked it from the creature's body. The familiar green liquid drooled from the wound. If I hadn't already profaned the rod of Moses, then this most likely had.

Now we had to figure out how to get into the BioGen facility. I straightened and scanned the area. Sweat sopped the front of my poncho. While I couldn't see any security cameras, I was sure Rothbard knew we were here.

The southwestern end of the property was laden in shadow. A shorting vapor lamp revealed more loading docks and several stairwells traveling up and down the expansive warehouse.

"Let's go." I motioned Allie to follow me and headed in that direction.

Our impending confrontation with Balfour Rothbard and Lex loomed in my mind like a raised guillotine. Discussing a plan of attack seemed almost pointless. Instead, I concentrated on convincing myself that I was worthy of—no, *serviceable* for—the job ahead.

"Where're the others?" Allie asked. "Shouldn't we wait for them?"

I glanced sideways at her.

"They're on their way," she said. "Right?"

I shrugged. "Probably."

"What?" she said.

"They're probably on their way."

"You say that like you don't want their help. C'mon, you can't be serious."

"Look, I just don't want anyone else dying. That's all."

"Do you have a death wish or something? Look, maybe there's a better chance no one else dies if we *can* get more help."

"Maybe. Or maybe we just give Rothbard a bigger target to shoot at."

"Wow." She shook her head and looked away. "I didn't realize that you were that big of a pessimist."

"I prefer to call myself a realist."

"Right. I'll make sure to add that to your bio. Sheesh."

I slowed as I reached the incline of the dock area. Corrugated metal roll-up doors bore thick padlocks. Stacks of pallets rose on either end. Stairwells led to and from metal doors with biometric scanners. Apparently, getting inside was going to pose a problem.

An indistinct sloughing sounded somewhere.

"Look!" Allie said, pointing to a misshapen figure bearing down on us from the lot.

More monsters!?

I raised the staff in hopes of fending off whatever threat we now faced.

"What the—" I gaped.

A metallic serpentine torso glinted in the light. Atop this frame rested something malformed, moving in and out of the shadows. I steadied myself and began drawing up the storm energy. However, the approaching form veered away from us towards a darkened archway below one of the docks. Whatever it was, we were not the object of its pursuit.

"What is that?" Allie asked.

"I'm not sure." I lowered the staff. "But it might give us some help."

We crept in the direction of the fleeting form.

It reached the docks and disappeared in shadow.

As we approached, the metallic vertebrae came into view. Along the spine were small moist gears. Atop this skeletal frame sat a canine head. It had detached from the torso. A trail of green liquid traced across the asphalt from the carcass of the Cerberus.

Just as K-111 had done, Fido had abandoned its neural skin. Now it was making its way home.

The archway that the creature writhed before was boarded up. Yet the jaws of the beast tore aimlessly at the wooden slats, spasmodically attempting to gnaw its way in. I approached and ripped several pieces of wood aside. Thick metal grates had been peeled back, revealing a spillway and a pitch-black passageway that stretched under the warehouse. The serpentine head sloughed through the opening and disappeared into the shaft. Its motion activated a series of lights, illuminating a series of tunnels that ran deep into the property.

Allie squeezed next to me, peering into the shaft. She leaned back.

"Well, here's our way in."

Setting the staff aside, I tore away several more boards. Debris littered the floor inside—plastic waste, cardboard, and tangled tree limbs—as if a flood had, at one time, rushed through the channel, accumulating at this exit. Indeed, several storm drains emptied here from opposite sides of the flume. However, the main tunnel rose in tiers and ascended further into the structure. Conduits of various sizes ran the length of this main tunnel. The walls here appeared to be stainless steel, mottled, yet still cast grotesque reflections of our forms across the surface.

The creature hadn't gone far. It was laboring to move, most likely because of the oversized cranium. We navigated through the debris and followed it into the second chamber, a rectangular tiled area. It struggled over a steel rib and thudded into the next tunnel, continuing its awful quest.

We followed several paces behind. As we proceeded, strange symbols and geometrical etchings appeared along the tile. Discarded surgical gloves and masks lay among ash and charred wood. Someone had made a fire here. Wax had pooled where candles once burned. I bent down and picked up a moldering hardcover copy of Dickens' *Great Expectations*. Apparently, someone was catching up on the classics during their stay under BioGen. Allie and I glanced at each other, and I laid the book back down. At the room's end a pneumatic door stood half-open. Dents and gouges marred its interior surface. It had been disabled and pried open by blunt force. Someone, or something, had wanted to get in. Or out.

The serpentine dog head slunk through the door and into another long passage. At the motion, more lights sprang to life. However, this section was much longer and more dimly lit than the last. At its far end, shorting electrical bulbs turned the tunnel into a funhouse of madness. This place was starting to give me the creeps.

"How long does it go?" Allie asked, staring down the tunnel.

"I'm not sure. Let's just stay on our toes."

It was the length of a football field, perhaps twelve feet wide and twenty high. A stink of mold assailed us. In fact, the patter of water increased ahead, dripping down concrete walls inset with steel girders.

Wherever this tunnel led, the robotic canine was not going to make it. A terrible gurgling issued from its neck as liquid pooled at the gullet. The neural spine jittered as it struggled to breech another structural ridge. As we approached, the creature's eyes rolled up to look at me. Its mouth opened in a voiceless howl.

"Poor thing," Allie said.

Even if the beast was made of nuts and bolts, and its mother had been born in a test tube, I couldn't just let it suffer. I thanked the dog for leading us this far and placed the tip of the staff at its ear. A big bloodshot eye turned my way. The mouth opened and closed. I looked away and drove my weight down into the staff. It punched easily into the skull. The creature seized and stopped moving.

And now I could add dog-killer to the moral infractions on my growing list of bad things I've done.

Our footsteps echoed in the tunnel as we proceeded. The pattering water was coming from a small drain in the wall and had formed a mossy puddle below. The word *aether* had been spray-painted across the wall along with Luciferian sigils and hermetic equations. As we approached the strobing lights, a fixed ladder with a safety cage came into view. It rose to a metal hatch. We stopped at its base and stared upward. I wasn't having a good feeling about this.

Allie turned to me, looking for direction. I shook my head and motioned us onward.

This section of tunnel ended at another set of pneumatic doors. These had been peeled back, revealing a spacious cubical of seamless metallic surfaces. A decontamination chamber, perhaps. Along one side, near the back, a ramp sloped from an indistinguishable entry point. As I stepped into this area, lights flickered to life. I stopped in my tracks because a desiccated torso lay with its back to us, not six feet away.

There was no question as to the status of this entity. It appeared near-mummified, skin shrunken and drawn tight over a knobby spine.

"Look," Allie whispered.

Other carcasses lay strewn about this area, all in various degrees of decomposition. However, rather than the stench of rot, there was only a trace of chemical residue. I approached the closest body and nudged it with the end of the staff. A dry hollow cracking sounded. Walking around the corpse, we discovered six small malformed limbs protruding from its gut. I squatted, balanced on the staff, to study this creature.

Its flesh lay sunken in parts, giving it the appearance of a deflated beachball or flotation device. Its head revealed a gruesome hybridization. Though the eyes had collapsed back into the withered brain, the upper cranium appeared human both in size and appearance. Yet a snout or proboscis protruded below the eyes, exposing feral teeth beneath the husk of skin.

"Gross," Allie said. "It's an animal."

"Or half of one. Look."

I pointed to large-knuckled appendages with bony, horn-like scales along its forearms. Was this some freakish reptile or a half-morphed anteater? The possibilities were endless. I rose, surveying the room. Shards of bone littered the area along with tufts of fur. Perhaps two dozen such bodies lay in various contorted array around us. We'd stumbled into a weird type of morgue, a depository for obsolete experimental species.

"Let's get outta here." Allie maneuvered her way through the freakish menagerie of biomechanical cadavers, heading towards the ramp.

Disquiet had seeped into my spirit. We were so outmatched in this battle. This was bigger than anything I'd yet faced. However, moving forward was the only way to throttle my dread. As much as I was conflicted about my new role in life and its multiple demands, bailing would not sedate my conscience. Rothbard was wrong. Opting out wasn't an option. I had to finish this. As hard, unpredictable, and as potentially fatal as this calling proved to be, I would follow it through.

I joined Allie at the base of the ramp and stared up its length.

"Tire tracks." She pointed to multiple tread smudges, both full size vehicles and forklift imprints, along the concrete incline. "They use it a lot."

"This is the place," I said. "We go in here."

The ramp rose to a large aluminum roll-up security door. Nearby, several biometric devices, along with two dome-like security cameras, were positioned.

I began trudging up the ramp, using the staff like a walking stick.

A faint electronic ticking sounded. Perhaps we had triggered a sensor. I was looking square at one of the cameras when a smooth female voice emerged from a console.

"Reagan Moon. We have been expecting you."

Something clicked, and the security door began to rise. Behind it was a vast shadowy warehouse. In the distance, the chugging of pistons sounded along with the clinking of metal. High above us, between open girders, spread an expanse of metal interspersed by large skylights. We reached the apex of the ramp and stared into a plain of hydraulic presses, water tanks, robotic assembly lines, and small amphitheaters of computer monitors. Lights glowed intermittently from terminals, illuminating stretches of aisles.

But perhaps it was the Victorian mansion on the second level that most captivated my attention.

CHAPTER 25

"**Y**ou are expected at the Rothbard Estate," the robotic voice sounded. "May I summon you a driver?"

I glanced at Allie and then up at the Victorian mansion. Lights flickered between two large columns, which I assumed marked the main entry. Upon closer inspection, the sprawling structure integrated several different thematic elements—steep gabled roofs, turrets, stained glass windows, asymmetrical facades, corbels, and even several gargoyles. Not that I'm an architectural snob, or anything. Nevertheless, the mansion contained both Medieval Gothic and Contemporary elements, consisting of clusters of buildings that possessed a haphazardly picturesque quality. In Los Angeles, such unusual architecture was not uncommon. However, this was the first such structure I'd ever encountered inside a robotics warehouse.

The synthetic voice appeared to have emerged from a console immediately below one of the domed cameras. I directed my question that way.

"Did you say the *Rothbard Estate*?" I asked.

"That is correct," the voice said pleasantly. "The estate occupies the veranda which overlooks the manufacturing floor of the BioGen facility."

I glanced at Allie. This was happening too fast. We needed time to talk, to get our bearings. We were on Rothbard's turf now. If the magician had been preparing for our arrival, we were way behind the eight ball. However, engaging our artificial host might be a good place to start.

I asked, "Excuse me, but do you have a name?"

"I have several names, depending upon the nature of your query."

"And your name, as of *this* query?"

"You may call me Randall."

Allie and I looked at each other, and I shrugged.

"Okay, Randall. What's the walking distance from here to the... Rothbard Estate?"

"There are several paths of approach and entry. Do you have one in particular you wish to calculate?"

"What's the most common approach from here?"

"The southern catwalk is a common access point from this location and will lead to the front entry. That path is approximately nine hundred meters, which is roughly one-thousand one-hundred and eighty-one steps."

"And who should we speak to when we reach the estate?"

"Flora will direct you when you arrive."

They were leading us straight into the lion's den. And we were accommodating them. There had to be a better approach. But at the moment, I would play along.

Allie had other plans, though. She looked away from the cameras, and we locked eyes. She wanted to say something but didn't want Randall, the feminine sounding AI, to overhear us. I peered at the girl, wondering if perhaps we should split up. Yet, as that thought crossed my mind, she nodded vigorously. Of course. Allie's gifts clustered in psionics. She was inside my head. Or was I in hers? Unless Rothbard's computerized butler could somehow read minds, communicating telepathically might keep our plans below the radar.

"Reagan Moon," Randall said in her soothing female intonation. "May I suggest that I summon a driver for you?"

"No," Allie said. "We'll walk."

"As you wish."

And Allie strode under the roll-up door into the BioGen warehouse.

There were no sirens or explosions that ensued. Rather, motion-activated lights came on, highlighting the grated metal catwalk along the perimeter of the warehouse floor. The girl followed the path at a brisk pace, her head swiveling from side to side. I assumed she was calculating alternate routes through the vast complex. Despite the sounds of metallic tapping and occasional bursts of steam, no one else was visible. The place looked mostly abandoned.

"Before you exit," Randall said, "please be aware that sentries monitor the entire facility. If you should venture into prohibited areas or exhibit inappropriate conduct you may be subject to detainment or arrest."

"What do you consider inappropriate conduct?" I asked.

"That list is quite extensive. Should I recite it?"

"No thank you. I just don't want to get shot for cussing or something."

"Using profanity is not considered inappropriate

conduct on the BioGen premises."

"Bitchin'."

Seeing as our conversation was proceeding well, I debated being more forthcoming with the affable AI.

"Randall, is L-3X at the estate?"

"I am not permitted to share that information with you."

"So... you know who L-3X is?"

A long pause. Finally, Randall answered, "I am aware of a biotic organism attached to that sequence."

"Is it on the premises?"

"I am not permitted to share that information with you."

I sighed. Then tried another approach. "How about this—is there a way to disable L-3X in the event that was required?"

As Randall processed my question, I watched Allie navigate the warehouse. She passed a series of small water towers, hurried down some steps, skipped into one of the aisles, and disappeared. Probably into the shadows. From the shadows, she could move more freely. Cover more ground with minimal detection. Apparently, no sentries were activated by her actions. Watching her leave sent a pang of fear through me. I was on my own—as I'd wanted.

I redirected my attention to the AI, who remained silent. Was she stuck in a loop?

"Randall," I said again. "Can L3-X be deactivated?"

"Deactivating one of our units would be a breach of conduct restrictions and could elicit severe consequences."

"Understood. Just checking." I peered ahead of

me, into the BioGen complex. "Randall, you've been very helpful."

"Thank you, Reagan."

"I have more questions, but I realize that you're prevented from answering those questions."

"I am sorry you feel that way."

"It's not your fault."

She paused again.

I said, "Will you let Mister Rothbard know that I'm on my way."

"I will."

Before I walked into the warehouse, I looked back on the mutant carcasses in the tunnel. Seeking justice for such grotesqueries was a noble, but likely misguided intention. Nevertheless, if justice could be had for the junkyard Cerberus and these pitiful hybrid monstrosities, then I hoped I could play a part in it.

I passed into the warehouse. Once inside, it seemed even more immense than I'd perceived. The roof loomed overhead, girders of steel stretching like a vast inverted plain. A buzzer sounded, and the rollup door rattled closed behind me.

I stopped for a moment, attempting to center myself and to summon the elusive powers that I'd been given. Being that I had no plan of attack, the next best thing was, at least, to head in the right direction. I followed the southern catwalk, as Randall had suggested I do, keeping my eyes and ears—and instincts—open to alternative routes.

The air was stale, musty. The facility had been out of use for some time. Small driverless trollies sat vacant at intervals along the perimeter of the floor. At one time, this had been the manufacturing center of the facility. However, assembly lines now sat dormant beneath lifeless robotic arms and scanners. Banks of computers interspersed the floor, rising like obtuse monoliths in the stagnant dark. Glass walls separated these terminals, as did ornate metal panels containing the BioGen logo.

Remaining on the southern catwalk, I followed it as it passed a series of massive hydraulic presses, some with tables the size of a truck bed. Twisted shards of metal and cable twined from nearby pits. A bin bulged with prosthetic limbs wrenched at disparate angles. Large magnets and swivel hooks also rested nearby, accessories of the overhead crane that ran along the girders above me. Water towers rose to my right, creating aisles of shadow. This was where Allie had disappeared. But she could be anywhere by now.

I allowed my gaze to ascend along the machinery and the banks of computers to the estate. It overlooked the floor with all the charm of the Psycho mansion smiling down on Bates' Motel. Invisibles swirled above it, fomenting like storm clouds. Some great evil must be drawing these devils. What in the hell was Rothbard doing here?

I glanced at the staff. It remained unchanged. No storm energy. No smoldering sigils. Nevertheless, I had to stay ready, alert.

I reached a circular metal stairwell at the end of the catwalk. This would take me up to the second tier. As I was about to grip the handrail to make my way up, the metallic clinking sounded again. I stopped. It was closer than before. And arhythmical. This indicated that it might not be mechanical, but human in origin.

As I stood there, I had the distinct sense that I was

being drawn to the house. No—*compelled.*

You are expected at the Rothbard estate, Randall had said. Of course, he was expecting me! Rothbard had been seeding my thinking all along, drawing me to himself... or to something worse. I was being led like a dumb ox to its own slaughter. The magician had spoken about such spells—spells of magnetism or attraction. In fact, he'd mentioned something about a Minor Draw. Was it still in effect? Well, at the moment, I would be the perfect, gullible subject to comply with such a spell.

But what better way to disrupt this enchantment than by changing course?

I turned around, heading back down the catwalk the way I'd come, until I reached a set of stairs descending to the factory floor. I took them. The metallic tapping I'd heard seemed to have been coming from the southernmost part of the facility. I went that way.

The warehouse remained mostly in shadow. The night sky shone through the skylights overhead. Between random LEDs and walls of computers, there was enough light to navigate the glass-encased aisles. I passed several autonomous gurneys strewn with robotic limbs. Past them rose a tier of exoskeletons and titanium spinal columns in various stages of assembly.

The Rothbard Estate now loomed above me. Its gables and wings meandered out, filling the upper level. From there, I got a better look at the demons and imps that swirled above, peering down upon me with perverted delight. As I'd learned, they couldn't touch me. They could only hope to evoke fear and dread. Thankfully, I was getting a little better at ignoring their theatrics.

The house brooded over the warehouse floor like an ogre guarding its treasure. A bannister consisting of finely detailed spindles stretched across this upper tier, creating the effect of a massive balcony. The flowers and foliage surrounding the property were likely artificial. Knowing Rothbard, he'd probably developed his own strain of synthetic geraniums. Carnivorous, perhaps. Immediately beneath this balcony spread a bank of tall, liquid-filled cylinders. They were much like the cryogenic tubes I'd encountered at Spiraplex. But other than indistinct, fleshy debris, these cylinders were empty.

I contemplated my next steps. That's when I recognized a trace of incense. It was not unlike the incense that Rothbard had kindled in the Asylum—woodsy and earthen. I followed the scent, passing along the cryotubes before reaching a narrow tunnel at the corner of the warehouse that descended into darkness. A thick track bracketed the opening upon which a heavy steel door hung. The door had been pulled open, and its scanning device had been disabled. The scanner's glass was shattered and wires protruded from the opening. Not only was the smell of incense stronger here, but cool air filtered up this tunnel. I peered down the passageway, listening. Had someone recently broken in? Allie maybe?

The metallic tapping rang out again. It was coming from down below. The sound was so close, so abrupt, that I about jumped out of my shoes. Following it came dull thumping, and then silence.

Adrenaline awakened inside me; storm energy pulsating into my limbs. I waited a moment, then I stepped through the doorway into the tunnel. No lights or alarms were triggered. None of the sentries that Randall had warned me about appeared. So I made my way slowly, allowing my eyes to adjust to the darkness.

Immediately, a sense of vertigo struck me.

I reached out to steady myself. What was this sensation? It was similar to the strange disorientation I'd experienced when entering the Sixth Circle of the Inferno. Had I passed an invisible barrier? I winced, biting back against the disequilibrium.

A rumbling sounded somewhere below. Turbines or generators. How deep did this facility go? I opened my eyes and focused my attention ahead. Some twenty feet ahead, a series of tunnels intersected this one. Further down, perhaps fifty feet ahead, an indistinct light source shone. There, the tunnel formed a T, each passageway veering in opposite directions. At this juncture, an unrecognizable plaster bust rested on a pedestal. I gathering my senses, steeling my mind against magic. For, indeed, this disorientation seemed supernatural in origin. Satisfied that the moment had passed, I drew a deep breath and continued forward. My footsteps echoed in the corridor as I went.

My eyes had adjusted enough, with the help of the aforementioned light, to better see my surroundings. The tunnel was eight feet in width, encased in a fine metal mesh. However, there were few signs that this passage was used often. By now, I had to be almost directly under the house. Claustrophobia began gnawing on the edges of my brain. I glanced back up the tunnel. I could escape quickly if need be. However, despite a growing paranoia, I felt like I was heading in the right direction.

I continued forward until I reached the intersecting tunnels, where I stopped. Runic symbols carved into stony plaques overhung the entryways. The darkness was denser in these tunnels. I peered down the passage on my left, then my right. Metallic clatter boomed forth from the tunnel to my right. I stumbled back, swinging the staff before me as if to ward off an attacker. But there was no attacker.

Apparently, the sound had triggered a light inside the corridor. Actually, it was a track of red lights that made the area look like a sleazy strip club. However, it was enough to reveal a single robotic arm convulsing on the floor. It flailed around before stopping. There was no sign of a corresponding torso. This was the source of the noise I'd heard above.

I cautiously stepped into the tunnel, making sure to keep my distance from the disembodied arm. The walls were plaster, aged and crumbling in spots. For a moment, I had the weird sense that I'd stepped into a time warp and been transported to a medieval museum. In fact, I was no longer sure this was a tunnel at all. The wall I faced contained large recessed niches, each of which displayed almost a dozen titanium robotic skulls. The exhibit appeared to have been intended to showcase the development of the design, as they moved from more crude to sleeker models. But why here, in the bowels of the warehouse?

I approached the skulls and studied them. Perhaps they contained some clue as to how to combat Lex. I tapped one of them with the staff of undoing. Nothing unusual happened. Then I slipped my hand into the recessed shelves and removed that same skull. It was much lighter than I would have thought. Turning it over revealed the Hebrew letters engraved at its base:

נִשְׁמַת חַיִּים

It was the same phrase Celeste had uttered—*nishmat chayyim*. She'd said it meant *Breath of life* or *spirit*, as I recalled.

Those words danced in my brain. There was a numerological significance here; or, at least, a combinational import that I was not yet seeing. Rothbard had used magic to animate the biots. No, it was more than *animation* he sought. The robotic elements of the biots were animated enough. It was *spirit*, self-awareness that the magician wanted.

Spiritus aetheris, Rothbard had said. *Just like God, I made the dust live.*

I peered at the skull, turning it over and back in my palm. But as I did, a faint blue light skittered along the titanium surface. I froze, staring at the object... before realizing that it was reflecting something nearby.

I turned to see blue storm energy shimmering at the near end of the tunnel. There was a large multi-colored window there, steepled at the top. Glass panels, both large and small and of different colors, conjoined to form an unrecognizable image in the panes. It looked like a... stained glass window. And at the moment, its frame sizzled with storm energy.

I returned the skull to its place, crept further down this tunnel toward the strange window. As I did, the neon charge intensified, turning the window into what looked like an electrical conductor.

This was the same phenomenon I'd experienced at Third Street Shul. The same energy that had dismantled the door was now present here. I glanced at the staff to see veins of electric blue now twining my fist and coiling along the wooden rod.

My next move seemed obvious.

I took a deep breath and raised my hand.

Should I speak something? I didn't have to. Energy crackled from my fingertips. Blue neon traced across the window's perimeter. Yet this time, confidence came with the phenomenon. I knew what would happen... and what I was capable of.

The window groaned and sagged inward. Shards of glass crackled and burst as the individual panels folded back. I turned away, covering my eyes. The window thudded to the ground, its frame now a molten skeleton. The concussion reverberated through the tunnel. Its sound echoed through the subterranean corridors, resonating down into the depths of the facility.

Dammit. So much for a surprise attack.

Cold air rushed through the window opening. Past it, I could see a domed ceiling with celestial designs and astrological symbols spread across it. Was that an observatory? It couldn't be; I was below ground here. At least, so I thought. Reflections of firelight flickered across the domed surface. Incense wafted from below, carried on the cool air, as did a pungent, faintly familiar odor.

Once the storm energy subsided from my body, I stepped around the crumpled window to the opening, crackling glass as I went. I peeked out.

As I suspected, I was not at floor level. In fact, I was likely some fifteen to twenty feet above the floor of the domed room. There was no sound coming from below, so I stepped closer to see a large oval floorspace. This was no observatory. In fact, it was more like a museum. Or a chapel. Gothic architectural themes appeared here—several ornate columns and archways

—which made me wonder if this was part of the house. Along its perimeter stood statuary—full body replicas of ancient figures; bearded men in robes wielding wands, globes, and fiery stars. Interspersed among them were winged entities, angels or demons. Some of the statues were separated by basins of glowing coals and blocks of incense. The floor itself was some sort of stone inset with a massive pentagram. Each of the star's five points contained burning black candles in tall brass menorahs laden with wax. Herbal smudges lay nearby. Sigils and symbols dotted the walls in seeming disarray, refracting the light from the candles. Yet there appeared no other doorways or exits other than the one I now occupied.

I realized I was gaping. This was no museum, either. It was the most elaborate occult temple I'd ever seen. In Los Angeles, that was saying a lot.

Somehow, I'd managed to break into Balfour Rothbard's own personal temple.

But there was something else, something even more startling than the esoteric grandeur of the place. At the center of the pentagram stood a large stone slab. Ten maybe twelve feet high, and thick as a castle wall. Runic symbols notched the slab. Its surface appeared roughly hewn and uneven. Had Rothbard managed to import a stone from Stonehenge, or what? I wouldn't be surprised. Yet it was the figure standing erect against this stone slab that most intrigued me.

It was Lex, the Third Golem.

The biot stood unmoving, eyes closed, as if lashed to the stone table by invisible cords. He appeared immobile, in hibernation mode. Did biots need to sleep? Or perhaps he was recharging. Nevertheless, the Mantle of Ur still blazed upon his loins, sending fractals of golden light shearing through the ascending plumes of incense.

I peered at the biot. I'd come here to destroy it. Or at least do as much damage as possible. This was my chance.

I leaned through the window, surveying my surroundings more closely. Directly below me stood a statue, its head perhaps two feet below the opening. This would be tricky, but unless I wanted to teleport, there was no other way to get down there. I hoisted myself on the ledge and sat there, watching Lex. He remained unmoving. It would be difficult scaling this statue while holding the rod, but I dared not release it. Thankfully, the statue below me was one of the few with wings, which would allow for greater ease— at least, more possible handholds—in descending the piece.

Before I went, I whispered for Bernard. Such attempts were becoming futile, as this one proved to be. I shook my head. I didn't get it. What was the sense in having a guardian angel if he just showed up whenever he wanted? Then again, maybe he just enjoyed watching me squirm.

I slowly put weight on the head of the statue. Once I was convinced it could hold me, I squatted and grappled my way down. As I'd guessed, the crook of the wings provided a perfect foothold, then handhold, as I went. Switching the rod to my other fist, and with help from the statue's serpentine tail, I lowered myself to the pedestal. From there, I pushed off and landed on the floor with a soft thud.

I quickly turned towards Lex with the rod extended before me. He remained stationary with his eyes closed.

From here, the room looked even bigger. The starry domed ceiling stretched overhead like some vast celestial umbrella. Another stained-glass window, like the one I'd just exited, was positioned directly opposite the room. A cephalopod-like image adorned the glass. Apparently, Cthulhu had reached divine status.

I stepped into the room and stood nearly in the middle of the giant pentagram. The statues looked down upon me, silent witnesses to some imminent event. What foul mysteries and rituals had they observed?

I approached Lex. My breath quickened. The biot's eyes still remained closed. Yet standing against that monstrous slab made him appear even more intimidating. Was he even alive? My question was answered when I saw the faint rising and falling of his chest beneath the Mantle. The biot was in some type of suspended animation. Or was it just a ploy?

Thick braided cords emerging from the stone traced to the robot's neck and groin. These sinewy ropes pulsated, much like an umbilical cord. Yet they seemed more synthetic than organic. It was the stone that appeared living: a dense yet slightly undulating material. Like an ancient root. A peculiar symbiosis existed between Lex and the monolith upon which he was bound.

The Mantle of Ur pulsated. Light, rather than heat, emanated from the mysterious object. I was tempted to reach out and touch it. This close, the glistening cloak appeared to be quite solid, stitched of fine shards of stone, diamonds and emeralds, pulverized and bound together into an impenetrable breastplate. It sparkled as I peered at it, hypnotic in its luster. Yet as I studied it, I could feel the storm energy churning in my gut.

The memory of Orphana's death replayed itself in my mind's eye.

Damn him.

I raised the staff of undoing before Lex. Slight charges of neon blue wound the rod.

Whatever is made, Klammer had said, *can be unmade.*

As powerful and intimidating as the creature was, it had been *made*. Steel and gel and lab-grown organs, all joined by magic. I'd done some demolition in my younger days, but unmaking something of this caliber involved more than just a sledgehammer and elbow grease. Nevertheless, a strange confidence grew in me that I could *unmake* the Third Golem.

I raised the staff, tilting its gnarled crest at Lex's chest. Words, numerical sequences, rambled about my mind. I drew a deep breath and lowered my eyes...

...when something lustrous flashed near my feet.

My second sight revealed that puddles of green mucus smeared the ground around me; large inhuman footprints smattered the stone. This slime existed in the Invisible realm, unseen to the normal human eye. It was the same phenomenon I'd seen at the Magic Dragon. Which meant that whatever had slaughtered Casey Song was here!

I straightened. The storm energy welled up inside me.

The footprints trailed away from the stone slab and disappeared behind a statue of a plump, scantily clad woman with ram's horns. I followed the footprints, crept around a fluming menorah, and stopped.

Balfour Rothbard lay crumpled at the base of the statue.

Was this a trick? No. He was hurt. In fact, he was in agony. Though not just from physical pain. The strange shadowy aura still entwined him. But now it roiled like a vortex, writhing in torment.

I did not approach the magician but stood off, unsure of my next move. Perhaps this was my opportunity. If I killed Rothbard, the robot would be unmoored from its master. But how should I kill him?

Wait a second!

I shook myself. *What was I thinking?!* When had I become a killer? Who was I kidding? I couldn't do this!

As I stared at the magician, I noticed something unusual. My heart pounded as I stepped closer to him.

Rothbard wore loose, plain linen apparel, much like his biots wore. However, the magician's clothing was torn in spots, shredded and singed. He'd endured a blast. Or had he been involved in a fight? His knuckles were bloody. And a thick knot bulged on his forehead. I was about to speak to him when he groaned.

I stepped back and glanced at Lex. The biot remained as still as a mummy. When I returned my gaze to Rothbard, he had opened his eyes. His gaze was distant, glassy. Finally, he realized that someone was there and he focused in on me.

"You... you f-fooled me," Rothbard slurred.

What did he mean?

"The Draw." He pushed himself into a sitting position. Pressing his palm against his thigh, he winced. "You... broke it. The spell. Good job, Reagan. It m-made me... it forced me—I had to rethink my plan when I-I... when you were coming here." He swallowed. "Then someone else woke up."

As he said that, the shadow aura swirled around him. A miasma of pain and anger.

I said, "So that thing is what killed Casey Song."

"Most likely." He forced an embarrassed chuckle. "It's an Id monster. That's as... it's the best I can say. It comes and goes. I don't have control of it. It shows up when... well, when things get bad. I think—" He swallowed. "It manifested at the Magic Dragon and gutted your friend."

He removed his hand from his thigh and that's when I saw it—pistons, and circuitry where flesh and muscle should have been. Bolt-like nodules fused his flesh. There was no blood, just traces of green fluid trailing from his thigh. He looked up at me.

"I know what you've come here to do," he said.

"I don't have any other choice."

"Choice. Interesting that you b-bring up choice. I didn't have a choice when the Black Council began their experiments on me. It was my father, Reagan. He's the one who gave them permission. They killed your father. And they stole mine."

The aura fumed above him.

"Here," He extended his hand. "Help me up."

I hesitated.

"Oh, c'mon," he said. "You have the advantage. Look, at me. And Lex..."

I glanced at the biot.

He said, "Lex is on pause."

He stretched his hand out to me. I shifted the rod to my other hand, approached, and helped him to his feet. I glanced at his thigh as he rose, and he covered it with his hand.

"It's not polite to stare, Reagan."

"You're a cyborg?"

"Heh. Worse. I'm a prototype. An alien experiment. A transhuman, you could say."

"I'm sorry, but..." I peered at him. "Look, that isn't enough to keep me from doing what I came here to do."

He shook his head. "You're not getting this, are you? Lex can help us. All the pieces are in place. All we needed was... *you*."

Rothbard limped to the biot.

"Easy cowboy," I said.

He ignored me and made his way to the stone slab. Bending down, he reached toward the biot's hip area and detached one of cords.

"Hey," I said. "Hey!"

I marched to the magician and drew him back, away from the biot. "Why don't you just leave Lex alone for right now. Stand back there. Let's see if we can work something out."

I stood between Rothbard and the biot. Coils of storm energy entwined my hands now.

The magician looked at me. At first, he seemed confused. And then he nodded and his gaze drifted from me. "You're right. Let's see if we can work something out."

A blur of motion behind me. Allie?!

No.

Lex seized my wrist in a death grip. It was the same hand that held the rod. With a single motion he shook the staff free from my hand and sent it clattering to the floor.

Either the robot had become lightning quick since I last saw him, or I was operating in slow motion. Both were probably true. As he stepped free of the stone slab, Lex slammed my hand against it. A cord whipped across the stone and then clamped my wrist, binding it to the monolith. I yelled out as storm energy exploded in my chest. But not before Lex grabbed my other hand and forced it to the slab. It too was clasped in place. A third cord coiled around my ankles, pinning me spread-eagle against the stone.

As I struggled against the restraints, Rothbard and the Third Golem stood before me.

I bellowed in protest. My solar plexus exploded in fiery retort.

Lex stepped closer, took hold of the collar of my poncho, and ripped it completely open, exposing my upper torso. They stood side-by-side staring at the Tau scar.

"Wow. I guess it *is* real." Rothbard stretched out his arm and said to the biot, "There it is, son—the gateway to the Crossroads of Time."

CHAPTER 26

I don't like being the center of attention and have, on occasion, gone to great lengths to avoid being such. It's not a matter of feigned humility. Neither is it fear of the public's eye. It's more like a profound awareness of my own fallibility and complete foolishness. However, lately, avoiding the center of attention had become more and more difficult. And with Balfour Rothbard and his supercharged golem staring straight at me while I stood pinned to the stone monolith, the prospects of leaving the center of attention any time soon seemed remote.

I strained against the bonds that held me lashed to the block. "You—mmph!—tricked me!"

Rothbard raised an eyebrow. "How did I trick you?"

"You were... hurt."

"I *am* hurt!" He rubbed his thigh. "I'm not *pretending*, if that's what you mean. Geez. You're the one who messed things up anyway."

"Lemme guess." I tugged against the restraints. "I was supposed to walk in the front door so you could whack me."

"Whack you?! Please. We need each other."

"Like hell we do."

Sweat dripped into my eyes. The storm energy seethed deep inside my veins. But I resisted its release. There had to be another way to get free from this torture rack than by jumping.

Rothbard stepped closer. "Go on, Reagan. You can do it. You can break free any time you want."

I peered at him. "You know what'll happen if I do that."

"You're right! The portal will expand! You'll make the way for my son." He extended his hand to Lex.

The biot still scrutinized the Tau scar. Its strange brilliance reflected in his cold metallic pupils.

"What the hell... are you talking about?" I panted.

Rothbard scanned the temple until he spotted something. He limped to one of the statues and removed an ornate mirror from the wall nearby it. He returned, holding the mirror in both hands.

"Have you seen what they've done to you?" Rothbard asked.

He stepped directly in front of me and turned the mirror toward my chest.

I hesitated.

"Look," he said. "Go on, Reagan. Look!"

My gaze lingered on Rothbard. Up to that point, I'd hesitated to study the Tao portal. Mostly out of fear. Truth was, I didn't want to know. As long as the ol' lungs worked and my heart was beating, I could avoid probing. But it was becoming inevitable; I couldn't ignore the reality of it any longer. Choices have consequences. My choice to listen to Ellie and protect the Tau had led to this. And my choice to use the storm gifts would only hasten this process.

"You're afraid," he said. "Aren't you?"

"Me? Afraid?" I forced a laugh. Then I gritted my teeth and turned my gaze to my reflection in the mirror.

The Tau scar was barely recognizable anymore. Whereas it had once occupied an eight-inch square plot in the dead center of my sternum, now the strands and fiery fingers had woven their way outward, consuming my flesh as they went. From my collar bones to my pectoral muscles and down to my upper abs, a portal of swirling gossamer opened inside me. Its fringes glowed with fiery tentacles, ashen and red. Blistered. Strands of inflamed scars webbed their way to my shoulder, disappearing under the poncho.

Yet it was the black hole in the center of my torso that most captivated me. As dense as an ice sheet, it shimmered with an odd luminescence. A window of deep space had opened inside me, a wormhole to God-knows-where. It created the illusion that my lower and upper body were detached, sheared in two.

A rush of disorientation was followed by nausea. What was happening to me? Was I still human, or becoming something... else?

"It's really incredible," Rothbard said, his eyes sparkling in the glow of the Tau.

I turned away, sickened by the reality of my state.

"Oh my." Rothbard set the mirror aside. "You're not well. I'm sorry. But you need to know the truth. This *is* the truth, dude..." He stepped closer and traced his fingers along the edges of the scar. "Reagan. You've become something... wonderful."

He reached toward my chest.

"Watch it," I cautioned.

"I am. Now stop wiggling."

"Well, stay away from me."

He didn't listen.

I winced as Rothbard dipped his fingers into the opening in my sternum. He quickly yanked them out.

"It's cold," he said, shaking his hand out. "Did you feel that?"

When I didn't respond, he said, "I guess not." Then he pressed his entire hand into the portal.

Surprisingly, other than a few butterflies, I didn't feel anything. Which apparently prompted him to press further.

Half of his forearm disappeared inside of me!

"Stop it!" I finally yelled, struggling to keep from releasing the storm energy. "Get out! No more! Get away from me!"

Rothbard pulled his arm out and staggered back. He stood, breathless. Then he studied his forearm and hand, turning it over and back. He showed it to Lex. The biot scanned his master's arm before turning his gaze back to the Tau.

"Then it's true," Rothbard said. "The prophecies. And now it's almost big enough for a man."

"You're crazy."

"Am I? You guys said it yourself. Felix said it—*the Tau created a dimensional portal.* Perhaps the lightning reconstituted its molecular fabric. Or it was the elemental composition of the pendant. Maybe it was even *divine.* Anyway, it's brilliant! What better way to reach the Crossroads of Time than through a living person?!"

I peered at him. Sweat trickled into my eyes, and I winced against the stinging.

Rothbard said, "All along, they thought the Cross-roads of Time was somewhere else; it could only be reached through some type of interstellar travel. Quantum gravity. Maybe a stargate or something. But no one thought this. My gods! Hey, maybe that should be your new superhero moniker—*Captain Stargate*. Ha!"

"Get me the hell outta here, Rothbard."

"I want you out of there too, Reagan. But you're going to have to do it yourself. It's the only way. Unless you want Lex to go through like that."

I glanced at the biot. It stood as poised as a lion ready to pounce. Rothbard's plan was slowly dawning on me.

I swallowed. "What d-do you mean?"

"You really don't know? See, you guys are wrong about me, Reagan. I've been trying to explain that. But you just refuse to believe. I'm not a tool for the Summu Nura, man. Got that? They're the ones we need to worry about. They did this to me." He gestured to his lower body. "They're the ones who took your father from you. They sent Etherea and the death angels. And they're preparing for something a lot bigger."

"Like what?"

"A savior." His voice was dispassionate. He wandered away from me, expounding as he went. "A god. A leader who'll rule the world and make us their slaves. He goes by different names. Lord Matraya. Wormwood. The Antichrist. He's a servant of Hail. He'll dream again the dream of history. Possess the body, turn humanity into his feast. You think I'm the enemy? Heh!" He turned and glared at me. "You are *so* wrong."

"If you're not the enemy, then why the hell do you have me strapped to this rock?"

He stroked his jaw. "That's a good point. But you're missing something. This isn't about power, Reagan. Get that outta your head. The golem legends were never about power. They were about protection. Agency. It's not a coincidence that the first golems were created during times of persecution. We Jews needed someone to protect us from our oppressors. We needed a defender. And who better than a giant clay man? But today's oppressors aren't the same; they aren't Nazis or anarchists—they're worse. The Black Council will make the Holocaust look like an afterthought.

"The Imperia had the right idea. I'll give 'em that. They anticipated a Seventh Guardian. One who would possess all power, rejuvenate the guardians, control the course of history. Yada yada yada. But their plan was flawed. Humans are flawed! I mean... just look at you. You're the best they've got? You're their... *messiah*? That's not meant as an insult, you know."

"'Course not."

"That's when I realized," Rothbard continued, "what we needed was a new golem. One for *our* age. Not of clay or stone. A perfect superintelligence. One whose processing power is near infinite. Its knowledge base —inexhaustible. It doesn't require deliberation and research. It doesn't get tired or angry. Don't you see what something like that can do for the world? A being who's unbound by emotion and sentiment, unbound by our quaint notion of morals. Standing at the nexus of universal power."

"The Crossroads of Time."

"Exactly." Rothbard nodded. "And you've opened the gateway. See, the prophecies... they had to do with a man. A human. *When a Seventh Guardian possesses their star chart*, they said, *the Crossroads are theirs*. But the prophets couldn't see beyond themselves. They couldn't see anyone but a human with that kind of power, even though that's exactly what was needed— *something other than a human.* An intelligence unbound by humanity. Lex is an entirely new genus. A new... category. Superior to man! With the Mantle, Lex's physical power is second only to his capacity for knowledge. And now you've created a way to the ultimate throne of power.

"Reagan." He stepped closer, his eyes tight with urgency. "*You are the gateway to the Crossroads of Time.*"

I had given up fighting against my bonds, enraptured by Rothbard's words. Their implications sent my mind reeling.

"Lex doesn't need a star chart. He's not human. See? With that power and knowledge, he can guide our species to the next stage of evolution. He can do what you can't—stand at the Crossroads without indecision and fear. Without weakness. He can calculate a way forward and do what it takes to get us there. You're looking for a way out anyway. Well, this'll do it. Let Lex be our Advocate. A perfectly indifferent being designed only to serve our needs. Between the three of us, we can have our revenge. The Summu Nura won't stand a chance."

Lex stood motionless, watching with lethal dispassion. The Mantle radiated across his frame, a thin sunlit shell that cloaked the biot. He was only waiting for the next command.

I had to admit, Rothbard's plan was brilliant. Of course, I was flawed! How could *any* human being be worthy to wield such power? But after seeing Lex lay waste to the guardians—and having watched the Terminator films enough to know the possible direction of self-aware AIs—the human option still seemed better.

"Do it, Reagan!" Rothbard demanded. "Release your power. Expand the portal. Open the gateway. It's what you're fated to do."

"No. Fate has nothing to do with it."

"You're mistaken. I've seen it. The map says so!"

"Then the map's wrong. Fate isn't inevitable, unless... unless I don't do anything."

Rothbard shook his head, clearly frustrated with my refusal.

"All right," he said. "Then Lex proceeds. I just can't guarantee you'll survive that."

"You're crazy."

"Use your magic!"

"It ain't magic," I muttered and turned away.

Where was Bernard? Or Allie? What a fool I was! I'd gotten my wish. I'd wanted to go it alone. Well, here I was—alone.

Seeing my inaction, Rothbard spat his disapproval. "So be it."

He raised his right hand, holding his index and middle fingers erect—the two-finger salute popularized by Luciferian practitioners. With his opposite hand, he gestured to the portal. "As above, so below. *Solve et Coagula.*" Then he said to Lex, "Take it."

The biot was upon me in four steps. He lowered his head and aimed straight at my chest.

"No!" The storm gifts exploded inside me. "No-o-o!"

With one hand, the biot gripped the interior of the portal and pulled himself partway into my body.

His head, then one shoulder, disappeared into my torso. However, his frame was much bigger than I'd anticipated. If he managed to fit through the aperture, the width of his shoulders alone would probably split my ribcage in two.

Pain tore down my abdomen and back as my anatomy distended to accommodate the intruder.

"Aghhhh!" I strained against my bonds. Icy bolts charged my limbs. Energy swirled in my sternum as if it was a living centrifuge. "Get out!"

Rothbard stepped back, his eyes wide with wonder, watching the Third Golem enter my body.

I must admit, part of me wondered what would actually happen here; I mean, basically, the physics of the thing. Was the portal elastic, and could it expand beyond the actual parameters of my body? And could my physical body sustain the punishment? Then what? Would Lex just disappear inside me? Where would he actually be when he reached the Crossroads of Time? Would this give him access to other portals, or would he have to climb back out of my body? The possibilities crashed upon my imagination, overwhelming me like an emotional avalanche. Did I just bear a portal, or did I actually constitute the space in which the Crossroads of Time occupied? If the latter, how in the world could a human being contain a vast swath of space?! Unless it wasn't space at all, but a wormhole between spaces. Despite my wonderment, one thing was glaringly obvious—I had to stop this insanity.

"No!" I bellowed. The words reverberated in the stone at my back. "Stop him!"

But Rothbard had no intention of stopping the biot.

Pain swelled into my shoulders, rising up from my spine, white heat that left me blinking back tears. A stench of mineral and vegetable filled the air. The bonds at my wrists and feet were smoldering.

Rothbard ducked as a crack of voltage sounded overhead.

Storm energy coursed my limbs... and kept increasing. The intensity was so great that heat vapors rippled off my flesh. I was becoming a dynamo of raw energy. Rage exploded in me. My space had, literally, been invaded. My body was countering the intruder. Yet this was more than just self-preservation. A confluence of energies—some of which I'd never experienced before—bubbled inside me.

Lex's feet had not yet left the ground. His torso remained awkwardly wedged, part inside and part outside me. However, he had stopped struggling. The surge of storm gifts had forced him to pull back.

The stink of flesh filled the air, merging with the other exotic scents. Braids of electric blue crackled around me, arcing off my body in concussive waves. Damn. What was happening to me? Should I try to contain it or let it rip?

Rothbard continued stumbling back. His gaze went from revelry to alarm as the black candles in the menorah near him exploded into flame. The brass stand tottered and crumpled into a molten heap. Ghost flames coiled upward. The atmosphere was alive.

A crimson incandescence now shone across the floor. It outlined the pentagram, turning the symbol into a pulsating red brand. It mirrored the summoning circle at the Magic Dragon, only this time I was the one in its center.

The constraints on my wrists and ankles sizzled and wilted, before dropping to the earth. I sagged to my knees while the biot wrestled to free himself from the portal.

I attempted to locate the position of the staff, but Lex's body prevented me. As I groped the ground in hopes of finding the rod, a distant rumble sounded. But it wasn't from anything I'd done. Another event had to be transpiring.

Tesseracts appeared around me. While I had not jumped, layers of dimensional worlds, demarcated by liquid curtains, seemed to unfold. An infinite succession of translucent veils stretched into the distance. Was I still in the temple, in the BioGen facility, in downtown Los Angeles? If so, what was I seeing? Could this be the Crossroads of Time?

Even though the physical pain had subsided, I sensed that the biot would remain in that other dimension, still wrestling in my chest. The conflagration around me slowed, becoming a hazy palette. Time sucked out of the room. Or was it I who was sucked out of the flow of time?

Then, came the voices.

Betwixt the world of futures' past...

They were voices from the Nether.

...and present almost gone...

No, it was just *one* voice. It was Ki. But, where was he? I hadn't yet jumped, at least not to my knowledge.

One stands alone and wields the pow'r...

A curtain of blackness dropped, delineating the outskirts of my vision. However, this darkness was alive with small. scuttling entities; demons, twisted and bent, crouched there, watching. A cluster of indistinct forms appeared in the near distance. Grappling, perhaps fighting.

Against this backdrop I watched Ki approach.

"Of destiny undone," he finished. He stopped in front of me, smiled, and extended his hand. "You're a lot tougher than I thought."

The noise and tumult faded. A vacuum of silence encased us.

I reluctantly took Ki's hand, and he pulled me up. I patted my chest.

"Where's Lex?" I asked, scanning the area.

"He's still there," Ki said. "Inside you. In that other dimension, I mean."

"But... I didn't jump! How'd I get here?"

"Maybe you don't have to jump to get to this place." He smiled.

Somehow, we were still inside the pentagram. Or maybe it was more accurate to say that the pentagram also existed here, in this dimension. Outside the periphery of the circle, the demonic horde still raged. Yet in this space, I could make out cuboid forms, opaque and leathery, rising and falling on gangly limbs. Cytomorphs. Drones for the Black Council. Of course, they were watching. They'd been watching all along.

Ki saw me staring at the creatures. "They can't enter the circle. Not now. Not with you in it. You act as a... barrier. Sort of like an anti-sorcerer."

I looked at him, puzzled.

"Listen," Ki said. "There's so much you can do. So much you don't even know. Right now, you're doing the right thing. You can't let this happen. You gotta possess the Crossroads, not the biot. Just like the prophecy says, 'One stands alone and wields the power.' *Alone*

—get that? No robot. No magician. Only the Seventh Guardian."

"Then why did you lead me to Rothbard?"

"I didn't lead you to him! You went to him yourself. Rothbard and I just struck a deal—the map for the Mantle. That's it! But with the map, we got the better end of it."

"We?"

"You know who I mean."

I tried to rise above the maelstrom of emotions. Finally, I said to him, "Why didn't you help us back there, in the Golem Prison?"

"I *did* help you! I brought the map. And I told you about using the air spell."

"I don't know how to use spells."

"You've *been* using them! Geez. And whaddyou think I'm here for right now—*to help you.* God! You are dense!"

I probed around my chest again. The biot was, indeed, no longer there. At least, not in *this* place, at *this* time.

"I'm sorry," he said. "I didn't mean to yell. Look —you have to listen carefully. Earth. Air. Fire. Water. *And aether.* Aether is the fifth element. The *quintessence.* The fifth essence! The merging of the physical and the spiritual, the material and the immaterial. Spirit. The *breath of life.* That's what the magician used to bring the golem to life. Technology and magic. It's the same magic that'll stop him."

"But—"

"Listen to me! Whatever's made can be unmade. And the unmaking is in your power, Reagan."

A slight smile curled the edges of Ki's lips. Confidence rose inside me, but with it came ambivalence. Something enigmatic surrounded the Wayward Guardian, a mystery that had yet to be unraveled.

"Why are you helping me?" I asked.

"Oh, so now I *am* helping you."

The smile left his features.

The roiling demonic curtain outside the pentagram swelled. In the distance, a faint rumbling sounded, invading our tranquility.

"Because I need *your* help," he said. "Nobody else can help me."

The voices of the lost, the ones I'd heard drifting up from Diades on our very first meeting, rose in my imagination. And one of those voices was that of Harleen, his sister. Frozen in the outer rim of hell. Hoping for the hands of the clock to be reversed.

Ki's features began to fade, as did the dimensional bubble we'd temporarily occupied. The rumbling changed frequency, moving from a low growl to a bellow. Someone nearby was screaming.

Ki's body slowly dematerialized as he said, "The fifth essence. Own it."

A great whooshing of air filled the atmosphere, and the pain exploded in my chest.

I was back on the floor, groping for the staff of undoing. The biot struggled to free himself from my chest.

Lex roared as his upper body burst from the portal. His cry was pained, animalistic. It almost made me feel sympathy for the biot. He wobbled, his pupils whirring in and out of focus. His shoulders and upper torso were blistered. Frost blanketed his head and rivulets of melting ice trailed his torso.

I doubled-up as a wave of pain tore through my body. Charges of storm energy whipped about me, wild and unstable. Chunks of plaster tumbled from several statues, and a large crack snaked its way along the floor.

Lex hunched forward, bracing himself against the voltage blazing from my body. The power coalesced and drew down upon him, a single stream of molten energy. Yet it didn't appear to be harming him.

The Mantle was absorbing the storm energy.

Lex's pupils blazed as his body assimilated the fiery blue electricity.

Rothbard's voice rose above the chaos. He was laughing. This is what he'd wanted all along. Chaos mantles absorbed energy and counter-spells.

I had to stop! By releasing the power, I was only making the biot stronger! This awareness immediately caused the storm energy to subside from my body. As it did, Lex straightened. Blue veins of electricity now skittered across his frame. Water pooled at his feet as the remainder of the ice melted. He rose like an ancient god.

"The Mantle," Rothbard said, breathlessly. "I knew it!"

I stared, dumbfounded. How could I counter this madness? According to Ki, aether was the key. The fifth essence. But how did I wield something I knew nothing about?

I sucked air between my teeth and tried to rise. I might get flattened, but at least I'd go down swinging. I immediately collapsed. Gripping my rib cage, I released a howl of pain.

I rolled over and tried to get up again.

The biot's gaze was now locked upon me. His

eyes burned with storm energy.

I was so screwed.

I frantically scanned the area for the staff of undoing. It lay eight to ten feet to my right. I'd never reach it in time.

But maybe I didn't have to.

It wasn't a thought as much as a decision. The staff had come to me in the Asylum, drawn to my hand during the sonic event. I could do it again. I knew I could do it again. I reached towards the staff and willed it to myself. In an instant, the rod was in my hand.

And just in time. At that moment, Lex lunged at me, raised his fists, and swung a hammer blow down on my head. I thrust the staff in front of me.

Such a blow by the Third Golem would, in real life, have snapped the wooden rod like a toothpick, pulverized my skull, and driven the remainder of my body halfway to China. Instead, the biot's impact reverberated off the staff, sending him arching backward like a rubber toy. Perhaps even more surprising was how little physical effort it took to stop his motion. The staff of undoing had completely absorbed the blow.

No wonder Moses was such a bad ass.

Buoyed by that confidence, I inhaled and forced myself to my feet. I bit back the pain and steadied myself. The edges of the Mexican poncho smoldered, but the storm energy had drawn up into the staff. Electric currents traced the shaft, and its sigils and pictographs blazed with luminescence. If Lex had not straightened and squared his shoulders to me, I would have studied the glowing syllabary.

"Ha-ha!" Rothbard proclaimed. "I knew you could do it!"

The biot remained unmoving. I can't say that he appeared cowed in any way. But the effect of the staff had definitely prompted some recalibration. And infused me with a bit of chutzpah.

"C'mon, Rothbard," I said, panting. "It ain't gonna happen. That… thing is not going through me."

"He's not a *thing*." Rothbard glanced at Lex. "And, anyway, you're wrong, Reagan. You can't stop him."

"You saw what this can do, right?" I extended the staff.

"I saw a rookie magician with a few good moves, a bitchin' relic, and a complete lack of confidence."

"My *confidence* is just fine."

"You waffle too much. One minute you're a gangsta and the next you're doubting yourself. Okay then. See what you can do with this. It's an old one. I think you'll remember."

He inhaled deeply. The Invisibles that swarmed the perimeter of the summoning circle agitated as Rothbard raised his eyes. Was he praying? If he was, it wasn't to any god I wanted to believe in. Suddenly, he pointed at me and shouted, "*Ayiqaz althaeban!*"

I braced myself. But his words did nothing. At least not immediately.

I repositioned the staff, waiting for something to happen. The biot held his ground. Other than the blisters that marred his upper body, he appeared unharmed from his impact with the staff. The storm energy had now subsided from his body. However, the Mantle still pulsated. Rothbard approached and stood next to the biot.

He looked at Lex and said casually, "He's all yours."

Lex rammed his fists together and stomped towards me. A renewed determination possessed his features.

But as I raised the staff of undoing, it grew limp in my hand. What the hell? I glanced at the piece. It was moving, slithering out of my grasp! What was happening?! The wooden grains diffused and became reptilian scales, while its rustic tones flushed and turned mottled green.

I seized the rod with both hands, attempting to keep it from wriggling free. When I saw its crest bulge and sprout two eyes and a forked tongue flick from its mouth, I yelled out and dropped the staff.

In that split second, Lex had me by the throat.

I was too stunned to react. From the corner of my eye, I saw the serpent whip across the floor and disappear in the rubble below a statue.

Rothbard laughed as Lex's hands clamped my throat like a vice.

The storm energy rose up in me and burst from my pores. However, with the biot now in my face, the Mantle was sucking the electric waves into itself. I struggled against his grip, but to no avail. No amount of physical strength could overcome the biot.

Rothbard kept his distance as charges of wild energy coiled me and Lex. Together, we were a conductor of raw energy.

"I learned it from a mage in the U.K.," Rothbard said. "Guy does a podcast and writes spell books. He swore it's the same spell Pharaoh's magicians used against Moses."

"Rrrff!" I wrestled against the biot's grip. As I did, he lifted me off the ground.

I gasped for breath and punched futilely at the robot. My blows did not faze him. His grip tightened around my throat. He was absorbing energy... as well as choking the life out of me.

"Careful, Lex. We need him alive." Rothbard limped to the stone slab and patted its surface.

Lex's face was inches away from mine. As I realized that my resistance was only fueling his power, the halo of energy subsided from around us. His synthetic skin shone with a glowing residue. His eyes still bore the brute mercilessness of a machine.

However, in his eyes I saw a spark.

I stopped flailing, gripped the robot's forearms, and steadied myself. A glint of life burned deep in his chemistry. A node of immaterial substance. Raw, but fused into the biot's micro-circuitry and mechanisms.

The *breath of life.*

The distant rumble sounded again. Only this time it was not emanating from our altercation. It was outside of the circle. Approaching the temple. Indeed, the demon swarm around the pentagram had become still. They hunched in dread anticipation of what was about to happen.

The magician promptly spun around, attempting to locate the source of the sound. He stared up at the starry dome. Then his gaze flicked toward the window opening that I'd entered the room through.

"Dammit!" he said. "Someone else is in here. They've been—" He pressed his fingertips into his temples. "They've been blocking me!"

That's when Allie laughed, as if she couldn't contain her amusement.

She whirled between shadows, vanishing and reappearing as she went. From in back of a statue, to the ceiling, to the crest of an archway, before tumbling out from behind the stone monolith. Quick as a wink, she bounced to her feet and faced Rothbard.

"You ain't the only one with skills," she said.

And with a rapid series of blows to the gut, she sent Rothbard writhing to the floor.

Lex immediately snatched away his attention from me. However, he didn't look at the girl, but at the molten boil that had appeared on a wall above us. Oddly, the phenomenon came with little sound. A massive bubble grew, dripping plasma, creating a circular aperture in the temple walls.

A twenty-foot section of plaster collapsed in a vapor of fire and dust.

Lex flung me aside and squared his body toward this new threat.

Dust billowed into the temple. The cavity, however, opened all the way into the BioGen warehouse. Its floor was above us some ten feet. Several steel structural beams had been exposed and sagged in twisted smoldering ruin.

Mace stepped to the ledge of the cavity and lowered the antimatter rifle with its muzzle still glowing.

"Now that's what I'm talkin' 'bout," he growled.

Behind him, the Imperia emerged—Rapha, Quinn, Celeste, and Kanya. But it was Len who stole the show. The biot ran to the edge and leapt off. His body glowed with cerulean blue.

He was going to engage his brother for the final time.

CHAPTER 27

I stumbled away from the clashing biots, trying to regain my breath.

Len had been thrashed by his brother before. He only had one arm to prove it. But even with that single arm, the biot was intimidating,

Because now he was girdled in an energy field.

I knew immediately what it was and glanced up at Celeste for confirmation. The woman's hands pulsed with healing energy as she handled a gaseous ball. Like a puppeteer, she manipulated an energy orb that cocooned Len from a distance. The biot now had a mantle of his own: an elemental shield.

Len raced at his brother and their collision released a burst of energy that rocked the room. I was flung backwards, off my feet, and skidded across the floor on my ass. I collided with a statue as it fragmented. Chunks of stone tumbled around me and I covered my head, hoping to not get beaned. Around the room, statues and basins trembled from the blast. A crack snaked through the monolith, top to bottom. The halves separated and fell, in seeming slow motion, in opposite directions.

Allie and the magician were lying side-by-side, having been thrust together by the impact. She struggled to her feet and glared down upon Rothbard. What degree of psychic powers did she have to possess to block a mage of his order?

The room swirled with motion as Len and Lex engaged in a brutal showdown of power. Yet what caught my eye was the serpentine form snaking its way along the base of the wall.

The staff of undoing! Could it be restored? If I remembered correctly, after its transformation, Moses' staff had returned to its original form. And to its original owner.

I struggled to my feet. The room thundered again as the biots exchanged blows. Celeste remained above, standing on the upper ledge of the crater alongside Mace, who kept the antimatter rifle aimed at Lex. Celeste's hair swirled about her face as she bent forward and deftly manipulated the energy field around Len.

Because of the cerulean shield, Lex was unable to get a significant grip on his brother. Not only did the energy bubble impede approach, but it seemed to energize its recipient. Len lowered his shoulder and drove his brother into the wall. Their impact ripped away the plaster and mortar, boring them six feet into the structure. The room quaked again, and ceramic tiles fell from the domed ceiling and shattered on the ground. Len stumbled out of the crevasse and quickly located me.

"Reagan Moon!" he yelled. "Now would be an exceptional time to demonstrate your famed abilities."

"No kidding!" I said, keeping an eye on the location of the serpent.

"I suspect that we do not have much time." The biot squared his shoulders with his adversary. "You must hurry!"

"I'm trying! Just keep him occupied."

Lex emerged from the rubble and shook himself. The Mantle pulsated its magical energy. Near him, a statue lay in ruins. Taking hold of its base, he raised it up, twisted at the waist, and flung the massive carved image like an Olympian athlete would his discus. The statue base rocketed through the air, striking Len, and fragmenting into pieces.

Len tumbled back as debris sprayed throughout the temple. Allie turned and flung her arms over her head as shards of stone battered her. However, she still managed to remove a dagger from her waistband and thrust it to Rothbard, who still lay sprawled upon the floor. He spat dust and slowly moved to a sitting position with his hands raised in surrender... and a smirk on his lips.

A section of the collapsed wall formed a crude slope upon which Quinn and Kanya made their way down to join Allie. Together, the trio surrounded Rothbard.

With the magician temporarily contained, I ran —more like, *hobbled*—in the direction where I'd last seen the serpent. It was coiled behind a basin of burning coals, its scales glinting in the firelight. I crept toward it, hoping not to startle the creature. I was not afraid of snakes. But knowing that this one had been magically transformed from the staff of Moses added a compelling twist to the possibilities. Would it flee my approach? Attempt to bite me? And, if so, was it poisonous?

The uniqueness of this particular reptile was confirmed for, as I approached, the glowing sigils that had appeared on the staff were radiating across the serpent's body.

An odd geometry was in play. These symbols were some form of equations, not mathematical, but… metaphysical. Having always been fascinated with numerology, the sequencing of these images intrigued me. Since the Accident, the idea of Symmetry, of a universal schematic, was increasingly plausible to me. All power or authority was an alignment with forces outside ourselves, whether good or bad. Choosing what force to align ourselves with could be the difference between life or death, heaven or hell. But in the case of magic or miracles, the issue was *alignment*. Being that I was neither a magician nor a miracle worker, whatever symmetry existed between myself and the power of the staff would likely require fortuity rather than actual competence.

Rapha made his way to the floor and joined Len battling the Third Golem. Lex roared as he prepared to attack. However, as he pushed off, his feet adhered to the floor, causing the biot to bend forward at an excruciating angle. Indeed, his feet appeared to be stone, as if they'd been fused with the floor itself! Rapha gritted his teeth as his arms swept forward in a repetitive circular motion. His motions were fluid, as if following an elegant choreography. The alchemist was employing some form of elemental manipulation.

With Lex temporarily detained, I inched toward the serpent. It did not attempt to flee. In fact, it slithered toward me. The reptile's head rose, and it peered at me as its tongue flecked the air. The sigils blazed along its body. The longer I looked, the more they appeared to change, to blend into new forms and shapes. Letters. And words.

Another concussion hammered the room. Tiles rained down from above and one of the basins split in two. Burning coals tumbled from the cauldron. I stumbled to my knees with my arms over my head.

The burst had come from Lex who was now standing free. Two small craters smoked where he had stood imprisoned in stone. His fists glowed from the energy he'd released to extricate himself. The biot's features had drawn into an angry cast.

Kanya and the others dragged Rothbard to the side, away from the melee. They continued to surround the magician. But their action came none too soon as Lex stormed to Rapha and hammered him with a succession of lightning quick blows.

I'd yet to see Rapha engage in hand to hand combat. Though he was bigger than Lex in height and girth, the sheer power of the robot sent Rapha struggling backwards against the blows. Len leapt upon his brother's back and locked his arm under the biot's throat. The elemental shield protecting Len was dissipating, however.

Someone yelled from above. It was Mace. Celeste had collapsed from maintaining the energy field in the midst of the battle. Mace now aimed the antimatter rifle directly at Lex. But if the rifle was fired, there's no telling how many of us would be zapped.

I had to do something.

Mace yelled again as Lex used his brother's body to leverage himself, arc his torso back and drive his feet into Rapha's chest. The guardian sailed through the air and struck the wall with a thunderous impact. He crumpled to the floor. In a single motion, the biot flipped backward with unparalleled dexterity. Len was the fulcrum for the backflip. The motion ended as Len's grip was broken and Lex drove him into the ground. It was a splendid move. The force was so great that huge blocks of stone tore loose from the floor and Len was buried below.

And that's when I saw it.

תיפסק נשימה

The words at the base of the biot's skull were glowing. The *Breath of life.*

Lex turned and squared himself at me. Rothbard laughed as the rest of my crew watched helplessly. Mace stomped the ground with his boot; he was itching to pull the trigger, but doing so would likely inflict unparalleled collateral damage on us.

Besides, we still had one more chance.

I didn't need to look far for the snake. The reptile was moving toward the biot, as if to strike. Apparently, the staff served a higher purpose and would fulfill that purpose in any form.

Lex lowered his head and barreled towards me. I winced against the radiance of the Mantle, which was now glowing furiously. Yet I bent down and snatched the serpent as it whisked past me. Upon contact, it transformed into the staff of undoing. However, its motion carried me forward, yanking me towards the onrushing biot. Perhaps the Cloak of Levitation had a real-world parallel in the staff of undoing.

I stretched the staff out and yelled as I drove straight into Lex. I prepared for a hellacious collision, but the moment the biot's hands touched the staff, a burst of energy flung him backwards. And again, the rod absorbed the blast.

Which bolstered my resolve.

Lex skidded across floor before slamming against the base of a column. I maneuvered around shattered ceramic tiles and shards of stone, making my way to the Third Golem. Carrying the staff, I moved with unusual confidence. Indeed, a divine power infused the moment. Lex scrabbled from the ground as I approached and swung the staff down upon him. The biot cried out as the rod struck his forearm. But rather than releasing energy, this time the impact extracted it.

I gripped the rod as power tore through it, siphoning magic from the biot. For a second, I thought the staff might leap from my hand. But I held it tightly.

The Mantle throbbed like dying coals as its glow drained away. Thin rivulets of crystal lava traced up the biot's arm and bled into the rod. Fine particles of gravel and ashen fragments crumbled from the creature's chest as the magical shield disassembled.

Finally, the Mantle faded and fell like dust.

The remaining energy coalesced into the rod, and then drained into me.

I absorbed the Mantle of Ur.

The hair on my arms stood on end. Static electricity swept through the air as a combustible sphere of energy now radiated from my being. Good God! How could any human being withstand such a thing? Ceramics melted as the atmosphere bristled. The remaining candles combusted. The pentagram glowed hot red.

Lex slowly rose.

But rather than charging me, he processed the event. His pupils whirred rapidly, as if scouring his memory bank for an appropriate response. He knew that the power of the staff could not be countered. Nor that he could defeat me.

Rothbard shouted, attempting to summon an incantation to assist his creation.

"Shut him up!" I turned and pointed at Rothbard. "And keep a good eye on him."

Quinn, Kanya, and Allie tightened around the magician.

I turned my attention back to Lex. Flumes of heat and sulphur rose between us. Shreds of the biot's clothing swept about him, singeing away into rags. His pupils continued spinning, caught in a chaotic loop. He made no move to defend himself. Could he sense what was happening inside me?

The staff has no inherent power, Allie had said. *It's just a conduit. The power's in the hand that holds it.*

"Speak it!" Celeste shouted from above. "Speak it out, Reagan!"

I didn't need to ask what she meant. Because that same primal energy that had given rise to the sonic event in the Asylum was again coalescing in my mind. Words and phrases of unknown origin skittered about my brain. Were they the tongues of angels or the words of God himself? All I knew was that I was a vessel to speak them.

Shouts emerged from nearby. Rothbard was struggling with his captors. The Invisible hordes at the periphery of the pentagram drew back.

What God had done through the spoken word, Rothbard had done through magick. *Spiritus aetheris.* The fifth element was spirit, the breath of life. But inside the summoning circle I was the anti-magician.

Lex's gaze bore down on me. He knew what I was about to do.

I watched, strangely detached, from within the

maelstrom swirling around me. I remained untouched, stationed in the eye of this storm. In that place of serenity, outside of myself, the phrases dawned upon me.

Breath begone.

spiritus et abierunt

At the moment, their source did not matter. The words blazed in my mind's eye like a universal equation, a language of the spirit that I was hearing, intuiting—a command that required only to be spoken.

In religious circles, some claimed to speak in tongues. *Glossolalia* was the technical term. But this was not glossolalia. At least, I hoped it wasn't. Being associated with wild-eyed Pentecostals was the last thing I hoped this superhero gig resulted in. However, the possibility that an unknown language could be spontaneously articulated suddenly didn't seem as weird as I'd previously thought.

I raised the staff before me. It was like a transmitter, taking my words into it and sending them forth. Is this what had happened to Moses when he stood before the Red Sea commanding it to separate?

Yet as I spoke the words, there was no implosion, no blast radius. If there was a blast, it was inside the Third Golem. For the spark that had gleamed in his eye snapped, and evaporated.

The breath of life—the one imparted by the magician—left the biot.

Lex wobbled. He opened his mouth to speak, but did not. Instead, he cast a perplexed glance at his maker. Rothbard cried out as the biot collapsed.

The dynamo of energy around me subsided and swirled into stillness. Sweat stung my eyes. Smoke trailed from charred strands of the poncho. Yet the Tao portal still seared beneath it. The staff looked the same. Perhaps a little more weathered, but undamaged.

I went to Lex and knelt down. I could have fallen down out of pain and pure exhaustion, but the adrenaline wouldn't let me. I studied the biot. No breathing was visible. I touched his flesh. It was cold. And once again, I wave of sorrow swept through me, not because the biot had been a formidable opponent, but for the anguish of being self-aware and yet bound to subservience.

Something sounded behind me, and I rose to see Rapha assisting Len from the depression in the floor. The biot moved haltingly. A deep indentation notched his forehead. His upper torso appeared misshapen and crushed. Across from them, Rothbard peered at me, still surrounded by the trio.

"Do you realize what you've done?" Rothbard's eyes glistened with moisture. "We could've changed history!"

I shrugged. "Maybe we are."

"You don't have the guts. Or the brains!"

"No. But I have a hell of team."

His eyes grew narrow. "What the hell are you?"

"Well," I replied, "I'm not fated to be your partner. That's for sure."

"Let's get him outta here," Quinn said, yanking the magician forward.

"Where are you taking me?" Rothbard objected. "To the police? Ha! They won't stop me. And neither can you."

"Oh yeah?" Allie pressed the dagger into his throat. "Let's go."

And they began leading Rothbard over the debris and up into the warehouse. When they reached the top, Mace switched out the antimatter rifle for a more stable gun. He leveled the weapon on Rothbard.

"Let's see you get out of this one, Houdini," Mace spat.

Rothbard laughed. "Oh, I'll play along. For now." As they proceeded to escort the magician out, he turned around and looked down at me. "Reagan! Reagan! The three of swords. Remember?"

"I remember," I said.

"Do you know what it signifies? The card—do you know what it means?"

The mention of the Tarot card brought pause.

"It's about pain," Rothbard said. "Pain and suffering. That's your lot in life, Reagan. It's your destiny now. The one you've chosen."

"Get'm outta here," Mace said.

As they dragged Rothbard away he yelled, "It's about your true nature. Reagan! Get out... while you have a chance!"

Celeste joined the others in leading the magician away.

Len limped to his brother's body, placed his foot on his brother's chest, gripped his throat, and yanked the biot's head out of his torso. The spinal column whipped from the neural sack, and Len stood holding it aloft like some mechanical barbarian.

"Reagan Moon," Len said. "There is one final thing we must do."

CHAPTER 28

Taking his brother's head and titanium spine, Len led Rapha and I up the debris field into the warehouse.

Kanya was waiting for us there.

"You sure they're gonna be all right?" I gestured to the others as they bustled the magician out of the warehouse.

"Rothbard's not going anywhere," she replied. "You okay?"

But when her gaze rested on my chest, still exposed from the torn poncho, her eyes widened.

"I'm gonna have to get this fixed," I said. "But as long as I'm still breathing...?" I shrugged.

Len limped badly as he guided us to the Western side of the warehouse. By the looks of it, his ribs had been crushed. Yet he trudged past the banks of computers and exoskeletons, clearly on a mission.

Many of the glass partitions had shattered during our struggle. The skylights, as well, were broken, and I could now see starlight twinkling through the empty panes.

"Len," I said. "Where are we going?"

The biot stopped. "We must complete this, Reagan Moon. As long as this technology remains in circulation," he held up Lex's cranium, "it can be duplicated, or regenerated to serve another's purpose."

"You're going to... destroy it?"

"Yes."

"How?"

He motioned to the large hydraulic presses that I'd passed on my way in.

Len said, "Goliath has been used to destroy similar technologies."

"Goliath?"

He pointed to the largest of the presses, a three-story green and yellow monstrosity.

"Goliath is what my father called it. At the time of its creation, it was the world's largest all-forged-steel closed-die hydraulic press, capable of exerting 90,000 tons of force."

"Damn."

"Our bodies are designed to endure much abuse, but such tonnage will render the frame of the L series unsalvageable."

Len turned and proceeded to the press, where he climbed the platform and placed Lex's head and spine across the blackened steel surface. It smelled of grease and oil. Metal shavings sprinkled the floor around us. Len manipulated some of the controls. A panel glowed and the machine roared to life.

Kanya covered her ears as Rapha stood, looking rather grim.

"Stand back!" Len said.

We moved further back and watched the biot crank a dial and then flip a switch.

The press roared like a jet engine. Its upper plate engaged and began its descent to the biot's body.

Sure, it was a shame to see that technology be

lost. But there were plenty of other mad scientists to redesign new and improved monsters. Besides, having seen the capabilities of the Third Golem firsthand, watching his destruction was a fitting resolution.

As the press reached the biot's body, its skull elongated, oozed liquid, and cracked. The spine crunched and flattened, unable to withstand Goliath's force. As the press met steel, rivulets of fleshy liquid and fluid seeped from the edges of the table and puddled on the floor.

Len watched, appearing melancholy. A horn sounded overhead as the press completed its action. The biot flipped another switch, and the massive block rose. When it stopped, the engine whined and came to a rest. Retrieving a long-handled poker, Len reached into the press, hooked his brother's body, and pulled it out. Setting the poker aside, he lifted the flattened torso. It was now nothing more than a thin, oily metal plate.

Len stared at the misshapen mass, as if in thought.

Finally, I said, "Len, what's wrong?"

He said, "I believe I'm experiencing what you call... sadness."

"I... I'm sorry."

We waited while the biot continued to stare at the malformed remains.

Rapha looked up. A helicopter sounded in the distance. It was heading our way.

"Brother Moon," he said. "We must go."

I nodded. "Len. He's right. We need to get out of here. The cops are on their way."

Len straightened and tossed the remains of his brother in one of the nearby scrap bins.

We began to calculate our route of escape when Len said, "Wait. We are not finished here."

The three of us turned back to the biot.

"Reagan's right," Kanya said. "We gotta get outta here."

I asked, hesitantly, "What do you mean, Len? What else do we have to do?"

Len stepped aside from the control panel. "For this, I will require your assistance, Reagan."

Then he moved to the press and stood with his back to it. "I am the last of the L series. As long as my technology remains, I too can be used to reproduce such technologies."

"No," Kanya said, slowly shaking her head. "No. Get away from there."

"He's right," I said, numbly. "If the police find him, they'll hand him to others, to scientists... they'll use him for the same thing."

Kanya bolted up the platform, took the biot's hand, and tried to pull him away. "Get away, Len. Let's go. You're not doin' that!"

She could barely budge him. Yet the biot did not resist her; he simply stood his ground.

"No one else needs to know," Kanya said, her voice faltering. "D'you hear me? You can... you can stay with us, at the Asylum. Mace'll like that anyway. You c-can help him with his weapons and stuff."

Len smiled, an obtuse crease in his dented skull. "That is kind of you. But I have calculated the probabilities that a similar ethical crossroads will be reached. Statistically speaking, the chances that my technology can be acquired and employed for nefarious ends is quite substantial. It is better for all of us to remove such possibilities. I am sorry, Kanya."

He freed himself from her grasp, turned, and tinkered with the controls.

"No!" Kanya grabbed his arm. "You are not doing this!"

Rapha climbed up the platform and put his arm around her. "I'm afraid he is correct, sister. It is how this must end."

Rapha gently, but firmly, drew Kanya away.

Len looked at me. "Being as I am programmed with a proscription against self-immolation, I will require your assistance."

I sighed deeply. Could I do this? Weren't there moral boundaries I would be transgressing by flipping that switch? But having just watched his brother get pulverized, whatever lines *did* exist were surely gray.

The sound of the helicopter grew louder, as did the approaching sirens.

I went to the control panel. Len showed me how to work Goliath and then climbed upon the press. He sat with his legs slung over the edge.

Kanya sobbed as Rapha kept her embraced in his thick arms.

"It has been a pleasure serving with you," Len said.

I said, "It's been our pleasure, Len."

He smiled. "You have expanded my perception of beauty as well as of baser, yet still enjoyable experiences. However, the comradery of pursuing justice and moral goodness is what I have profited the most from."

He scooted back onto the press. But before he lay down, he turned to me.

"Reagan Moon?"

"Yes, Len."

"As I have sought to bring good into the world, do you believe I came close to being... *human*?"

I smiled. "You were more than *close*."

He nodded, as if satisfied. Then he lay his head on the plate and he stretched his body out. I activated the press and it roared to life.

"Farewell, friends!" the biot yelled.

None of us were able to watch as the press came down and crushed Len's body. Kanya drew into Rapha's chest, still sobbing. I hung my head, numb from the events of the last several days. My body ached from head to toe. And there was so much that remained a mystery, but there was no time to mourn or contemplate.

The rotors of the helicopter sounded outside and a spotlight beam whipped through the skylights above. Had I been a bit more alert, we might have avoided the police. Instead, they burst into the warehouse from multiple entries. We made no attempt to hide or flee. In fact, I just walked towards the closest ones with my hands lifted.

"Stop!" The voice echoed through a megaphone. "Hands up! All of you. Do not move."

Several units approached and then halted, with their guns leveled at us.

One officer demanded, "You. You're Reagan Moon."

"That's me." I tightened my poncho so the Tau scar wouldn't be too visible.

"Hands up!" he barked. "You're wanted for questioning regarding the Magic Dragon murder."

"Yeah. I know."

"And for evading police."

"I wasn't—" I shook my head. "Whatever."

"And for damage done to a police cruiser."

"Oh, for Pete's sake," I exclaimed. "I didn't even go near the cruiser."

They ushered us out. Half the police force was waiting outside. Talk about overkill.

We spent the evening into late morning being interrogated at the police station. The police brought the remainder of the team in for questioning while they sorted things out. Thankfully, Klammer still had some pull and got us out of there by afternoon.

Being free did nothing to assuage our grief about Len. That wound would take some time to heal. In the meantime, I could only hope that no one else got the fancy idea of using the wormhole in my chest as an airlock into eternity.

CHAPTER 29

F all was in the air. Although you couldn't tell by the low ninety-degree heat. We buried Orphana in a small cemetery near the coast, up past Ventura in a farming community. Adobe structures dotted the property, as did citrus and sprawling avocado trees. A small salmon-colored chapel with a Spanish tiled roof marked the center of property. Apparently, other earth guardians had been buried here.

Felix Klammer footed the bill. He even made an appearance before most of the others arrived. Blondie remained at Klammer's car looking as humorless as a bag of potatoes. It wasn't the time for questions. But boy did I have them.

A modest crowd attended, nearly filling the small chapel. I must admit, many of the people I did not know. But, by their looks, they knew me.

Rapha eulogized Orphana, telling about their first encounter and her inclusion into the Imperia. He also told a funny story about a time they rescued a lady from a burning building and inadvertently learned it was one of Orphana's half-sisters. Rapha was an optimist and his speech bore that in spades. She died in service to a much higher cause, he said. He concluded by placing Orphana's cane upon the casket to be buried with her. Celeste had some good stories, of course. And an elderly black gentleman whom they called Quince told of his and Orphana's romance and how her 'calling' kept them from ever tying the knot. It was all very bittersweet.

After the funeral, the Imperia gathered at a fountain outside the chapel, where Rapha extended Orphana's Tau to Allie. The girl blushed.

"*Estas bromeando!*" she exclaimed. "For real?"

Rapha smiled. "Our sister would have wanted you to have it. To carry the torch."

"Oh, wow." Allie studied the piece. She couldn't stop gaping. Finally, she said, "This means I'll have to make a trading card of myself. I hadn't planned on that."

She giggled and then slipped the Tau on.

"My condolences," Quinn said, extending his hand and smiling.

As she shook it, Allie asked the others, "Is he always so sarcastic?"

"Always," Celeste said, before hugging the girl and wishing her welcome.

But I knew where Quinn was coming from and, in a way, felt bad for the girl. Although, it was cool knowing she was officially on *our* side.

A couple reporters tracked us down and snapped pictures. They hounded us for statements regarding Rothbard's trial. The magician was being held without bail in a maximum-security detention facility, awaiting trial for violating AIC guidelines. Of course, they couldn't stick him with the murder of Casey Song, and the general consensus was that he'd receive a light sentence... if *any* sentence. With his unmatched legal team and support from fellow technocrats, Rothbard's acquittal and release seemed inevitable. Before a film crew could arrive to get us on record, Mace got into a scuffle with one of the reporters and we split.

Although I told no one, Orphana's words to me, the poem she'd recited, played on repeat in my head all day:

> Betwixt the world of futures' past,
>   and present almost gone;
> One stands alone and wields the pow'r,
>   of destiny undone.

It was a mystery yet to be revealed. And, perhaps worse, it left me feeling in debt to another person who'd dearly sacrificed for me.

Later that day, I went by Jimmy's house. The thought of visiting him, using my powers to try to remove his cancer, had been bugging me. Sure, it was a crazy idea. But I couldn't shake it. I needed to see him.

They'd put him on leave as he underwent chemo. Most likely, any connection I'd had with the LAPD was going with him, but he encouraged me again to introduce myself to the new boss. He said her name was Romena and reminded me that the office staff had taken to calling her Mrs. Mantis. Then his tone turned somber.

"Somethin's going on over there, Moon," he cautioned. "And it ain't good."

It was difficult to focus on my future involvement with the LAPD after seeing Jimmy. He looked like shit—sunken cheeks, dark circles under his eyes.

I'm reluctant to use the word *prayer*, but that's the best term for what I did for Jimmy. I placed my hands on his gut and willed the storm energy to life. I'd healed someone before and watched Celeste do the same. However, the blue energy didn't manifest. And unlike some popular televangelists, I didn't feel the need to fake it. So, I just bowed my head and stated that I'd like his life spared.

Jimmy thanked me. "I ain't a religious, man. But I'll be damned if I'm goin' to the grave with unfinished business." He cleared his throat. "So, I called the ex and apologized for bein' a thick-headed son-of-a-bitch who was AWOL for most of our married life. She took it surprisingly well. Whaddya know."

"And your son?" I asked.

"One step at a time, Moon. One step at a time."

I patted his arm and told him I'd check on him later that week.

When I met the others at the Asylum that evening, Quinn surprised us all by apologizing.

"I said things I shouldn't have." His gaze was downturned. When he looked up, his words were resolute. "I'm sorry."

I couldn't say whether this would heal the rift between him and Rapha. But the emotion was genuine.

Celeste hugged Quinn, followed by Rapha who laid his hand on the psion's shoulder and drew him to himself.

I'd already decided that I was heading back to my apartment. Mace and Kanya both implored me to stay. In fact, they requested me to move in.

"You told my father you'd watch after the place," Kanya said.

"I know, I know."

"Well?"

Mace chimed in. "And why pay for that overpriced dump when you can live here?"

"It isn't a dump," I objected. "Besides, Klammer is

basically paying my rent."

I told them I'd sleep on it, but I'd mostly made up my mind. Truth be told, I was starting to have some feelings for Kanya. Not that she reciprocated. But the last thing either of us needed was to start mucking around in romance. And moving into the same pad she lived in would only complicate things. Besides, I didn't know the first thing about having a shapeshifter for a girlfriend.

Nevertheless, I think that Ellie would've approved.

Upon seeing the Tau scar, Quinn and Rapha vowed to design something to keep the portal from swallowing me alive. At this stage, I was convinced only a suit the size of an iron lung would stop its spread. Like a black star that had exploded in my solar plexus, the blazing scar had now consumed most of my chest and made its way into my abdomen and shoulders. After the incident in Rothbard's temple, I dreaded to look upon the wound ever again.

You are the gateway to the Crossroads of Time, Rothbard had said. I wasn't sure everything that implied. But knew it mattered.

We stored the staff of undoing in the Asylum, along with the key to the Golem prison. I hoped neither would have to be used again. But the way things were going, anything was possible.

When I left, Rapha was sitting down with Allie, explaining what it was like to be part of the team. Celeste joined them as Mace retreated to his workshop, most likely to work the bugs out of his new weapon—the antimatter rifle.

Kanya followed me to the freight elevator and

then to ground level.

She said, "Well, think about it, at least."

"Think about…?"

"About staying here. We could use the help. And I'm just not sure how safe you'll be at your place."

"Yeah. Well, for now, I need to spend some time at the Crescent. I've got an article to write and Arlette has been riding me hard."

"What's the article about?"

"You don't want to know. Okay. Extraterrestrials. In Laurel Canyon, no less."

"That's your favorite topic, isn't it?"

"Funny."

I unlocked the Cammy and climbed in.

"Hey," she said, leaning on the open door. "I meant what I said the other day—I believe in you."

She stood for a moment as if to let that sink in. Her eyes were the color of burnished copper. Underneath them was fire. She pushed the door shut, went to the freight elevator, and descended into the Asylum.

As I drove home, I called Arlette to make sure the map was safe, which she assured me it was. Of course, she reminded me that the stories were piling up… along with deadlines. I said I'd get right on them. Although, getting the star chart was the next item on my to-do list. Where things went from there was anyone's guess.

I arrived home to discover that Mrs. Richardson had left a Tupperware container of fresh pecan sugar cookies at my apartment door. Bernard showed up to watch me eat half a dozen of them. We didn't say much. When I queried why he'd not shown up for my last exchange with Rothbard and the Third Golem, my guardian angel indicated that I didn't need him. It felt like a compliment, so I left it unchallenged. He stood watch at my bedside that night.

I think about Len often. Mostly when things get bad and I'm tempted to complain about my lot in life. The biot suffered no such despair. He looked for beauty in the world, and added a bit of his own. I really hope that, one day, I can do the same.

$$\tau$$

ON THE WRITING OF THIS NOVEL

The Third Golem has, for various reasons, been a very difficult book to write. Some of that difficulty had to do with content. Researching artificial intelligence, robotics, as well as chaos magic and Hebrew mythology, has been fascinating as well as grueling.

The most difficult aspects of this book, however, have been personal.

In May of 2018 I underwent open heart surgery for valve replacement. It was unexpected and threw me for an emotional loop. Early that next year, one of my granddaughters was diagnosed with cancer and began receiving chemotherapy. Then in the winter of 2020, the coronavirus pandemic ensued and I, like everyone else, was quarantined amidst much economic and global uncertainty. During that quarantine, protests and riots broke out regarding alleged racism and police brutality. The world was in a chaotic state, both personally and globally. It was in the wake of these dynamics, that I was finally able to complete this book.

Anyway, it really feels like an accomplishment and represents a significant period of my life. I hope the effort shows.

GLOSSARY

ALLIE: Psionic shadow-jumper assigned to guard Third Street Shul, eventually becoming the Third Guardian of the Imperia

ARCADIUM: Earth's higher dimensions

ARLETTE: Senior editor of the Blue Crescent

ASYLUM, THE: Massive storehouse for occult and accursed items from around the world; in Los Angeles, south of Little Tokyo in the Warehouse District

AUDRA: Kanya's mother; one of the Hydra Sisters

AZRAEL: The Archangel of Death

BALFOUR ROTHBARD: Heir to the BioGen technological dynasty; billionaire hipster and chaos magician who's made a pact with Ki to acquire the Mantle of Ur and join Moon in defeating the Summu Nura

BERNARD: Reagan Moon's guardian angel

BIOT: An artificial biological organism; different from robots and cyborgs (which are inorganic or a combination of mechanical parts and organic tissues)

BIOGEN: Robotics corporation run by the Rothbard Estate

BLACK COUNCIL, THE: The body of Summu Nura overlords who plot the merger of all dimensions

CASEY SONG: Chinatown shop owner who possesses key to the golem prison under Third Street Shul

CELESTE: The Fourth Guardian of the Imperia; Archivist and Healer

COSMAGON: Genetically enhanced henchmen developed by Volden Megacorps

CROSSROADS OF TIME, THE: The legendary intersection of past, present, and future

CYTOMORPHS: Synthetic dimensional scouts made of Nefarium and used by the Summu Nura

DIADES: Earth's lower dimensions

DIEDRA: One of the Hydra Sisters

ETHEREA: Evolved lerium user able to correspond with the Black Council, summon ice nymphs, and harness Santa Muerte for releasing the Tenth Plague

FELIX KLAMMER: The First Guardian of the Imperia; exists in two dimensions—earth and Arcadium; possesses Foresight

FIFTH ESSENCE, THE: A universal element that can only be possessed by a Seventh Guardian, thereby allowing them to control the Crossroads of Time

GOLEM PRISON, THE: Legendary magical prison under Third Street Shul which houses the Third Golem

HAIL: A demigod of the Nether, lower realms of Diades

HOLLOW, THE: The lowest realms of Diades

IMPERIA, THE: Seven earth guardians; empowered by Heaven to battle evil on earth and counter influence of the Summu Nura

JIMMY PASTORELLI: Lead investigator for LAPD Special Crime unit

KANYA: Matisse's adopted daughter; possesses therianthropic abilities; Audra is her mother

KI: The Sixth Guardian of the Imperia; the Wayward Guardian; allegedly defected to the Summu Nura; through his pact with Balfour Rothbard allows Moon to acquire his star chart

L3N: Biot developed by Rothbard, Nicknamed Len

L3X: Biot developed by Rothbard, nicknamed Lex;

LERIUM: Smart drug being illegally produced and distributed; some users develop psychic abilities

MACE: Cryptid big-game hunter; arms / weapons expert; helps catalog and collect for the Asylum; Friend of the Imperia

MAELOHIM: Death angels; lower caste of Harvester angels; precursor to Azrael

MANTLE OF UR: A chaos mantle; makes the wearer impervious to magic

MATISSE: Founder of the Asylum; Kanya's adoptive father

MRS. RICHARDSON: Moon's neighbor for whom he cat-sits

NDOCRON: Organic material mined from the dimensional skin of Arcadium

NEFARIUM: Material forged from Diades; indestructible on earth, except to Reagan Moon

Neokor: Urban developing conglomerates that re-opened the downtown subway project

NETHERWORLD: Another term used to describe the lower levels of Diades

NEUROS: A class of lerium user who has harnessed the smart drug and developed psychic abilities

NEVILLE: Moon's co-worker at the Blue Crescent

NOMLIES: Term used by the public to describe humans with supernatural abilities

NORMALS: Term used by Nomlies to describe the average human

ORPHANA: The Third Guardian of the Imperia; gifted with Agglomeration and Lore

PENNY: Moon's co-worker at the Blue Crescent

QUINN RODGERS: The Fifth Guardian of the Imperia; gifted in Psionics; coder, developer, tattoo artist

R.G. PENTECOST: Angelologist living in Venice Beach; possesses the Seraph's Wing

RAPHA: The Second Guardian of the Imperia; gifted in Alchemy, ability to manipulate matter

REAGAN MOON: The Seventh Guardian of the Imperia; possessor of the Fifth Essence; possesses flight gifts, dimensional transit, healing, telepathic groupings, commutation, and others; also referred to as Storm-soul and the Twelfth-borne of Chaos

REPTOIDS: The lost Lizard People living in the tunnels under Los Angeles

SAUCY: Rapha's mastiff, short for Sausalito

SHROUD, THE: Five muses of the Netherworld; ice nymphs; summoned by Etherea to invoke Azrael, the Angel of Death

SIDRA: One of the Hydra sisters, killed by Kanya

SOREN VOLDEN: Founder of Volden Megacorps; pioneered Dream Chamber technology and Spiraplex

STAFF OF UNDOING, THE: a magical item designed to counter the Mantle of Ur; rumored to be the rod of Moses

STAR CHART, THE: Tabula Lumen, a map of each human life from beginning to end, vaulted in the celestial Archive; the Seventh Guardian who possesses their star chart is then capable of controlling the Crossroads of Time

STELLARS: Term used by Lizard People to describe humans with supernatural abilities

STORMSOUL: Another title for the Seventh Guardian who will possess the Crossroads of Time

SUMMU NURA, THE: Bodiless astral vampires seeking incarnation and energy; plotting to merge all dimensions and harvest human beings

TAU, THE: A symbol of the cross of Christ, named after the Greek letter it resembles, worn by all members of the Imperia; Moon's icon was fused into his body from the Accident

TENTH PLAGUE, THE: The invocation of the Archangel of Death for indiscriminate slaughter

THIRD GOLEM, THE: A legendary golem, impervious to magic, housed in the Golem Prison; also, the role that L-3X filled in servitude to Balfour Rothbard

TWELFTH-BORNE OF CHAOS, THE: One of several titles attributed to the Prophesied One, the Seventh Guardian who will possess the Crossroads of Time

WARPERS: Term used to describe those who can traverse different dimensions

WHETHERWERES: Conflagration demons held in the Netherworld; contained by ice muses

DID YOU LIKE
THIS BOOK?

If so, there's a couple ways you can help me and we can stay connected.

Without reviews, indie books like this one are almost impossible to market. Leaving a review will only take a minute —it doesn't have to be long or involved, just a sentence or two that tells people what you liked about this book, to help other readers know why they might like it, too, and to help me write more of what you might love. The truth is, VERY few readers leave reviews. Can you help me by being the exception? Thank you in advance!

I also have a mailing list. Signing up is simple (just your name and email addy). It's called *Mike Duran's Infrequent Updates* for a reason, as I promise not to clog your email with daily or weekly info. Signing up will keep you abreast of my new projects and give you opportunity to get discounts on some of my books and products. You can sign up for my mailing list at my website: www.mikeduran.com.

If you liked THE THIRD GOLEM, you'd probably enjoy the first two books in the series THE GHOST BOX: A Reagan Moon Novel, which was selected by Publishers Weekly as one of the best indie novels of 2015 and SAINT DEATH. SUBTERRANEA: NINE TALES OF DREAD AND WONDER is an anthology of my short fiction that stylistically ranges from literary to pulp. It is available in ebook or in print. CHRISTIAN HORROR: ON THE COMPATIBILITY OF A BIBLICAL WORLDVIEW AND THE HORROR GENRE is a non-fiction exploration of reli-